Praise for

Ebba and the Green Dresses of Olivia Gomez in a Time of Conflict and War

To read *Ebba and the Green Dresses of Olivia Gomez in a Time of Conflict and War* is an overwhelming experience. Joan Tewkesbury has crafted a novel of luminous originality, creativity and resonance. It is driven by a unique narrative freedom and by characters that are immensely touching. They will stay with the reader for a long, long time. A rare sense of wonder permeates this novel. Its picaresque tone, unusual sense of humor and capacity to rebound will surprise you on every page. Cervantes and Marquéz may come to mind, but Joan Tewkesbury novel's operates on its own terms. *Ebba....* is an unforgettable novel and a brilliant achievement.

> – Walter Salles, award winning director, "Central Station,"
> "The Motorcycle Diaries" and "Linha de Passe"

This beautiful book is ebullient, irresistible storytelling from Joan Tewkesbury, who takes us on a complex and mesmerizing journey with Ebba. In her first novel, the screenwriter who redefined cinema with the masterpiece "Nashville" proves that written fiction can affect and enchant you even more deeply than film.

> – Joan Juliet Buck, writer, editor and actress

Ebba, growing up orphaned in a small Mexican village, comes of age in this delicious, surprising and powerful first novel by one of our great Hollywood screenwriters. Tewkesbury brings an exquisite eye, a sly humor, and a flair for details to an eccentric group of characters. Unforgettable and deeply resonant, the novel weaves the human and the political with lyricism, sensuality and grace.

> – Michelle Satter, Founding Director, Sundance Institute Feature Film Program

The themes and characters of Joan Tewkesbury's remarkable book are steeped in the spices and flavors of Latin American magic realism. She can turn on a centavo from comic absurdity to gossamer romance, sweep through envy, betrayal, and revenge, and then plunge down a nightmare hole into things terrible to contemplate. This book has the freshness of a first novel told with the assurance of a master.

> – Jonathan Richards, author of *Nick & Jake*

What a fierce, bawdy, wonderfully inventive novel! Somewhere in time in South America the enchanting Ebba and her beleaguered village are upended by the power and greed of a ridiculous tyrant. Spun as a fable in a style both grotesque and lyrical, Tewkesbury clearly stands with the kind, the decent, the daring. She does so with so much humor and charm that we the readers are swept breathlessly along and feel triumphant at the astonishing outcome. *Ebba and the Green Dresses* is a captivating tale of innocence struggling against evil, a far too familiar story in this sorry world, but told here with fearlessness and defiant hope. A delighting book.

– Kathryn Walker, author of *A Stopover in Venice*

EBBA
AND
THE GREEN DRESSES
OF
OLIVIA GOMEZ
IN
A TIME
OF
CONFLICT
AND
WAR

a novel by

JOAN TEWKESBURY

HAND TO HAND

Hand to Hand is a community based endeavor that supports independently published works and public events, free of the restrictions that arise from commercial and political concerns. It is a forum for artists who are in dynamic and reciprocal relationship with their communities for the sake of peacemaking, restoring culture and the planet. For further information regarding Hand to Hand please write to us at: P.O. Box 186, Topanga, CA, 90290, USA. Or visit us on the web at:

www.handtohandpublishing.com

Donations to organizations have been made to replenish the trees that were used to create the paper in this book.

"XXIX"(A Little Friendly Advice") by Nicanor Parra, translated by W.S. Merwin, from ANTIPOEMS: NEW AND SELECTED, copyright ©1985 by Nicanor Parra. Reprinted by permission of New Directions Publishing Corp.

Book and Cover Design: Stephan David Hewitt
Author Photo by Catherine Ledner

Ebba and the Green Dresses of Olivia Gomez in a Time of Conflict and War
© 2011 Joan Tewkesbury
ISBN: 978-0-9720718-8-8
Manufactured in the USA by Hand to Hand
Hand to Hand First Edition, October 2011
05 04 03 02

Hand to Hand Publishing, P.O. Box 186, Topanga, CA 90290

www.handtohandpublishing.com

Publisher's Cataloging-in-Publication Data

Tewkesbury, Joan.
    Ebba and the green dresses of Olivia Gomez in a time of conflict and war : a novel / by Joan Tewkesbury.
        p. cm.
        ISBN-13: 978-0-9720718-8-8
        ISBN-10: 0-9720718-8-1

    1. Teenage girls–Latin America–Fiction. 2. Political corruption–Latin America–Fiction. 3. Latin America–Politics and government–Fiction. 4. Bildungsromans. 5. Suspense fiction. I. Title.

PS3620.E98E23 2011   813'.6
                           QBI11-600171

For
Robin and Peter

ACKNOWLEDGMENTS

With gratitude to good friends... Marguerite Gordon, who introduced me to some of the world of this story and her flock of dogs. To Karen Gottlieb, Konni Corriere and Signe Lohman who were generous enough to read early on.

To Peter Dimock who read the manuscript at its first "finish" and provided encouragement with intelligent, sensitive guidance. To Paige Bernhardt who took on my failings in the rudiments of the English language with her expertise and sense of humor. To JoAnn Carney and Jean Pagliuso whose images were evidence that characters imagined could exist. To Tony Etz for his continued interest and support. To my children, Robin and Peter Maguire, who provided encouragement, honest appraisal, a wary eye and relevant information. To Stephan David Hewitt, the editor of this book who collaborated with an open mind, also with a sense of humor and his composer's sensibility.

To the unknown South American authors whose accounts of survival despite political imprisonment and the dark realities of torture are a testament to the power of personal voice. To Alma Guillermoprieto. Her *New Yorker* articles and non-fiction books provided exposure to facts in the Central and South Americas more inconceivable than fiction. To Carolyn Forché. Her anthology, *Against Forgetting, Twentieth Century Poetry of Witness* presented authors from all over the world who transformed unjustified political oppression and cruelty into heart-stopping resonance. To the Chilean poet, anarchist, professor of physics and unrepentant Dadaist, Nicanor Parra, whose wit and humor impacts overwhelming chaos with truth and ironic wisdom. And to the French poet, novelist, mathematician, Raymond Queneau, whose approach to reality, including war, is verbal juggling and black humor with a Buster Keaton touch.

But most of all, to Deena Metzger who opened the door to my outrage. Her belief and encouragement allowed me to access the world of my imagination to be used as a tool to examine the often absurd and incomprehensible events of the human condition.

"The birds went silent in collective anticipation of disaster."
Author Unknown

Before, When the Village Was Called
Viento de Costado Tormentoso

The village of Viento de Costado Tormentoso (roughly translated, stormy winds, troubled and turbulent) sat perched precariously on the top of a mountain like a basket of eggs. It was old and dusty and dry. There were passing clouds that cluttered the sky, but it hardly ever rained and the wind howled constantly.

"Just like Elena Cordova," all fifty-four residents of Viento de Costado Tormentoso sniped.

Fifty-four... the exact number of inches around Elena Cordova's two hundred and seventy pound waist.

Fifty-four... the exact age of Elena Cordova when she came to Josefina from Spain to sing selections from "Madame Butterfly" for the Kind Predecessor's sixtieth birthday celebration. Jorge Maximo, who insisted on being called Kind Predecessor because he thought of himself as benevolent, loved opera. The self-appointed authority figure of Spanish and German descent was very rich and governed a narrow district squeezed between two bigger districts that produced coffee, trees, rumor, and dangerous confusion. Josefina, the capital of his domain, was a modest, made-up municipality nestled next to the sea and situated at the very bottom of the mountain.

The distinguished opera singer had arrived by boat on July 26th and immediately lost her voice because the climate was humid and damp. In a desperate attempt to get it back, she wrote "higher, dryer air" on a piece of paper and handed it to the musical director, Manuel Martinez.

At first he'd panicked but after blowing into a paper bag to calm himself down, he arranged for a quiet young man named Juan Ernesto, who played bass violin and piano and was the only member of the orchestra owning a car large enough to accommodate the opera singer's commodious assets, to drive her up the mountain to the village of Viento de Costado Tormentoso. It was the highest, dry place he could think of.

Legend has it that as soon as they arrived at the top of the peak, Elena Cordova stepped out of the four-door sedan, walked to the center of the village square and sang...

"*Un bel di vedreme... e poi la appear...*" (One fine day the ship will appear...) to perfection. And because the wind was always blowing, the grand sound of her large voice drifted down into the brief-green valley where everyone, including the animals and birds, stopped doing whatever they were doing to listen.

"Magnificent!" someone shouted.

"A singing angel is filling the air," a son remembered his mother saying. Others, with more pessimistic views, determined that the beautiful music had apocalyptic overtones and could only mean that the world as they knew it was about to come to an end, which as it turned out was true, but not until a little later.

From that day forward, anyone wanting to hear the thrilling voice of Elena Cordova had to journey up the treacherous road to the top of the mountain because the two hundred and seventy pound, hypochondriacal singer refused to budge. She told three newspaper reporters who braved the trip that her voice had never sounded better and from now on she would only be singing up there in the sky.

Due to her decision, and because the Kind Predecessor loved opera or anything artistic, he commissioned the erection of an outdoor bandstand in the center of the square with a reinforced stage strong enough to support Elena Cordova's enormous weight. He also provided free bus transportation from Josefina to Viento de Costado Tormentoso three times a week and Juan Ernesto, who really preferred the company of men, was recruited, actually blackmailed, into being the soprano's permanent pianist. The Kind Predecessor also made arrangements to airlift, by helicopter, his very own baby grand piano so Elena Cordova would have the best instrument money could buy to underscore her glorious voice. He even postponed his government duties on the day of the piano's arrival to oversee the tuning of the keyboard. In truth, he had high hopes of getting a little on the side, but Elena Cordova graciously declined, saying it was bad policy to mix politics and art.

After a few weeks into her singing schedule, a small post office was built not far from the church, so she could receive fan mail and, at her insistence, a well-known medical practitioner, Dr. Lorenzo Vidal, was imported from Mexico City to check the singer's throat and pulses on a daily basis. In order to have light on the stage, Elena Cordova herself taught Juan Ernesto how to bootleg electricity from the one and only power pole in the village, abandoned after plans for a state of the art, three-lane highway went belly up.

However, because of the paranoid political climate and because Elena Cordova remained un-seducible, all of this robust activity began to make the Kind Predecessor nervous. What if everyone in Viento de Costado Tormentoso decided to become creative and have ideas of his or her own?

For three nights in a row, as the Kind Predecessor slept next to his extremely flat-chested wife, he dreamt he climbed to the top of Elena Cordova's gigantic breasts. So on the fourth morning, after his first cup of coffee, the Kind Predecessor had an idea. He sent a message to Octavio Gomez, the unambitious husband of Olivia Gomez, the Kind Predecessor's ambitious third cousin. Octavio was a man of medium expectations, a man you could count on to do exactly what he was told. So on that very day at exactly twelve noon, under a tree in the garden, Octavio Gomez placed his chubby hand on the family bible and became the first official mayor of Viento de Costado Tormentoso.

For a while everything went pretty smoothly except for the howling wind and an occasional raid by rebel splinter groups hoping to find someone worth kidnapping status, but who always gave up because the soprano was really the only person of value and she was too fat. Basically, life on top of the mountain was constant, predictable and a little bit boring so when two really unusual events occurred on the same day back-to-back, it threw everyone for a loop.

Event One. At precisely 2:00 p.m. in Josefina, during a publicity stunt arranged to promote progress by Benny Rodriguez, the Kind Predecessor's aggressive public relations person, the Kind Predecessor, while attempting to shift the gears of a gigantic Caterpillar tractor, slipped off the seat, fell to the ground and was crushed under two tons of tread. Rodriguez, a short, self-important man with bad skin, bad breath, a nasty disposition and who liked to call himself The General, made several seriously wrong, protracted attempts to pull the Kind Predecessor out from under the tractor's tonnage. As a result, instead of being rescued, the Kind Predecessor died a hideous death while crying out in excruciating pain. The headline in the evening paper, written ahead of time by Benny Rodriguez himself, read: A TRAGIC ACCIDENT.

Event Two. In Viento de Costado Tormentoso, at exactly 2:05 the same afternoon, Elena Cordova, dressed in a brand new green satin dress, singing B-flat above high C in a complicated aria by some contemporary composer, burst a blood vessel in her brain and dropped dead, face down on the reinforced stage. Unfortunately, all two hundred and seventy pounds of the singer's girth landed on Juan Ernesto's foot, which broke with a resounding snap. His screams of pain were mistaken for grief until Dr. Vidal from Mexico City had the presence of mind to ask someone to roll the dead soprano off the poor man's foot. After close examination the doctor put Ernesto's whole leg in a cast. Three days later in a grand ceremony, organized and managed by Juan Ernesto from a wheelchair borrowed from Dr. Vidal, the dead soprano, wearing her "Madame Butterfly" kimono, was eulogized and laid to rest in the Viento de Costado Tormentoso Cemetery. Her custom-made coffin took up three plots.

Fortunately for everyone, Benny Rodriguez, now proclaiming himself the successor to his predecessor, couldn't make it but he did send a large wreath of purple plastic flowers. It seems he was much too busy working with an out-of-town lawyer to officially change his name to "General" before taking over the government. His first order of business was to install Pepe Montano, a beefy, self-important military man with well-publicized takeover ambitions of his own, as next in line in case of emergency. The "General" even gave him a title... "Commander after Me." Then after booting out the kind Predecessor's flat-chested wife when she spurned the General's advances, he moved himself into the official mansion and, to completely cover his backside, the General staged a memorable memorial for his ex-boss. Most importantly he was making sure the Kind Predecessor's coffin was nailed shut so no one would see the state of his mangled body.

Everyone up on the mountain or down by the beach was convinced that the tractor accident was no accident at all, just an unnecessary event staged by Rodriguez to elevate himself into power. Everyone knows a tragedy is cheaper than a coup. And Benny, now only answering to General when being addressed, kept rubbing his eyes to keep them irritated so he could drip tears of grief. The pessimists with apocalyptic leanings just shook their heads and said, "We told you so."

Meanwhile, on the day after Elena Cordova's splendid sendoff, Juan Ernesto, even though his foot was throbbing in its hip-high cast, packed up his four-door sedan and drove down the mountain to the house of the musical director, Manuel Martinez. After drinking a beer and some idle chitchat, Juan gave Martinez the car and a jar of homemade apricot jam. Then he asked if Manuel could please give him a ride to the harbor where he helped Juan adjust his crutches, said goodbye and watched Juan Ernesto board the boat to Cuba. He was never heard from again.

Later, when the mayor stood on the reinforced stage and read Elena Cordova's will to all fifty-four residents, they discovered that in a ploy to deter the romantic advances of the Kind Predecessor, she had secretly married Juan Ernesto, even though he preferred the company of men but all Juan got for his trouble was the unused portion of a boat ticket to Cuba.

The rest of her estate, including her sheet music and costumes, she bequeathed to the people of Viento de Costado Tormentoso to use however they wished. Everyone in the village was stunned. They were certainly grateful, but not quite sure what it meant. Finally, Dr. Vidal from Mexico City suggested that the name Viento de Costado Tormentoso was such a mouthful, they should rename the village Elena in honor of the dead diva. After a brief discussion and a show of hands, the decision was unanimous. So Father Lyle said a few things in Latin, sprinkled a little water from his holy-water sprinkler, waved his incense ball and announced that from now on the name of the village would be Elena.

Almost immediately the howling wind died down to a breeze and in a few days, except for the occasional gust, it stopped blowing altogether. It even started to rain. After a week and a half it stopped like someone had turned off a spigot, but when the sun came out, a double rainbow blasted across the reinforced stage in an arc.

Convinced that this was a sign with mystical meaning, the soprano's fans, despite the political risks, streamed up the mountain to visit the bandstand like it was some sort of shrine. But when the roads clogged with the spiritually inclined, the General, running the district whether anyone wanted him to or not, stopped the free bus and issued citations for walking. He wasn't interested in opera or anything artistic or the slightest hint of a miracle because miracles had the potential to upstage him and his brand new prominent position.

"Waste of money and gas," he announced. "Besides, she's dead," he said, blowing his nose. "A bandstand is a bandstand, not some kind of shrine. You want religion, go to church. You want singing entertainment, go buy a record."

Eventually the fans stopped coming up the mountain but the residents continued to call their village Elena even when the General issued an order to stop the name change at once. "But you changed your name," they reminded, delighted to turn his proclamation inside out and since the General couldn't find a loophole to get around that fact, he made an announcement in the paper as if the whole thing had been his idea. "Because," he was quoted, "the wind had stopped blowing on top of the mountain, the name, Viento de Costado Tormentoso, (stormy winds, troubled and turbulent) didn't really apply. So, from now on the village will be called Elena, after my mother." The mother part was a lie but she was dead so he figured he could get away with it.

Then, in a campaign to win favor by improving his looks, the General

EBBA, HER MOTHER WHO IS DYING, AND THE SMOKE OF HER FATHER

Ebba stood coiled in the corner saturated with sun in a perfect square of pale heat. A hot dusty wind lifted the hem of her blue cotton dress, blew it around her skinny body making music on the curves and hollows of her frame. She watched a large yellow spider creep across a clump of bright blue lobelia growing in the kitchen wall and disappear into a jagged crack. Ebba sighed. Her mother was dying. Nothing dramatic, just bit-by-bit. A slow, orderly erosion of all the particles that make up a human being. Her father was already dead. Gone without much ceremony, which seemed appropriate since all she'd ever known was the smoke of him, a mirage he'd chiseled out of silence and fury.

Her parents had come together over a flat front tire on Ebba's mother's bike. Ebba's mother's girlfriend, Lucy, had a brother who could solve problems and was good with his hands so after he improvised a patch for the puncture, he'd walked Ebba's mother home where they engaged in what Ebba's mother called "her appreciation." Nine months later "appreciation" produced a daughter, whether Lucy's brother liked it or not.

Ebba's father had always been trouble and she knew it. Risky business with no foundation. She'd figured it out crouched down beside him as he pulled weeds he didn't want to pull in the garden of a house he didn't want to live in. Somewhere between the onions and tomatoes, he'd flung out his arm and smacked Ebba across the mouth with the screwdriver he used as a trowel. "You look just like your mother," he'd growled then whispered to his delicate hands, "And she's no saint."

After that he went back to weeding, clammed right up, shut himself off like a radio, let the quiet hang in the air like an old rag while Ebba's lip took on a life of its own and puffed up purple. She'd stayed glued to the spot waiting for an explanation. Surely her father would feel ashamed and give her a reason, feel sorry for what he'd done... but he didn't. It wasn't her fault she looked like her mother. Her mother was her mother and Ebba didn't like it any better than he did.

Finally, when the silence was so silent it felt really loud, Ebba grabbed the screwdriver out of his hand and flung it into the ravine. Then she got up and ran away quick so he couldn't catch her, but much to her surprise he never looked up, never got up, never moved a muscle except to sit back on his heels and stare at the ground.

After that her father lost his allure, lost the upper hand so to speak. He'd poked too many holes in her heart, used it once too often to launch the rockets of his rage. The last time she saw him was on the Sunday morning before Ash Wednesday when he walked out the door. He was carrying his sister's suitcase and he didn't say a word as he walked out of there fast.

Ebba had followed him out to the road, watched him not look back or wave a single wave but she didn't call out. She just waited for him to disappear. Oddly, his departure didn't make her sad. Truth be told, she felt relieved and after a few days it seemed as if he'd never been there at all.

Ebba looked up at the sky from the perfect square of pale heat and waited for the sound of Bernardo DeVille's truck as it strained its way up the winding dirt road that pointed to her house like an old bony finger. Bernardo DeVille called his truck "Gloria" in honor of his sister Gloria DeVille, a school teacher who, after being dragged from her house at three in the morning by a group of uniformed men, was never seen again. Everything in her house, nailed down or not, had been torn apart or taken. Clothes, pictures, furniture, letters, kitchen cupboards, even her bobby pins and metal curlers. Dishes were smashed on the kitchen floor. Her books shredded and burned. The bathtub was ripped out of the wall and the commode off its mooring. Bloody sheets were ripped to shreds and thrown over the bedroom door. The only thing left was the icebox and a bottle of sour milk.

With no husband or children except for her young students, nothing of Gloria's spirit remained. No namesake, no keepsakes, no stuff to show that she ever existed and, worst of all, no one knew why. There was a lengthy, halfhearted search but finally, out of frustration and because Gloria's body was never recovered, Bernardo made a coffin and buried it in the family plot across from the shrine dedicated to Elena Cordova. He pounded her headstone out of tin with trimmings and it said...

Missing...
Gloria Rodriguez DeVille
Devoted daughter-sister-teacher
1953 - 198...

The neighbors were convinced it was all a mistake. Another Gloria, the Gloria who sold poppy pods out of her kitchen window to avoid paying government taxes, lived right down the road and the neighbors said that that other Gloria left on a trip right after the abduction to visit her boyfriend in Guadalajara and never came back. But Bernardo didn't buy it. His sister was a threat. Fierce and smart, she taught her students to use birth control and to question authority. She taught them foreign languages and how to speak out if they had something to say. On the day after he buried the empty coffin Bernardo painted his temperamental pickup truck candy apple red and airbrushed "GLORIA" in high-gloss gold across the hood. When he was finished, he drank a toast in her honor, smashed the glass on the ground and went to search for her or her body.

He looked everywhere. He even announced he would pay the kidnappers big bucks for her return, but nothing ever showed up. Finally he decided that his search was futile so he drove "Gloria" to his cousin-in-law, Octavio Gomez, the mayor's office, parked her right in front and sat in the flatbed carving *milagros* of his sister out of wood or soap to give away to anyone passing by who was interested enough to want one.

Crowds gathered daily to collect the tokens of Gloria's spirit and as long as there was a clear path to the front door, the authorities didn't seem to care. But after three weeks Bernardo got so fed up with everyone's lack of effort or interest he walked into the mayor's office with a machete and threatened to cut off the legs of the Chief of Police.

Outraged at the intrusion, the Chief went into action to "disappear" and torture Bernardo DeVille's entire family, but had to give up the idea when he was reminded by his superiors that Bernardo's dead father was Hernaldo DeVille, renowned photographer and distant cousin of Olivia Gomez, wife of the mayor. Besides that, Bernardo, renowned furniture maker and creator of religious objects he made for the church, was the only person licensed to use wood from the local forests which were dwindling fast because the General decided that cutting down trees was important for progress. In other words they said, Bernardo, unlike his sister who was just a teacher with a big mouth, would be missed. Needless to say, the Chief was encouraged by his superiors to address the problem in a more creative way. Three days later the Chief of Police penned the following statement which was printed in the paper, and posted on the front door of the mayor's office.

"Regarding Gloria DeVille...

We are inclined to think that perhaps there has been some sort of Gloria mix-up, but to show Bernardo DeVille that there are no hard feelings for his threatening tone to the Chief of Police, the General, current president of Josefina and all surrounding territories, would be happy to happily accept a lovely banquet table and twenty chairs that Bernardo DeVille will carve especially for him. And that because Bernardo DeVille is so respected in his field, the General will be honored to honor Bernardo with the honor of making the General this special gift so they can put the entire 'Gloria' business behind them."

In other words, given the current political climate, Bernardo had better pay attention because he was putting the rest of his family at risk if he continued this threatening trend in his behavior. Not really having a choice, Bernardo made a banquet table and carved twenty chairs for the General, but only after choosing wood that was wormy and infested with termites.

How Bernardo DeVille met Phillipa Marie

To calm his fury, Bernardo started to raise chickens and pigs. Not to eat or sell but for the love of it. Sensing they were bored in their pens, he would put them in his truck every Saturday after confession and take them for a ride to soothe their senses. Driving down the rutted road rimming Elena, he would enter the brief-green valley and turn them loose by a shallow pond to wander in the weeds and wallow in the water. Then after he read the paper and smoked a cigar and felt certain they were cooler and calmer and eager for a nap, he would load them back in the truck and drive home.

One afternoon during a heat wave, Gloria ran out of water and stopped under the tree that Ebba had climbed to escape from her mother and to make up songs that she shared with the birds and leaves. Before Bernardo could get out of the truck to unlatch Gloria's hood, the two pigs and eleven chickens and two friendly dogs picked up Ebba's song and responded with ones of their own. Her voice was high and thin like a wire so she used it to hang the laundry of her soul, to let it flap in the breeze. The animals' noise was so god-awful Bernardo told them to be still, that he couldn't think with all that racket, but they didn't listen. Ebba's tone was thrilling and it inspired them. Not sure from where the song was being sung, Bernardo left Gloria's dehydrated engine and looked up in the tree. Surrounded by a cluster of pale green leaves, Ebba's skinny brown legs, framed by her blue cotton dress, dangled from a limb. Bernardo waited for a space between the notes and then called out.

"Hello..." he shouted. Taken by surprise, Ebba stopped singing and heard the noisy animal choir. She looked down through the leafy branches and saw Bernardo looking up, the open hood of the red truck right behind him. He had a long braid trailing down his back and his skin was the color of coffee with a little milk. His prominent nose looked like a broken branch sitting on a plate.

"What's your song?" Bernardo called out.

"My what?" Ebba flung back.

"Your song," he asked. "My animals seem to know it."

Ebba tucked her dress under her legs. She didn't want him to see her white cotton underpants. "Just a song," she shrugged. All of a sudden the animals stopped their racket so it was quiet and Bernardo didn't have to shout.

"Do you live in the tree?"

Ebba looked at him like he was crazy and pointed from her perch.

"I live over there."

Bernardo glanced at the sloping adobe house that seemed to be sinking into the ground but growing bright blue lobelia in all of its crevices and cracks.

"Do you live alone?"

Ebba shook her head.

"With my mother, Carlotta Pavon." Bernardo thought for a moment but he couldn't place her.

"Who are you?" Ebba asked.

"Bernardo," Bernardo said. "Bernardo DeVille."

"The guy who carves his sister?" Bernardo nodded and wondered how she knew.

"I took one when you weren't looking," Ebba smiled and started to climb down the tree. "I'm Phillipa Marie, but I call myself Ebba. I like the way it feels on my lips when I say the beeees."

Bernardo nodded again then remembered why he was there.

"Well Ebba, I'd like to borrow some water. My truck is thirsty."

He pointed to Gloria's yawning hood.

"Do you have a bucket?"

Ebba was gripping the trunk with her big bare feet and when she got to the ground Bernardo took a step back. He hadn't expected someone so short. Up on the limb Ebba seemed older but she was just a kid, yet not exactly. She was young but weary. Eager but wary. Skinny and dark from the sun, she had round brown eyes that looked out from a delicate face and a thick black braid that hung down her back like a rope. Bernardo realized he hadn't been listening.

"I beg your pardon?"

"A bucket," she said, pushing through Bernardo's preoccupation.

"How old are you?" he pressed.

"None of your business," Ebba replied.

"I'm thirty-seven," Bernardo offered.

She looked thoughtful then shrugged.

"Maybe eleven almost twelve, or twelve going on thirteen. My mother doesn't remember."

Bernardo was taken aback.

"Your mother doesn't remember? How could she forget?"

Ebba ignored the question, though she'd often wondered herself.

Joan Tewkesbury

"There's water at the pump," she pointed.

Finally Bernardo snapped to, forced himself to pay attention and off they went to the truck where Ebba climbed into the flatbed with the black and white pigs who let her scratch behind their ears and the eleven brown chickens Ebba let walk across her feet and the two friendly dogs who jumped out of the truck barking and rolling in the dirt while Bernardo filled Gloria's emergency radiator can with water.

Finally when he turned the key in the ignition to coax the parched plugs into action, Ebba patted the gold, airbrushed "Gloria" on the hood and spoke softly, encouragingly, convincingly, letting the truck know it was all right to belch black smoke as it sputtered to life. So as not to kill what he just got started, Bernardo kept his foot on the gas as he released the hand brake and shouted his thanks, promising to come back to take Ebba to meet his wife, Hortence Grace and their three children. Then he lurched up the mountain as Ebba waved goodbye from the middle of the road.

EBBA'S DREAM

That night, after the rescue of the truck, Ebba dreamt she flew up the road and landed in Bernardo's kitchen where his entire family was eating vegetable soup with freshly baked bread. After she joined them for dinner, she helped Hortence Grace, whom she'd never met, with the dishes and then after that she helped Hortence Grace wash Bernardo's long black hair in the kitchen sink with rain water and cider vinegar. As she watched the long black tendrils cascade down the white porcelain bowl, she stuck her hands in the water to let the slick wet slippery ribbons slide through her fingers like eels and as Hortence Grace talked about the benefits of drinking cider vinegar for arthritis or gout, a thrill sensation started running up and down the inside of Ebba's legs like the vibration after the ring of a bell and she started to tremble with throbbing tingles rising and falling in wavy rhythms, throbbing and talking and thrilling and talking and tingle thrillings... thrilling and talking... thrilling and throbbing and rising and floating and falling and ringing and rhythmy waving and thrilling until at the very peak of the pinnacle of the thrill sensation, when Ebba thought she was about to explode, she jolted awake with a jerk and shivered. Not a cold shiver, but an internal shimmery shiver, subtle and remarkable all at once. Just as mysteriously as the whole business had started, the tingling and thrilling started to slip away. Smaller and smaller... fewer and fewer... less and less... faint, more faintly thrilling... drifting... until the only thing left was the fragrance of the night blooming jasmine growing outside Ebba's bedroom window and she sat up in bed and blurted out, "What in the world was that?"

Since there was no one there to answer, the words just bounced around in the dark and as the last miniscule of tickle twitched a final tingle in her left little toe, Ebba laid back down and went straight to sleep.

"Phillipa Marie?" Ebba's mother called out.

"What?" Ebba was watching the yellow spider creep out of one crack in the wall and into another.

"I need you," her mother whined.

Ebba sighed and hurried to her mother who was propped up in bed, lost in a cluster of poinsettia printed pillows.

"I need my will," she whispered.

"Again?" Ebba whined. She sounded just like her mother.

Carlotta Pavon didn't bother with an answer. She just glared until all the air in the room seemed to freeze. As a girl, she'd had high hopes of becoming an actress and practiced different looks in the mirror. When nothing came of her acting efforts she became a singer three nights a week at the local cantina where her intense expressions became legendary.

Ebba moved the small table next to her mother's bed off two loose bricks in the floor. She picked them up one by one and removed a metal box, opened the lid, took out the worn stack of papers wrapped with a red rubber band and handed them to her mother who clutched them to her chest.

"Thank you," Ebba's mother said dramatically, like she'd just received a basket of diamonds, but the edge in her voice meant the retrieval hadn't been fast enough.

"It gives me comfort just to hold these in my hands."

"I don't know why," Ebba yawned.

"Because it's our security," her mother snapped.

Ebba looked doubtful and studied the light haloing her mother's hair, making her look pale and fragile against the pillows.

"You get the house no matter what anyone tells you, including your father's relatives who will be sure to show up to get something for nothing. This house belongs to you and that is that."

Ebba stared straight ahead. She'd heard this "will" business over and over. Where the will was, where her mother wanted to be buried, who was not to be told she was dead after she died so Ebba wouldn't be robbed or coerced by Mrs. Marquez, their desperately possessive, meddlesome neighbor, into handing over the three green satin dresses purchased by Ebba's mother at the annual yard sale of Olivia Gomez.

By some stroke of luck, Ebba's mother had been first in line at Olivia's gate on the morning of the sale and spotted the dresses made from the green satin costume Elena Cordova was wearing on the day of her death. Because the sun was shining on the satin it made them enormously attractive and greener than Olivia's hopeless little patch of dried up lawn. Unfortunately for Ebba's mother, Mrs. Marquez, their aggressive neighbor, was second in line so she spotted them too.

The dresses had been commissioned by the mayor's wife, Olivia Gomez, after they cut the costume off the fat soprano because she wasn't breathing. All that green satin was too good to waste and because Olivia couldn't decide which style would make her look thin and be best to entertain a visiting German professor and his wife, she'd had the seamstress create three different concoctions.

When Olivia was informed that the German professor hated the color green, she'd worn her old, substantial, brown silk file with a fishtail skirt and a neckline that showed her cleavage. Then after entertaining was halted due to a rash of homemade bombs exploding at parties, the green satin dresses had been shoved to the back of the closet and forgotten. Finally, in an effort to show that neither she nor the mayor were frivolous, but mostly to make more room in her closet, Olivia had included the dresses in her once-a-year sale. After a very long wait, Olivia's maid had finally unlocked the gate and Ebba's mother rushed in ahead of everyone else. But just as she reached out to touch the shiny green sleeves, Mrs. Marquez had shouted, "Don't touch those dresses, Carlotta Pavon! Olivia put those dresses out there for me, just for me! All mine! I have big plans for those dresses!"

That's when Ebba's mother, who had no plans for the dresses whatsoever, reached down, gathered the gowns and bought them all... one, two, three. Not only did Ebba's mother hate Mrs. Marquez with all her heart for no reason in particular, but more importantly Ebba's mother felt that the dresses shouldn't be separated. She believed that everything had a life of its own and as far as she was concerned, these dresses had lived a long time crammed in the closet so they would be lonely living apart. Mrs. Marquez went crazy and kept screaming as Ebba's mother counted out the pesos for her purchase.

"Those dresses don't give a shit about being separated. They don't have feelings. They're not people!" she yelled.

But Ebba's mother deliberately ignored Mrs. Marquez' raging manifesto and walked out of Olivia's yard with the green garments carefully folded

Joan Tewkesbury

over her arm.

Needless to say, Mrs. Marquez hadn't spoken to Ebba's mother since and on those occasions when she saw Ebba's mother wearing all three dresses, one on top of the other, to work in the garden, she spent endless hours thinking of ways to get even. Ebba's mother, knowing the color green to be healing, wore the green gowns to water and plant and rub Mrs. Marquez' nose in envy.

Poor Mrs. Marquez. Ever since her husband died, she'd been trying to seduce Raymond Valdez, the plumber, into marriage and was strongly convinced that any one of the three dresses would do the job. But it was not to be in life or death if Ebba's mother had anything to do with it.

"I promise," Ebba uttered listlessly. Ebba was certain that this constant review of death was because her mother relished the details of dying. It seemed as though she could hardly wait.

"I'm so bored," she would sigh.

"There are things to do," Ebba always said.

"Nothing that hasn't been done before," her mother would bark.

Then she'd roll over and turn on the tiny radio beside her bed to listen to her favorite soap opera starring Tootsie Quieler. That was Ebba's cue to walk out of the room as her mother yelled, "Where do you think you're going?"

Ebba never answered. It was safer. No explanation. No lies. Once, when Ebba tried to explain how she had met Bernardo and why she liked going for rides in his truck, her mother had flown into a fury. "He's a man and there's nothing worse," she'd shouted.

"So was my father," Ebba had tried to point out.

"Yes, and look where it got us," her mother shot back.

"Then why were you married?" Ebba demanded.

This question was always met with silence and no reply because Ebba's parents had never been married which gave Ebba the latitude to press on.

"And why was I born?"

This too met with resounding silence, giving Ebba the edge. She'd learned if she asked those two questions back to back she could shut her mother up with no possibility of any more discussion about anything at all. This was extremely important because with the exception of her own two feet, Bernardo and his truck Gloria were Ebba's only means of escape.

Bernardo, sensing Ebba was as bored as his livestock, started to include Ebba in all of the animal outings. He even took her up the top of the mountain to spend time with his wife, Hortence Grace, and their children,

Ariel, Rebecca and Tobias. She'd even met Bernardo's cousin, Olivia Gomez when all of them went halfway down the mountain into the brief-green valley to cool off and heard Olivia screaming from her house across the pond. It seems she had just been informed her that her husband, Octavio the Mayor, had been assassinated in cold blood.

Octavio Gomez had been sunbathing nude in the garden of his Oriental mistress, Li Choo. She lived on the far side of Josefina and since she wasn't around, he'd propped up his feet on a low stone wall by Li Choo's pond bordered in bright pink bougainvillea and full of belching frogs, to let the sun work its magic on his privates. The mayor was a great believer in magic, which included the properties of the sun, the moon, and predestination. He consulted oracles, astrologers, numerologists and tarot card readers on a regular basis but somehow none of them had foreseen this particular event.

According to the papers, the mayor lived long enough to whisper the details of what had happened, but in fact none of what the paper reported was true. In order to make the mayor seem a little bit brave, a friendly journalist wrote the following words and pretended they had come out of the mayor's mouth. "Awakened from sleep, I thought I had been struck by rotten mangoes falling from the tree. A natural mistake until I opened my eyes and saw that blood was pulsing out of six gunshot wounds in my belly. Looking up, I saw six men with drawn guns and bandana-covered faces."

In truth, the mayor had looked down at his friendly member shriveled with fright and succumbed without a word.

The paper also didn't report that the assassins had to jump over the garden wall to escape Li Choo's two old bow-legged servants who rushed at the men yelling and waving very large swords. Only when they were sure that the killers were gone had they dropped their weapons and carried the mayor into the shade where they covered his privates with a linen napkin left over from lunch and dabbed at his face with chilled champagne. They fanned him with a stack of city planning papers regarding homes for the poor, but he never regained consciousness. By the time the ambulance arrived the two old servants had managed to slip the mayor into a black satin bathrobe, one of several he kept in Li Choo's closet, and tied the belt in a knot. It was a thoughtful gesture considering that two newspaper reporters accompanied the dead mayor in the ambulance all the way to the hospital where he was pronounced dead on arrival.

BERNARDO'S DREAM

The night after the mayor's assassination, Bernardo had a dream so intense that he threw himself out of bed. Desperate sounds crept up from the bottom of his throat and marched out of his mouth in shout after shout waking Hortence Grace, who managed to grab hold of him before he could run out the door. She shook him as hard as she could but when Bernardo finally opened his eyes, they were shiny and blank. Not sure how to bring him back, she spoke in a firm, clear voice.

"Bernardo... what is it? Bernardo... what's wrong?"

That's when he started to sob.

"The children are gone," he rasped and tried to get up and run outside, but Hortence Grace held him firmly by his braid and this time she spoke in a low dark voice.

"Bernardo, stop! You're trapped in a dream."

Then she took hold of his hands and steered him back to the edge of their bed, sat him down gently, crawled around behind him until she was in back of his back and pulled him into her roomy couch of a body, held him close, rocked him, patted him even though he was still clutched in a knot making desperate sounds and shaking.

"You are here. You're at home with the children and me."

And she didn't stop holding and patting and rocking until slowly, ever so slowly, Bernardo unwound himself from the grip of his night terror and she coaxed him into the nest of their bed where he opened his eyes, sighed then fell back to sleep nursing Hortence Grace's giant vanilla breasts like a baby.

Now wide awake, Hortence Grace puzzled Bernardo's dream long into the night, puzzled it over and over in her extra sixth sense but nothing came to mind. Finally, sure that Bernardo was deeply asleep, she released herself from the bed's tangle where two of their children, Tobias and Rebecca, had been created. Ariel, their third, had burst into being on a pink blanket under the stars, but that was another story. She picked one of Bernardo's old shirts up off the floor, pulled it over her head and padded outside into the garden where it was quiet except for insect armies doing night work.

The air was soft and made her feel calm so she undid her braid and shook out her hair as star after star showered across the sky. She made a pouch with Bernardo's shirt, gathered petals from the rose bushes and

Joan Tewkesbury

carried them into the kitchen, put them in an earthenware crock and filled it with water. In the morning she would make a special rose petal tea so Bernardo could drink to new beginnings. Then she would sprinkle all three children with what was left over, to wash away the ghost of Bernardo's dream.

BACK IN LI CHOO'S GARDEN

On the morning of the day after the assassination, Olivia Gomez walked into Li Choo's garden and looked around. She told herself that she wasn't there to find scraps of her foolish husband, but she was. She needed proof, some trace of him, a fingernail or a hunk of hair, a drop of blood, a sliver of skin. Without asking permission or making sure she was in the right place, she began to dig into the crumbling grout in the low stone wall, but the only thing she discovered was decay.

She pulled apart the bushes and hedges, studied the leaves and petals of flowers, searched the pond and the pool, but nothing jumped out that she could recognize. Finally when she was tired from trying and had sighed a sigh of resignation and started to the gate she saw a tiny glint on the ground, bent down and picked up the last scrap of her husband. It was a chip of his tooth. First she cradled it in the palm of her hand. Then she held it up to the light and studied it carefully, wondered exactly when it had broken, examined the yellow enamel hoping for an answer written in code, but nothing revealed itself.

Olivia sighed and looked around the orderly garden. It certainly wasn't like her overrun yard featuring a rusty car carcass, a washing machine and other electric appliances the mayor purchased on business trips that sat like decaying trophies on her tiny scrap of lawn. Although her house boasted three electrical outlets, using them all at once guaranteed blown fuses in the ancient fuse box illegally attached to the one and only power pole not far from her kitchen window.

All of a sudden there was a terrible crash of breaking glass and Olivia was jolted out of the peace and quiet by a woman shouting in shrill Chinese at two bowlegged servants running out of the house dragging suitcases so heavy they could barely get to the gate topped with broken glass, barbed wire and vines.

Afraid of being seen, Olivia stepped behind the arbor covered in purple passionflowers and watched a pale slip of a woman hidden in a cyclone of black hair, appear in the doorway. Olivia inhaled sharply. This was the competition. This was Li Choo, the Oriental mistress of her late husband Octavio, the Mayor. Olivia tucked the chip of her husband's tooth in the small sack of stones she wore around her neck to encourage magic. Then she peered through the passionflowers just as Li Choo's orange and pale green silk robe fell open and revealed her naked body.

Olivia turned away. She really didn't want to see what her husband had been into, so to speak, what he had touched, caressed and penetrated on a regular basis, but she couldn't resist. The desire to compare her own flesh with this other woman's flesh was too tempting. She stepped out of the arbor just as Li Choo, framed in fluttering silk, stormed after the escaping servants. Oriental sounds spilled out of her mouth like an opera, but her body seemed very ordinary. In fact, it seemed less the body Olivia had expected a mistress to have. Small breasts, no waist, legs stick thin and not a hint of hair. Olivia wondered if that had that been the main attraction.

Olivia looked down, reacquainted herself with the valleys and vistas of her curves, her peaks and mounds. For the first time in a long time, she found her own terrain interesting, even scenic compared to the panorama before her. Then something happened that made her forget all about the female playground that her husband had visited on a regular basis. One of the servants had stopped, removed his leather belt and stood waiting for the flapping Oriental to come a little closer.

Li Choo was so caught up in her own fury she didn't see what was coming. Didn't see the strap lash out until it struck her like a snake, stopping her, stunning her, scaring her, shutting her up. Again and again, over and over the old servant let the belt rip Li Choo's silk robe to shreds and tear into her pale white flesh and lash lines across her face. Li Choo covered her eyes to protect them, but the bow legged servant moved closer and delivered a powerful highflying kick. Terrified, Li Choo lost her footing and slipped, fell backwards and hit her head on the sharp corner of the low wall where Olivia's husband had raised his feet to let the sun work its magic on his privates. That's when Olivia stepped forward and shouted "Stop!" as loudly as she could.

Startled, the bowlegged servants looked up as Olivia approached the unconscious mistress. "Don't come any closer," they said.

"I'll do what I want," Olivia answered and kept walking. The servant with the belt put it back on.

"We're sorry for you," he said, "but your husband was a fool."

This was no surprise to Olivia.

"Besides, you're too late."

Olivia looked down at Li Choo lying on the ground. Seeping blood was circling her head in a dark red halo and the silk robe fluttered around her body like a flag. Olivia turned back to the man buckling his belt and before she could ask any more questions, the couple ducked out the gate without another word. Olivia heard Li Choo moan so she knelt down and listened for a breath. Ignoring the business of mistress or wife, Olivia pulled a blue striped cushion off a nearby chair and lifted Li Choo's head which was soft and mushy like the overripe mangoes lying on the ground. Olivia leaned closer, looked into the almond-shaped eyes of her dead husband's object of love.

"Your husband was shy," Li Choo whispered.

Then she shuddered, exhaled deeply and died as blood continued to pulse out of the back of her head. Olivia leaned even closer to listen for any sign of life, but it was over. She grabbed hold of the billowing robe and pulled it across Li Choo's pale, ordinary body. She tucked it so tight Li Choo looked like a mummy. All that fluttered now were the wispy ends of Li Choo's long black hair.

Olivia sat back on her heels and after a moment pulled a few strands of hair from Li Choo's head, wound them into a figure eight and placed them in the sack with the stones and the chip of her husband's tooth. Then she got up and washed her blood-covered hands in the turquoise tiled pool, watched as threads of red streaked the pale blue water. That's when she heard a metallic clunk and saw something that looked like an oblong nut rolling toward her. For a moment she thought about running away, but reached down instead and picked up the whatever-it-was. It filled the palm of her hand and was much heavier than she expected. Since nothing about it was familiar she hurled it out of the garden without thinking twice.

The explosion was immediate and so intense it blew a hole in the wall, threw Olivia onto the ground and reverberated through her body as the noise rang in her ears and reshaped her future.

ANOTHER GARDEN

I n the General's garden, Sergeant Chavez stood behind his young wife Juanita seated at the small table under a plum tree loaded with fragrant fruit. Desperate to have a baby herself, Juanita was poring over baby pictures entered in a contest to become "the baby" whose face would appear on every label of every jar of government dispensed baby food. For two years Sergeant Chavez and Juanita had tried to conceive a child of their own. It was all Juanita wanted. They had exhausted themselves in continuous copulation, replaced desire with charts and thermometers and accusations of shooting blanks into a barren womb. Juanita was the Sergeant's third wife and at eighteen, the youngest. His first wife, Alma, had died, buried in the rubble of the awful August earthquake and his second wife, Stella, was so bored after three months of marriage to him, she ran off to Panama City and became a cocktail waitress.

Sergeant Chavez and Juanita had been in the garden all morning with a dozen other childless couples from the military. They had been appointed to be official judges of the "Baby Food Picture" contest featuring a thousand pesos prize to the winning baby picture and a year's supply of disposable diapers.

"Who better," the General had said. "Who better to choose the face for a baby food label then a childless couple who wanted to have a baby of their own? A couple desperate for their own little face, their own little replica of themselves, their own little angel. Who better then these barren couples to make the selection?"

Then the General, who still kept the heart of the Kind Predecessor in a jar and carried it with him wherever he went, shed a tear. Basically, he was a sentimental man without feelings who loved how the sound of his own voice moved him, made him believe that whatever he was saying was for the good of the people even though the contest was a lie to cover up giving stolen children, taken for back taxes or their parents' so-called political violations or to get even for some personal infraction, to impotent military couples to adopt.

Juanita studied each picture carefully while the Sergeant shifted from one foot to the other and worried about the seventh race at the dog track. He'd bet heavily on a hound named "Savior" hoping to cover his mounting gambling debts. Finally, Juanita placed the pictures in three piles. Yes, No and Maybe. After much deliberation, she chose one and held it up for the

Sergeant to look at. He bent over and adjusted his glasses, ran his fingers through the greasy strands of his thinning black hair. In truth, babies didn't interest him much. In fact, children really didn't interest him at all. He'd spent far too much of his military career herding and transferring other people's traumatized kids from one place to another. Not at all what a man of his experience and stature should be involved in. Law and order was more his style.

How he longed to be dealing with dissidents. For a man who had been trained in the refinements of torture, this current assignment seemed a demeaning waste of time. He was sick and tired of grandmothers chasing him wherever he went. Yelling and crying, blaming him for everything that was wrong. No matter how much he explained he was only carrying out orders, just doing what the General told him to do, they wouldn't listen.

"He looks very sweet," Juanita said.

Sergeant Chavez squinted then shrugged, told her to choose because she knew more about babies than he ever would. So Juanita held up a small sign printed with a number ten and smiled at Rosa Guillermo, the woman from Social Services in a worn-too-often, navy blue suit, who rushed right over to gush her approval about Juanita's choice.

"A lovely child," she trilled. "I'm sure he can be available in a few weeks."

Juanita looked puzzled. She glanced up at her husband who shook his head at Rosa Guillermo and lit a tiny brown hand-rolled cigar he pulled out of his pocket. God, he hated women with college degrees. They always talked too much and filled in the details. They always let the cat out of the bag.

Rosa Guillermo was confused. Surely the Sergeant had discussed this covert adoption with his wife. Yes, some baby's picture would be put on a label to put on a jar, but these were pictures of babies owned by the government for redistribution. Instant offspring to fill the void in the barren couple's home, the patter of little feet to guarantee the couple a military pension, not to mention the General's insurance policy for the future of his reconstructed army.

Rosa Guillermo sighed. God, she hated men who judged women by the size of their breasts. The world was full of them dressed in one uniform or another, wearing arrogance and avoidance of truth like decorations on their overstuffed chests. As Sergeant Chavez exhaled smoke rings over Rosa Guillermo's head, she realized he hadn't told his young wife anything at all.

"But not until after the contest," was all Rosa Guillermo could think of to say.

She certainly didn't want to go into detail. Besides, it wasn't her job to clarify what was really going on. All her years in government and Social Service had taught her two things: stay detached and don't finish other people's unfinished business.

"I don't understand," Juanita said looking from one to the other.

Juanita wasn't terribly quick about worldly matters, which was precisely why the Sergeant had launched an all out campaign with Juanita's mother to make Juanita his wife. Especially after he'd glimpsed Juanita's large, upright breasts under the clinging wet dress she wore to wash clothes in the river. Right then and there he'd decided he had to have them. Her too, of course, but those upright breasts preceded everything else in his list of wifely qualifications. Besides, after his last wife Stella, who had opinions and a mind of her own, he vowed never again to have a wife who knew more than he did. It could spoil any marriage. But a wife with those breasts, who was young and grateful, obedient and maybe a little dim... that was exactly what he wanted, what he required.

Rosa Guillermo was determined to avoid any sort of definitive explanation. "Perhaps your husband can fill in the details, but in the meantime go home and prepare a room for your son."

That did it. Never mind the details. Juanita was so overjoyed she started to tremble. Then she burst into tears, threw her arms around her startled husband's waist and knocked over the small table spilling baby pictures everywhere. But Rosa Guillermo didn't mind. She glanced at the Sergeant as she righted the table. A glance that said, "She's all yours. Tell her anything you like."

Sergeant Chavez turned away, pretended he hadn't gotten the message and decided that when the baby was delivered he would just tell Juanita that the "little bundle of joy" had crawled right off the baby food label and into their home. It would be all right, he knew it would. After all, Juanita believed in the Virgin birth and she was excitable and she had those upright breasts and she was just dim enough, in his opinion, to believe anything he told her.

THE UNDERWEAR WAR

"No doctors!" Ebba's mother shouted, as Ebba pulled at the pale colored quilt covering her wispy mother. "I won't go!" she continued fiercely, eyes blazing, pounding "NO" like a nail into the heart of Ebba's mission.

Ebba grabbed an unguarded corner of the quilt and threw it back, exposed her mother's thin little legs as she said, "Yes you will," in a low forceful tone and won the first round in this battle of wills.

Now her mother screwed up her face in a pucker and started to cry, eked out a few tears, but Ebba wasn't moved by the display.

"I hate doctors!" her mother whimpered.

"So do I," Ebba said as she looked in vain for a pair of underpants to cover Carlotta Pavon's private gray garden.

"I hid them!" her mother yelled at the top of her lungs, straining the still air with the weight of her rebellion.

After a moment Ebba pulled up her blue cotton dress and stepped out of her step-ins, held them in her hand and waved them at her horrified mother.

"You shit!" Her mother yelled and slapped Ebba's hand. "Put those on right now!"

"Only if you put on yours," Ebba shouted defiantly and waited. Finally, having no other choice, the furious Carlotta Pavon pulled her white cotton underpants out from under the mattress and together, mother and daughter slid into their respective shorts just as Bernardo drove up in front of the house and honked Gloria's horn.

Carlotta Pavon sat in Gloria's front seat huddled between Bernardo and Ebba like an old turd. As they banged and bounced down the rutted road she sucked in her fear so sharply she whistled. And Ebba, trying to avoid any contact with her mother whatsoever, leaned out the window to let the wind blow in her face. In fact, she leaned out so far Bernardo shouted at her to get back.

"If you fall out, you'll land on your head."

Ebba did as she was told, but gave Bernardo a dirty look. "A blessing," she mumbled as her mother started to weep.

"Mothers and daughters," Bernardo said to himself then belched a soft male belch to round out the theatrical performance of the women. He leaned toward Ebba to make his point.

"You hurt your mother's feelings when you discount your life."

Ebba pretended to look at the passing scenery.

"You take away her only accomplishment," Bernardo continued.

"I am not," Ebba said after a moment or two.

Bernardo sighed and shook his head. "In every mother's list of accomplishments there is only one that counts in her heart..."

Ebba didn't answer, so Bernardo continued.

"She alone knows the inventory that came out of her body and it soothes her in her old age."

Ebba rolled her eyes just as her mother shouted, "Unless she has a child like you."

"Or if the mother hates the child," Bernardo interjected.

Ebba turned as Bernardo jerked Gloria around an unexpected boulder and poked her mother in the shoulder. "According to her I was a mistake!"

Ebba's mother smacked Ebba's hand as Bernardo rolled his eyes, reached into his shirt pocket and popped two Chiclets into his mouth. This was more information than he needed to know, but he continued philosophically. "There are no mistakes in destiny," he said as he chewed.

Then, trying to smooth out all the hurt feelings, he passed the box of gum to Ebba's mother, who shook her head showing him her loose, intermittent teeth and passed the box to Ebba, who took four figuring it would be all right to chew the two her mother couldn't.

"We're all mistakes," Bernardo said. "No matter where we were born or what our mothers told us, we are just hiccups between breathing in and out, a chance combustion between two particles that should never have met."

Uncertain of where this was going, Ebba and her mother turned and looked at Bernardo. At last he had their attention so he continued his rumination while he still had the floor. "Forget all that business that you were a mistake and don't be so judgmental. It's like a mosquito bite. It makes you itch so you scratch, but it doesn't stop itching so you scratch and scratch until you are so busy scratching you miss what you need to see."

Ebba leaned back in the seat. She wasn't buying the mosquito bite business. Bernardo didn't have to live with her mother. But Bernardo was so pleased with his logic he began to hum and finally her mother stopped sniffing. Figuring the discussion had come to a close, Ebba looked out the window at the passing houses huddled together like a chorus of gossips whispering in the wind.

The Clinic of Dr. Lorenzo Vidal

It was dusty and hot and a long line of patients spilled out the door of Dr. Vidal's clinic into the street. A fierce looking woman in a yellow turban sat at a small desk enjoying the blast of electric breeze coming from a tiny fan in the corner as Ebba tripped over a spotted dog sprawled across the threshold.

"Outside. Outside. Wait outside!" she snapped at Ebba.

But Ebba snapped back. "Who are you?"

"I am Mercedes, the doctor's assistant," Mercedes said, pointing to a small sign on her cluttered desk. "Now, go outside. There is a line and you have to wait your turn."

Ebba looked at the row of obedient people sagging in the heat.

"The doctor is very busy. Besides, what did you bring?"

"My mother," Ebba replied.

Mercedes gave her a jaundiced look. "For the doctor. What did you bring to give to the doctor?" she said, getting right to the point.

Ebba looked around, saw a bundle of carrots, crates of oranges, four patched inner tubes, two blue water lilies in a bucket, four small squid alive in a bowl and a basket of speckled eggs. All of these contributions made the tiny room seem even smaller.

"I have brought my mother," Ebba repeated. "She's sick and needs help." Mercedes looked at Ebba and pointed to the line.

"What about them? They all need help too. Anyway, how do you plan to pay the doctor?"

"With money." Ebba was emphatic.

Mercedes laughed. "Then you better go home. We don't take no money no more."

Mercedes leaned across the messy desk and grabbed a bottle of tomato-red nail polish called "Flash." She twisted off the top, using her back teeth, and started to brush thick red polish on each well-tended nail.

"Since when and why not?" Ebba wanted to know.

"Since money is worthless and you're too young to use that tone with me. I am a woman of refinement and grace."

Suddenly Bernardo was at Ebba's side.

"I have something the doctor will want," Bernardo said.

Mercedes looked up from her red, wet task, took note of Bernardo's shiny black braid, his smooth skin and sturdy stance.

"How do you know what the doctor wants?" she asked as she blew on her nails.

"Only he will understand," Bernardo said softly and smiled.

A hush fell over the room. You could hear the clock tick, the fan blow, the dog snore and the irregular breathing of the old man at the front of the line. Mercedes adjusted her turban only using the palms of her hands and crossed her legs. She leaned back against the wall seductively and looked into Bernardo's eyes.

"So," she said. "Where is this, what the doctor will want?" That's when Bernardo led Ebba's mother into the tiny room and Mercedes sat up straight, leaving her seductive pose by the wall.

"Now just you wait just a minute..." Mercedes shouted. But Bernardo ignored her. He pulled a parcel wrapped in purple satin from a soft leather pouch hanging from Ebba's mother's shoulder. He untied the orange ties, removed a photograph framed in sterling silver, pushed aside some of the mess and placed it on the desk. Mercedes squinted at the image. "So... what's so hot about a picture of a couple of guys on horses? Besides, this thing is so old it could be moldy. Nobody cares about old junk. Go back outside and get in line."

Suddenly, the green velvet curtain separating the tiny room from whatever was behind it opened a crack and an old man's pink face peered out much lower down than expected.

"Where is the photograph?" he demanded. Dr. Vidal's deep voice seemed buried somewhere in the back of his throat, but his blue eyes darted around the room energetically.

"It's nothing. Old junk," Mercedes said, trying to hide the nail polish. "They're just trying to get to the head of the line."

The old man sniffed the stale air.

"And what's that smell?" he asked.

"Human decay," Mercedes shot back.

"Not that smell, the other smell," he said.

"Nail polish," Ebba interrupted even though Bernardo placed his hand over her mouth, but too late. The words had escaped already.

Mercedes looked at Ebba, her fury rising, getting itself ready for the explosion to come.

"Nail polish?!"

The old man's voice blasted out like a horn as he propelled himself into the room. He was in a wheelchair, making clear the low placement of his face, and he rolled to a stop as Ebba shouted through Bernardo's fingers.

"I brought it to her," she lied.

Ebba's mother rolled her eyes at her daughter and everyone in line looked at Mercedes to see what she would do, but she was too surprised to speak.

"Where did you get this ridiculous paint?" the old man asked Ebba in a much softer tone.

"At the dump," Ebba shrugged. Now Bernardo rolled his eyes, but he picked up the photograph and placed it in the old man's lap.

"Here," Bernardo smiled. "See if you remember."

The old man closed his eyes and didn't move. It was as if he was preparing himself to see what he was about to see. Finally he put on his glasses and stared at the picture while everyone listened to the ticking clock, the snoring dog, the irregular breathing of the man at the head of the line and someone else who coughed. After a moment the old man's face softened. The nail polish incident was forgotten. Tears rimmed his pale blue eyes and fell down his droopy pink cheeks. Bernardo smiled.

"My father gave it to me to give to you. It was one of his favorites."

The old man looked up at Bernardo and shook his head. "You never said you were the son of Hernaldo DeVille." Bernardo nodded yes and the old man sighed.

"I remember the day he took this picture."

Mercedes was fit to be tied. She wasn't prepared for the unraveling of her power base. Ebba's mother coughed from the door as the old man looked up at Bernardo.

"Your father took this just before the explosion."

"Yes," Bernardo nodded. "He told me the story."

Mercedes snapped to attention. "You mean that's you?!" she shrilled. You had two legs to stand and walk on?" The old man looked at her dismissively. Mercedes was gathering speed and volume, but the old doctor wouldn't be torn from the image of his youth.

"And a leg between your other two that worked, stood up on its own without coaxing?" The doctor had had enough. He rolled his chair over to the messy desk and smacked her hard with the back of his hand. Then he grabbed the bottle of nail polish and handed it to Ebba.

"Take this back to wherever you found it. I hate red and I can't stand the smell."

After that he rolled himself to the green velvet curtain, looked at Ebba's mother sweetly and spoke in his most soft gentle tone.

"The doctor will see you now."

HEALTHY AS A HORSE

The examining room, the color of peaches, was bordered with window boxes full of plump blue hydrangea that he'd planted as soon as he arrived from Mexico City to take care of the fat opera singer's throat. Actually, it was rumored he'd come to escape some sort of scandal involving medical birth control procedures and the Catholic Church. Once he'd settled in, the Kind Predecessor commissioned Dr. Vidal to execute those same sorts of procedures for friends of friends of his. After that, he moved Dr. Vidal into the clinic recently vacated by the previous doctor who it seems had flatly refused to perform any sort of medical maneuver for anyone, even in an emergency, so the Kind Predecessor had seen to it that he was "disappeared."

Dr. Vidal motioned to Ebba's mother to sit in the chair with arms hand carved to look like claws, handed her a black satin pillow embroidered with "Buenas Noches" in purple and green and told her to put it in her lap. Ebba's mother looked at it closely before she did what he asked.

"A gift from my first wife," he said.

"Where is she?" Ebba's mother asked.

"Dead," the doctor responded and handed Ebba's mother a pair of copper rods attached to wires in a large black box crowded with knobs and dials and needles that bounced from side to side.

"Hold one in each hand and think of what troubles you most."

"Ebba," Ebba's mother said without a moment's hesitation.

"Troubles about your own health," the doctor said loudly. "And don't speak. Just keep whatever it is to yourself as you grip the rods."

Ebba's mother wasn't listening. She was pointing at the box. "What kind of thing is that?"

"A diagnostic invention that came from Budapest."

He slipped a rubber cover over his thumb and dipped it into a copper bowl filled with water.

"And in order for it to work you have to be quiet." Sensing she was about to register a few more complaints, he looked at her darkly, smacked the table the same way he'd slapped Mercedes and yelled. "Absolute quiet!" For the first time that Ebba could ever remember, her mother did exactly what she was told. Then the doctor strummed his wet, rubber covered thumb across the conductor pad next to the diagnostic device and watched the needles jump.

Rub, rub, rub... Jump, jump, jump. He wrote some numbers down in a column and looked at his watch.

"Strong as an ox," he mumbled under his breath. "How old did you say..."

"None of your damn business," Ebba's mother interrupted.

"By all accounts, forty-six," the doctor announced.

Ebba's mother's mouth shut closed like a trap.

"Gallstones, early rickets, one live child, three stillborn, bunions, boils at twenty-three, a major mishap with a horse, never married in church, prone to bronchitis, halitosis, early menopause, measles, mumps and chicken pox."

Ebba's mother was stunned into silence. His accuracy was uncanny. She started to have palpitations.

"Strong cerebellum, weak heart, liver and kidneys."

The doctor pulled off the rubber thumb protector, handed Ebba's mother a glass of water and took her pulse. Everyone sat absolutely still and watched him open several little drawers in a tall cabinet full of herbs, dried geckos and snakes, watched closely as he dropped a little of this and a little of that into a bowl and ground it into a powder which he placed in a cheesecloth bag.

"Brew this tea and drink full strength," he said to Ebba's mother but he handed the concoction to Ebba.

"You keep it. She'll just toss it out the window," he said, "And let me know how she responds." Then he looked up at Bernardo and smiled. "Thank you Bernardo. Your generosity lets me relive the past." After that Dr. Vidal rolled himself to the green velvet curtain, did a little nod with his head then held it open so they could leave.

THE PLAN

A few days later Olivia Gomez stood at Ebba's front door with Mrs. Marquez, Ebba's neighbor, a round tub of a woman in a dull purple dress, "yoo-hooing" for someone to answer. Finally, after stalling in the hopes they would just go away, Ebba opened the door a crack.

"What do you want?" she demanded.

"It's us." Mrs. Marquez replied. "Me with Olivia Gomez, widow of the late mayor. We'd like to come in."

"I'd like to come in," Olivia interrupted.

Ebba looked at the women, shading their eyes from the sun.

"Why?" Ebba asked.

"We have a proposition," Mrs. Marquez said, trying to ooze charm.

"A what?" Ebba stalled. She didn't trust Mrs. Marquez any more than her mother did.

Mrs. Marquez jerked her head in Olivia's direction and batted her eyes for effect. "Something that needs to be a secret and you're the only one who can do it."

Ebba knew in her heart Mrs. Marquez wasn't telling the truth but she was bored and curious so she slipped out the door, closed it behind her and motioned the women into the dried up garden.

"Can't we go inside?" Olivia whined. "I'm awfully hot."

Ebba looked at her sternly and shook her head no.

"My mother is trying to sleep," she lied.

"You're very rude," Olivia said, but Ebba just shrugged.

"You're the ones who came without asking."

Olivia decided to ignore her. She looked around for some shade and a place to sit down while Mrs. Marquez went to the well, found a tin cup and filled it with water.

"Why me?" Ebba asked. She pulled up an old metal chair peeling white paint so Olivia could sit.

Olivia dusted the seat with her dainty lace hankie, gulped down the water and launched into her request. "Well..." she paused dramatically, "since my husband was killed..."

"In the garden of his Chinese mistress," Ebba nodded.

Olivia gave her a sour look and removed her high heels to rub her swollen feet as Mrs. Marquez reprimanded. "Nobody asked you to fill in the blanks, so shut your mouth and listen."

Ebba looked at Mrs. Marquez darkly as Olivia continued.

"I need you to take my place to go see a particular person instead of me."

Ebba looked at Olivia like she was crazy. "Why? I don't know you and you don't know me." Ebba answered her sternly.

"But my green dresses are hanging in your mother's closet."

"So?" Ebba shrugged.

"You owe me a favor."

"I didn't buy them."

"But your mother did."

"Just get to the point," Mrs. Marquez interjected and poked Olivia's arm. She didn't like being reminded of the dresses she wanted so much.

Olivia took the bag of stones with the chipped tooth and Li Choo's hair from around her neck, wrapped it with some paper money and handed it to Ebba. "If I go I'll be followed and people could get suspicious. You're a kid so if you go, no one will care."

"Go where?" Ebba was confused.

"To see Lilly Narada."

"Who?"

Mrs. Marquez was becoming impatient. "Who she is doesn't matter. You just go, give Lilly the bag and she'll know why."

"Why?" Ebba was curious.

"That's not your business," Olivia said, losing patience. Ebba looked at Olivia, shook her head no and gave the bag back.

Olivia sighed. Realizing she'd been a little harsh, she pulled out some more money and rewrapped the bag.

"There. There's a little something for you," she said and extended her hand. Ebba didn't move.

"It's better not to know details," Olivia said in a mysterious tone.

"She doesn't want to put you in danger," Mrs. Marquez offered. Ebba was still suspicious but she shrugged and took the bag.

"Okay, I don't get it, but where do I go?"

Olivia smiled. At last, a slight opening to ease the tension. She pulled a small map out of her cleavage. "It's at the top of the mountain."

"Bernardo and Hortence Grace live at the top," Ebba replied.

"Damn it. Not the top of the top," Mrs. Marquez snarled. She knew Ebba was smarter than she was letting on. "I'm showing you. Here!" Olivia accidentally pierced the paper with her fingernail as she pointed to the map. Ebba looked at the wiggly lines and recognized the location.

"Where Sofia Hernandez was hit by a truck?"

"Exactly," Olivia brightened. Finally they were getting somewhere.

"And died..." Ebba said finishing her sentence.

"Of course she died," Mrs. Marquez fumed. "She got smashed."

Olivia stood up and accidentally knocked over the chair. "I have to go," she announced.

"But after she gets the bag, then what?"

Mrs. Marquez stuck out her arm to give Ebba a swat, but Olivia stopped her and smiled tightly. "She'll tell you things and then you'll come back and tell me."

"But what if she doesn't?" Ebba asked.

"Lilly Narada always has something to say," Olivia said as she struggled into her patent leather pumps.

Then without another word or even saying goodbye, the two women turned around and hurried down the path to the bright pink bicycle with the rusty bell where Olivia, intent on keeping her high heels out of the spokes, hiked up her skirt and climbed onto the seat behind Mrs. Marquez. Then she tucked up her legs after Mrs. Marquez got off to a shaky start but finally managed to get control and keep the bike upright as they disappeared down the rutted road.

At exactly twelve noon the next day, Ebba stood at the gate of a makeshift barbed wire fence in the blaring sun. On the other side, a pack of mangy dogs stood barking nonstop in the dirt. Shifting from one foot to the other, Ebba watched the wind kick up dust devils around a short woman wearing black clothes that strained over her fleshy folds like a twin sheet trying to cover a double bed. She was puffing on a cigarette as she gathered flapping laundry off the rickety clothesline.

"Hello?" Ebba called out.

The woman didn't answer. She looked at Ebba once, but didn't stop what she was doing.

"Are you Lilly?" Ebba called out again. The woman screwed her face into a squint and shaded her eyes.

"Lilly Narada?" Ebba yelled impatiently.

The woman ignored her, turned her back and moved briskly to avoid stepping on stacks of rubber tires, old car parts and a rusty tub full of water. When she shoved two goats out of the way the dogs barked louder and more frenzied than before. One even bared his teeth.

"Who wants to know?" the woman finally decided to answer. She sounded a lot like the dogs so Ebba said the first thing that came into her mind. "My mother is dying." The woman laughed and adjusted her unruly hair. "Everyone's mother is dying or already dead. You'll have to do better than that." The barking dogs kept barking and the woman lost her temper, used the laundry as a shield as she stepped closer to the gate, attacked them with her bare feet and her bare voice and Ebba noticed that most of her teeth were gold.

"Shut up, stupid dogs!" After a few intense moments the dogs whimpered and ran off to cower in a scrap of shade.

"Who are you?" the woman snapped.

"Ebba," Ebba said.

"You sure cause a lot of trouble."

Ebba didn't answer. She was studying the dark purple lipstick arching above the woman's lips.

"Who sent you for what?"

"Olivia Gomez," Ebba replied.

The woman laughed. "Now, there's a real mess. Why you?"

"She said you'd know why."

"Olivia is full of mystical horseshit."

"But are you Lilly?" Ebba asked.

"So what?" the woman replied. "I don't have time for games."

Ebba pulled Olivia's sack wrapped in money from around her neck. "She said to give you this."

The woman reached through the fence and grabbed it.

"What for?"

Ebba had had enough of the heat and the dust and noise. "Could I please have a drink of water?"

The woman put the sack in her pocket and released the latch on the gate. "Why didn't you say so in the first place." Then she looked around at the dogs. "Just slide in and stand still."

"But are you Lilly?" Ebba wanted confirmation. The woman gave her a dirty look.

"Who the hell else would I be? Now get inside."

Ebba did exactly what Lilly said, but the dogs rushed her anyway, jumped up and down. They almost knocked her over. Randomly bred, they were skinny and scared and mean. Then, from a long shed made entirely of old kitchen doors, a cowbell rang and the snarling dogs bolted off toward the sound.

"Run!" Lilly shouted and took off across the yard to an old bread truck painted gold with metallic flecks that sent sparkles back to the sun like squeaks. Ebba followed, ran fast to the heavy metal screen door that Lilly struggled to open.

"Hurry up!" Lilly yelled and disappeared inside just as Ebba tripped over a rusty bike and crash landed in a sprawl, alerting the dogs to renew their chase.

"Clumsy girl!" Lilly sniped from behind the screen. Ebba managed to climb out of the tangle, even though her knees were skinned and starting to bleed. She dragged open the door and rushed inside as the dogs hurled themselves against the mesh. Once under the shell of the truck, Ebba stood at the top of steep steps bordered with glass jars of fruit that went down to the dirt floor where Lilly stood waiting.

"No wonder you fell, you got big feet."

Still juggling the laundry, she motioned to Ebba to follow as she opened a door topped with a dirty glass window and walked into a room dug in the dirt like a gopher hole. Overhead, a sheet of corrugated metal served as the roof and a thin layer of adobe covered the irregular walls. A radio played romantic songs and a pot of black beans was cooking on a hot plate.

The whole place smelled of stale beer, cigarettes and Tabu cologne.

The narrow window over the sink was level with the yard. Screened with scraps of mesh it swung out and rested on a stick stuck in the ground to keep it open. There was an icebox, a water cooler and a wood burning stove with a stovepipe chimney. A small TV with rabbit ears sat in an alcove full of family photos, religious relics, and voodoo dolls. The orange velvet couch, boasting stiffly starched, hand crocheted doilies, was crushed in another corner.

Lilly walked past a hand-painted screen and dumped the laundry on her round, red chenille-covered bed that looked like a bleeding heart.

"Don't trip your big feet on the extension cord, 'cause everything will blow..." Then she filled a jelly glass with water from the cooler.

"You want ice in your drink?"

"Please," Ebba replied as she spit on her knee. Lilly opened the icebox and hacked off a hunk from the block.

"Olivia's got her wires crossed cause she's full of discontent."

Ebba squashed an ant crossing the sink. Lilly spun around and smacked Ebba's hand. It was loud, but it didn't hurt. "Don't squish ants! They're God's perfect creatures," she shouted. After the exchange between Lilly and the dogs, her remark surprised Ebba more than the smack.

"What about the dogs?" Ebba asked.

"Dogs are dogs," Lilly was emphatic. "They deserve what they get. So do humans. Humans are dogs too."

"I'm not a dog," Ebba said and gulped down the water. Lilly laughed. She laughed so hard she had to sit down.

"You sound just like my mother," Ebba said.

Lilly stopped laughing and blew her nose. Then she walked to the pile of clean clothes and started folding big black brassieres and boxer shorts. "Olivia's been dancing in the dark for a long time."

"What's that supposed to mean?"

Ebba couldn't take her eyes off the laundry. She'd never seen such big underwear before. "She don't want to see the world beyond the back yard but she'd like to know more about the Chinky woman her dead husband was with." Lilly stopped folding and pointed at Ebba. "She's a lazy woman. Answers don't grow on trees you know." Then she laughed.

"That's why she sent you. I scare her to death. She's afraid I'll contaminate her high hopes with facts and she's right." Lilly lifted a clean pink sheet, flapped it over the bed, let it unfurl like a tongue in the air.

"Maybe I should go," Ebba said. Something about that pink sheet made her nervous.

"Why? You just got here."

"It's a long walk back."

"So. What did you expect... a limousine to take you home? Some nice words to make Olivia feel better? Some nice words for you?"

Ebba put her empty glass on the wooden sink next to a pair of false eyelashes, curled to perfection.

"Olivia said you were wise."

Lilly stopped folding clothes and got serious. "This is the wisdom I got for you, whatever your name is. You're a kid, act like one. Taking care of grown women means you're missing the boat."

Suddenly Ebba was on the verge of tears. "I don't know what you're talking about."

Lilly shook her head, reapplied her purple lipstick and lit a cigarette. She clamped the filter between her gold teeth and rolled it around with her tongue. "That's because you're puny."

"And you're fat," Ebba shot back.

That did it. Lilly started for the door. "Okay. Time to go."

"But what's the big whatever it is Olivia wants to know?" Ebba asked. Lilly took a drag off her cigarette and blew the smoke over Ebba's head. "You tell Olivia the 'wise' woman who lives under the ground and sees the future, had nothing to say. So, nobody learned nothing." Then Lilly opened the door.

"That's it?" Ebba asked, knowing Olivia would be mad.

"That's plenty," Lilly said and took another puff.

"But what about the dogs?"

"You're the one that spoke out on their behalf."

"Couldn't you just walk me to the gate?" Ebba's fear of the mangy dogs was mounting.

"Can't. Got too much work. Besides... coming and going is all part of your experiment with wisdom," Lilly grinned.

Ebba gave Lilly a dirty look. Lilly's gold teeth made her look like one of the snarling dogs.

"Pleasure to meet you," Lilly said, extending her fat little hand. But Ebba was on her way out. "And tell Olivia not to send a girl to do a woman's work." Lilly said. Then she slammed the door shut behind Ebba and locked it. She even pulled down the shade over the window and turned the radio up louder.

"Battle-ax, bitch," Ebba muttered as she ran up the stairs and scraped the metal screen against the step causing every dog to growl and jerk to attention. By the time she stepped into the yard all of them were on the run. Every kind thought Ebba had about dogs flew right out the window. She picked up a handful full of rocks, but the dogs were coming too fast so she started to run but tripped over the rusty bike and re-skinned her knee.

"Son of a bitch!" she yelled. But she picked herself up and grabbed the clumsy two-wheeler, crashed it upright on its big balloon tires and continued to smash it up and down, making so much noise she surprised the dogs and they backed off. No more messing around. Ebba was mad. She looked at the dogs and shouted. "Son of a bitch, son of a bitch, son of a bitch!" She sounded so fierce, the dogs turned and ran, except for one at the gate who snarled, but Ebba didn't care. She used the bike like a battering ram and yelled, "MOVE!" so loud the dog yelped and ran away.

That's when Lilly stepped out of the bakery truck door and watched Ebba unlatch the gate. Applauding vigorously, she hollered. "Keep the bike. I don't want it."

Ebba didn't even look at Lilly. She threw the bike on the ground and squeezed out the gate. "I don't want nothing to remember I was here," she yelled.

Lilly just laughed her cigarette cough laugh and shouted. "But you will. Like it or not, kid... you'll remember." Then she began to whistle, "You're My Everything," terribly off key and went back inside.

FATHER LYLE AND THE MIRACLE DIRT

Exhausted and hot, Ebba walked into the tiny dark chapel at the Church of Martyrs, genuflected to Christ on the cross and looked up at crutches and leg-braces hung on hooks for display. Tied on each, a note with descriptive details of the miracle performed and a prayer of thanks. Reading them back to back made each miracle seem more miraculous than the last. Requests for "yet-to-be-miracles" were stuffed in the metal box next to an Offering Tree made out of chicken wire where paper money dangled from clothespin clips.

Rows of scented candles flickered brightly in red jelly jars and overwhelmed the room with heat and the smell of sweat and incense and marijuana. Covering the walls, photographs of faces gleamed in the soft flickering light. Face after face draped in black ribbon and dead flowers. Babies, children, mothers, fathers, and above the photographs, a hand-painted banner that said, "Missing." Ebba picked up a jelly jar candle and looked into each pair of eyes as Father Lyle's thin, uncertain voice seemed to float out of the dark.

"Bless you my child," he said.

Startled, Ebba put the candle back on the rack. The overlapping smells and heat were beginning to make her dizzy.

"Someone you know on the wall?"

Ebba turned to the angular man wearing a dirty lace vestment that covered his robe and shook her head no. "I came in because it's hot."

"Not here for the miracle dirt?" The priest smiled tightly as he bent down and scooped a handful out of the hole in the floor and let it dribble through his fingers, never mentioning that each day before dawn the Barella brothers brought it new from the riverbed in their old green truck and dumped it down a make shift chute through the chapel window into that very hole. Never mentioned that each day, after they delivered the dirt, they went home to help their grandmother sell poppy out of the kitchen window in her double-wide trailer and tithed ten percent of the profit to the church. Never mentioned that collecting dirt was their penitence for selling poppy in the first place.

Father Lyle gestured at the crutches and braces hanging from the ceiling. "This evidence of the holy miracle proves believing makes it true. To be touched by the soil is to be healed. To be healed is to be blessed. To be blessed is to be saved." Then he crossed himself quickly. "In the name of the Father, the Son and the Holy Ghost."

Ebba just looked at him, didn't say a word. Her mother had never been big on church. After a moment, Ebba pointed to the pictures on wall. "What about them?"

Father Lyle looked away, bent down and rubbed an invisible dust smudge on his shoes. "I'm afraid I don't have an answer."

Ebba looked at him in disbelief. "Why not?" she asked.

"Everything is in transition," he cleared his throat.

"Where is that?"

He was desperate to be evasive.

"Grandmothers come every day like amputees praying for lost limbs. They hope God will reunite them."

"What's that supposed to mean?"

Father Lyle sighed, then leaned in close and whispered, "They practice their religion, but I never see you in church."

Ebba looked at his dirty frock and kept what she was thinking to herself. Then before she could stop him, Father Lyle reached out and touched her forehead with red dirt, left the imprint of his thumb right between her eyes. "Bless you my child," he said.

Expecting her to be grateful, he waited for her to kneel down on one knee for the rest of the blessing. Instead Ebba looked at her reflection in a glass case full of neck braces and baby shoes. She raised her hand to wipe away the smudge, but Father Lyle stopped her.

"It's to keep you safe," he said sincerely.

"Safe from what?" Ebba asked in a loud voice.

Father Lyle scraped his shoe on the ground to cover the unavoidable sound of gas blasting out of his bowels with a lingering whine.

Embarrassed, Ebba stepped back, moved down the wall of faces until she saw a picture of Renaldo Rodriguez' mule and stopped.

"Is he missing too?" she asked.

Grateful for the change of subject, the priest shook his head and stayed where he was in case of another attack of gas. "Oh no," Father Lyle said. "The mule died and señor Rodriguez is in mourning."

Ebba nodded solemnly and deliberately and crossed herself twice.

This cheered the priest a little. At least she wasn't a total loss. "May Jesus hear your sincere heart," he said quietly. Then he closed his eyes to let the spirit fill him, but Ebba had already bolted out the door.

JOHNNY ORTEEZ

Outside, Ebba sneezed three times in a row and sucked in sunshine to replace the oppressive odor of church. She was wiping the dirt off her forehead when the pop of a flash bulb turned her world into pinpoint dots. Now the only thing she could see clearly was a camera spitting out a Polaroid square.

"Stop that!" Ebba demanded as she rubbed her eyes. Cameras scared her, especially after all those faces on the wall. A man not much taller than Ebba and grinning from ear to ear stuck out his hand.

"Johnny Orteez. I'm running for mayor."

Ebba blinked and took a step back. The dots had turned into rings, but she still couldn't see. Johnny Orteez just laughed and took another picture before Ebba could cover her face with her hand.

"Stop doing that!" she shouted. But he just kept grinning as he adjusted his tight orange iridescent shirt.

"After I'm elected you can show this to your friends, tell them about the day the mayor stopped and took your picture." Then he handed her the Polaroid, but she couldn't see it. The dots were back and dancing in front of her eyes.

"Olivia Gomez is the mayor, not you."

"She's the widow, not really the mayor."

Ebba decided not to say any more, so Johnny Orteez kept talking.

"You want an Orteez T-shirt, stop by the Johnny-mobile..." He pointed across the street to a Volkswagen bus, painted the same iridescent orange as his shirt with "JOHNNY ORTEEZ FOR MAYOR" scrawled across the side in black. "You Ain't Nothin' But a Hound Dog," began to blare out of the loudspeakers mounted on top, but before Johnny could continue his one-on-one political campaign, Ebba darted across the street to the drinking fountain next to the outdoor stage where Elena Cordova had dropped dead.

If Johnny Orteez taking her picture was any indication of what could happen after you were smudged with miracle dirt, Ebba wasn't interested. She tore the Polaroid picture into tiny pieces, tossed them in the air then stuck her hands in the trickle of water and washed her face until every trace of holy dirt was gone. That's when she remembered Olivia's little black sack. In her hurry to leave, she'd forgotten and left it with Lilly. But as she wiped her face on the sleeve of her dress she determined she would not, under any circumstances whatsoever, go back to the house scooped out of the ground.

Joan Tewkesbury

Ebba squared off under the tree in front of her mother's house against Olivia Gomez who was not taking no for an answer.

"She said you got your wires crossed..."

"She did not!" Olivia squawked. Olivia didn't want to believe what she was hearing.

"She said you've been dancing in the dark and that answers don't grow on trees. She said you were lazy and full of mystical horseshit."

Olivia's jaw dropped dumbly, but Ebba continued, leaving nothing out as she hurried to get to the end. "Lilly said you were afraid she would contaminate your high hopes with facts and that's why you sent me and to be sure and tell you that I didn't learn a thing from the 'wise woman' who lives under the ground."

Olivia was too stunned to speak. She leaned against the wall and after she caught her breath, she lashed out.

"You're a liar!" she shrilled. "Mrs. Marquez was right. You and your mother are evil!"

Ebba shrugged. "She called me puny," Ebba offered.

Olivia narrowed her eyes and glared. "I bet you didn't go. I am a poor widow and I bet you made up this story to have me in your clutches. Ebba looked at her like she was crazy, but Olivia just kept going. "And I know you stole the money, so just give back my magic sack." Ebba didn't move. Unlike her mother, Olivia's wrath was shaky. Her voice went up and down, rose and fell. It didn't blare out in a steady stream of self-righteous rage. It was full of cracks.

Ebba lifted the hem of her dress and pointed to her knee. "That's where I fell getting away from her hideous dogs."

"Bullshit!" Olivia parried.

"And that?" Ebba pointed to her ankle. "That's where one of her dogs bit me and I don't have your stupid sack because she put it in her big black brassiere and I'm not going back!"

Olivia had a momentary sag. She tried to rev herself up all over again, but in her bones she knew Ebba was telling the truth. The dogs, the house dug under the ground, the big black brassiere. Olivia swallowed her pride and high hopes. She even pushed aside her belief in outcomes. "Son of a bitch," she muttered. Then she took a deep breath and started down the path to Mrs. Marquez who was waiting on the bike. After a few steps in her wobbly high heels she turned back and shouted. "If you ever tell anyone about this discussion..."

But Ebba jumped in before Olivia could finish her sentence. "I'm not telling nobody nothing. I'm sorry I went and I'm sorry Bernardo has you for a cousin."

For a moment the insult hovered around Olivia like a fly, but she decided not to respond so Ebba turned and climbed the tree to watch Olivia hoist herself onto the bike behind Mrs. Marquez struggling, as always, to keep them upright as they took off down the road.

MR. LOBOS

M r. Lobos was younger than he looked and old beyond his years. His gaze was so direct that it crowded your thoughts and took over, made you forget what you wanted to ask him in the first place. He had a fine full mouth, but he didn't speak unless it was absolutely necessary and always so softly that you had to strain to hear what he was saying.

Mr. Lobos thought of himself as a ladies' man, but he had a mother who was small and fierce and loomed over him like a giant grasshopper chomping through his private thoughts searching for secrets. Mr. Lobos had a first name, but no one knew what it was except his mother who he threatened to kill if she ever told anyone. And he meant it, but in truth she ran the show and she was mean.

Secrets clogged Mr. Lobos' heart and truth choked his soul but every now and then, one of those truths, desperate to escape, would reveal itself and scare him to death. These unpredictable breakouts were extremely unsettling because he couldn't control them. So, fearing that someone might demand to know more, he excised himself from himself. It was deliberate and precise like a surgeon with a scalpel. Whole parts of himself were so well hidden they were lost and no matter how hard he tried, he couldn't retrieve them. He was convinced that somewhere there was a map, but he had no idea how to find it.

His loss pleased his mother so much it made her proud. As far as she was concerned, her son was a model of self-discipline and discrimination. He was pragmatic and restrained, a realist with both feet on the ground, but boy was she wrong. Mr. Lobos was really a dreamer. When his father died, Mr. Lobos was only eleven, but the demands of his mother and her mother and his father's sisters engulfed him in a cluster of female clutter. Their invasion was so severe he lost track of everything that he thought about or wanted and if something did cross his mind, he pushed it back, swept it out of the way of the women until he stripped himself of his imagination and there was nothing left to call his own or for anyone else to find. Not even his tears.

Overnight, all of those women turned him into a shell of a man. He was everything to all of them, all of the time. They constantly fought about who needed him most, loved him the most, who he should love the most. All but one. His cousin Theresa. She was eighteen with shiny black hair and berry-colored lips, wide set brown eyes and laughter that shimmered.

On the day of his father's funeral, just before the procession, she kissed him on the lips. It was a deep meaningful kiss and she told him that, heart and soul, she would always be there just for him. Always, she whispered, to comfort him whenever he needed her. The declaration set off a pause so profound in Mr. Lobos' psyche that a sob, lodged in his chest, sprang into his throat and flew out of his mouth like a bird.

Enchanted, Mr. Lobos turned to receive another kiss, but his mother swooped down instead and whirled him around with so much force he fell to the floor. She came at him like an eggbeater, flailing like a deranged spider caught its own web.

"Men do not sob," she sobbed. "Men do not... kiss cousins on the mouth... Men do not..."

On and on she shrilled at the top of her lungs as his beautiful cousin Theresa stepped behind a pillar and watched him recant his sob. But watching her watch him, allowed Mr. Lobos to send the swallowed sound in her direction as the only gift, the only fragment of himself that he could give her and she accepted. Looking at him, Theresa began to cry and cried the tears Mr. Lobos' mother wouldn't allow him to shed. Her cheeks were wet with his tears and his spirit soared, so he didn't notice the grave state of his widowed mother's rage or feel the impact of her hand slapping his face or anywhere else she could strike a blow.

Finally, Mr. Lobos' dead father's mother pulled his wailing mother away, pulled Mrs. Lobos off her son, pushed her outside into the sun to force a little light into the situation, to bring the widow up short and shut her up. Wailing only worked in the dark.

Inside, still on the floor, Mr. Lobos was coming apart in a sea of conflicting currents. His heart airborne with his beautiful cousin or buried with the wrath of his mother who, if she could have, would have eaten him alive to feed her grief.

In that moment, Mr. Lobos' heart imploded and made him uncertain but convinced him that joy would only be his if he couldn't have it or if he gave it away. The only thing he knew for sure was that his mother, forever and always, would try to consume him, leaving no room for anyone to enter the dreams of a dreamer.

Joan Tewkesbury

WHAT HAPPENED DURING SIESTA

Shutters were drawn against the afternoon sun and things were quiet and lifeless because everyone in Elena was taking a nap, everyone but Ebba. So bored she thought she would die, she sat under the post office portal watching a shiny black, bullet-shaped, Mercury sedan maneuver around three sleeping dogs in the middle of the road.

When the car finally stopped, Mr. Lobos wearing his usual black suit, white shirt and black tie stepped out of the back seat and a dry breeze rearranged his dark hair. Ebba didn't know who he was but decided that he must be awfully hot in a suit. She climbed onto the wide wooden handrail that bordered the sidewalk squaring the square. She reached up, touched the top of the portal with her fingers, felt the dry breeze lift her skirt as Mr. Lobos turned just in time to see Ebba's long brown legs framed by the billowing blue cotton dress like a theatre curtain. It was an unexpected surprise.

She wasn't particularly pretty or one of those beautiful beauties, but her eyes claimed him from the narrow framework of her face as she stood on the wooden rail swaying softly in the hot breeze. Mr. Lobos dropped his eyes and looked at the ground as he walked across the square of dusty green lawn. Ebba, seeing that he was coming in her direction, swung herself up to the beam over her head and hung upside down by her knees. She gathered her dress between her legs and held it tight as Mr. Lobos stopped right in front of her, letting her long braid touch his hand when he placed it on the rail.

Ebba cocked her head, studied Mr. Lobos' almond shaped eyes, his smooth skin the color of coffee with milk and his cheeks that were a little bit rosy. After a moment she let her head drop but he just kept his eyes glued to hers and stepped forward another step until they were nose-to-nose. Then he put his finger in the center of her chest and pushed. Ebba swung back and forth on the beam. Her mouth, upside down, close to his, then far away, close to his, then far away. Neither of them spoke. They just kept looking into each other's eyes locking themselves into a history they didn't have. Then Ebba stopped swinging and unhinged her legs with the grace of a cat, stood on the handrail and placed her bare feet between Mr. Lobos' hands, felt his nose touch the hem of her blue cotton dress and dropped to a squat, balanced herself perfectly on the wooden rail as she pulled her dress over the peaks of her knees. Now they were face to face,

Ebba and the Green Dresses of Olivia Gomez in a Time of Conflict and War   53

engaged in some sort of contest without touching until Mr. Lobos took a step back and put his hands in his pockets. Ebba unfolded the wings of her legs, sat down on the rail, making her exactly his height, and fluffed out her dress like a queen.

The driver of the black sedan was getting impatient. He honked the horn twice and started the engine, drove around the square forcing the three sleeping dogs to get up and move or get run over. Mr. Lobos turned toward the car but turned right back and spoke to Ebba.

"I am Mr. Lobos," he said in a low soft voice.

Ebba just nodded, didn't say a word, just waited to see what he would do next and in the silence he raised his large beautifully shaped hand and placed it on the promise of Ebba's chest, spread his long graceful fingers out like a rising sun, moved his little finger and thumb across the pebbles her nipples had become. Ebba inhaled her surprise, but she never stopped looking into his eyes. She even arched her back and leaned into his hand, pushed against it, imagined she had the breasts of Hortence Grace until the horn honked again and Mr. Lobos stopped what he was doing, withdrew his hand and walked to the mailbox, pulled a letter out of his pocket and dropped it down the chute.

After that, he hurried to the waiting car but before he stepped inside he turned back, saw the hot dry breeze lift the bottom of Ebba's blue dress exposing her long brown legs rimmed by white cotton underpants, watched her watch him as he got into the back seat of the black, bullet-shaped car and was driven away.

Joan Tewkesbury

A THOUSAND DONKEYS BRAYING

At four o'clock in the morning, when it was pitch dark and quiet, and people were sound asleep, there was a loud thud, then a shake and a severe jolt that seemed extremely out of place and all-wrong, as if someone had dropped a car out of the sky. Then there was another shake, a terrible bang that shook all the windows, and more shaking before a savage shudder made the ground cry out like a thousand donkeys braying. Deep inside the earth things were erupting whether anyone liked it or not.

Ebba woke by being flung back and forth in her bed and jerking in spastic jerks as the groaning noise became more intense with rumbling and screeching and Ebba wondered why a freight train had decided to come through the house.

Doors slammed, plates broke in the kitchen, canned goods spilled out of the cupboards and scattered as a terrible scraping sound came from the ancient mirror in the hall that threatened to lose its grip on the wall and crash onto the floor. The framed photo of Consuelo Bolivia, the soap opera star, slammed against the chest of drawers in Ebba's mother's room and shattered into splinters but Ebba's mother never surfaced from her sleep.

Ebba clutched the covers over her head to dodge plaster falling from the ceiling but finally she was pitched out of bed, capsized under the mattress, marooned in a tangle of sheets and springs and then as suddenly as it began, the quaking stopped. It was over and still, as if nothing had happened.

All Ebba could hear was the loud rasp of her mother's snore and when she looked out the window, she saw birds flying in the dark.

THE VICTROLA

The morning after the quake, Ebba rushed out of the house to see if there were any cracks in the ground where she might fall and be trapped like a cockroach caught in a crevice, but everything looked exactly the same as before except for the dead birds.

Every few feet a bloody carcass lay in the dirt. Sometime in the night it had rained birds and all of their beaks were open in a last cry or gasping for air. Ebba bent down and picked one up by its wing, looked for bullet holes or arrows, some reason for this bird to fall because it was big, almost as long, wing-tip to wing-tip as Ebba was tall and it wasn't a hawk or an eagle or a crow or an owl. It was a seagull.

Ebba continued to hold the bird by its wing. The bloody mash of feathers and tiny broken bones made her sad. Why would sea birds fly to the top of the mountain at night and why hadn't she heard them? Surely something dropping out of the sky made a sound.

Ebba heard a scrape and then crunching. Still holding the gull by the tip of its wing, she turned and saw Mr. Lobos standing among the dead birds in his black suit holding a three-legged stool and a wind-up Victrola. Ebba was startled at first but not surprised. It seemed as if she'd run out of the house expecting to find him. "Do you know why they died?" she asked. Mr. Lobos put down the stool.

"Maybe they got tired of flapping their wings," he said, never taking his eyes away from hers.

"Do you think they felt the quake?" Ebba asked.

Mr. Lobos didn't answer. Instead he placed the Victrola on top of the stool and opened the latch. He took a record out of the pocket in the lid, put it on the turntable and began to crank the handle. Mystified, Ebba watched the turntable go faster and faster and, when it was turning at just the right speed, Mr. Lobos lifted the metal arm and set the needle down on the disc. After a moment or two, Erik Satie leaked out of the tinny speaker, a light blanket of thin sound to cover the dead birds. Then Mr. Lobos held out his hand.

"I thought we could dance."

Ebba looked at the still figure in the black suit. Something about him made her feel like she knew him. So, trailing the dead bird behind her like a gown, she used her feet to feel her way across the lumpy gap to Mr. Lobos, wreathed in the music and holding out his hand until she stopped in front of him and he released the bird from her grip, let it fall to the ground on top of all the others. After that, Mr. Lobos took Ebba's blood-covered fingers and put them one by one in his mouth to suck away the red, and when he had licked them clean he took out his handkerchief and, in perfect time to the music, dried each shaft as Ebba stood speechless in sensation.

When he was finished, Mr. Lobos put his handkerchief back in his pocket and placed his right hand around the back of Ebba's neck, his thumb keeping time to the music on her soft earlobe. Pretty soon she was breathing in time to the beat and his touch and they started to dance on top of the dead sea gulls in the pink dirt. Mr. Lobos didn't feel them, he had on his shoes and gradually Ebba, so captured by Mr. Lobos' steady stare and Erik Satie and the blue cloudless sky, lost track and didn't feel them either until a horn honked in the distance and broke the spell.

Ebba pulled her hand back from Mr. Lobos' chest where he had placed it and stopped dancing, watched as the bullet-shaped car she'd seen in the square stopped under the tree at the end of the path. Mr. Lobos sighed and stopped dancing too.

"I have to go," he said and withdrew his hand from around her neck.

Ebba looked at him steadily; she didn't even blink. Finally, Mr. Lobos smiled a perfect white smile, walked to the Victrola, cranked it round and round and placed the needle back at the beginning.

"Keep the music," he said, gently touching her cheek with his fingers as he walked away, started down the path, didn't look back until he reached the shiny black car, turned around and called out, "A woman at the post office pointed out your house." Then he waved, stepped into the car and was driven away, leaving Ebba confused and alone on the carpet of dead birds with her senses soaring to the tinny strains of Erik Satie.

BAD NEWS

Sergeant Chavez towered over Juanita as they stood on the front porch of the low rent military casita provided for married personnel. She was dressed in a loose yellow dress she'd bought for the maternity that never came. Sergeant Chavez was in uniform. A uniform of his own design, made up of other uniforms he'd picked off the dead. Men he'd killed in various guerilla skirmishes, bloodstained souvenirs of his expertise that Juanita was not allowed to wash. He was convinced the stains made him invincible and death proof.

At that moment, Rosa Guillermo was delivering the bad news. The child whose picture Juanita had chosen had died. It seems he'd been born with a weak heart, a fact no one bothered to pass on to the baby selection committee. Juanita could hardly believe what she was hearing.

"Oh, that poor little boy," she whispered and lapsed into sobs.

Startled, the Sergeant put his arm around his wife and patted her shoulder in a way that kept her tears from falling on his uniform shirt. To avoid the further emotional escalation of loss, Rosa Guillermo rushed to open her briefcase and grabbed the envelope she'd just received from Johnny Orteez containing new pictures he'd taken of children ready for adoption.

"Wait... Mrs. Chavez, I have all of these others," Rosa Guillermo said.

"Those are the rejects," Juanita wailed.

"No. All of these are new," Rosa Guillermo replied.

To prove it, she placed all of the photos she had in her hand in a fan and waved them at Juanita, but Juanita wasn't interested. She dug her head into her husband's waist, mingling her fountain of tears with the mojo of blood and death from the killing fields. Because the Sergeant didn't want to expose his uniform to female outbursts of any kind, he encouraged Juanita gruffly. "Just have a look," he said. And as gently as he could, he pushed her toward Rosa Guillermo's glossy black and whites while he untangled himself and his garment from all of that crying.

Gulping for air between sobs, Juanita did as she was told. After all, obedience was her finest attribute and the Sergeant never tired of reminding her what an important asset it was, along with her upright breasts. Rosa Guillermo held the pictures at eye level so Juanita could get a better look, but after a moment or two Juanita cried out. "These aren't babies. These are old. These are big kids. How can you have a baby without a baby?" Rosa Guillermo rolled her eyes, but was quick on her feet.

"These pictures are part of another contest. One of these faces will be featured on a government nutritious cereal box."

Now the Sergeant rolled his eyes and looked at Rosa Guillermo as if she'd lost her mind, but Rosa Guillermo just glared at the Sergeant. If he hadn't lied by omission in the first place, they wouldn't have to continue this charade.

"But I want to choose a baby," Juanita pouted. Then she stamped her foot, grabbed the fan of photographs and threw them on the ground.

"All right, all right." Rosa Guillermo acquiesced. "But there may not be any newborns for a while. You may have to take what you can get."

"Why?" Juanita cried. "Newborns are born all the time except for me."

Sergeant Chavez took out a big white handkerchief and blew his nose while Juanita stooped down to pick up a picture that landed by her foot. She thrust it at Rosa Guillermo like a sword.

"Look at this... look! This is a girl. A great big girl. What would any one want with something as big as that?"

Rosa Guillermo looked down at a picture of Ebba, the one taken by Johnny Orteez, and wondered what it was doing in the stack of available adoptions.

"Surely there's been a mistake," she murmured as she tossed it back in her briefcase and snapped it shut just as Sergeant Chavez decided to exercise a little control.

"A boy is what we want. A boy to carry on the family name," he said emphatically.

"Fine," Rosa Guillermo replied. "I'll see what I can do."

"And don't come back until you've found what we want. When you upset my wife... you upset me."

Then he put his arm around Juanita, walked her into the casita and slammed the door.

Rosa Guillermo sighed and shook her head. She hated this part of the job. No matter how hard she tried it was never right. She bent down and picked up the rest of the pictures and hurried to the Volkswagen bus parked in front where Johnny Orteez sat talking to Mrs. Marquez, his cousin by marriage.

Once she was in the back seat, Rosa Guillermo removed her shoes so her bunioned feet, trapped in elastic hose, could breathe and gratefully accepted the thermos of lemonade Mrs. Marquez passed from the front as Johnny Orteez revved up the engine and drove through the military base with his loud speakers blaring "You Ain't Nothin' But a Hound Dog."

THE CLOSET

Olivia sat on the red velvet Victorian couch in Li Choo's living room wearing Li Choo's bright yellow silk kimono. From the window she could see the garden with pool and pond and the hole in the wall blown open from the hand grenade Olivia had returned to its unknown messenger. Ever since that day, Olivia had been coming to Li Choo's house on a regular basis. At first, she'd been a little nervous. After all, two deaths in the same garden, she could be number three. But after a while, visiting the house became a ritual, the only thing Olivia looked forward to. She was obsessed. There was so much she didn't know.

It started with the closet. On the day of Li Choo's death, when Olivia looked inside to find a suitable something to cover up her dead husband's mistress's body, she'd been confronted with such a profusion of quantity and color that it haunted her. That night, she hadn't been able to sleep so she'd slipped out of bed and left her house and sleeping children.

Making sure she hadn't been followed, which was an ongoing occurrence since the assassination of her husband, she'd entered the side door of Li Choo's house and went straight for the closet. First, she'd rummaged through the dressing gowns made out of silk or satin or chiffon with trimmings of marabou or fur or embroidered with lace. Next, she'd inspected every crotchless panty, every rhinestoned G-string, every garter belt and nippleless brassiere even though Olivia had no idea what these clothes were for. Unfortunately, the sun had broken over the horizon just as she found the mail-order catalog with pictures of models in the mysterious lingerie. Knowing she wouldn't be able to stay away because the closet and its contents had grabbed hold of her imagination and wouldn't leave, Olivia stacked everything in stacks by category and color so things would be easier to find when she came back.

At home, Olivia fixed breakfast for her children and went about her usual routine, but the closet and its contents bore into her psyche like a drill. Then, because she was the dead mayor's widow and had been followed, she marched straight into the office of the Chief of Investigation and ordered him to order Li Choo's house and all of its contents, "off limits." Nothing was to be looked at or touched. Nothing was to disturb the essence of her late husband the mayor and since the Chief knew exactly where she would be, he could stop having her followed. Her request was odd, but convincing and, frankly, the Chief of Investigation was greatly relieved. Fearing of finding something he might have to investigate filled him with panic. So, if Olivia was too distracted to make them search for assassins, so much the better. Any excuse she wanted to use was all right with him and he could stop wasting all that man power documenting her every move.

Olivia's obsession with the closet was fierce. Night after night she went back to plow through Li Choo's belongings. She was so infatuated with what she couldn't figure out, she went without sleep for weeks and when she appeared a little vague and groggy everyone just assumed she was in mourning. In truth, discovery was exhausting. This was a whole new world, a world she never knew existed.

After a few visits she couldn't restrain herself and began to try on all the lacy contraptions using the catalog as a guide. At first it made her feel very important, as if she'd tapped into some sort of secret very few women would ever be able to understand. Certainly neither Mrs. Marquez nor any of the others in Elena would be smart enough to decipher the details.

Finally, Olivia felt so confident, she decided to inspect her mastery in front of the full-length mirror surrounded by electric lights on Li Choo's bathroom wall. It was a mirror fit for a movie star, but unfortunately Olivia's reflection didn't cooperate. Her voluptuous body spilled out over the garments like a pudding trussed with multicolored string and none of the paraphernalia fit, which was very confusing because all they were made of were spaces.

Olivia wept in utter frustration. Attempting to try on the crotchless underwear, she hopped around on one leg only to discover both legs were trapped in the same opening and crushing her enormous black pubic bush with a tight pink stripe. Not to mention her voluminous breasts that spilled out of and on top of and underneath the two skimpy triangles of white rabbit fur linked by a line of lime green sequins that cut off her breathing. Furious, Olivia ripped the band of lace off her leg, tore off the top and sobbed angrily at her naked reflection. After that, she picked up the pile of spider web undies and threw them into the fireplace, lit a match and watched them go up in flames. Something about the blaze seemed to calm her. Looking through the kitchen cupboards, she discovered an assortment of exotic teas. She picked something with rosebuds and violets and let the fragrance pacify her confusion. Restored, Olivia went back to the closet and found a fine ivory satin robe. Not realizing it had belonged to her husband, she slipped into its smooth coolness and let it soothe her vanity. A robe was something she could understand and just before Olivia let

THE DANCE

$\mathcal{E}$bba had seen them in the moonlight from the top of her tree, watched as the women dressed in white descended the hillside like giant moths drawn to the pinpoints of colored light dotting the portable dance floor perched in a field of wildflowers. On the fourth Saturday of every month, at exactly nine o'clock at night, Bernardo's mother's musician cousins would park their bus under the criss-cross canopy of Christmas lights and climb on its roof to play the national anthem which signaled that the dance was about to begin.

On this particular fourth Saturday, Hortence Grace had invited Ebba to come along with her daughter Rebecca and at the last minute made each of them a new white dress out of her old bedroom curtains. Fueled by the excitement of the music, the rushing women engulfed the girls until all of them flocked onto the floor like a colony of chattering birds.

There was laughing but deliberately no discussion of anything of importance. No conversations about illness or broken hearts or kidnappings or thefts or accidental deaths or murders. No mention of grandmother Barilla's refrigerator full of poppy tar being confiscated or how many of her grandsons and their friends she'd turned on to the pipe. And no speculation about Olivia Gomez, who never attended the dance, or what she might be doing at Li Choo's house. Only conversations about the balmy air, the countless stars filling the sky, the moon gleaming above like a beacon or the pinpoints of light that dotted the women's white dresses like colored raindrops.

Ebba's mother wasn't there. In fact, Ebba's mother was retreating further and further into her illness and losing track. Sometimes she even forgot that Ebba was her daughter. Carlotta Pavon was living in a twilight world between here and heaven, which is why Hortence Grace insisted that Ebba leave the house for a few hours of escape. She gave Ebba every assurance that when it was time for her mother to pass away, it wouldn't matter if Ebba was there or not. Ebba just hoped that her mother wouldn't die while she was gone because she didn't want to come home and find her.

At nine o'clock, after they'd rushed down the hill with all of the others, Hortence Grace gathered the girls into the cluster of women curling in a circle and singing in time to the music. Ebba had never experienced anything like this before. The only dance Ebba had ever danced was with

Mr. Lobos and that certainly wasn't this. The shuffling feet and arched backs and laughing and smiling faces with parted lips and glistening eyes, like an army of cats excited by what they could see in the dark which turned out to be all the men who were coming down the hillside, first in trickles then in torrents, rushing, running, twisting and turning with their hair slicked back, bathed and perfumed, wearing clean clothes and sandals. They were in a hurry to meet the women dancing on the wooden square who called out to them without ever using their voices and when they entered the white swirl with their bright colored shirts it was like splatters of paint on freshly fallen snow.

Ebba and Rebecca were pushed around the floor in time to the music as Bernardo, his shiny black hair combed loose and floating down his back, smiled his big white smile and joined Hortence Grace and Rebecca and Ebba circling tighter and tighter until they were at the very center of the swirl. For the first time in Ebba's life she felt like she was part of everything all at once.

"Thwap-thwap-thwap..."

"Thwap-thwap-thwap..."

A steady pounding rotary noise began to pulse through the music, began to push its way onto the dance floor. Gradually everyone stopped moving and looked around as the ground started to shake. The band stopped playing, halted mid-phrase.

"Thwap-thwap-thwap..."

Everything started to blow. Dirt, flowers, strings of overhead lights arching up and down like volts of electricity until out of the dark, and barely visible, a black helicopter dropped down from the sky.

The crowd on the dance floor crouched to their knees and tried to shield themselves from the flying dirt and debris. The musicians bent low and gripped their chairs hoping not to be blown off the bus but Ebba was transfixed and remained upright and rigid as a rod. She'd never seen anything that compared to this. Finally Hortence Grace reached up, grabbed Ebba's hand and pulled her down with the others.

When the helicopter landed, the rotary blades slowed but didn't stop and the passenger door flew open. Father Lyle, his white lace tunic spattered with blood, stepped out into the whirling dirt followed by a military policeman holding a gun and hurried toward the bewildered crowd shouting against the noise.

"Ernesto... Ernesto Miguel!"

Father Lyle looked desperate and his nose was bleeding. No one spoke.

"Ernesto!"

The priest was frantic, but everyone on the dance floor remained silent against the slow, thwap-thwap-thwap. He decided to wade into the crowd to try to part it like the sea. He pushed and pawed, mauled everyone he touched until finally he fell down calling Ernesto Miguel's name over and over. Ebba huddled against Hortence Grace and Rebecca. Fear was spilling out all over the place, you could smell it. Bernardo mumbled to Ernesto Miguel, who was blind and kneeling right beside him, not to say a word to the flailing priest.

"I have news of your mother," Father Lyle said as he got up then tripped again and collapsed into the crowd. For a moment it seemed as though he'd been swallowed by people but when the military policeman shot his gun in the air, Father Lyle lurched to his feet and gasped.

"Ernesto!"

Ernesto didn't flinch as the priest, stinking of sweat, used Ernesto's shoulder to lean on before he pushed his way back to the military policeman who continued to shoot his gun in the air. When they got to the helicopter door, Father Lyle climbed up the fold-down steps and looked back.

"I have news of your mother!" he shouted. But no one answered so the military policeman holstered his gun and shoved the priest inside. Then he pulled up the stairs as the helicopter resumed rotary speed and sucked itself back up into the sky, silhouetted itself against the moon for just a moment, then disappeared in the dark.

When the thwapping diminished to a plodding pound, the musicians examined the bullet hole in the marimba player's hat. But after a short conversation, they all laughed, resumed playing the exact same note where they'd left off and everyone got up off the floor, dusted themselves off and went back to dancing.

Everyone but Ebba, who had no idea what had just happened and stayed glued to her spot. Bernardo reached out and took her hand as he shouted over the noise of the band. "Ernesto doesn't have a mother."

Ebba didn't understand. "Everybody has a mother."

"Ernesto's mother is already dead."

"Then why did he say...?"

"A policeman's trick," Bernardo explained. Holding onto Bernardo's hand, Ebba watched Ernesto move to the music.

"Ernesto was a painter before they scooped out his eyes and gave them to a Commander's blind son."

Ebba looked at Bernardo in disbelief.

"They thought Ernesto's eyes would give the boy talent."

Bernardo smiled sadly and shook his head. "All it did was give the blind boy second sight, so he hung himself in his closet because he thought he was going crazy. Every now and then, someone in government decides it was Ernesto's fault so they try to trick him about his mother but we all know that she died right after Ernesto's operation."

Ebba was stunned by the story but Rebecca took hold of her hand and they joined Hortence Grace and Bernardo to circle the square under the dancing lights in the field of wild flowers bobbing in time to the music.

When Ebba got home from the dance, she tiptoed into her mother's room and knelt down to listen for the sound of her mother's breath. Thankfully it was still there.

In... out. In... out. In... out.

Ebba leaned over to kiss her mother's angry cheeks and in the middle of the kiss she imagined her mother turning over and putting her arms around Ebba's neck to tell Ebba, the same way Hortence Grace always whispered to Rebecca, how much she'd missed her while she was gone and that Ebba was her very own sweet angel. Ebba also imagined her mother sitting up to stroke Ebba's hair the way Ebba had seen Hortence Grace stroke Rebecca's hair and asking Ebba for all of the interesting details of everything that had happened at the dance, saying that she hoped that Ebba had had a nice time.

Ebba was smiling in her imagination, grinning from ear to ear when her cheek caught the back of her mother's hand.

"Where have you been?" her mother shouted.

"At the dance," Ebba said softly.

Angry that she'd fallen under the spell of her own wish, she rubbed her cheek stinging from the impact of her mother's slap.

"You said I could go. You said it would be all right."

Ebba didn't want to, but she started to cry so she moved away. But her mother grabbed a handful of Ebba's hair to stop her and didn't let go.

"Don't you dare talk back," her mother snapped. "In fact, don't you dare talk at all." With her other hand, she ripped a square of white adhesive tape off the bedpost and slapped it across Ebba's mouth. A white square to lock Ebba's lips, but it didn't stop the bewilderment in her daughter's eyes or the sounds that leaked out of the white trap she'd placed over her daughter's mouth. Ebba's mother laughed. It was a nasty laugh, filled with winning. Cutting her daughter down to size, even for a moment, with a strip of adhesive tape was a victory as far as she was concerned.

"And don't take it off," she ordered.

Humiliated, Ebba pulled free of her mother's grasp, ran out of the room and down the hall where she caught a glimpse of herself in the old mirror looking haunted.

In the Morning

In the gray dawn, Ebba said goodbye to the unhappy woman who had been her mother, watched her die, watched her slip away on the sagging bed dressed in all three of the Olivia Gomez' green satin yard sale dresses... all three at once, one on top of the other.

"I'm going," she'd called out, after the incident with the tape. "Get out the green gowns."

Even in death she wasn't willing to part with those good time garments designed for cocktails and Lester Lanin's orchestra and orderly chicken dinners served by uniformed waiters to diplomats at round tables of ten where husbands did not sit with their wives.

What a letdown for those garments. Whole gown lives had been lived out in closets, first in cedar, then mud. Gowns ready to attend coronations and weddings had ended up, stacked one on top of the other, covering the thin withered body of Carlotta Pavon on her final journey into the ground.

Ebba looked closely at the shell of her mother who was cold and empty like she'd been in life. Ebba ran her finger over the tips of her mother's eyelashes then down her mother's right cheek, traced the rim of her mother's lips, all things she would have never have dared to do if her mother was alive. Then Ebba combed and arranged her mother's hair, spreading it out over a lilac velvet pillow with "Guadalajara" hand embroidered in red. She tucked a white rose from the garden behind her mother's ear and since her mother's feet were too swollen to fit into shoes, Ebba slid her mother's fuzzy pink slippers over her toes.

The whole time that Ebba powdered her mother's face, rouged her cheeks and put "Black Orchid" lipstick on her mother's lips, a fly buzzed around Ebba's head to remind her of how her mother had really been so Ebba wouldn't get too sentimental. But she sensed something in the doorway. Whatever it was wasn't substantial like a person, but it was tall and dark and definitely there. At first Ebba pretended not to notice and picked up the lipstick to add a little more of the dark color to her mother's lips. But the whatever-it-was in the doorway crept into the room and stood at the foot of her mother's bed. Terrified, Ebba froze. If she had known how, she would have crawled back up into her mother's womb. Instead, she got down by the bed, buried herself in her own arms and tried to hide in her blue cotton dress.

"Ebba..." the whatever-it-was whispered.

Ebba screamed and jumped up on the bed. She threw herself around her mother's cold, stiff body and begged for protection.

"Oh, my mother," she cried. "Hold me. Help me, please," she sobbed.

Ebba worked her way around her mother's body, but just like in life Carlotta Pavon did nothing to comfort her frightened daughter. No solace came from those "Black Orchid" lips and Ebba's scream, "Mother!" cut across the hot gray dawn and she woke up. She'd been dreaming.

Ebba looked around the tiny room. There was no whatever-it-was, only Carlotta Pavon silent and dressed in all three green satin dresses with Ebba tucked into the hollow of her dead mother's hip trying to squeeze some small bit of something from the woman who had given her birth.

Ebba touched her mother's cold cheek and leaned closer, listened carefully to be sure she still wasn't dreaming. But it was true, Carlotta Pavon was gone, nothing of her was left. Finally, Ebba lay back down, stretched her arm across her mother's chest and patted her gently as she gazed out the window dull with dust.

LATER IN THE MORNING

"Oh, Phillipa Marie!" Mrs. Marquez called out.

She walked in Ebba's back door and made her way toward the bedroom.

"Where are you dear?" she trilled.

Ebba slid off the bed, grabbed the old pink chenille bathrobe from the floor, flung it across her mother's body and ran out of the room, pulled the tablecloth curtain across her mother's doorway and waited. When Mrs. Marquez rounded the corner she extended her fat arms in Ebba's direction and Ebba began to cry. She couldn't help it.

"Oh, poor dear," Mrs. Marquez cooed.

She gobbled Ebba up in a hug and pressed Ebba against her "Mum" scented armpit. "Poor dear, poor dear, poor dear," Mrs. Marquez continued, all the while trying hard to see what was going on behind the curtain. Ebba, knowing exactly what Mrs. Marquez was up to, managed to keep moving around.

"Is she dead, dear?" Mrs. Marquez asked.

Ebba didn't answer, just kept sending up sobs, one after the other, like black balloons. Camouflage for the green dresses.

"Oh, you poor dear," Mrs. Marquez started all over again.

But this time she managed to touch the tablecloth curtain with her chubby little hand.

"Stop that!" Ebba shouted and pulled out of Mrs. Marquez' clutch.

"Stop what, dear?" Mrs. Marquez responded innocently, pretending not to realize that Ebba realized exactly what she was up to.

"Trying to look into my mother's room."

"Your mother? I don't even like your mother. I only came to see if you were all right."

"You only came to see what was going on." Ebba said.

Mrs. Marquez put her hands over her heart and looked hurt. "I only came to help you."

"You came to see what you could get."

"Impudent brat," Mrs. Marquez snarled and reached out as if to smack Ebba, but managed to grab the tablecloth curtain instead, pushed it open and saw the pink chenille lump on the bed.

"Ah-ha!" she shouted. "I was right! I knew when I opened my eyes this morning, your mother was dead."

Without stopping to bat an eyelash, Mrs. Marquez marched straight to the bathrobe-covered corpse on the bed.

"Don't you dare," Ebba yelled.

But Mrs. Marquez was not about to be stopped. Once she reached the bed, she whipped the chenille robe off Carlotta Pavon and shouted, "Son-of-a-bitch!" at the top of her lungs. "Look what she's done!" The still form of Ebba's mother seemed to smile from deep inside her three-tiered green satin coffin.

"I'll kill her!" Mrs. Marquez shouted and grabbed the corpse by the throat. "How could she be so selfish!"

Ebba threw herself around Mrs. Marquez' middle to try to pull her off her mother, but she wouldn't budge.

Then from the doorway came a voice that sounded like a cello.

"That will be enough."

It was Hortence Grace and the sound of her was ominous yet thrilling against the shrill greed of Mrs. Marquez who stopped dead in her tracks. Ebba let go and stepped back as Hortence Grace spoke quietly, but with all her heart. "Go home, Mrs. Marquez, and don't come back."

Mrs. Marquez was so startled she looked around and her face pinched into a knot. After a moment, she let her fury explode all over the room. "You don't give me orders, Mrs.!"

"I'm afraid I do," Hortence Grace continued in that same cello tone. Mrs. Marquez was fit to be tied so she continued with her explosion.

"Then you'll pay for sticking your nose in. I'll see to that. You will pay and Bernardo will pay and your children will pay and your animals will pay and this brat..." Mrs. Marquez turned and pointed her chubby finger in Ebba's face. "This brat will pay too..."

Ebba grabbed Mrs. Marquez' finger and bit down as hard as she could.

After a moment of shocked silence, Mrs. Marquez let out a howl and ran out of the room screaming, screaming down the hall, screaming out of the house and down the road still screaming. Hortence Grace looked at Ebba and shook her head.

"Oh, Ebba..." she said. Just the tone of her voice encompassed everything... Ebba had gone too far, Ebba had done the right thing and even though Ebba would probably be better off, Hortence Grace was very sorry Ebba's mother was dead.

"Oh, Ebba..." she said again. "I am so sorry." Then she opened her arms, held them out for Ebba to run into and Hortence Grace rocked Ebba back and forth when she started to cry and held onto her until she stopped.

After that, Bernardo stepped into the bedroom and they filled the floor with dishes, placed a white candle on each which they lit as they backed into the hall in order to watch Ebba's mother's soul struggle out of the cocoon of green satin dresses and depart in the flickering light while Hortence Grace whispered in her low, melodious voice...

"May she rest in peace."

OLIVIA TELLS MRS. MARQUEZ TO GET A LIFE

Olivia hired an Asian couple from Kowloon who'd run out of money on a cruise from Buenos Aries to take care of Li Choo's house and keep it stocked with the same things, the same way as it was when Olivia found it. She had them prepare the exotic foods that she ate whether she liked them or not. She took naps between the satin sheets in Li Choo's bed and hired another woman to look after her children. She also took over some of her dead husband's mayoral duties and the officials in power didn't seem to mind. After all, the mayor had only been in charge of parties, carnivals, new holidays and parades. In truth, his city planning plans had never been taken seriously so any of his leftover duties were never an issue.

Secure in her new position, Olivia took to holding court on Li Choo's Victorian couch while wearing one of the robes from Li Choo's closet letting her naked abundant body run amok under the soft folds of fabric, allowing glimpses, hints, flashes of her flesh and private crevices to leak out when least expected. Olivia's children began to miss her, but confronting the issues of her sons and daughters was boring at best. Everything Olivia did at home was done in a rush so she could hurry back to her residency on the couch where nothing but a thin layer of fine fabric separated her from her guests.

On this particular day it was Mrs. Marquez bleating about the green satin dresses. "I want the body exhumed," she shrilled.

"Oh, why bother," Olivia yawned. She stretched out in a languid sprawl that made Mrs. Marquez aware of the rise and fall of Olivia's breasts and the fleeting pubic patch that whizzed by whenever Olivia crossed and uncrossed her sturdy bare brown legs. Just like her late husband the mayor, she'd taken to sunbathing naked by the pool.

"Have one of these robes," Olivia said, motioning toward the closet. She still hadn't figured out that the ones large enough to accommodate her girth had belonged to her husband. "Or one of my old gowns. Why would you want something that somebody dead has been in?"

"It's the principle of the thing," Mrs. Marquez persisted as she met Olivia's yawn.

"The rotten brat is just like her mother. If you ask me, someone should just take her away."

Olivia adjusted the robe and leaned forward, propped her giant breasts on her folded arms to display her canyon cleavage and her patch in passing as the robe parted at her knees. Mrs. Marquez was shocked. "And I certainly don't want any damn robe that falls open like that."

Olivia smiled. She liked making Mrs. Marquez nervous. "Well..." she said as she stood, deliberately letting the robe fall open and stay that way. "Go look in my closet at home and take anything you want, but I don't want any more discussion about green satin dresses. There are bigger problems than you and your obsession with the plumber." Furious, Mrs. Marquez got up, mumbling obscenities and left the same way she came through the hole in the garden wall. Olivia shook her head and stretched.

"Silly woman," she said.

Then she reached under the couch cushion for the stack of photographs she'd found of the Oriental mistress in provocative pornographic poses. Suddenly motivated, she took them into the bathroom and turned on the movie star lights around the full-length mirror. She pulled up a stool and after careful study, began to mimic the poses, abandoning her voluptuousness to the full-length mirror in a way that would have shocked her dead husband.

Every day, Ebba went to the cemetery where her mother was buried under a blanket of fading flowers. Every day, Ebba picked a dark red geranium from the plant that grew on the spot commemorating the place where Louisa Ortega had been struck by lightning and died when she was eight. Every day, Ebba walked to her mother's grave, cleared a spot and stuck the new geranium into the dirt, doused it with water and wondered what her mother was doing under the ground.

"Been dancing?"

Ebba turned around. Mr. Lobos was standing at the other end of her mother's mound with his hands in the pockets of his black suit. After a moment she shook her head, no.

"You still have the phonograph?"

Ebba nodded and squinted into the sun. "My mother died," she said softly, digging her toes in the dirt.

"I heard," Mr. Lobos said softly. "I'm very sorry."

Ebba didn't say a word, just looked at his slicked back hair glistening in the sun and wondered who his mother was, wondered if he'd always worn a black suit.

"I thought you might like to go for a ride?"

"A ride?" Ebba used her hand to shade her eyes.

"To see the sea," he said, looking over the grave. "I thought that you might like a change."

Ebba turned toward the cemetery dotted with headstones and crosses and surrounded by a barbed wire fence. A change would be nice. She'd been hanging around her silent house and before that, staying with Bernardo and Hortence Grace until they'd received unsigned letters, which they assumed were coming from Mrs. Marquez, threatening to burn down their house. Finally, Olivia had taken Bernardo aside and told him that Mrs. Marquez was so angry about the outcome of the green satin dresses, she wouldn't put anything past her, including her threat to move into Ebba's mother's house. So, in order to nip Mrs. Marquez' moving-in plans in the bud, Ebba had hurried home, settled in, and made sure that Mrs. Marquez knew it.

"We can go right now if you like," Mr. Lobos said.

Ebba looked at Mr. Lobos from under her lashes and nodded yes.

"This way then," he smiled and motioned for her to follow.

So Ebba knelt down, kissed the damp dirt on her mother's grave, told her she would be fine and hurried to catch up, just missing Hortence Grace on her way to Ebba's mother's grave with an armful of wild sweet peas and calla lilies from the garden. By the time Hortence Grace saw Ebba she was getting into Mr. Lobos' shiny black car. Hortence Grace called out, but the car was already pulling away.

After a moment, she put the flowers in a jar filled with water and placed it next to the geraniums Ebba had pushed into the earth but all Hortence Grace could think of was Bernardo's sister Gloria and Bernardo's nightmare about the children and the letters threatening to burn down their house. Filled with foreboding, Hortence Grace got up and ran all the way home.

THE RIDE

Ebba sat in the front seat of Mr. Lobo's car. All the way down the steep mountain road she leaned out the open window as far as she could to let the hot air whiz past her face. Once they got closer to Josefina she could hear the waves crash in the distance and she felt like she was flying right into the smell of the ocean until beckoning fingers of fog stretched out in front of them and covered the car in a filmy cocoon of cool.

Through the mist Ebba could see rows of corn and tall stick crosses dressed in white shirts flapping limply in the dense air, a feeble attempt to frighten carnivorous crows hovering over an open trench that boys, younger than Ebba and dressed in military uniforms, were digging with pickaxes and shovels. Older uniformed men holding rifles, stood around a canvas-covered truck, laughing and eating donuts and smoking cigarettes.

Before Ebba could ask any questions they had already passed whatever it was that was going on and the fog lifted as they passed thirty- two statues of the Virgin Mary lined up by the side of the road. Then, sitting all by itself on a man-made hill was an enormous plaster head, covered in empty shotgun shells. It was the brand new, official monument of the General, three stories tall. A perfect replica of Benny Rodriguez' fat face, the General who, it was rumored, kept a jar of human ears under his bed.

"Who's the head?" Ebba asked.

Mr. Lobos thought for a minute before he answered. The General wasn't easy to explain.

"A relative. Not close, you understand." Mr. Lobos hated his uncle.

"A relative?"

Mr. Lobos nodded. "My uncle thinks he's a king."

Ebba studied the oversized representation as they turned onto another road. "He doesn't look like a king and not very friendly."

Mr. Lobos smiled at the truth. "He was more acquainted with my father," Mr. Lobos said.

Suddenly, Mr. Lobos stepped on the brakes and threw out his arm so Ebba wouldn't fly through the windshield. Unexpectedly, a small brass band wearing donkey heads made out of papier-mâché and playing a march had stepped onto the road from out of the bushes and were crossing in front of the car. Mr. Lobos stuck his head out of the window and shouted.

"Are you crazy? You could have been killed!"

But the band didn't hear him because they were still playing. Ebba leaned out of the window to watch them disappear in the scraggly trees and glimpsed the ocean where fishermen's nets flapped in the breeze like laundry. Ebba turned from the window.

"Would you mind?" Ebba pointed to the front right fender. "I'd like to ride out there."

Mr. Lobos actually laughed and stopped the car.

"Go ahead. I'll drive slowly."

So, Ebba slipped outside and closed the door, climbed onto the fender and spread out her blue dress so she could pretend she was a queen. As promised, Mr. Lobos started off and drove carefully. Ebba was thrilled. This was much better than riding inside, even better than riding in the back of Bernardo's truck. Out here on the fender she could get to where they were going first. Majestic and regal like a hood ornament, Ebba and her blue dress flapped like a flag announcing their arrival.

Hortence Grace ran through the courtyard calling for her children, but nobody came. She called out for Bernardo, but he didn't come either. Panic-stricken, she ran through the house room by room, closet by closet. She ran into the woodshop and then the kitchen, rushed past the new yellow curtains billowing in silence and the empty glass jars waiting to be filled with green chilies from the garden and the sink full of flowers, the wire basket with eighteen fresh eggs that Rebecca had gathered at dawn and Bernardo's loaded shotgun hanging on the wall.

She ran outside and tripped over a watering can she'd left by the gate. She fell face down in the gravel and was so afraid she started to cry. What if all of them were gone? What if something had happened? What if she never saw them again? What if they'd been taken away and what if, whoever it was, came for her too? She dug her fingers into the dirt and sobbed. That's when she heard Gloria's horn honk two shorts and a long. Hortence Grace sprang to her feet. Wiping her eyes on the hem of her dress, she ran to the middle of courtyard waving her arms, forcing Bernardo to slam on his brakes and skid to a stop so he wouldn't run her over. He'd never seen her so panicked.

Quietly, Bernardo told the children to hurry into the house so he could tend to their mother's fear. Then he ran to Hortence Grace and gathered her in his arms to calm her.

"I thought all of you were gone," she sobbed. Bernardo shook his head. He didn't understand this outburst.

"Why on earth would you think that?"

"Ebba's gone... at the cemetery... Ebba... Ebba got into a car with a man who drove her away... I was afraid all of you were gone too..."

Before Hortence Grace could continue or Bernardo could say a word, Mr. Bravo, the special occasion photographer and barber, drove into the courtyard in his old black truck hauling a sandwich board trailer filled with hair tonics, instruments for pulling teeth, herbal remedies and a portable barber's chair that had belonged to General Zapata. At the sound of his muffled horn Hortence Grace gripped Bernardo's arm. "What is that?" she asked in a panic.

"Mr. Bravo. You asked him to come," Bernardo said softly and soothingly, stroking her back as he said it.

"When? Why did I do that?"

Hortence Grace was so frightened she'd completely forgotten about the occasion of Ariel's first communion and his first professional photograph and his first professional haircut. Normally, she cut her youngest son's hair in the courtyard, using an old blue bowl to guide the trim.

In the meantime Mr. Bravo, who was so short that even sitting on two cushions, one green the other purple made for him by Carmelite nuns, wasn't high enough for him to see over the steering wheel, so he was about to drive right into the chicken coop. Tobias, realizing what was going to happen, ran to the truck, jumped on the running board, reached in the window, grabbed the wheel and turned it hard to the left. Grateful for the intervention, Mr. Bravo reached down and using both hands to pull up on the emergency brake caused the truck to jerk to a stop.

"It's over. I stopped!" Mr. Bravo shouted.

Tobias laughed and helped him get out from behind the wheel as the chickens cackled hysterical relief and knocked over the water trough. Somehow, all the noise and confusion helped Hortence Grace get her bearings and gather her thoughts, pull them together and remember all the plans of her life before she saw Ebba get into that shiny black car.

She wiped her eyes and started to laugh. She patted Bernardo's arm in a way that let him know she was all right and hurried to help Mr. Bravo unfold the portable barber's chair.

"Oh, Mr. Bravo," she said in her cello voice. "Thank you for coming."

Mr. Bravo just smiled. Being around Hortence Grace always made him shy, so he got right down to business. "The pleasure is certainly all mine on this splendid occasion." He paused. "So... The Communion cut for your youngest?"

Hortence Grace nodded.

"And Tobias... a trim?"

"Yes, but not for Rebecca or me..." Hortence Grace smiled.

"Or me," Bernardo said, tucking his braid into the neck of his shirt as everyone laughed.

Momentarily relieved, Hortence Grace hurried inside to make lemonade as Mr. Bravo flapped the blue and white striped drape over Tobias and sneezed. Once in the kitchen Hortence Grace squeezed the lemons into the water, added sugar and a few rose petals, but the image of Ebba continued to haunt her and when she glanced at the red geraniums in the window, silent tears filled her eyes and fell into the lemonade giving it a slightly salty flavor.

Joan Tewkesbury

RAYMOND VALDEZ AND ROSA GUILLERMO'S PLUMBING

Raymond Valdez, the even-tempered, sweet-faced plumber with dimples in his cheeks that Mrs. Marquez convinced herself were the size of dimes, and the object of Mrs. Marquez' obsessive desire, was on his belly under Rosa Guillermo's kitchen sink with a wrench and a bucket and a flashlight. He was trying to unblock a blockage that was plugging up her pipes while she stood nearby with Mrs. Marquez drinking iced tea and constantly checking her watch. Mrs. Marquez had arranged this emergency visit after running into Rosa Guillermo in the post office at the peak of her plumbing problem.

"Indoor plumbing is nice," Rosa Guillermo had said, "but things fall down and get stuck." Then she'd launched into a rant over the loss of her mother's gold wedding ring, explaining how it had slipped off her finger in the soapy water, slid down the drain and lodged itself in the crook of the pipe.

"Poor dear," Mrs. Marquez had said, but brightened. Knowing Rosa Guillermo was desperate for help only a plumber could provide, and knowing that she, Mrs. Marquez, could put all of that help into motion, she had volunteered Raymond Valdez' services so she could further a plan of her own.

In truth, Mrs. Marquez thought Rosa Guillermo was boring and bossy, a real "by the book" bureaucrat whose only purpose was to interfere in everyone's business. Because Rosa Guillermo's brother, Ricardo, was a lazy, mid-level politician who lived with an airline stewardess in the capital, he never came home. He couldn't stand his insecure sister and had, out of sheer machismo and perversity, screwed up her one chance at marriage. Then to make sure she stayed in Josefina maintaining his government apartment on a busy street, he got her one of those "all title no power" government jobs with a minimum wage paycheck and his absent presence to hide behind.

But for all of her management skills, Rosa Guillermo's house was a mess. She'd gotten used to the leak in the roof, the broken shelves, the cracks in the caulking, a toilet that never stopped running and the broken love seat in the living room, but her mother's wedding ring sliding down the drain was the last straw and left her incapable of anything but confusion. Remembering Johnny Orteez' mention that Mrs. Marquez had a friend who was a plumber made Rosa Guillermo feel like it was divine intervention that she was in the post office the same afternoon Mrs. Marquez was getting her mail. Mrs. Marquez couldn't have been nicer or more understanding or more compassionate about the problem with her pipes, but what Rosa Guillermo couldn't possibly know was the extent of Mrs. Marquez' obsession with Raymond Valdez. If Rosa Guillermo thought the chance meeting in the post office was by chance it was because she couldn't begin to imagine the grand scale of Mrs. Marquez' Machiavellian intention to carry out her plan regarding the fate of the three green satin dresses now buried and going to waste.

"I can't thank you enough," Rosa Guillermo kept saying over and over as she checked her watch again and again. She was running late for a meeting of bureaucrats. "There must be something I can do to repay this great favor."

At last, there it was. The opening to open the way to the opportunity Mrs. Marquez had been aching to discuss.

"Well... now that you're bringing it up," Mrs. Marquez said, smiling shyly. She was trying as best she could to show a little restraint before revealing her scheme, but Rosa Guillermo was no fool. She'd already caught a whiff of conniving in Mrs. Marquez' tone as she attempted to disguise her homegrown intrigue.

"Anything. Almost, anything at all," Rosa Guillermo replied, managing to sidestep something someone could pin down. "As long as it's inside my jurisdiction," she added.

Mrs. Marquez caught the gist of the finesse and it only made her more determined. "There is a situation," she whispered, "to benefit your human resource bank."

Rosa Guillermo looked at her oddly and blinked. "My what?" There was no way Rosa Guillermo was about to say anything specific about anything significant to a distant cousin of Johnny Orteez. "I don't think I understand."

Mrs. Marquez finished the iced tea and cleared her throat, motioned to Rosa Guillermo to step into the hall. Now that the opportunity had arrived she was not about to be deterred.

"There has been an incident," Mrs. Marquez started to whisper as if she was in a detective movie, but Rosa Guillermo wasn't taking the bait and whispered right back.

"Mrs. Marquez, before you go any further, I want you to know that this house is bugged."

It was a bold-faced lie, but Mrs. Marquez looked around the room as if she was expecting an army of cockroaches to march out of the walls.

"Maybe another time," Rosa Guillermo said, and patted Mrs. Marquez' arm. Before Mrs. Marquez could come up with anything else there was a sudden clink and a great big splash.

"Here it is!" Raymond Valdez shouted from under the sink.

After a few twists of the wrench, he turned off his high-powered flashlight, wiggled out backwards on his belly, reached into the bucket and held up the wedding band.

"Oh God! It's a miracle," Rosa Guillermo exclaimed, clapping her hands.

"No. It was just caught in the joint," Raymond said as he stood up tall and straight, smiled a smile that lit up his face and washed the ring off under the faucet.

Smiling over a thick layer of frustration, Mrs. Marquez handed Raymond a dishtowel so he could wipe his capable hands and polish the ring. After it was shiny, he took hold of Rosa Guillermo's left hand and gently slipped the wedding ring onto her ring finger making her blush and Mrs. Marquez really mad.

"Okay, it's time to go," Mrs. Marquez snapped, even though Raymond was already packing his equipment.

"Oh... well... maybe you could stay for some refreshment," Rosa Guillermo fumbled, forgetting all about being late.

But before Raymond Valdez could ask for a glass of water, Mrs. Marquez cut to the chase.

"Too late, gotta go." She'd seen the look in Rosa Guillermo's mind's eye. A handyman who was tall with an even temper and a smile, including dimples, who knew about plumbing...

"Oh... Well, let me get my purse."

"Won't be necessary," Mrs. Marquez jumped in, much to Raymond's surprise. Mrs. Marquez turned to Rosa Guillermo with a steely smile.

"But... if you'd like to get together for a little chat..."

Rosa Guillermo got the "hands off he's mine" message loud and clear and decided to let Mrs. Marquez' secret request dangle.

"Anytime after my trip," Rosa Guillermo oozed condescendingly.

Then she stepped forward and gave Raymond a little peck on the cheek as she whispered, "Thank you so much," in his ear and waved at Mrs. Marquez doing a slow burn as she followed Raymond out the kitchen door.

A Day at the Beach

Ebba ran across the bright white sand, past the rows of fishing poles and nets billowing in the wind, past the ancient banyan tree with its rambling roots. With her heart leaping in her chest, Ebba ran to meet the sea. Eager to embrace all of it at once, she ran in and out of the water, let the waves crash against her body until she was soaked and the blue cotton dress clung to her like extra skin. After that, she ran along the shore with her arms outstretched, pretending she was a bird that could slip into the sky. Then she stopped and pulled off her wet dress, pulled off the white cotton underpants and dove into the water, gave herself up to the crashing waves. Up and down... up and down... She laid down in the water, rolled over and over, let the sand stick to her skin then let the water wash it clean. Her sleek, naked brown body shimmered in the sun and her long black hair spilled over her chest and down her back in luxurious vines that clung to her face and neck.

Mr. Lobos reached down and picked up Ebba's wet clothes. He hung them on the stake of a fisherman's net. He even took off his shoes and socks and sat down to watch her dance with the water. She watched Mr. Lobos, too. Watched him watching her out of the corner of his eye, watching her flight, her breakout freedom, her feeling of all-out joy.

Ebba stood naked in front of Mr. Lobos. Drops of water on her brown skin caught the sun like jewels, her black hair plastered against her body as she stuck out her arm and walked in a circle, head held high, slowly, deliberately displaying the authority of her straight sturdy body. Mr. Lobos watched her closely. The arch of her back, the lift of her haunch, the hint of breasts, the perfect unadorned slit of her entryway, a neat incision like a surprise in her brown body. Ebba started to turn cartwheels end over end, a confusion of hair and legs and feet far too big for her body. Suddenly, she stopped and walked toward Mr. Lobos again. He had removed his coat and his white shirt, laid them neatly by his shoes and socks, rolled up his pant legs and sat back on his haunches as he brushed his hands together to get rid of the sand. He looked younger without his clothes, more vulnerable, more willing, but he never took his eyes off Ebba standing in front of him with her arms stretched over her head like a diver.

Mr. Lobos shifted his weight and fell forward onto his knees. His head was level with Ebba's chest and so close that his breath whispered against her skin. He opened his hand and spread it across her chest. Just like that first day, his fingers reached her nipples, but this time they skimmed the dark pigment... thumb on one, little finger on the other. Ebba ducked down, doubled over, laughed, then folded her arms across her chest and studied the shirtless man kneeling before her and started to move from one hip to the other... side-to-side, side-to-side. Then she stopped, stood just out of reach with her legs apart digging her toes in the sand, but Mr. Lobos surprised her. He reached out and put his hand through her legs, cupped the small distance from her front to back. Four fingers held her naked backside while his thumb rested on her neat slit in front.

Ebba's eyes opened wide. This was not what she had expected. She started to move away, but Mr. Lobos didn't release his grip and as she shifted from side to front to back, his thumb slid into her crease and found its destination, the source of the shivery sensations in her dream about Bernardo's wet hair. Ebba looked at Mr. Lobos. Her mouth opened to speak, but nothing came out and she stopped trying to move away, started to push against his thumb as he continued to hold her in the palm of his hand. When the shivery feeling started to echo around his thumb and tingle down her legs, Ebba reached out and put her hands on Mr. Lobos' shoulders for balance and leverage until his thumb and her thrust performed a miracle of shimmery sensation leaving Ebba breathing faster and faster and shuddering in shivers. Gripping his shoulders, hoping the feeling would last, not caring what happened as long as it continued going on and on and on, she was caught, captured, wrapped up in sensation... but then... it started... to... fade... and ... came to an ... end.

Still breathing hard, Ebba closed her eyes then opened them slowly. Mr. Lobos smiled softly and watched her slide into surprise as he slowly removed his hand. It was a shock and now she felt naked. Suddenly the sea breeze blowing between her legs was cold, a chill instead of an embrace. Ebba started to cry, she couldn't help it and Mr. Lobos, bewildered by her tears, didn't know what to do. Ebba turned and ran away, ran into the ocean, ran into the waves.

That's when Mr. Lobos caught her, picked her up and swung her around, held her naked body against his bare chest and rocked her back and forth like a baby. Mr. Lobos kissed away her tears and Ebba threw her arms around his neck just like she'd thrown herself around the body of her dead mother, only this body was different. It was answering back. It was hard and warm and holding her too, rocking her gently...

Ebba curled up in the nest of his neck and kissed him all the thousands of kisses her mother had refused to receive and all the thousands of kisses her father had never wanted or perhaps had been afraid to take, let alone give.

Problems With the Darkroom Drain

Inside the tiny darkroom, Mr. Bravo stood on a wooden box in the infrared light developing pictures in the various combinations of chemicals. Tray number one for two minutes, tray number two for four; bit by bit the images swam onto the surface of the wet paper to be captured permanently for posterity. Mr. Bravo thought of himself as a keeper of records and a barber who occasionally pulled teeth if it was absolutely necessary. He certainly never thought of himself as an artist, but he was particularly pleased with the portrait of Bernardo and Hortence Grace and the children. He especially liked the photograph of Ariel who looked proud and earnest even though he was holding his pet mouse.

"Full of mischief like his grandfather," Mr. Bravo said to the chemicals swirling in their pans.

Mr. Bravo always spoke out loud in the darkroom, sharing his hopes and dreams and secrets and theories with his surroundings. It was a habit he'd picked up from Bernardo's father who'd taught Mr. Bravo everything he knew about photography because his son had shown no interest in learning how to capture images in a box. Bernardo liked working with his hands. He liked things he could hold on to. Tangible things that were solid. As far as he was concerned, all the trees in the forest were just waiting to be turned into something else, houses or buildings or fences or furniture molded or shaped or carved, which meant that you didn't have to be a slave to the whim of the light or chemicals or an unexpected turn of the lens. You didn't have to wait and hope that the image that rose up through the water was the image you wanted to retrieve. Wood wasn't mysterious. It was right there, ready to go. Besides, you couldn't sit in a photograph or use it for a table.

Mr. Bravo met Bernardo's father, Hernaldo DeVille, when Mr. Bravo was in the circus with his parents and Bernardo's father came to take their picture for a magazine. Mr. Bravo was fourteen and besides juggling and balancing on top of a ball, he could fix anything that was broken. Cars, radios, watches, guns, musical instruments, bicycles. He could even take apart a camera and put it back together again. Bernardo's father, who was looking for an apprentice, noticed that the boy was interested and curious so he asked Mr. Bravo what he wanted to do for a living. Mr. Bravo said anything was fine with him as long as he didn't have to spend the rest of his life being a midget in the freak show circus.

After a few days of serious negotiation with Mr. Bravo's mother and father, Mr. Bravo became the apprentice of Hernaldo DeVille and learned that it didn't matter how tall you were to take a picture. You could always stand on a box. Mr. Bravo remained with Bernardo's father until Bernardo's father was blown to bits. In fact, it was Mr. Bravo that saved the camera and film and developed the final frames including the one of Dr. Vidal on his horse and the picture of the blast... the "grand finale" of Hernaldo DeVille's life and career.

Just as the timer buzzed in the darkroom, there was a knock at the door.

"Don't come in!" Mr. Bravo shouted. "I'll be right out."

"We'll wait right here," came the muffled answer.

Mr. Bravo pulled the photographs out of the bath, hung them on the drying rack he'd devised out of clothespins and wire, flicked off the lights and carried the rack with him into the kitchen where he secured it onto the clothesline strung across the tiny sink. Then he opened the kitchen door and said hello to Raymond Valdez and Mrs. Marquez, invited them to come in and sit down and poured each of them a glass of beer. After a brief discussion about the weather, Mr. Bravo took Raymond into the darkroom to show him the problem he was having with his drain.

Bored, Mrs. Marquez stood up and looked around the room. There was really nothing to see, so she edged her way to the newly printed pictures Mr. Bravo had hung up to dry. She put on her glasses to have a better look and couldn't believe her good fortune. Opportunity had dropped in her lap and who was she to turn it down.

Without thinking twice, she reached out and unclipped one of the two damp pictures of Ariel holding his mouse and dropped it into her gigantic patent leather purse along with her glasses and snapped it shut. Then she sat back down on the kitchen chair like nothing had happened and was sipping beer when the men emerged from the infrared room filling the air with their discussion of valves and gaskets and filters and copper tubing and how to create more pressure to the pump for a steady flow of water from the well.

NIGHT NOISE

A hot, dry wind tore through the curtains and banged around Ebba's house slamming doors, knocking things over and blowing memories all over the place. Dirt and feathery puffs from the cottonwood tree swarmed in circles across the yard, flew in the open windows and ricocheted around the corners leaving layers of fluff on the floor.

Ebba sat up rigid as a rod in her narrow bed. She hated this kind of wind. So did the coyotes that yapped and the sleepless birds clinging to branches that slapped against each other chaotically. Ebba sneezed; her throat felt ragged, her head and chest tight. She threw back the sheet and ran to the window, looked out at the full moon blazing in the sky. It was hot as noon and now there was screaming.

At first she thought it was peacocks. They always screamed when it was time to mate, but these screams were the kind of screams that sent fear rippling across the canyon. Ebba sat down on the floor under the window and curled into a ball. She wrapped her arms around her legs and hummed three choruses of "Rosalie, I Love Your Curling Lips," but it didn't help.

A volley of gunshots pecked through the shrill screams, so Ebba got up and ran to the room of her dead mother, laid down on her dead mother's bed and sank into the shape her dead mother had worn into the mattress. She tried to concentrate on times tables by twelve and division by nine. She closed her eyes and tried to picture Hortence Grace's comfortable face, tried to hear her low cello voice telling her not to worry. She tried to imagine herself in Bernardo's house with Hortence Grace and the children and the dogs and pigs and chickens...

Suddenly, there was loud pounding. Not from the wind, but fists pounding on the door and shouting.

"Come out, Ebba!" a hoarse voice shouted. Ebba sat up frozen with fright.

"Come out now!"

Instead, Ebba lay back down, burrowed deep in the bed and waited for the ragged voice to quit calling her name.

"Please, Ebba... It's Bernardo!"

Without thinking if it was Bernardo or not, Ebba got up, ran to the front door and flung it open.

Without saying a word Bernardo reached in like a thief and pulled Ebba out of the house, slammed the door, picked her up, carried her through the hot lashing wind to his truck Gloria and put her in the front seat. Then he turned the key in the ignition and when the engine turned over he ground the gears and tore up the steep road, praying that they wouldn't be blown off the mountain.

Finally, when they reached the top, Bernardo pulled into the courtyard, slammed on the brakes and turned off the engine.

"Someone murdered the pig," he said. Ebba just looked at him; she didn't understand.

"After that, they took Ariel." Before she could say a word, a sob ripped through Bernardo, but he reached out and opened Gloria's door. Then they climbed out and ran through the hot wind into the house.

OLIVIA'S CALLER

A day or so later, Mr. Lobos stood in front of Li Choo's gate littered with leaves and broken branches. It was hot and bright and still. Frogs belched from the pond and a long row of tuberose trumpeted a symphony of scent that hung in the air like a curtain. Mr. Lobos found the bell and rattled the clapper. After a long wait, a small door in the gate opened a crack and revealed the arthritic cook who peered out like an old bird.

"What do you want?" she rasped. Mr. Lobos stared at the large black mole on her nose instead of giving an answer.

"Are you deaf?" she shouted. She didn't like his looks and Mr. Lobos didn't like her tone, but he took a step back and replied in a respectful manner.

"The mayor's wife, is she in?"

"She's always in," the cook said, rolling her eyes.

"I'd like to see her."

"For what?" Suddenly, the cook was curious, a man at the gate for Olivia Gomez.

"My business, not yours," Mr. Lobos said firmly.

"Who are you?"

"Mr. Lobos," Mr. Lobos said, looking into her slightly crossed eye. The cook studied him darkly.

"You got weapons? Two accidents is already enough."

Mr. Lobos raised his arms. "No weapons," he announced.

Finally, the cook, who had better things to do, opened the door a little further, but stuck out her hand.

"Wait right here," she said with authority. Mr. Lobos nodded and she disappeared into the maze of magazines and shoebox stacks forming pillars along the hall. A fat, gray cat struggling with the lizard dangling from its mouth darted inside and disappeared. Mr. Lobos tried to see beyond the piles of paper, but it was as hopeless as it was hot. He mopped his face with the white handkerchief his mother ironed just for him with her own two hands. Finally, from somewhere way down the hall the cook called out.

"Okay... come in."

Mr. Lobos tried not to touch anything as he picked his way along the narrow path of consumption. The curtains were closed and it was so dark he almost fell down the three steps to an even darker living room.

"She hates the light," the cook hissed from the corner.

After a moment, when his eyes finally adjusted to the dim, he saw Olivia. Actually, he smelled her first. She was saturated in "Joy" perfume and spread out like Goya's Maja on a red velvet couch that seemed to be sinking into the floor. Fortunately, she was covered, kimonoed in mint silk with touches of tangerine trim and surrounded by a forest of lit candles that made the hot room even hotter. "Don't be afraid," she said speaking with the newly acquired, affected voice she was trying to perfect. She'd been listening to BBC broadcasts on Li Choo's overseas radio and had no idea what anyone was saying, but she liked the lilt and tone and was convinced it made her sound exotic. She peered at Mr. Lobos, took note of his hand tailored suit, his high cheekbones and smooth skin, his dark eyes and black hair. She also took note of the fact that he was standing directly in front of the tiny electric fan, blocking the flow of air she used to create a billowing, fluttery effect that made the silk robe seem like it was in constant motion.

"Could you step aside," she motioned with her fat little hand.

Mr. Lobos did as he was told but kept a corner of the cool for himself. Olivia leaned back on the couch and spread her arms like a large predatory bird in flight.

"What is it you want?" she asked just above a whisper in her BBC voice. Mr. Lobos looked at her for a moment before he spoke.

"I have a proposition."

Olivia lowered her eyes and lifted her expectations. Her bright pink lips started to part with a smile. She was an inch away from enchantment. At last, a man had come to her door with a proposition. Fortunately, some small bit of sanity poked itself up through the rushing rapids of her illusion and alerted her to remember that Mr. Lobos was Hermina Lobos' son.

"A business arrangement," Mr. Lobos said.

He'd caught wind of the passing fantasy on the back of her perfume about the time Olivia caught wind of his catching her fantasy. She dropped the curve of her mouth and refolded the folds of the mint silk kimono with the tangerine trim.

"What kind of arrangement?" she asked, suddenly all business.

"Some perspective on the death of your husband," Mr. Lobos said.

Olivia interrupted with a yawn. "Why would I want that? "

"You must have wondered..."

Olivia looked at him blankly and shrugged. "Listen. What's done is done," she said, remembering at the last minute to use her BBC voice.

The last thing Olivia wanted was somebody shining a light on the past and ruining her present state of "self-discovery."

Mr. Lobos decided to go in a different direction. "If they murdered the mistress, they're sure to come after you and your family."

"She wasn't murdered," Olivia interrupted. "She fell and hit her head."

"How can you be so sure?"

"Because I was here. I watched it happen," Olivia blurted.

Mr. Lobos smiled. "Maybe you planned it."

"What?" Olivia said sharply, losing the BBC voice altogether.

"I've heard that you're running for mayor?"

"Who in the world told you that?" she bristled. She'd only mentioned the idea to a very few people.

Sacrificing what breeze there was from the fan, Mr. Lobos stepped a tiny bit closer and whispered. "Given the number of child abductions you must worry that your children could be taken for back taxes."

Olivia gave him a jaundiced look. "Not a chance," she replied flatly and without a hint of BBC tone.

Secretly, she wished all children everywhere would disappear. She was sick to death of children, especially her own. "What exactly do you want?" Olivia snapped, she'd had enough dancing around.

Mr. Lobos took a step back but didn't say a word so his silence had time to tweak Olivia's curiosity.

Dying to know what it was that he wanted she leaned forward and reverted to her not-so-hot BBC voice. "Forgive me," she demurred. "I was a little bit hasty. What is it you know that you think that I should know too?"

Mr. Lobos let more moments slip into the hot room as Olivia's impatience progressed.

"Because if it's one of Mrs. Marquez' rumors..."

Mr. Lobos shook his head reproachfully as he interjected, "This is not a morsel from bored women who review rumors over cocktails and cards."

Olivia leaned back confidently and scratched her head with the nail file she kept on the arm of the couch.

"Well I don't drink cocktails or play cards so I'm sure I already know whatever it is."

"But what if you don't?" Mr. Lobos replied in his softest voice.

Realizing she'd gotten off track, Olivia leaned forward and readjusted the robe as Mr. Lobos moved to catch a few whispers of wind from the fan.

"Okay, Lobos. What is it?"

"There is talk of the General coming to take over this house." Olivia dropped the nail file on the floor. She couldn't believe what she was hearing.

"But I have the authority to stop them," he lied.

Olivia was speechless, all pretense gone. She'd die if she had to move back into her old life. Having captured her attention, Mr. Lobos went on with authority.

"In exchange for protection..."

"Protection?" she whispered still in shock.

"...for a girl...Phillipa Marie..."

Olivia looked at him like he was crazy. "That horrible brat?"

The combination of the heat and Olivia's perfume was beginning to be overwhelming.

"May I have a glass of water?" Mr. Lobos asked.

Olivia grabbed the pitcher of water with fresh lemon and mint, filled a nearby glass to the rim. Mr. Lobos nodded his thanks and drank it down without stopping. "She's not exactly hurting," Olivia said. "She's got a roof over her head, thanks to her crazy mother..." Olivia stopped mid-sentence and realized that whatever Mr. Lobos wasn't really saying was perverted. She brightened and looked at him coyly. "Am I to understand..."

"What?" Mr. Lobos replied in a tone of practiced innocence.

"Have you discussed this with your mother?"

Mr. Lobos stopped her with a look and put the glass back down on the table without making a sound. "And you Mrs. Mayor... all wrapped up in the robe of your dead husband's mistress?" There was a very long pause while Olivia and Mr. Lobos mulled over their private interests in the oppressive heat.

"So what is it that you want?" Olivia finally asked.

"The assurance that you won't let anyone harm a hair on her head."

Olivia looked at him with amazement and started to laugh, but he countered. "A terrible loss if this house burned to the ground."

That did it. Olivia stood up and wrapped the kimono around her battleship body, covered herself completely from knee to neck. "How dare you threaten me," she snarled.

"But it got you up off the couch," Mr. Lobos said with a smile. After a moment Olivia's eyes narrowed. She had a plan.

"Do what you want, but don't ever tell anyone we spoke. Tell the church that whatever it is that you want was her mother's dying wish. Tell them you were a friend of her father's..."

"I was," Mr. Lobos interjected.

"Then it won't be a lie," Olivia continued. "And remind Father Lyle that you're the General's nephew but get out of my house and don't ever come back and if you don't leave right now... I will call your mother."

Mr. Lobos started to laugh.

"What's so damn funny?" Olivia sniped. "She might like to know what you've been up to."

Olivia pointed at the door and shouted, "Out!"

"No reason to raise your voice, Mrs. Gomez. I'm on my way."

Mr. Lobos turned and passed the arthritic cook who sneered "pervert" as he walked out of the house into the symphony of tuberose and croaking frogs. But when Mr. Lobos finally closed Olivia's gate behind him and stood in the dusty street he took a deep breath and started to whistle, "I Only Have Eyes For You."

Bernardo sang the whole time he painted his truck Gloria government green. He crooned to her in a soothing voice, assured her that it was only a matter of time until he returned her to her rightful state of red. According to Mr. Bravo, as told to him by Dr. Vidal as Mr. Bravo was cutting his hair, Bernardo had been seen by certain authorities as he wandered across the countryside night after night looking for his missing son. They had watched him through binoculars driving in his red truck until he ran out of reasonable road. They also watched him lift his son's rusty bike out of Gloria's flatbed to continue his search.

"Tell him to count the blessings he's got," Dr. Vidal had told Mr. Bravo to tell Bernardo. "Tell him, too much discovery can kill a man." So with every brush stroke, Bernardo reassured Gloria that everything would be all right while he tried to reassure himself that there was dignity in doing duty that required camouflage.

Ebba, eager to be part of the plan, helped paint Gloria's bumper and hubcaps regimental gray even though Bernardo forbade her to participate in the search. He'd already brought her back three times when she tried to follow.

"I could really help," she whined on those bring-back occasions.

But Bernardo never budged. He'd just point to the kitchen door and wait until Ebba was safely inside with Hortence Grace before he'd leave to retrace his route.

"I'm like a bug in a jar," Ebba pouted. But Hortence Grace didn't budge either. Soldiering on with a hole in her heart, she made sure Ebba said twenty-four Hail Marys before she crawled into bed next to Rebecca who was already sound asleep. No matter how hard Ebba stared at the stars through the tiny bedroom window or listened to the clicking gecko as it ran across the bedroom ceiling, all she could think of was escape. In the meantime, Hortence Grace ironed Bernardo's shirts in the kitchen and sang the same love songs her father had sung to her mother and tried to pretend that everything would be all right. Finally, Ebba would be lulled to sleep, but not Hortence Grace. She waited, alert and wide awake until she heard the sound of Gloria struggling up the hill, hoping always hoping for good news... but it never came.

Haggard and despondent, Bernardo would make his way across the courtyard and into the house then into bed with Hortence Grace where he slid into her roomy back, her comfortable-as-a-couch body, running his hand down her haunch and across her belly, holding the weight of her giant breast in his hand, letting the vanilla flesh seep through his fingers until his breathing grew slow and deep and he fell asleep. Then Hortence Grace would slip out of bed, wrap her white robe around her naked body and pad into the kitchen where she sat down and cried softly among the familiar domestic objects etched against the pink dawn.

PIG BREAKOUT AND A BIG MISTAKE

A week or so later, Bernardo's surviving black and white pig rebelled. Not only had his companion of many years been slaughtered but everything pleasant had come to a halt. No one thought to scratch behind his ears anymore or sing to him or take him for rides into the brief-green valley, so on a sweltering Thursday afternoon he knocked down his pen, charged the fence and ran away.

After Bernardo drove Gloria all over the place, using Tobias and Ebba as scouts, the pig was finally spotted having a nap next to the wooden dance floor in the field of wildflowers. It took every melon rind, some stale bread and the sound of Ebba singing, to lure the pig back to the truck where all of them had to struggle to hoist him onto the ramp and into Gloria's flatbed. Once he was captured, Bernardo put up the green canvas bonnet Hortence Grace had sewn on the sewing machine so Gloria would look official. Furious about being trapped, the pig who hated any kind of cover, demonstrated his discontent loudly. The whole point of being outside was to look up at the sky. After a lot of promises and sweet talk and more singing, Ebba and Tobias finally gave up and climbed into the flatbed so they could start for home.

The sun had set but a sliver of new moon shone brightly against the afterglow and off in the distance a pair of headlights flicked on and off like some sort of signal so Bernardo slowed down and gripped the wheel. He pulled his old work bandana up over his nose and tucked his braid down the back of his shirt. He clapped his hat low on his head and knocked on the window behind him. This was the signal for Ebba and Tobias to hide under the tarp. The flashing headlights got closer and closer then stopped in the middle of the road. Fear nicked Bernardo's usual calm as he rolled to a standstill but kept Gloria's engine running and watched Sergeant Chavez climb out of the government truck with a revolving machine gun mounted on top, take a step or two, then stagger and trip before he smoothed his fine greasy hair, put on his uniform hat then suddenly remembered to go back and take the key out of the ignition. Sergeant Chavez was preoccupied, wishing with all his heart that Rosa Guillermo had never delivered that kid the other night. Ever since the boy's arrival he'd hardly seen Juanita at all. She was too busy trying to calm the kid down. Besides the kid was too old. Sergeant Chavez' story about a baby crawling off the baby food label to come live with them didn't hold water.

Worst of all, Juanita had told him not to touch her upright breasts in front of the boy they decided to name Pablito after Juanita's brother who died when he was four. Somehow Juanita had convinced herself that this kid was him come back to finish his life.

"You're late," Sergeant Chavez growled at Bernardo's bandana covered face.

"I had to catch my pig," Bernardo answered truthfully, trying to keep his voice steady. Sergeant Chavez grunted his reply then checked under Gloria's canvas bonnet, poked his flashlight into the dark and turned it on. The pig complained loudly. Bad enough to be captured but worse to be blinded by a probing light. Didn't anyone know about his sensitive eyes? But the pig's shrieks of annoyance deterred the drunken Sergeant from further inspection so he blew his military whistle and after a moment or two the jeep doors opened and a stream of haggard children in mud-caked Children's Association clothes spilled into the road.

Bernardo's heart started to pound but he forced himself to stare straight ahead and pretend to know exactly what he was doing. Not really paying attention to how the children were dressed, he studied every size and shape and managed to convince himself, just like Juanita, that God had delivered a miracle. God had helped the pig escape so Bernardo would be at this very spot on this very evening at this very time to retrieve his son.

"Hurry up," the Sergeant yelled at the dazed little faces.

He lifted Gloria's green-canvas-bonnet and motioned the children to get in with the pig who set up a racket more frightening than the Sergeant waving his gun. Underneath the tarp, Ebba and Tobias were stepped on and crushed but managed to stay absolutely quiet. Finally, after the last child struggled inside, Sergeant Chavez slammed Gloria's gate, yanked the canvas closed, hit the truck's back fender and yelled, "Giddy-up," as if Gloria was a horse.

She responded with a blast of thick smoke, but the Sergeant didn't notice. He walked to the center of the rutted road, took off his bullet proof vest and used it to execute a perfect Veronica in a perfect imitation of his nephew the bullfighter before he was gored. It was a ridiculous flourish considering the outrageous mistake the Sergeant was in the middle of making.

"Take them away," Sergeant Chavez shouted over the last twirl of his make-believe cape.

So Bernardo nodded grimly and prayed as he ground Gloria's gears and drove in circles around the Sergeant's still turning body to make him confused and lose his sense of direction. Finally on the last turn, when Gloria was pointed toward town and the Sergeant was tangled up in his feet, Bernardo stepped on the gas and Gloria rose to the occasion giving him everything she had in order to get away fast.

Ebba and Tobias counted to seventy-five before they crawled out from under the tarp causing the disoriented children to scream which scared the pig already full of complaints. Unfortunately, the more Tobias tried to explain, the louder the children's terror. Finally in an effort to calm things down, Ebba started to sing filling the air with high pure notes and pretty soon, the children stopped their noise and used Ebba's voice like a rope to hang onto.

Even the pig was delighted. This was more like it. Rides and singing. It was just like the old days, except for the crowd.

AFTER THE VERONICAS

Several hours later, after four Scotch whiskeys and seven shots of Russian vodka, Sergeant Chavez discovered that his uniform was streaked with government green paint and on closer inspection found it was all over his hands. He decided, because somewhere he'd heard that was how you removed paint from brushes, to clean it off with kerosene.

He was a bit unsteady, but Sergeant Chavez took out his handkerchief, reached across the desk and grabbed hold of the hurricane lamp. He removed the glass chimney and with utmost care tilted the glass base toward his handkerchief for a few drops of what he now considered cleaning solution but somehow he lost his grip and the glass base slipped on the shiny surface of the desk and spilled kerosene all over the place.

In an effort to shed more light on the situation, Sergeant Chavez decided to place the lamp upright and light the wick so he struck a match, which he accidentally dropped on the desk in one of the pools of kerosene and inadvertently set himself on fire.

At first he was mesmerized by the leaping orange flames, but then it started to burn the sleeve of his uniform and get hot. Convinced that he knew exactly how to get the flames under control he reached for the bottle of Russian vodka and poured it on his burning clothes, which, of course, only made the flames leap higher. At that point he began to shout. In desperation he grabbed a stack of government papers and began to slap himself, but they caught fire too and soon he was a human torch shrieking in pain.

Eventually one of his fellow soldiers, who couldn't bear the piercing screams of the Sergeant and was too dumb to know to throw him on the floor and roll him in the rug, shot the Sergeant dead and considered the killing an act of mercy as it was the quickest way to provide relief from the misery at hand and all future miseries in perpetuity.

Bernardo rattled into Elena honking Gloria's horn. He couldn't help himself. He was ecstatic. With this capture and seizure he had outwitted the enemy and regained his beloved son. He was so filled with anticipation and joy that he stopped in front of the church, ran to the back of the truck, threw open the canvas curtain and announced:

"You can go!"

The black and white pig squealed with discontent but oddly the children didn't move. They just stared at Bernardo with vacant eyes as he tried to match each face with the face of his son. After a few minutes Bernardo got confused. It hadn't been that long, he thought. Surely he hadn't forgotten what his youngest son looked like.

"Ariel?" Bernardo called out.

Tobias jumped to the ground and unlatched Gloria's gate.

"Ariel..." Bernardo repeated, full of conviction.

"He's not here," Tobias said calmly. "He's not one of them. These children are from someplace else."

Bernardo looked at Tobias in disbelief. He tried to take in what his son was saying but his denial was so strong he was certain Tobias had made a mistake, had said no such thing, that the words coming out of Tobias' mouth was the wind blowing or maybe someone tooting a horn or a barking dog. He turned back to the grim little faces.

"Ariel?" he called out one more time.

Now the children were bounding out of the truck, bumping into one another and falling down as they tried to figure out where they were but none of them uttered a sound. Bernardo stepped onto Gloria's bumper and looked inside.

"Ariel?" The pig answered back with a grunt and Ebba, looking closely at Bernardo's hope, spoke softly but firmly.

"He's not here." Bernardo looked at Ebba. This time he couldn't pretend that the truth was the wind or a barking dog. Then they heard Father Lyle shout.

"What's going on?"

Awakened from a sound sleep, the priest walked out of the rectory disheveled and barely alert. Tobias slipped into Gloria's cab and curled up on the floor as Bernardo slammed down the canvas curtain so the priest wouldn't see Ebba. "I found them," Bernardo choked. He had been so sure.

Father Lyle peered at the shapes standing by the truck. "Children? These are children." Father Lyle whined. Still half asleep, the priest was having a hard time putting things in context. He'd taken a pill to ease the pain of his badly set broken nose so he was groggy.

"I found them on the road where I found my pig," Bernardo lied.

"On the road? What were they doing on the road?"

"I have no idea," Bernardo said sadly. "So I brought them back. I thought you'd know what to do."

Bernardo's voice was flat, but Father Lyle's blue eyes were dancing with terrible anticipation.

"Me? Why should I know what to do?"

"Because you're the priest."

"Well of course, that's who I am."

Father Lyle fingered his rosary nervously and adjusted his privates all in one gesture.

"But what do I do with them?"

The silent children clustered around Father Lyle as if at attention and watched him scratch his sleep-matted hair with lifeless eyes.

Bernardo wanted to shout at the priest. It was all he could do to keep himself from reaching down and patting each child's dusty head. His heart was breaking. He even looked down at his chest to make sure blood wasn't seeping out of the wound of his loss and staining his shirt. When he discovered it wasn't, he pointed to the chapel and opened Gloria's door.

"Maybe their pictures are on your wall. They may not remember who they belong to but their grandmothers will."

Father Lyle started to come to just as Bernardo was getting in the truck.

"Where did you say they were?" Bernardo just shrugged and started Gloria's engine.

"But these children aren't missing. These are military recruits," the priest shouted, "part of the Children's Army..." It was too late. Bernardo was already driving away fast, abusing what little horsepower Gloria had left.

At home, everyone went to work restoring Gloria to her rightful state of red as Bernardo fought back the dreadful burden of self-deception, chastising himself for trying to make things seem what they were not and finally, after attacking every Gloria crevice to make sure all the government green was gone, he reached out for Tobias and held him close. Ebba watched as they walked away, both of them silent until they reached the grape arbor and Bernardo fell to his knees and began to sob, so Tobias

Joan Tewkesbury

knelt down beside his father and held him in his arms. Ebba turned away from Bernardo's anguish, sat on the ground and tried to think about other things like Mr. Lobos and where he might be at this very moment. And while she wondered she dipped her brush into the can of bright red paint and painted the nails of her fingers and toes.

Scorched Chavez

Juanita hovered over the body of her dead husband like a bird of prey drifting from one end of him to the other. What remained of Sergeant Chavez was a mess. Fire is not kind to the flesh, but Juanita kept fluttering her fingers over the charred parts she had loved and lingered over the bullet hole in his heart. She insisted he be brought home and put onto the bed where they had traveled together in good times and bad, in ecstasy or rage. The bed had been their war zone and peacetime passion.

Unfortunately the scorched carcass of Sergeant Chavez arrived at exactly the same time Rosa Guillermo pulled up in front of the house to check on how the family was getting along with their brand new "Pablito." Horrified, Rosa Guillermo watched as the fully exposed, burned-up corpse was lifted out of the government ambulance on a stretcher and carried onto the porch past the wide-eyed little boy that no one bothered to shield from the sight.

Rosa Guillermo had run to the child protectively and turned him away from the gruesome goings-on. She realized Juanita was in shock, but surely, she thought, her mothering instincts would take over to comfort the child and tell the men to put the Sergeant somewhere out of sight.

Unfortunately, Juanita had done nothing to inspire maternal confidence. After glimpsing the burnt up body, Juanita let out a sob then turned away and gave her "Pablito" a ringing slap. "It's all your fault," she screamed. Then she saw Rosa Guillermo and shifted her wrath.

"We wanted a baby and you gave us this," she shouted and pointed menacingly at the little boy. Poor Ariel. He looked as if he'd been kicked by a mule.

"I'm not sure I understand," Rosa Guillermo tried to interject.

She knew Juanita was upset and not terribly bright, but to slap a child?

"I gave him too much of my time," Juanita shouted. "All of my attention and devotion. I left nothing for him." Juanita turned and pointed at the charred remains.

"But that wasn't necessary," Rosa Guillermo said. "I'm sure 'Pablito' didn't want all of your time... Did you, Pablito?"

Ariel looked at Rosa Guillermo as if she was crazy, but he shook his head no. That's when Juanita grabbed Ariel by the shoulders and shook him as hard as she could. It was violent and nasty, but he didn't make a sound. Juanita, on the other hand, was shouting. "See what I mean! He never talked, never said a word!!"

At this point Rosa Guillermo intervened. She pulled Ariel away from Juanita and pointed to the car.

"Run along and get inside," she said to him calmly. Tears spilled down his cheeks, but he did what he was told.

"Don't ever come back!" Juanita screamed. Then she picked up a nearby broom and started after him determined to beat the boy to death. Quickly, Rosa Guillermo grabbed Juanita and stopped her.

"You're in shock!" Rosa Guillermo shouted at the top of her lungs.

After a moment, Juanita took a step back, dropped the broom and blankly watched Ariel get into the car and slam the door.

"Now," Rosa Guillermo said, "go inside and tend to your dead husband. I'll take the child home with me and in a few days we'll talk."

But before Rosa Guillermo could finish the sentence, Juanita turned to the men holding the body and opened the screen door, pointed to the bedroom and said. "Take him in there."

After the men left and Rosa Guillermo drove away, Juanita started to cry, but then she went dry and when she couldn't bring up another sob she locked the door. She pulled the white lace cover that had been their wedding blanket out of the cedar chest and spread it over the Sergeant's burned up body. She drew it up under his singed chin, kissed the bullet hole in his heart through the delicate lace. Then in the absolute quiet, she pulled a chair up to the foot of the bed and stood on the seat. She wanted to be sure her husband could see her while she took off all of her clothes, piece by piece, like a show. And finally, when she was absolutely naked, she ran her fingers up over her large upright breasts and began to sob... "Oh Alberto, my Alberto. Alberto, Alberto..."

Holy Celebration and Bad Pork

On top of everything else, it was the celebration of St. Augustine and the procession to the church was late getting started due to rain. When the sun finally came out, soldiers with their guns slung over their shoulders helped Mr. Bravo stretch a sheet over the street in front of the post office, so when it got dark he could set up his projector and show a movie.

Every child in the village was dressed as an angel with wings and wire halos covered with chicken feathers and foil. Except for Father Lyle and the soldiers, every adult, including the musicians, had powdered their faces with flour in order to be holy. Four donkeys draped with hand-embroidered silk shawls wore leis of red paper flowers and preceded the flatbed truck driven by Raymond Valdez that carried anyone who was too old or unable to walk. That included Dr. Vidal and his assistant Mercedes who'd polished her fingernails white whether the doctor liked it or not. Each of the elderly carried a four-foot candle and waved to their white faced friends standing by the side of the road.

Mrs. Marquez sat beside Raymond Valdez like a large orange moth in a borrowed Li Choo kimono that she'd pinned at the neck so that it would stay closed, and sitting beside her was Olivia Gomez. Still obliged to be in mourning, Olivia was wearing one of her own, now too tight, black dresses with all of the dead mayor's military medals pinned on her chest. Mr. Lobos, who hadn't bothered dusting his face with flour and his mother Mrs. Lobos, who was a distant cousin of Father Lyle and wearing a veiled hat that covered her face completely, were already in the church courtyard where she kept crossing herself over and over.

"In the name of the Father and the Son and the Holy Ghost..."

Others were dipping their hands in bowls of bull blood to make red handprints on the newly whitewashed walls. Younger boys and some of the men climbed up ladders to the top of the courtyard wall where they formed a fringe of red paint fingers against the bright blue cloudless sky. Excess blood dribbled down the white walls to meet the bright orange poppies below and the horn and drum band played while altar boys swung great balls of incense that filled the air with smoky perfume.

One of the soldiers deliberately shot his gun in the air to scare off a flock of noisy crows that begrudgingly took flight and clacked across the sky and when it was finally time, everyone lit a candle and walked into the

Joan Tewkesbury

church where it was so hot that all the flour faces started to melt and turn to paste. Even the children's chicken feather halos began to droop.

Father Lyle intoned his communion prayer and looked around the room before providing wafers to the congregation's protruding tongues and wondered where all the children Bernardo had delivered to the church had gone the following day in a government bus. He'd meant to make an announcement to the congregation but decided it would only cause panic. Best to ignore any military situation most especially the recruitment of children exchanged for the release of their imprisoned relatives.

"In the name of the Father and the Son and the Holy Ghost," he said to each trembling tongue waiting for a wafer.

Then another round of "Father and Son" as he held the wine-filled chalice to every pair of the lips including Mr. Lobos and his mother, who dipped her wafer into the drink. Then to Hortence Grace and Bernardo and Tobias and Rebecca and Ebba and Mr. Bravo and Dr. Vidal with his assistant's hand draped on top of his.

"Surely he doesn't," thought the priest, letting his mind wander as he looked at the old man's tongue then moved on to Mrs. Marquez in the orange robe safety-pinned at the neck. Then to Raymond Valdez and Rosa Guillermo, who kept trying to catch the plumber's eye, then to Olivia Gomez as he thought to himself that she was beginning to look like a couch and withdrew the chalice hastily from her bright pink lips. After that he turned and passed a little wind leaving its lingering fragrance as he climbed the pulpit steps to launch into the history of St. Augustine and the church, reminding the congregation to remember how thankful they should be for their Lord Jesus Christ.

After he delivered the homily, something about "progress" for the son of God, he scanned the sea of melting flour faces nestled amongst the homemade wings. But he never mentioned the gunshots at night or the screaming children torn from their parents' arms or the children already missing or the children's army or his broken nose or anything against peddling poppy or cutting down trees. No comfort or caring or mention of fear. Instead, he spread out catechism and doctrine like a doily on the arm of a chair to cover the wear and tear of everyone's loss. As far as he was concerned, rituals kept people busy and if they were busy they were relatively safe. Most of all it kept Father Lyle, who was passing wind profusely, from answering any questions that he, unfortunately, might know the answers to.

Suddenly, the band struck up a hymn usually played on the organ by señora Avila to signify the end of the sermon. It scared him out of his wits, but he managed to recover and held up the money tree made out of wire where a few paper pesos flapped from clothespins and paper clips. Then he declared a serious blessing on all of those about to make serious donations. Turning to face Jesus on the cross, he worried if the tripe and pozole he'd eaten last night was tainted, so he missed seeing Mr. Lobos watch Ebba as she watched him from under the rim of her halo, secretly wishing he would take her away from this roasting hot room so they could go to the beach.

Father Lyle crossed himself for the last time and rose from his knees while trying to contain another wave of wind escaping from his bowels. Instead it trumpeted out with unforeseen force. Those at the altar exchanged discreet looks and waved their incense balls vigorously as the priest looked heavenward and cleared his throat one last time.

"In the name of the Father, the Son and the Holy Ghost, world without end. Amen."

Then he hurried up the aisle disturbing a couple of peacocks and a flock of chickens that had wandered inside and hoped to make it to the bathroom before anything serious happened. He picked up the pace and shielded his eyes from the glare of the mayor's medals pinned on Olivia's chest as she forced her swollen feet back into her patent-leather pumps.

After Father Lyle left the vestibule everyone blew out their candles and started outside. Olivia, tottering unsteadily, was first, then Hortence Grace and Bernardo, their children and Ebba not noticing Mr. Lobos watching her as he handed his mother off to Hectoro the driver and hurried out a side door to intercept the priest as he was on a direct approach to the bathroom.

"Excuse me, Father." Mr. Lobos said.

"What?" the startled priest exclaimed. He was really quite desperate.

"I only need a moment of your time."

"Then you'll have to wait. In fact, wait right here."

Then Father Lyle opened a very narrow door down the hall and hurried into a tiny cubicle painted red, barely making it to a small white commode underneath the stained glass window depicting Moses holding a sacrificial lamb.

CALVADOS AND INDIGESTION

Father Lyle entered his office first. He felt much better, but wasn't convinced that the bout with his bowels was over. Mr. Lobos followed at a respectful distance. He didn't like churches or priests or religion but he was eager to put forward his proposition. Father Lyle picked up two paper-thin glasses that glistened in the sun and poured a generous amount of Calvados into each.

"For the digestion," he said as he drank his down and poured himself another.

Mr. Lobos took one sip and looked at the priest intently before launching into why he was there.

Father Lyle leaned back in his chair to feel the breeze drifting in the open window and as he listened to Mr. Lobos, he sipped his second drink slowly and watched a large black beetle work its way across the polished wood floor toward the toe of one of Mr. Lobos' shiny black shoes.

After Mr. Lobos finished speaking there was a very long pause. Father Lyle leaned forward and refilled his glass. Mr. Lobos' request unnerved him. Getting involved with children unnerved him. Invariably it set off a flurry of questions regarding responsibility and accountability that he didn't want to be asked or have to answer. Not certain how to respond, he took his time to collect an answer, but nothing surfaced so he stalled.

"Why?" was the best he could come up with.

"Why what?" Mr. Lobos replied.

"I'm not sure I understand."

Mr. Lobos looked at Father Lyle and smiled.

"I'm not sure you have to."

Father Lyle sighed. "I suppose you've talked to the General?" he stalled again.

"At length," Mr. Lobos lied.

"And did you discuss a donation?"

"No. No donations," Mr. Lobos was emphatic.

"But with so much loss... it would be a consideration of revenue for the church."

Mr. Lobos shrugged. Whatever losses Father Lyle was talking about had nothing to do with Mr. Lobos or Ebba, so he wasn't about to let the priest pressure him with guilt for a bribe.

"This isn't a loss," Mr. Lobos interjected.

"Not for you," the priest interjected right back. "The arduous task of incorporating loss into the fabric of everyone's daily life has taken some getting used to. A sudden reappearance of what has disappeared could be overwhelming and to what purpose?"

"Sending children to school instead of selling their organs or turning them into soldiers or awarding them to infertile military men."

Father Lyle choked mid-sip on the truth of Mr. Lobos' statement and coughed, took a sip of water to recover. Not wanting to get into anything specific, Father Lyle decided to go in another direction. He began to traverse the truth.

"How would you, psychologically of course, explain any kind of a return to stabilization...?" Mr. Lobos let his mind wander around the priest's circular route and smiled.

"You could say it was a miracle," he said. But Father Lyle didn't hear him; he was on to his next thought.

"People have gotten used to the disappearing..."

Mr. Lobos interrupted, "No, they haven't."

The priest's stomach rumbled loudly as Mr. Lobos leaned back and took a sip of the apple brandy, watched the large black beetle bump its way across the multicolored landscape of the Persian rug to the open toe of Father Lyle's sandal.

Suddenly the priest's bowels rolled over and squeezed into a knot. Mr. Lobos watched him go pale.

"Something wrong?" he asked.

"A touch of indigestion," Father Lyle gasped as his bowel gripped hard when he tried to get up.

"Perhaps I should get the doctor," Mr. Lobos looked concerned.

"No. It won't be necessary," Father Lyle whispered. Father Lyle didn't want to be looked at or touched by Dr. Vidal. He couldn't stand him. "There's a bottle of paregoric in the desk."

Mr. Lobos stepped over the black beetle settling into a patch of bright red on the rug and made his way to the desk. He opened a drawer, found the bottle of chalky white relief and placed it in Father Lyle's trembling hand. The desperate priest took a long swig. After a moment he caught his breath, grabbed hold of the arm of the chair. He pulled a handkerchief out of his robe pocket to wipe the cold sweat off his face and thanked Mr. Lobos profusely for his help. Then after he got his bearings he leaned back and announced that he would meditate on Mr. Lobos' request.

Having had his fill of ambiguity, Mr. Lobos nodded and started to the door, but the priest stopped him.

"Beg your pardon, Mr. Lobos," he called out weakly. "Which one is this girl?"

Knowing that Father Lyle was lily-livered and weak and would do anything to save his own skin, Mr. Lobos shrugged. "Just one of your angels," he smiled.

Though feeling poorly, Father Lyle sensed Mr. Lobos sensing him, so he tried to smile back but it was shaky and he felt another stab in his stomach so he gave up his pursuit for details. Now he only hoped that Mr. Lobos would exit quickly so he could hurry back to the white commode.

"Fine," he whispered and waved him on. "We'll leave it at that."

Mr. Lobos genuflected a small genuflection to the crucifix hanging over Father Lyle's door as the sound of Nelson Eddy singing to Jeanette McDonald drifted through the open window. Once out in the hall, Mr. Lobos shut the door and walked away wondering why Mr. Bravo had started the movie when it wasn't even dark, but he hummed along tunelessly to the song of love.

ESCAPE

Ebba felt like a rat in a trap. She lay in bed in the dark next to Rebecca waiting for her to fall asleep. Home with her mother hadn't been much, but she'd always managed to escape whenever she wanted. Now ever since the pig was killed and Ariel snatched, her come-and-go world had been replaced with Bernardo's rules and regulations and "NO." Ebba and Rebecca could not stay to see the nighttime movie, absolutely not. And "NO," Ebba was not allowed to wander all over the countryside at night. But the biggest "NO" of all was riding in someone's car without Bernardo's permission.

Finally, when the sound of Bernardo snoring came drifting through the open window with the breeze, Ebba moved closer to Rebecca to check to see how deeply she was breathing and when Rebecca didn't move, Ebba slipped out of bed, pulled on her angel dress with wings and tiptoed out the door.

Outside, the moon was full and bright as daytime so Ebba managed to hurry out of the courtyard without waking the dogs and ran down the winding road, passing her house and then the house of Mrs. Marquez, then down, down, down the mountain. In truth, she didn't care about the movie at all. She just wanted to see if she could find Mr. Lobos. She'd watched him watching her at mass and remembering that made her run faster until she tripped over a discarded tambourine and fell in the dirt, rolled over and over. But she got up quick, dusted off her dress, readjusted her wings and continued running until she reached the center of the village.

$\mathcal{E}$bba arrived as Nelson Eddy and Jeanette McDonald were kissing on the billowing sheet. They burst into song just as Ebba found a place to sit down. Nearby, two drunken soldiers got into a fight. Bone crunching punch after bone crunching punch until one of them stuck his finger in the left eye of the other and it popped right out of the socket where it dangled on the soldier's cheek. Horrified, Ebba watched as he was carried to the clinic on a stretcher of human hands. Overhead, Nelson Eddy and the Royal Mounted Police marched across the movie sheet and vanished into the movie mountains signifying the beginning of the end of the story.

As Ebba adjusted her dress she caught sight of Mrs. Marquez pressed against the Courthouse wall kissing Raymond Valdez. She'd obviously given up on the safety pin at the neck of the kimono because it was wide open and Raymond Valdez had his hands full of everything Mrs. Marquez had to offer. Ebba thought about letting Mrs. Marquez know that she was watching but decided to see if she could find Mr. Lobos instead. But right at the most memorable movie moment when Jeanette McDonald was waving her handkerchief out the window and weeping, Ebba felt someone grab her braid, give it a hard yank and use it to pull her up to her feet.

Ebba cried out in pain and shouted, "Stop!" But no one paid any attention as the high-ranking military man twisted Ebba around by her hair and slammed her hard against his stomach. Then he pushed her through the crowd, banged her into people's beer bottles and belts. All through the swelling movie music, Ebba kept shouting, "Let me go!" But everyone was so full of celebration and numbing refreshment they assumed an angry father was punishing his disobedient daughter. Even if they thought otherwise they wouldn't have stepped in to stop him. They were all too afraid of his uniform and his rank. Finally, the uniformed man slammed Ebba against a chain link fence near the deserted church courtyard. He wrapped her hair around his fist and when she started screaming desperately for help, he clapped his hand across her mouth then squeezed her nostrils between his thumb and finger until she couldn't breathe. He wasn't even drunk but he spit in her face and called her a little whore with wings. Then he lifted her up off the ground by the fist full of hair, turned her round and round and laughed as her muffled screams traveled in a circle.

"Little Puta," he shouted over her noise. "Little Puta in an angel dress."

Ebba could feel her hair ripping out of her head until all of a sudden the man fell to the ground taking Ebba with him.

"Let go of the girl," said Mr. Lobos in a dark low voice. He grabbed the ear of the uniformed man still holding Ebba by her hair and gave it a twist, twisted and twisted it until the high-ranking military man was screaming like a girl and lost his grip. That's when Ebba collapsed, just blacked out in the dirt. Mr. Lobos kneed the uniformed man in the groin and watched him double up with pain. Then he kicked the man over and over as the man moaned and rolled around and finally passed out. Then when Mr. Lobos was sure the man wasn't going to get back up, he bent down, gathered Ebba in his arms and lifted her off the ground.

"What the hell's going on?" Olivia yelled from the crowd. Due to the scuffle, Mr. Bravo had stopped the movie and now the noise of an oncoming helicopter was causing the crowd to scatter, but Mr. Lobos wasn't paying any attention. He pulled Ebba close against his chest like an old coat and ran right past Olivia to his car. He laid Ebba down in the back seat, got in front and nodded to the driver even though Olivia was running, trying to catch up as she shouted.

"Wait! Can you give me a ride?"

But it was too late. The car was already halfway down the street.

Olivia was furious. The movie had stopped just before the end and she hadn't been able to find her shoes, so there she was in her stocking feet stumbling along with all of the others trying to hide from the helicopter's relentless roving light.

"Do you know how the movie ends?" she yelled, trying to catch her breath. But no one bothered to answer. They just kept running because something was fluttering down from the sky. She looked up and so did everyone else. They seemed to be caught in a storm of whirling paper and on each piece of paper a picture and all of the pictures were swirling like snow. Paper faces with something hand-stamped across the bottom in red, just a flurry of children's faces printed in black and white.

But Mrs. Marquez hadn't noticed, nor did she care. She and Raymond Valdez were in back of the church, tucked inside the Jesus manger alongside Joseph and Mary in the Christmas crèche, frantically fucking in the hay when the Xerox copied picture of Ariel taken for his first communion, floated down through the dark sky and landed on Raymond's bare backside, eventually getting lost under the plaster of Paris "Son of God."

Joan Tewkesbury

E bba came to just as the picture shower started dropping out of the sky. Not sure where she was or how she got there, Ebba stayed still until she was certain it was Mr. Lobos sitting in the front seat watching whatever it was fall around them like rain. She listened when he asked the driver what it was, but the man just shrugged. He didn't know either. Frankly, Ebba didn't care. What she had hoped for had happened, so nothing else mattered. She was in Mr. Lobo's car with Mr. Lobos speeding down the mountain and it was even thrilling but her head did hurt.

She sat up just as Mr. Lobos turned around looking very worried.

"Are you all right?" he asked.

Surprised by his concerned tone, Ebba nodded.

"I heard you scream," he said. Ebba just kept nodding. She didn't know what to say.

"Do you know who was trying to take you?"

Ebba shook her head no. "I was watching the movie," she whispered.

Mr. Lobos looked at her for a moment longer then turned around as Ebba rolled down the window to get some air. Instead, paper pictures with "DESAPARECIDO" hand-stamped across the bottom flew into the back seat like a flurry of bats. Before she could gather them up, Mr. Lobos turned back.

"Did he hurt you?" He asked looking more concerned than before.

"Just my hair," Ebba said and rubbed the back of her head. Mr. Lobos nodded and mumbled something to the driver who nodded as Ebba rolled up the window and spread all the pictures she'd captured beside her on the seat. It took a moment, but in the bright-as-day moon she began to make out faces. Mr. Lobos turned again.

"What is all that?" he asked.

"Faces," Ebba replied, remembering the faces she'd seen in the chapel and bent down to get one of the pictures on the floor. If it was a picture of Ariel maybe Mr. Lobos could save him too, but when Ebba turned it over she let out a little cry.

"What?" Mr. Lobos asked. Ebba was too startled to speak so she handed it to him instead.

Mr. Lobos looked in the glove box for the flashlight, turned it on and held the paper up to the light. It was the picture of Ebba taken by Johnny Orteez. "DESAPARECIDO" was stamped on it too. Mr. Lobos inhaled his surprise sharply and turned off the light. He put the picture in his pocket then looked at Ebba in the back seat and reached out his hand.

"Don't be frightened," he said softly. "I'll take care of the rest."

Ebba leaned toward the curve of his hand, lingered looking at his long fingers then handed him the rest of the stack, which he glimpsed and tossed out the window. She was so exhausted she leaned back in the seat and lay back down, undid her braid; let her hair fall over her like a curtain and closed her eyes. So much for escape and adventure.

What Bernardo Found in the Courtyard

Bernardo moved silently from one room of the house to another, careful not to wake Hortence Grace, careful to have her keep her sixth sense locked up in her dreams. He checked and rechecked and checked again, retraced his steps but Ebba was gone.

He walked outside and stood in the courtyard. The air was so soft it took him by surprise, but the wind shifted and he heard a whispering sound. He took a step back towards the portal and looked up at the sky. Drifting along in the breeze and swirling in circles, black and white pieces of paper had started floating to the ground. Bernardo reached out to catch the papers hovering in midair then bent down and scooped up the rest. He even went after the derelicts that landed in the vegetable garden. When he was sure he had collected every paper in sight, he took them inside and sat down at the kitchen table.

After he lit a candle, he stacked the papers in piles like playing cards and turned them over one at a time. Every piece of paper announced a face and the word "Desaparecido" in red: baby faces, children's faces, face after face, but thankfully none were familiar. These were pictures of other people's children, but when he turned over the last piece of paper he froze. Ariel with his brand new first communion haircut was smiling up at him from the table.

Bernardo didn't move for the longest time. Finally, he lifted up the picture to kiss his son and as the paper touched his lips the scent of roses, peppery and sweet, filled the air all around him. Bernardo turned expecting to see Hortence Grace in the doorway, her nightgown full of freshly picked petals, but she wasn't there and when he turned back the fragrance was gone. Exhausted, Bernardo sighed and blew out the candle, made his way back to bed and his wife. The mystery of Ebba would have to wait until morning.

Hortence Grace stirred in her sleep and turned over, opened in her sleep for Bernardo who slid into her darkness, her well, her reservoir and they made love in semiconscious cascades. They were one over and over so many times before they drifted into sleep, deeply asleep, a sleep so deep they had no memory of how well they had known each other in the night.

Almost Light

I t was almost dawn when they reached Mr. Lobos' mother's house by the ocean and Mr. Lobos lifted Ebba out of the back seat trying not to wake her. He motioned to the driver to untie his shoes and slipped them off by the door before stepping onto the tile floor of the large house in his white stocking feet.

He carried Ebba up the stairs and entered a small white room at the end of the hall and laid her down on a feather bed that faced a window bordered in blue where morning sunlight from the sparkly sea would play around the walls like music. After that, he knelt down by the bed to help the still sleeping Ebba out of her dress. He looked around, found a white crocheted blanket that he placed over her thin, sturdy body and watched her sleep.

A storm of dark hair surrounded her face in a halo and fanned across the pillowcase embroidered with yellow lemons. He reached out to touch her but withdrew his hand and got up off his knees. She was so still he didn't want to leave her alone. Finally, he leaned down and placed his cheek next to her nose to make sure she was breathing, which she was at regular intervals. Mr. Lobos sighed. Then in the half-light he walked to the window and closed the shutter so the sun wouldn't wake her as it crept up over the horizon.

Joan Tewkesbury

In the morning Bernardo found everyone sitting around the kitchen table, the paper pictures spread out in front of them like a game. Four Ricky Romero, three Marguerita Lopez, two Luan Rey, three Gotera, one Martinez, two Sandoval, one Cortez, one Ariel...

Bernardo was too tired to speak. He filled a cup with water from the silver pitcher, a wedding present from his great aunt and uncle, and kissed Rebecca and Tobias noisily. He picked up Ariel's orange cat named Tomato, who lived outdoors and hunted mice, and held her next to his chest so the rumble of her purring could soothe his sadness. After a few moments Tobias turned to his father and asked.

"Where's Ebba?" For a moment there was only the sound of the purring cat.

"Papa?" Tobias insisted. Bernardo sighed and shook his head.

"Papa..." Rebecca persisted.

Bernardo looked at the cat and just as he was working up the courage to open his mouth and speak, Hortence Grace walked into the kitchen with a basket of laundry that smelled fresh from drying in the sun. She put the basket down on a chair and pulled a piece of paper out of her pocket. Then she pushed all the paper pictures aside except for the one of Ariel which she tenderly kissed before she put the only picture Bernardo hadn't found last night in the center of the table.

It was the picture of Ebba taken by Johnny Orteez with the word "DESAPARECIDO" hand-stamped across the bottom in red.

Men in the Bed

Ebba woke up with a start and looked around the white room. Nothing was familiar and a man was sitting at the foot of the bed facing the window. She closed her eyes and shook her head. Maybe she was dreaming but when she looked up the man was still there. Hoping he wouldn't notice, Ebba eased out of bed just as the man turned and looked at her sternly.

"Why are you here?" he asked. It was her father, but his hair had turned white. "In this bed?" Ebba was so startled she didn't move or say a word.

"Your mother let you run wild."

"My mother's dead," Ebba whispered.

Her father shook his head. "She was always dead. She just wouldn't lie down."

Ebba sat back on the bed. She pulled her knees to her chest and let her hair fall over her face and legs like a curtain.

"Is this where you live?" Ebba asked. Her father laughed. His eyes were shiny and bright and piercing in the dim light. Ebba moved to the foot of the bed and stood in front of him. She reached out with both hands and touched her father's face, took his face in her hands and held it. His cheeks were smooth and he smelled of imported cologne.

"Where did you go?" she asked, but he didn't answer.

"You could have taken me with you," she said.

"You never asked," he answered. He leaned forward and she felt the touch of his mouth on her cheek, felt his warm breath on her skin.

Ebba woke up tangled in her tears and her hair in the white featherbed with the white hand-crocheted blanket, the smell of her father's cologne all around her, his warm breath all around her, holding her, protecting her, touching her wet cheeks, her cheeks against his...

Mr. Lobos was on the bed wrapped around Ebba, swimming into Ebba on the tide of her tears and she was curled into him, clinging, needing his soft brown skin to be next to hers. Mr. Lobos was careful, took his time. Nothing quick or irregular, nothing harsh, nothing but the gentle reassurance of protection, letting Ebba cry on currents of grief, letting her spill into his hands... He held her as he'd held her before. He held her in the palm of his hand, letting her ride with her tears as she moved into him to see this other thing that he had that she had touched in passing and now she was holding and didn't understand.

Joan Tewkesbury

Mr. Lobos wasn't thinking. Not about Ebba's virtue or virginity or what would happen next. He was lost in the right now of Ebba's grip, holding onto him hard, not letting go, pushing, pulling until she pulled too hard. Mr. Lobos was silent, but he grimaced in pain, couldn't help himself. Frightened, Ebba withdrew her hand, but Mr. Lobos found it, held onto it, drew a circle in her palm with his thumb... round and round, over and over. He kissed the spot gently and Ebba stopped crying. She sat up in bed, her hair falling over her shoulders like a shawl. She looked at Mr. Lobos and he looked at her, felt her flat bare chest as she lay down on his bare chest, her hair covering them like water.

Ebba twisted herself around and looked down through the veil of her hair to see his event that rose up, stood up all by itself, separate yet attached. She poked it with her finger and it wagged ever so slightly like the tail of Bernardo's dog. Ebba withdrew her hand and turned toward the shuttered window, remembered that she had run away and thought about how worried Bernardo and Hortence Grace must be.

Ebba untangled her body from his, got up and opened the shutter, looked out at the sparkling sea, listened to the sound of the waves crashing against the shore and the people talking in the courtyard below.

"I should go," she said, gazing at the shimmering water.

Mr. Lobos pushed himself up on one of the hand embroidered pillows and watched her naked brown body against the smooth white wall.

"All right," he said softly.

Ebba turned and looked at him then dropped to her haunches, wrapped her arms around her bony legs and rocked back and forth watching Mr. Lobos watching her, never taking his eyes off her.

"But in a while," he said.

Then he got up, walked to where she was, bent down, pushed her hair back over her shoulders and Ebba never stopped looking at him and rocking and watching, rocking and watching.

Mr. Lobos gently brought Ebba to her feet. He lifted her up and she wrapped her legs around his waist and they stood naked and pressed tightly together at the window, looking at the shimmering sea, seeming every bit like an affectionate father holding his long legged daughter, humming a lullaby to his daughter, softly stroking Ebba's hair as his stiffness, alert and pointing straight ahead was hidden from view by the brilliant orange geraniums growing in the window box, shouting from their green leaves.

EBBA'S NEW DRESS AND AN OLD SILK SHAWL

Mr. Lobos gave Ebba's white angel costume and three yards of bright pink cotton that he found at the bottom of his mother's linen closet to Graciella Toledo, his mother's seamstress, and asked her to make Ebba a new dress while she was sleeping. By late morning everything was finished but the hem. After a snack of fresh mango and *sopaipilla* with honey, Ebba stood barefoot on top of the wooden table in the courtyard turning slowly, inch by inch while Graciella, with a mouth full of pins, measured the distance from Ebba's knee to the top of the table with a yardstick.

Ebba looked down at the new dress, smoothed the tucked bodice then scratched an itch in the middle of her back. Graciella stopped measuring and waited for Ebba to finish twisting so she could complete her work and take a nap. She took the pins out of her mouth and yawned. Mr. Lobos had awakened her out of a dead sleep just before dawn. Ebba looked down at Graciella and noticed her dumpling cheeks were the same pink as the dress. "It's scratchy," Ebba said. Graciella shrugged.

"It's new. It'll scratch till it's washed." She took up the yardstick again and started pinning.

"It's awfully bright..." Ebba said. She tried to make it sound like a question so she wouldn't seem ungrateful, but the color called out like a loud voice.

"It's new. It'll fade when it's washed," Graciella shrugged.

Ebba sighed, lifted her arms and stretched. Graciella rapped the yardstick several times on the table. "Please, hands at your sides till I'm done." Ebba dropped her arms and did as she was told. In a few minutes the pinning was finished.

"There," Graciella said. "You can step down and give me the dress."

Delighted, Ebba jumped off the table, pulled the garment over her head and wrapped herself up in a pale yellow silk shawl with long fringe that she found draped over a chair in the corner. Then she twirled herself around the courtyard until she got dizzy and sat down on the bench that faced a green shuttered window that suddenly opened with a bang and revealed a wiry looking woman of sixty standing in a dark room behind a row of white geraniums growing in another window box. She ran her fingers through the wisps of silver hair escaping from the tight bun on top of her head and looked at Ebba with displeasure.

"That's my shawl," she barked.

"It's very soft," Ebba replied.

"I know, that's why it's mine and I'd rather you didn't play with it."

"I'm not. I'm waiting for my dress."

"What dress?" the woman seemed very surprised.

"That dress," Ebba said pointing to Graciella sitting at the treadle sewing machine in the open window behind her.

The wiry woman adjusted her glasses and peered across the courtyard at the seamstress.

"What's all that racket?" she shouted.

"Almost done," Graciella shouted back.

"Well, see that you are. And you..." the woman pointed at Ebba. "Put that shawl back on the chair where you found it and don't let me catch you with it again." Ebba looked at the formidable hooknose bursting out of the woman's tiny face.

"Who are you?" Ebba asked. The woman slammed the shutters shut and dropped the inside bolt with a thud as the sewing machine stopped and Graciella called out.

"Come and get it."

Ebba got up and dropped the shawl in the wicker chair, touching it one last time before she hurried into the cool dark hall where the smooth tiles soothed her bare feet.

Graciella helped Ebba into the dress and turned her toward the full-length mirror. Ebba stared at herself in the glass, stepped closer to her image and tried to put herself together with all this pink. She looked at her brown skin, her long braid, her bare feet. Ebba was used to blue.

"Well?" Graciella asked. "Have you heard of thank you?"

"Thank you," Ebba replied, but her heart wasn't in it.

"Ungrateful girl," Graciella muttered and shuffled off to get some sleep.

Ebba sat down on the floor sadly. She hated pink. Besides, she didn't know anyone except Mr. Lobos and he was nowhere in sight.

Somewhere in the house a parrot screamed shrilly and scared Ebba to death. She stood up to run outside, but she started to itch so she stopped to scratch around her waist and noticed her hands had turned pink from the dye, which gave her a wonderful idea. She darted out of the room and down the dark hall to an open door forming a square of white light and rushed outside.

The parrot screamed again. This time it was louder. Ebba jumped then looked up in the tree right above her and the bright red bird started to laugh as shrilly as it had screamed. Ebba covered her ears and ran through the oval arch and across the white sand to the sea.

Once at the shore Ebba marched into the ocean to meet the oncoming waves that crashed on her then over her, caused her to lose her footing and fall into the salty water. At first she was afraid, but the continuous rhythm of the water lulled her into submission and soon she was floating in the spaces between the waves with the brand new dress billowing all around her, tinting the white frothy foam pink as the dye bled into the ocean. It bled down Ebba's arms and legs and belly and white cotton underpants and as she jumped up and down the dress became heavier and heavier, but at least it had stopped itching.

"Ebba... Ebba?"

Someone was calling her name in the distance. She stood up and turned toward the shore unable to see a thing because it was so bright.

"Ebba! Ebba!"

The sound got closer and closer and she saw the top of a black umbrella appear over a dune and then Mr. Lobos hurrying through the white sand holding it like a lid to protect a small wiry woman dressed in black from the sun. Ebba stood in the shallow shore break and watched pink dye lines leak down her arms. The wet dress hung heavily against her legs, but she started to walk to where Mr. Lobos stood waiting at the water's edge.

This was not at all the way he had planned it. He cleared his throat. So did the woman standing next to him.

"I see you got the dress," he said.

"It was a little bright," Ebba replied, not knowing what else to say. He decided not to dwell on what was done. "Well... there is someone I'd like you to meet." Ebba stopped a short distance from Mr. Lobos who lowered the umbrella to shield the older woman from the harsh rays of heat and the water's glittering reflection. Ebba recognized the woman's formidable hooked nose bursting out of her tiny face as the woman adjusted her glasses. Nothing but silence passed between them.

"My mother, Mrs. Lobos," Mr. Lobos said and shifted the umbrella. A shiver went right up Ebba's back.

"We've met before," Mrs. Lobos announced. "Now take me back. I've seen enough."

Then she grabbed the umbrella out of her son's hand and started across the sand to the house. Mr. Lobos didn't move, just stood staring at Ebba dripping pink dye.

"Join us for lunch?" he asked.

"Are you coming?" Mrs. Lobos shrilled in the distance. She sounded just like the red parrot in the tree.

"Coming," Mr. Lobos called out over his shoulder, but turned right back to Ebba. "I'll tell Graciella to give you something to wear."

And off he went, hurrying after his mother leaving Ebba as she watched the dripping water from the pink dress form a ring of pink dots all around her in the white sand.

LUNCH

"No!" Graciella shouted.

Ebba had stripped off the soggy pink dress and was standing unabashedly bare on top of the pile of wet clothes.

"You cannot eat lunch in the dining room like that!"

Ebba watched the large brown mole on Graciella's chin rise and fall.

"Why did you walk into the ocean in your brand new dress?"

"It was too bright," Ebba replied, "and it itched."

She folded her arms across her naked chest and tried to see if the pale yellow silk shawl was still draped over the chair outside.

"I could wear that ugly old shawl on the chair," Ebba hinted.

Graciella gave her a withering look and pulled Ebba's angel costume out of the trash.

"Just put this on and come with me."

Mrs. Lobos sat smugly at the head of a long table in the cool dark dining room. The coveted yellow silk shawl was wrapped tightly around her narrow shoulders and the shiny fringe trickled down her widow's back like a waterfall. Mr. Lobos sat on her right, a large white napkin tucked into his shirtfront like a bib. He stared straight ahead at the painting of Spanish conquistadors dressed in armor, riding their horses in a stately line across the new world. Mrs. Lobos adjusted her glasses and looked down the long table at Olivia who was belching quietly into her napkin. Except for the occasional scream of the red parrot in the vestibule, silence soaked up every inch of space in the large room like a sponge.

Finally Ebba, dressed like an angel, came in through the patio door. Her arms and legs were still stained with rivulets of pink from the faded dress, but Graciella had combed and braided her hair. Olivia took one look at Ebba and gasped but managed to swallow her recognition. Ebba just pretended she'd never seen Olivia before and since no one spoke, she slid into the remaining chair across from Mr. Lobos.

Before Ebba had time to wonder why Olivia was there, Mrs. Lobos rang a silver bell and the cook entered with bowls of chicken and cilantro soup on a sterling silver tray. She plunked them down in front of Mrs. Lobos and the others without much ceremony and hurried back to the kitchen as Ebba picked up her spoon, but Mrs. Lobos bowed her head and announced, "We're going to pray."

Ebba looked across the table at Mr. Lobos, but his head was already down and his eyes were closed tight.

"In the name of the Father, the Son and the Holy Ghost..."

Ebba leaned back on her wings, watched Mr. Lobos and his mother cross themselves devoutly and saw Olivia slip two white tablets into her mouth which she chewed throughout the prayer. Finally, everyone said "Amen" and began to eat without conversation, just random slurps and Olivia's continuous soft belching into her napkin.

The harder Ebba tried to catch Mr. Lobos' eye, the lower he kept his gaze on the soup, his thoughts held captive behind the barricade of his eyelashes as Mrs. Lobos rang the silver bell again which cut through the silence sharply.

The cook came back, replacing each empty bowl with a plate of tamales wrapped in banana leaves. Before Ebba could undo them with her fingers, Mr. Lobos reached across the table and took her plate, undid the steamy bundles with his knife and fork, removed the tough green leaves, slipped the delicate contents onto his mother's Limoges china and handed the plate back to Ebba as if it were a present.

"Thank you," Ebba whispered.

The tone of Ebba's response only fueled the fury Mrs. Lobos was suffering as she watched her son and Ebba. Olivia had missed the whole tamale episode because she was busy removing her patent leather pumps and relishing the liberation of her swollen feet on the cool tile floor. So she was startled, to say the least, at the crash of glass.

In a gesture of uncontrolled rage, Mrs. Lobos' hand had swept through the air and sent her water glass flying into space then smashing onto the tile floor where it lay shattered in tiny pieces like her heart. The parrot screeched from the vestibule and Ebba was terrified but Mr. Lobos wasn't shaken and continued to eat his favorite white corn and green chili tamales. When Olivia was certain nothing else was going to break she too resumed eating, smacking her lips, savoring the delicate pleasure passing over her palate. Crash or no crash, the food was very good.

"How could you?" Mrs. Lobos shrilled and pushed away from the table.

Then she got up and walked into the kitchen, the leather soles of her shoes crunching across the broken glass, grinding it into the tile floor. The parrot shrieked with laughter in the vestibule and Ebba shuddered in spite of herself.

"Just eat your lunch," Mr. Lobos looked at Ebba and said softly, matter of factly, as if nothing had happened. So Ebba picked up her fork and took a bite, then another and another. She was very hungry.

"How could you?"

Mrs. Lobos was back. This time she stood beside her son. Mr. Lobos sighed heavily and put down his fork. He looked up at the conquistadors riding above Ebba's head imagining, as he had his entire life in similar dining room episodes, that he was one of them on top of a horse, exploring the new world.

Mrs. Lobos shrieked at Ebba. "How dare you come to my table!"

Ebba wasn't quite sure how to respond.

"Do you know why she's here?" Mrs. Lobos shouted at Olivia.

Olivia shrugged and pretended to be clueless as she pushed the last bite of tamale into her greedy lipsticked mouth. Mrs. Lobos leaned across the table, stabbed her finger toward Ebba who shifted in her seat.

"This woman is Olivia Gomez, the mayor's wife."

"The mayor is dead," Ebba said quietly.

"Precisely!" Mrs. Lobos shouted louder than before.

"I didn't kill him if that's what you mean," Ebba said politely.

"I didn't say that!"

Mrs. Lobos was so mad she'd lost her train of thought and Olivia was completely confused about what was really going on. She looked at Mr. Lobos staring at the painting then his mother quaking with rage and pulled the bright red "mistress" kimono more securely around her black widow's dress.

"It's all your fault," Mrs. Lobos said fiercely to Ebba.

"What?" Ebba asked innocently and a little more loudly.

"Liar..." Mrs. Lobos hissed.

"I am not," Ebba snapped back.

"Don't tell me what you're not!" Mrs. Lobos yelled.

This conversation was beginning to feel very familiar. Mothers, Ebba thought, are all alike. She looked Mrs. Lobos dead in the eye and hoped that she'd cut herself on the shattered glass.

"Don't tell me what I do if I don't." Ebba replied.

Mrs. Lobos was shocked. "How dare you speak to me in that tone."

"You started it," Ebba pointed out.

Mrs. Lobos' dark glare flew down the table like a crow ready to pluck out Ebba's eyes, but Ebba hurled it right back with a dark stare of her own and smiled at the discord. After all, Ebba had had a lot of practice, a lot of training with a mother who perpetually laid in wait to pounce on the slightest infraction of childhood. In fact, thinking about the combat between her dead mother and herself made Ebba feel very strong. The parrot in the vestibule screamed again and Olivia lifted her napkin and picked her teeth with the gold toothpick that had belonged to her husband, but Mr. Lobos didn't move. He continued to sit still as a statue. Mrs. Lobos was becoming more and more frustrated. Her attempt to intimidate Ebba wasn't working. She thought for a moment then shouted. "You are a very ugly girl!"

"And you are old and mean," Ebba shot back. She'd had enough. Ebba picked up her plate and walked outside to sit on the patio so she could finish her lunch. Mrs. Lobos was beside herself with rage.

"How could you?" she yelled at her son for the third time.

Finally, Mr. Lobos turned and looked at his mother, but he didn't speak. He just studied her black eyes pecking at him from deep inside her hurt. A high-pitched whine escaped from Mrs. Lobos' constricted heart, flew out of her bird's beak mouth as she slapped her son's face so hard the sound of it rang out around the room in concentric circles. For a moment no one moved or took a breath. Mr. Lobos' eyes filled with tears, not crying tears, but tears from the sting of the slap.

Instantly repentant, his mother whimpered, "Oh my God," and fled. Again the leather soles of her shoes crunched across the shattered glass, grinding it further into the tile. Stunned, Olivia sat completely still and didn't move a muscle. From the vestibule the parrot laughed its awful parrot laugh and called out, "Dance with me honey," three times in a row.

Mr. Lobos turned back toward the painting across the room and Olivia saw the imprint of Mrs. Lobos' hand swelling up red on her son's cheek. Something about that handprint frightened her. She forced her swollen feet into her patent leather pumps, excused herself softly and hobbled out across the shattered glass, leaving Mr. Lobos with the ring of his mother's slap echoing in his ears, making him deaf to the sounds of his mother sobbing in the kitchen and the red parrot in the vestibule who continued to scream, "Dance with me honey," at the top of his lungs.

The parrot kept up its high-pitched chant as Olivia hurried out of the house without saying goodbye. She slid into her dead husband's Packard and turned the key in the ignition, ground the gears and gripped the wheel tightly as she lurched out of the driveway to the road.

"What a mess," she said out loud. Then something caught her eye in the rearview mirror.

Mrs. Lobos was running out of the front gate shaking her fist at Olivia's car and shouting, "Come back!" It was a frightening sight. For a split

Hortence Grace Talks to Carlotta Pavon

I n the distance a guitar played the same refrain over and over. The precise, delicate notes fanned out over the cemetery where Hortence Grace was tending the dark red geraniums she'd planted on the grave of Ebba's mother. Tenderly, she troweled around the plants' roots, whispering softly to the woman buried beneath the flowers.

"No one ever tells you how it will be to be a mother," she sighed. "No one ever speaks about the loneliness."

Hortence Grace stopped digging and sat back on her heels. She looked out across the cemetery's patchy green grass and too few trees as the musician playing the guitar moved on to the next refrain, repeating it over and over with meticulous precision. Hortence Grace shook her head and continued her conversation with the woman under the ground.

"Mr. Escalante comes here every day to practice. His wife is deaf, so he plays to the souls who are waiting in purgatory. He and his wife had four children and they were taken just like Ariel. They say his wife is deaf because she can still hear them screaming."

Hortence Grace put down her trowel and unwrapped a brown paper package full of pink rose petals and yellow lemon rinds. She picked up the watering can, moistened the newly turned earth and pushed the rinds and petals into the dirt creating sweet smelling compost.

"I planted these geraniums so Ebba wouldn't forget you. I didn't know what color you liked, but I thought red would be better than orange or pink." Hortence Grace began kneading the soil, squishing it between her strong fingers and continued to talk.

"I know Ebba had more freedom with you, but we have more children. More children, more rules..."

Hortence Grace shut her eyes for a moment and listened to Mr. Escalante move on to the next refrain full of poignant low tones that sounded like a woman weeping. Before she could stop herself, Hortence Grace leaned down and whispered to the dirt.

"I wasn't going to tell you because I didn't want you to worry, but I'm sure you'd want to know. Ebba is gone and I am so sorry." The guitar continued to mourn and big slow tears started to roll down Hortence Grace's wide, smooth cheeks.

"It was St. Augustine's Day so I made her a dress with wings and a halo. It wasn't like Ariel. I'm pretty sure she ran away." Hortence Grace dried her tears with the hem of her skirt and continued. "She's not like my Rebecca. Ebba's spirit is pure and proud, but she's willful."

Hortence Grace smiled just as a little sob caught in her throat and rang out with the guitar.

Suddenly a hot, dry wind blew across the grave and the bell in the cemetery tower tolled random and hollow, not the time or a tune, just a response to the wind. Hortence Grace tucked her flapping, flowered skirt under her knees as the brown wrapping paper flew away, sailed along a row of crosses and slapped itself against the gray granite headstone of the mayor. She pushed the petals and rinds further down under the geraniums so they couldn't blow away and doused the dirt with more water, watched it turn from brown to black as it swallowed the yellow and pink mix. After that, the wind stopped blowing as suddenly as it had started.

Hortence Grace smoothed her hair with the back of her hand and looked at the dark blossoms that spread the length of Ebba's mother's coffin. "In honor of a mother's blood," she said out loud. She was addressing the crosses and tombstones all around her before she leaned down and whispered to the wet ground. "Ebba left her blue dress. All that's left of Ariel is the smell of him on his pillow, but it's almost gone. Every night Bernardo holds that pillow up to his face to try to inhale our son back into our arms and every day we work so we don't drown in our sorrow, but the loss is so big..."

Hortence Grace leaned down closer to the dark dirt.

"I was wondering," she asked, "I don't want to burden you, but it would mean so much to Bernardo..." She looked around quickly before she continued. "Could you... could you give me a sign, something that would let us know that he isn't there...where you are? I know it's a lot to ask and it doesn't need to be much, but just to let us know..."

A large black and gray moth fluttered past and landed on one of the red geraniums. It opened and closed its wings, displaying its elegant decoration. Startled, but grateful, Hortence Grace whispered her excited response. "Oh my... Oh, thank you..." but the moth opened its wings and flew off mid-sentence. Hortence Grace got up quickly to watch the moth's flight, but it was gone. Hortence Grace shook her head and tried not to be disappointed.

"I'm sorry. It was wrong to ask." She lowered herself back down to her knees, made the sign of the cross, kissed her fingers and touched the dirt. She picked up her trowel and got ready to go, but stopped. Water was oozing up from the ground forming a rosy pink and yellow halo the exact length of Carlotta Pavon. It shimmered in the blindingly bright sunlight and seemed to lift up off the ground then after a moment it disappeared into thin air but left a ring of sparkling pink and yellow foam. Humbled, Hortence Grace bowed her head, made the sign of the cross and whispered "Thank you," to Ebba's mother.

When the bells in the cemetery tower chimed four times the guitar music stopped and Mr. Escalante walked across the graveyard holding his guitar next to his heart like a baby. His eyes were downcast so he wouldn't step on the dead.

"Buenos tardes, señor Escalante," Hortence Grace called out with a new lightness in her voice. "Buenos tardes, señora," he replied, his tone resonate and raspy.

"Your music is soothing, señor Escalante."

"It's for the souls," he shrugged.

"Our souls, too," Hortence Grace replied. A hint of a smile slipped across Mr. Escalante's face. "If you think so," he said. Then he waved a little wave and left, patting his guitar as if it were crying.

JUANITA VISITS THE GENERAL'S COMMANDER

Juanita stood in the General's Commander's living room. He was watching the Miss Central Committee Beauty Pageant on TV. As the master of ceremonies read off the names of the five finalists, the Commander picked up a bottle of purple liquid and dropped twenty-five drops of whatever it was into a glass of purified water, stirred it with his thumb and offered it to Juanita. When she declined, he shrugged and drank it himself, shuddering as it slid down his throat.

"Best thing to ward off smallpox," he said.

He plopped the glass down on the marble-topped table edged in gold leaf and patted the cushion next to him on the sofa. Juanita waited a moment then took a deep breath and sat down beside him even though she didn't want to.

"Look at those dogs!" the Commander shouted. He was referring to the final five beauty pageant contestants.

"Where's that soap opera actress or that blonde who sells toothpaste in the ads? These are dogs. Peasant dogs. How can you give a prize to ugly women like that?"

He turned and gave Juanita his full attention, looked into her eyes, then down to her lovely full lips then back up to the feathery mustache of delicate fur she had ceased to wax since her husband, the Sergeant, had burned up and died. It was something her mother had insisted she do when it started to flourish at puberty. Her brother had hated her because he hardly had any mustache at all.

The Commander couldn't take his eyes off Juanita's upper lip.

"You see," he boasted, "it is one of my duties to wine and dine whoever wins. She will come to this house for an evening with me and none of those dogs are worthy..."

"Commander..." Juanita interrupted, but he just kept talking.

"... Unlike you, Mrs. Chavez." The General's Commander stretched, lifted his arms and moved toward Juanita on the couch. He was totally transfixed by her furry mustache. Juanita moved to the very edge of the cushion as the bathing suit competition continued to blare on TV.

"Commander, I have come to ask..."

"Anything," the Commander interrupted in a whisper. He began leaning forward, tilting his head closer to hers, completely captivated by the dense, dark growth spreading a hairy frame for her mouth.

"Do you know, Mrs. Chavez, that I have fathered one hundred and eighteen children?" Juanita ignored the remark and continued in a firm voice.

"About my dead husband..."

"How can I be of help?" the Commander interrupted again and smiled.

"I would like to see..."

Unable to restrain himself any longer he lifted his hand.

"Excuse me," he interrupted, "but there is something right there..." The Commander leaning forward further moved his finger toward her mouth, but Juanita didn't stop talking.

"I would like to see that my husband receives a hero's..." At that exact moment the Commander's fingers reached their destination.

"Oh my..." he said, feeling the fuzz.

"Memorial!" Juanita blurted, simultaneously with the touch.

Recoiling reflexively, she said very loudly, "What the hell are you doing?!" This took the Commander by surprise. He wasn't used to being questioned about anything he wanted to do, but he managed to recover and save face by delicately feathering his fingers, as if he was removing something unseemly from under her nose. He made it seem as if he had saved her a great embarrassment. He even went so far as to drop the imaginary thing into an overflowing beanbag ashtray clinging to the arm of the couch, as he looked Juanita straight in the eye and clucked condescendingly.

"A little something caught in the hair." Then he leaned back and waited for her to be embarrassed, but he'd miscalculated. Juanita didn't give a shit. She only cared about getting what she came for, so she stood.

"I want to give my dead husband, Sergeant Alberto Chavez, a military memorial for dying in the line of duty."

The Commander blinked and tried to recall Chavez. Finally, when he did, the Commander spread his short pudgy arms across the back of the white leather couch. Sergeant Chavez had been a total fuck-up, taken off regular duty because he fell asleep and deserted his men, which was why he'd been relegated to Orphan Patrol, the Children's Army and family redistribution. The Commander smiled.

"I'm afraid that's not possible," he said.

All of a sudden his tone was official and he turned back to the contest on TV, taking note of the third finalist's bathing suit as it crept up her haunch revealing a lot of backside that should have stayed covered.

"What do you mean, not possible?" Juanita wanted to know.

"No real rank," he replied and kept his focus on the television set.

"What do you mean 'no real rank?' He fought for you..."

Her eyes were filling with angry tears as the Commander smiled unkindly. "Maybe that's what he told you to feel important, but I can verify whatever war stories he boasted were not true."

"Liar!" Juanita shouted and stamped her foot.

The Commander sighed. This was growing tedious. Then he remembered. "I hear you sent the boy we gave you away."

"Of course I sent him away. It was all his fault. If I hadn't been so busy day and night... too busy for my husband..."

"My dear, it wasn't as if you gave birth to him or nursed him day and night. He was only with you a short time..."

"So what?" Juanita interrupted.

"So, you will be moving out of the casita," the General's Commander announced. Stunned, Juanita stopped her fury and stared at the Commander.

"What?" was all she could manage to say.

"We have to make room for his replacement. Besides, we don't have casitas for widows. Casitas are for military personnel in the General's service. We've let you stay on a bit longer out of consideration for the circumstances of his death... a terrible shock. But since you don't have any children and you gave the one you had away... One person to a casita is extravagant... unless of course you'd like to think about some sort of arrangement... "

Before the Commander could continue with the rest of proposition, Juanita turned and stormed out of his living room to the front door which she slammed so hard the General's portrait fell off the wall and knocked over the flag.

In the living room, the Commander lit another cigarette and waited to see which one of the unfortunate, "peasant dogs" would be crowned Miss Central Committee.

E bba was sitting on an old bench in the kitchen courtyard between flat baskets of freshly picked green peppers drying red in the sun.

"You could live here," Mr. Lobos said so softly he could barely be heard. Ebba looked up and studied his face, but she didn't say a word.

"With me," he said, just as quietly as before. Ebba shook her head no, so Mr. Lobos sat down on the bench and leaned closer. "Why not?" Ebba shifted her wings and looked him uncertainly.

"Why?"

Mr. Lobos sighed and tried to think of the right kind of answer. He stood up again and looked at the vibrant fuchsia bougainvillea growing up the kitchen wall, listened to the rattle of pots and pans being washed in the kitchen sink. Now Ebba stood up on the bench in order to look Mr. Lobos in the eye.

"Why?" she asked again. Mr. Lobos looked at her steadily.

"Because."

"Because is no answer," Ebba said and readjusted her wings.

"What if you were my... my..." His voice trailed off. He didn't know how to say it.

"What? What if I was your what?" Ebba wanted to know.

Mr. Lobos searched for a word, a phrase, some sort of definition. Finally he blurted out, "My constant companion."

Ebba looked at him as if he were crazy. Mr. Lobos turned away, but then he looked back, shifted from one foot to the other growing more nervous and impatient as he watched her try to figure it out.

"You mean like a wife?" Ebba exclaimed, louder than expected. The full impact of his request had finally registered and words had flown out of her mouth before she could stop them.

Mr. Lobos looked around to see if anyone had heard, then he put his finger to his lips, an indication to talk quietly, and whispered.

"Maybe when you're older."

"Is a wife a mother?" Ebba whispered back. She was still standing on the bench.

"Sometimes," he said.

"Then I don't want to do it," Ebba replied.

"Why not?" Mr. Lobos was genuinely surprised.

"I don't like mothers."

Mr. Lobos was puzzled. "But every girl wants to be a mother."

"Not me." Ebba shook her head emphatically.

"You don't really mean that..."

"Mothers are mean," Ebba interrupted, "except for Hortence Grace. I hate mothers," Ebba said. She looked at the lingering fingerprints on Mr. Lobos' cheek. "You do too, you just won't say it."

Without another word, Ebba jumped off the bench and started across the courtyard. Mr. Lobos was stunned. He hadn't counted on being turned down.

"Where are you going?" he asked. But Ebba just continued walking and didn't answer.

"Wait!" he called out and hurried to catch her.

Ebba started to run, got as far as the gate before he grabbed her arm and spun her around.

"Stop!" Ebba yelled.

"Stop!" the red parrot echoed from inside the house.

"You're acting just like a mother!" Ebba shouted.

Mr. Lobos was so surprised; he slapped her across the face. It wasn't as hard a slap as the slap his mother had slapped when she slapped him, but it was a slap nonetheless. Without giving it a second thought, Ebba grabbed his hand and bit down hard.

"Ow!" Mr. Lobos cried out in pain and let go of her arm.

"Ow!" The red parrot echoed from inside the house.

Ebba ran out of the gate fast and onto the beach.

Mr. Lobos was furious. No more fooling around. She'd broken the skin. He started after her, out the gate, across the sand toward Ebba who was running as fast as she could to the ocean. Her cheek didn't even sting. Her own dead mother had hit her harder dozens of times, but Mr. Lobos wasn't her mother and he had no right to do that.

The two of them zigzagged across the white sand... a man in a black suit chasing an angel with droopy wings. It looked pretty silly to the three men fishing in the surf, but not to Mrs. Lobos who was watching the whole thing through binoculars from her bedroom window and mumbled, "I hope she drowns," under her breath.

Ebba jumped over a clump of seaweed then slid down a dune. She turned just in time to see Mr. Lobos lose his footing and fall and she started to laugh; she couldn't help herself. He was rolling down the dune like a log, reaching for her with outstretched arms, more angry now than before. She dodged his grasp, but Mr. Lobos managed to grab the hem of her dress

Joan Tewkesbury

and pulled it tight against her legs until she tripped and sprawled face down in the sand. Ebba screamed once before Mr. Lobos flung himself on top of her and pinned her down.

"Let me up," she wailed. "I can't breathe."

But Mr. Lobos continued to lie on top of her, panting harshly into her wings as he tried to catch his breath. In an effort to get up, Ebba lifted her backside, pushed it up against the front of Mr. Lobos. Her strength surprised him. She was only a girl. He was a man and had overpowered her completely, but he found himself pushing back, thrusting his hips against her, panting and thrusting until that other part of himself took over and started to creep up Ebba's back and he moaned.

He didn't mean to but he did. It had escaped from him like vapor. Ebba froze and stopped pushing and twisted around.

"What's growing?" she asked.

Mr. Lobos froze. He stopped panting and thrusting and in that moment Ebba attempted to get out from under him, but it didn't work. Before she knew what had happened, Mr. Lobos got to his feet, slipped his hands under her arms and lifted her up, swung her legs off to the side and over his shoulder so they trailed down his back and Ebba found herself hanging face down with her nose brushing the buckle on his belt. And because he wasn't answering her question, Ebba reached out and took hold of everything she could get her hands on that was attached to his body down below the zipper on his pants and held it tight. She was certain that whatever had grown along her back lived inside his black pants and was now in her hands. "Oh my God," Mr. Lobos gasped.

What Ebba was doing didn't really hurt, but the potential for pain was imminent, almost more than Mr. Lobos could possibly imagine. He stopped walking and stood very still, but Ebba didn't let go. Obviously she'd found Mr. Lobos' most important part.

"Ebba," Mr. Lobos said quite calmly for a man in his position. "I'm going to put you down." Ebba didn't respond, just continued to hold onto his privates.

It was an intricate feat, an acrobatic maneuver, but Mr. Lobos managed to get Ebba off his shoulder even though her hands were still wrapped around his cock and balls. Now they stood face-to-face, toe-to-toe in the sand. Ebba gave Mr. Lobos' privates a little squeeze.

"Oh no," Mr. Lobos groaned.

Like the moan, the sound had escaped before he could do anything about it. Suddenly, Ebba felt everything in her hands contract; recede like a tortoise protecting itself against danger. Ebba looked up at Mr. Lobos who continued to stand still as a statue.

"Don't you ever slap me again," Ebba said. She addressed him firmly, clearly, loudly so he would be sure to hear her against the pounding surf. Mr. Lobos nodded his head immediately, afraid of what she might do next, but he was sincerely apologetic. "I am very sorry," he said. "It was a reaction, I never meant to do that."

"I don't believe you," she insisted. "Say it louder if you mean it."

"I won't ever slap you again," Mr. Lobos said firmly, clearly, loudly against the pounding surf.

"Or hurt me in any way," Ebba continued.

Mr. Lobos sighed. This was going much differently than he had expected.

"Say it." Ebba was firm.

"I will never hurt you in any way."

"You really have to mean it."

"I do. I really do," he replied and really did mean it. Ebba held on for just a moment longer then opened her hand and released him.

"Good," she said and started back along the shore.

Mr. Lobos exhaled, but he didn't move. What if Ebba came back and grabbed him again. But she didn't. Instead, Ebba turned and walked backwards as she shouted over the surf.

"Why should I be your constant companion?" she asked. Mr. Lobos just looked at her and wished that he could formulate the right words to tell her what triggered his desire, his obsession, his sudden capacity to care, but all he could manage was a bewildered sigh full of longing. So Ebba, unable to interpret his meaning, shrugged and did a series of cartwheels before she took off down the beach, leaving Mr. Lobos alone with his desire.

THE YARD SALE

On the morning of Olivia's once-a-year yard sale, Hortence Grace woke before dawn, slipped out of bed, dressed quickly and hurried through the courtyard, shutting the gate behind her so the chickens and new potbellied pig wouldn't follow. In the shadowy light the dirt road was starting to fill with rushing women, each determined to arrive at Olivia's gate before anyone else. Rumor had it that some of Li Choo's lingerie was up for sale. Not that any of the robust ladies hurrying along the road would fit into or be able to figure out the garments any better than Olivia had but the lacy contraptions would certainly be interesting to see.

The sun was up by the time the women reached Olivia's house and after an elbow-stabbing crush to get through the narrow iron gate, the pushing and shoving stopped. There was nothing there. No table laden with sequined dresses or shoes or tools or old radios or tires or unwanted gifts from visiting dignitaries of silver-plated plates let alone the G-strings of a Chinese mistress. The only thing in the uncared-for yard was a mango tree full of rotting fruit and a trellis burdened with uncared for passionflowers.

The women were confused and began to talk amongst themselves. Had they come at the wrong hour on the wrong day? After a few minutes the front door opened a crack and the women stopped talking. The silence was substantial. Then the door opened a little wider and Olivia's Spanish maid from Barcelona looked out at the crowd and began speaking with a Barcelona lisp.

"No thale," she said. "Nothing to thell this year, maybe next time, but not today. No thale today." The women were shocked. How could there not be a sale?

Someone shouted that it wasn't fair, but the thin maid shrugged. "Is no unfair. Is her thuff! If she doesn't want to thell, thell your own thuff. Have your own thale. Besides, you know already. Mrs. Marquez already tole you, no thale. You just come to make big aggravation and meth up the front yard." A murmur began to circulate among the crowd.

"Mrs. Marquez?"

What was Mrs. Marquez supposed to tell them? They looked around. She certainly wasn't there. Normally she would have slept by the front gate so she would be the first one inside.

"What was Mrs. Marquez supposed to tell us?" someone asked.

"No thale!" The maid was losing patience.

"When? When was she supposed to tell us, no sale?" The maid waved disgustedly. She couldn't remember.

"Lath week," she lisped.

"Last week!!!" The women were working themselves into an angry frenzy.

"Mrs. Marquez thay Mrs. Olivia don't have nothing thee want anyway so probably the thame for you womans too. Thee thay what thee wan is buried six feet down. Tho go away or I turn the hoth on you."

Then the maid from Barcelona shut the door and slid the dead bolt into place.

Now the women were furious. They shouted and fumed. They tramped across the dying lawn, poured out the front gate to find Mrs. Marquez and demand an explanation. But when all of the others turned at the corner, Hortence Grace doubled back and went in the other direction. Her sixth sense was itching and she knew that she had to be quick.

Juanita Takes a Shower

Juanita stood in the shower. It was the last time she would have the luxury of a shower indoors. The last time the water would be hot, not cold. The last time in a series of last times for a lot of things she had become accustomed to. No more sleeping in a room of her own, in a bed of her own, having a closet or a kitchen. Her few possessions, the things she'd brought with her when she married Sergeant Chavez were packed in three boxes waiting for her brother to come. She was going back to her mother's house where she would sleep three to a bed and shower under a spigot in the yard. There would be no more military soap, the kind she had just lathered into a great froth and was lavishing all over her wet body, sudsing her upright breasts in circles, something her late husband had done with enthusiastic gusto. She started to weep. How she missed his insatiable delight.

She turned back into the cascading water, closed her eyes, bent her soapy head under the shower's steady stream, letting the hot water run through her hair as she cried and cried, getting soap in her eyes just as the water abruptly stopped flowing. Stopped period, not another drop, leaving her covered in suds with her eyes shut tight and stinging. She screamed then screamed again. It was bloodcurdling and loud, piercing right to the heart of Juanita's rage. Cutting off the water without any warning was the final insult, the very last straw.

Raymond Valdez almost had a heart attack. Except for the heavy wrench he'd just used to turn off the main water connector he dropped his tools and ran to the front of the casita. Surely someone was being murdered because the screaming continued as he tried to open the front door, but it was locked. He tried the window that was open, pushed it up and squeezed inside, tried to avoid the stacked boxes, but tripped and fell. However, he managed to get to his feet and run to the screams coming from the bathroom. He threw open the bathroom door and stepped inside, his wrench raised to do damage, but he saw Juanita instead. Aphrodite on the half shell. Eyes tightly shut, wet hair streaming down her back, her abundant body covered in bubbles, her arms outstretched, looking for something to wipe the soap out of her eyes, her upright breasts tweaked with cold and bouncing in time to her screams. She was Venus rising up from the froth. Raymond Valdez grabbed a towel, thrust it into her hand and tried to be reassuring though he could hardly stand to part with the sight of her naked body.

"I'll be right back with the water," he said.

Juanita had been screaming so loud she hadn't heard him charge through the door. Now she screamed with fright, panicking Raymond Valdez who ran out of the room and shut the door, then ran outside to the water main where he twisted the handle with the wrench and turned everything back on.

Inside the bathroom, after a few struggling sputters and spurts, the water started to flow. Juanita blotted her eyes and looked around. No one was there. She shivered. It was just a chill, but Juanita convinced herself that the ghost of her dead husband was present. That Sergeant Chavez himself had come down from heaven, handed her the towel and turned on the water. She stepped back under the shower. In minutes Juanita grew calm in the warm water, luxuriously rinsing every inch of her skin and hair. Finally, when she was slippery as silk she turned off the faucet and wrapped herself in the Sergeant's old robe.

As she moved to the sink there was a knock at the front door. Certain that it was her brother she hurried down the hall and opened the door. Raymond Valdez stood on the porch with a single red rose he'd stolen from somebody's garden. He held it out for Juanita to take.

"Please accept my apology," he said calmly, earnestly and in his most charming tone. Juanita was surprised speechless, but she accepted the flower.

"I am Raymond Valdez the plumber sent to turn off the water, so I had no way of knowing you were in the shower and I want to tell you I am so sorry to have caused you a moment of terrible inconvenience."

Juanita gulped. "Are you the one who handed me the towel?" Raymond lowered his eyes and nodded. He couldn't get the image of her naked body, slippery with suds, out of his mind.

"I was afraid you were being killed," he said. "Then I was afraid you'd go blind from the soap..." He looked up, looked deeply into her large brown eyes and sank because she allowed him to.

"I am so sorry to have intruded..."

Juanita just nodded and kept staring back as she twirled the rose in front of her upper lip, which she vowed to wax again.

"I should have knocked on the door."

"No, no, no," she said softly. "You saved my life," she whispered and she meant it. A real Raymond Valdez was certainly a lot more interesting than some ghost of Sergeant Chavez. Besides, Raymond Valdez had kind eyes and they never left hers, so she opened the door a little wider along with her robe, ever so slightly, as she said...

"Won't you come in?"

DIGGING FOR DRESSES

Hortence Grace heard the commotion as soon as she reached the cemetery and stepped over the geraniums growing where Louisa Ortega had been struck by lightning. Her sixth sense had been right. Mrs. Marquez was standing impatiently by a tombstone watching three old men and a boy dig up the grave of Ebba's dead mother. The dark red flowers Hortence Grace had so carefully planted were already buried in a mountain of dirt and Mrs. Marquez, clutching her patent leather purse, just kept shouting, "Hurry up! Hurry up!"

Before Hortence Grace could stop herself, a command as electrifying as the bolt of lightning that killed Louisa Ortega exploded right out of her mouth.

"Stop! Just stop what you're doing right now!!" And they did. Scared to death, the men dropped their shovels and ran away fast. Mrs. Marquez froze like a statue in front of the tombstone and Hortence Grace was so surprised by her own sound she looked behind her to see if it had come from somebody else. But no one was there, just a bunch of birds flying out of the pepper tree away from the command.

Hortence Grace cleared her throat, but Mrs. Marquez, seeing it was only Hortence Grace, started to shout to the men to come back and keep digging.

"What do you think you are doing?" Hortence Grace demanded.

"Nothing that concerns you."

"Yes, it concerns me. Why are you digging up Ebba's mother?"

Mrs. Marquez ignored the question. Instead she shrieked at the gravediggers peeking out from behind the tomb of Elena Cordova. "I'm not paying one red cent until you finish the job."

Slowly, ever so slowly, they began to shuffle back to their shovels. Without saying another word, Hortence Grace marched over to the grave, slid into the hole and laid down on top of what little dirt was still covering Ebba's mother's coffin.

Mrs. Marquez was stunned. "What do you think you're doing?" Hortence Grace didn't speak, just folded her arms across her chest.

"Get out of there," Mrs. Marquez yelled. "This is mine."

"No, it's not," Hortence Grace answered, barely moving a muscle.

The gravediggers stopped right where they were and refused to come any closer. Frustrated, Mrs. Marquez commanded.

"Go on. Get going!"

But they wouldn't budge. Hortence Grace noticed Juan Alessandro, the oldest, most toothless of the men who often worked for Bernardo polishing furniture by hand.

"Buenas tardes, señor Alessandro."

"Buenas tardes, señora," he answered shyly. "Buen tiempo."

"Yes, the weather is very nice," Hortence Grace replied. Furious, Mrs. Marquez grabbed the shovel out of his hand to do some digging herself, but one of the other men restrained her.

"Don't stop me!" she cried out. "What's in there belongs to me!"

There was a struggle, but Hortence Grace didn't flinch. Mrs. Marquez, on the other hand, became hysterical.

"Mine. They're mine!" she cried over and over. She flailed at the dirt with the shovel, but Juan Alessandro managed to pull it out of her hands and toss it out of reach. When Hortence Grace was sure Mrs. Marquez had worn herself out, she sat up. Only her head was showing over the edge of the grave.

"Taking clothes off the dead is a sin," she admonished.

"I know," Mrs. Marquez wailed, "but I paid Father Lyle for absolution."

"Father Lyle has no power over dresses. They have a life of their own."

"That's not what he said to me."

Hortence Grace shook her head. "Father Lyle doesn't understand dresses. He isn't a woman. He's a priest. All he understands is the color of your cash." Mrs. Marquez sat down in the dirt and started to sob.

"Raymond's favorite color is green."

Hortence Grace rolled her eyes. "If all you want is a green satin dress, I'll make you one." Mrs. Marquez looked up mid-sob.

"But only if..." Hortence Grace thought for a moment and then paused dramatically.

"If what?" Mrs. Marquez snapped.

"If you'll take me to see Olivia Gomez."

Mrs. Marquez lifted her eyebrow. "You go see Olivia. She's your cousin."

"No. She's Bernardo's cousin," Hortence Grace answered calmly.

"Why do you want to see Olivia?"

"Nothing that concerns you," Hortence Grace said quietly and continued. "And you will pay Juan Alessandro and the others to put the dirt and all of the flowers back the way it was before."

"No," Mrs. Marquez said indignantly. "Absolutely not." She pulled a handkerchief out of her patent leather purse and blew her nose.

"There will be no charge for making the dress. The dress will be free."

Mrs. Marquez stopped blowing her nose. "Free?"

"Free," Hortence Grace nodded.

Mrs. Marquez wasn't buying it. "Why? You don't like me and I don't like you."

"True, but I want you to take me to Olivia," Hortence Grace said evenly. "Besides, why would Raymond want to be close to death's smell? No matter how much perfume, you can't disguise decay."

Mrs. Marquez sighed. She hated giving up getting even with Ebba's mother, but deep down she knew that Hortence Grace was right.

"Otherwise," Hortence Grace continued quietly, "I will stay right here and when the Castillo widows come to sweep their husband's markers, I will tell them to tell all the women from the yard sale what you were up to." Mrs. Marquez looked at Hortence Grace and didn't say a word. She didn't want to get tangled in her own web. Hortence Grace continued, "The women in the village are very, very angry." Mrs. Marquez glanced at the gate anxiously. One of the men coughed, another sneezed.

Finally Mrs. Marquez sighed. "All right," she said grumpily, "but it had better be a better dress than any of those other dresses ever thought of being."

Hortence Grace nodded and stood up on Ebba's mother's coffin. She brushed herself off and let the young boy help her out of the hole. Then she turned to Mrs. Marquez.

"Don't worry," she said. "It will be the finest, most enduring green dress you've ever seen."

A Visit to Lilly in the Tan Packard

Olivia was still having trouble driving her dead husband's tan Packard. The simultaneity of steering, using the clutch and shifting the gears was really a challenge. She finally managed to step on the brake, not the clutch, and stopped at Lilly's rusty gate without knocking it down but the dogs barked ferociously and attacked the flimsy fence as they tried to get at the huge car. Olivia looked at Mrs. Lobos in the rearview mirror. She was sitting in the back seat with the pale yellow silk shawl wrapped tight around her bony frame. This trip to Lilly's was payback for Olivia leaving in the middle of lunch the other day.

"Cockroach," Olivia thought to herself as Mrs. Lobos rolled down the window and shouted at the dogs.

"Heathens!" But they kept barking and snarling and baring their teeth. Mrs. Lobos rolled up the window and poked Olivia's shoulder sharply with her bony finger. "Honk your horn, stupid woman. Let her know we're here."

Olivia did as she was told. Three loud blasts, then three more and more after that. Honk-honk-honk. Bark, bark, bark. Honk, bark-bark. Finally, Lilly Narada emerged from the screen door dressed in red. She looked like a bell pepper with matching high heels. She shaded her eyes and peered across the junk-strewn yard.

"What the hell is going on?" she shouted. Olivia rolled down her window and waved nervously.

"It's us Lilly," she trilled. Mrs. Lobos moaned her disgust, rolled down her window again and shouted. "It's not us! It's me and I expect some answers!"

Lilly whistled sharply at the dogs. They turned away from the gate and bounded toward her as she picked up a couple of rocks which she threw in their direction, so they sat down in the dirt but growled as Lilly walked to the gate scowling enviously at the Packard.

"Where'd you get that?" she asked in a demanding tone.

"It was the mayor's," Olivia replied and ground the gears as Lilly opened the gate.

"Hell of a car," Lilly said watching Olivia lurch toward a sleeping pig. "Watch out for the pig!" Lilly shouted.

Instantly, Olivia slammed on the brakes, throwing Mrs. Lobos forward with whiplash force, and barely missed killing three of the dogs who hightailed it to a distant part of the yard. Lilly laughed darkly as she closed the gate and locked it.

"Hell of a car..."

Orange and red candles in Guadeloupe glasses burned all over the tiny room. Lilly sat with her eyes shut and spread her pudgy fingers covered in rings on the card table. The Marlboro cigarette, clenched tight in Lilly's teeth, sent ribbons of smoke toward Mrs. Lobos who fanned the air furiously as she shuffled and reshuffled the worn deck of cards. Olivia sat on the couch behind Mrs. Lobos under the shelf of religious relics and rubbed her swollen feet.

"Make a wish and cut the cards," Lilly ordered.

Apprehensively, Mrs. Lobos stopped shuffling and did as she was told. Then she sat back and watched Lilly crackle the cards to life, slapping them against each other purposefully, re-snapping them on the table and forcefully fanning the entire deck across the table draped with purple velvet.

"Pick ten," she commanded.

Again, Mrs. Lobos did as she was told. She slid the cards out of the fan, leaving them face down on the velvet. In the background, the dull din of guitar music played on the radio as Lilly stacked the rest of the deck neatly beside her and turned over the first card.

"Who's the brat?"

Mrs. Lobos jerked to attention.

"What brat?"

"And a wedding," Lilly said, turning over the second card.

"Somebody's getting married... somebody next to you, close. Your son maybe? Anyway, there's a dance floor and a lot of people... poor people. A lot of people you're not used to. Who's the kid with wings?" Mrs. Lobos looked up from her tightly wrapped shawl.

"What kid with wings?"

"The one I see in your cards. A real pain in the backside this kid. She got something to do with your son?"

Olivia opened a box of Chiclets and popped two into her mouth, then two more and leaned back on the gold and red crocheted pillow.

"No one has anything to do with my son but me," Mrs. Lobos shouted.

"That's what you think," Lilly said.

Mrs. Lobos snapped around in her chair and pointed at Olivia. "Have you been telling this woman my business?" Surprised by the outburst, Olivia's only reply was the loud crack of her gum.

"I don't talk to nobody about nothing," Lilly boomed. "I got a gift to see the future of your puny little life. Now... if you want to see it too, we'll continue. If you can't take it, we'll stop, but I don't put up with insults."

"How dare you speak to me in that tone," Mrs. Lobos snapped.

Lilly let her long cigarette ash fall on Mrs. Lobos' upturned card, then leaned across the table. "My house, my tone. You want me to go on with this or not?"

It was silent except for Olivia cracking her gum. She was enjoying every uncomfortable moment.

Mrs. Lobos jerked around again in her chair. "Stop that chewing," she said. Which Olivia did, but only for a moment.

"Yes or no?" Lilly demanded.

"Continue," Mrs. Lobos said imperiously.

Lilly turned over cards four, five and six.

"Trouble with relatives. Disruption and tempers flying. You got anybody around you with a lot of money?"

"None of your business," Mrs. Lobos said. Lilly arched an eyebrow and stubbed her cigarette in the overflowing ashtray.

"Next time you say good-bye, they will be in a big lie."

Mrs. Lobos shook her head. "Wouldn't be the first time."

Lilly took a longtime drink of her Dr. Pepper then turned over cards seven and eight as Olivia dabbed at her face and neck with a Kleenex. She was having a hot flash.

"Bad weather on the horizon," Lilly said then belched. "An unpleasant discovery... You got friends in church?"

"Everyone has friends in church," Mrs. Lobos said.

"Well, you got enemies, so watch your step, Mrs."

Lilly flipped over card nine and ten quickly.

"Here's that kid again with the wings."

Lilly looked up, but Mrs. Lobos didn't meet her gaze. Instead her eyes rolled back up in her head as she gasped and fell backwards in her chair with such force it banged into Olivia's knees.

"Ouch!" Olivia squawked, more surprised than hurt. Even Lilly was surprised.

"My God, check her pulse," she said.

"You check her pulse, I can't move," Olivia said. Lilly looked at her with disgust.

"You're good for nothing, Olivia. Ever since you started dabbling in that dead Chinkie's underwear."

Lilly got up and placed her fingers on Mrs. Lobos' carotid artery. It was thumping along rhythmically.

"Strong as a swine," she diagnosed. "Let's get her into the car before she comes to. The cards just got more bad news." Olivia nodded and found her shoes as Lilly righted the chair. Outside the dogs began to bark.

"When she wakes up you can tell her all of it was a dream. By the way, I need to get four hundred fifty pesos."

Olivia gave her a dirty look, then opened Mrs. Lobos' money purse and counted out the money.

"It should be free. You almost killed her."

Instead, Lilly pulled a few more bills out of the purse before Olivia could snap it shut.

"It's not my fault her son's a fool. She made him like that."

Mrs. Lobos started to snore and the door into the kitchen opened with a bang. Salvador Magna, Lilly's short bowlegged boyfriend, was grinning from ear to ear absolutely thrilled to see the object of his desire dressed in such a tight red dress.

"Aie-eee, Lilly, you look like a million bucks!"

His low gravelly voice was accentuated by a tubercular cough but Lilly and Olivia shushed him. Poor Salvador's desire retracted like a wilted balloon. Fortunately, Mrs. Lobos continued to snore.

"Who's that?" he whispered hoarsely.

"Bad news," Lilly volunteered. Then she directed him to carry Mrs. Lobos outside to the Packard and put her in the back seat.

"Such a fine Packard," he said. "Is it hers?"

"No," Olivia answered. "It's mine," she said seductively, which Lilly squelched with a dirty look.

"Never mind the Packard, Salvador. You carry, I'll get the dogs and Olivia..." Lilly turned to Olivia and meant every word. "Don't bring her back and don't ever send that brat back here either. She's trouble. They're all trouble. I don't want them around."

Lilly started outside with Salvador who eased Mrs. Lobos into his arms.

"Light as paper," he said to Olivia who opened the door. But before she shut it behind her, she stole a handful of hard candy from the dish on the sink to calm her nerves and followed them out to the car.

€ bba stood before Dr. Vidal who sat in his wheelchair listening to Ebba's
heart with a stethoscope. He looked down her throat and in her ears
then he lifted one of her arms and looked at it carefully.

"What's all this?"

"Blood," Ebba replied.

"Blood isn't magenta."

"I'm young so it's pink," Ebba said. She kept shifting back and forth
from one leg to the other. The doctor ignored the remark. They were in
the spare room next to the sewing room where the dreaded pink dress had
originated in the first place. Mrs. Lobos' low folding table, complete with
metal brackets used for the occasional doctor visit, stood in the center of
the floor and was covered with a sheet. The doctor looked into Ebba's eyes
with a light.

"Your mother is well?"

"My mother is dead," Ebba said. The doctor pulled out a thermometer,
shook it and stuck it under her tongue.

"I'm sorry for your loss," he said softly.

"I'm not," Ebba mumbled. "She was mean."

The doctor looked her in the eye. "She had her reasons and don't bite
down on the glass."

"All she did was yell," Ebba mumbled, "A mother's shout can stab your
heart."

The doctor gave Ebba a withering look and checked his watch. "Don't
be dramatic. All of us have endured a mother of one kind or another."
Then he adjusted his glasses and removed the thermometer. Getting her
temperature wasn't really important.

"She got the last word then died her perfect death asleep and mad at
me."

The doctor rolled his eyes and turned his attention back to Ebba's
arms.

"The stains will disappear with fresh lemon," he said.

"But I like the design."

The doctor changed the subject. "Bernardo got a new pig." Ebba
shrugged and pretended not to be interested. The doctor leaned back in
his wheelchair and sighed.

"Phillipa Marie..."

"Ebba," she corrected the doctor bluntly.

"Ebba, I want you to take off your underpants and get up on the table."

Ebba was shocked but the doctor turned around in his wheelchair and faced the wall.

"You'll be covered with a sheet. Now do as you are told."

"No," Ebba said and started out of the room until the doctor reached out, snatched her skirt and reeled her in like a fish.

"Hey!" Ebba yelled, but the doctor didn't let go.

The door opened and Mercedes, the doctor's assistant, entered chewing gum. She walked to the table and dropped two metal stirrups into the waiting brackets. Ebba continued to shout, so Mercedes shoved a washcloth in Ebba's mouth to the muffle the noise, grabbed Ebba's flailing arms, hoisted her onto the low table and strapped her down. Then she grabbed the bottom of Ebba's angel dress, pulled the skirt up over Ebba's head covering her face and with her other hand, she pulled off Ebba's underpants and dropped them on a chair by the open window.

Gagged and bound, Ebba tried lunging. Not only were her private parts bare, she couldn't see what was going on. She tried to scream, but gagged on the washcloth and found herself unable to breathe. She started to kick but Mercedes shoved Ebba's right foot into the metal stirrup, remarking on their enormous size to Dr. Vidal who was busy preparing his instruments on a metal tray.

As she strapped Ebba's left foot into the other stirrup the doctor ordered Mercedes to remove the washcloth from Ebba's mouth.

"She'll only scream louder," Mercedes said, chewing her gum vigorously.

The doctor put the metal tray with his tools on his lap and wheeled around angrily. "She's choking!" he shouted. Then he pushed himself forward to confront Ebba's bald slit bucking up and down between her bent knobby knees and looked away. "And drape her for God's sake. She's still a child."

"I can't do everything at once!" Mercedes yelled back. But she did lift the dress off Ebba's panic-stricken face and yanked the washcloth out of her mouth.

Ebba choked, gasped for breath, lifted her head and looked over the bunched skirt around her belly to the exposed place where she peed and on down to the doctor's saggy face framed between her legs.

"The sheet," he snarled, deliberately avoiding Ebba's eyes as he adjusted the light attached to a metal band like a hat on his head and snapped on a pair of thin rubber gloves.

A white sheet unfurled with a snap, billowed in the air before it drifted down onto Ebba covering her belly and knees and formed a barrier so Ebba couldn't see Dr. Vidal smear K-Y jelly all over his rubber-gloved second-to-index finger. Ebba felt the sheet get tucked around her thighs, felt her rear end lifted to accommodate the pillow that raised her up so her slit met the doctor's gaze like a piece of rare fruit on display. Mercedes wheeled the doctor closer so he could see.

Ebba was beside herself with confusion. Why all this focus on the thing her mother always told her never to touch or show and to always keep covered?

"If my mother was here she would kill you," Ebba yelled.

"But she's not," Mercedes snapped as the doctor picked up the metal speculum.

"I want my mother," Ebba wailed. She'd never uttered those words in her life.

"You mentioned she was dead," the doctor said and spread more goo on his glove.

Ebba lifted her head, but was blinded by the doctor's light so she lay back down. Her arms and hands were falling asleep under the strap.

"I want my mother," she sobbed as the doctor parted her lower lips and tried to insert the cold, metal instrument into her private corridor.

Ebba screamed so loud that everything on the doctor's lap dropped onto the floor with a resounding clang. Even Mercedes jumped, then smacked Ebba's magenta stained arm as hard as she could which made the doctor so angry he ordered her out of the room. As a result, Ebba cried and Mercedes shouted obscenities on the other side of the door while Dr. Vidal continued the invasion with his jelly-smeared finger.

"Now just relax," he said looking over the sheet gravely.

Instead, Ebba froze and her opening shut like a vice. All the intrinsic muscles between her legs contracted and locked and that was that. The doctor grimaced.

"I don't like this either," he growled.

"Then stop!" Ebba yelled.

In that split second she let down her guard and wasn't holding on for dear life, so the devious doctor plunged his gloved little finger into her reluctant hole. Ebba shouted out and the doctor withdrew as quickly as he'd entered. He'd been stopped dead by her virginity.

"She's intact!" he shouted at the top of his lungs.

Suddenly the door flew open and in came Mrs. Lobos wrapped up tight in the pale yellow silk shawl.

"You're lying," she shrilled. She marched right over to the doctor and leaned in to look. "Let me see." But the doctor pulled the sheet down and covered Ebba completely.

"Show's over," the doctor said in a low dark voice. Then he held up his rubber-gloved hand and let his little finger catch the light. It was rimmed bright red with blood.

"Ah ha!" Mrs. Lobos shouted, pleased with what she saw. "You've ripped the virgin's seal so she's no longer intact. No vows for a woman whose not a virgin. So, that settles that." She turned and said this to her son who stood just outside the door with his eyes downcast so he wouldn't have to see Ebba on the table in the room.

"Wrong!" the doctor bellowed. His voice was so loud two water glasses on the bureau rang all by themselves.

"Her virginity is taut as a tightrope. This," he shouted wheeling his chair with one hand toward Mrs. Lobos menacingly, "this is the hint of her menses to come and declare she is a woman." He stuck his little finger in front of Mrs. Lobos' face so she would have to see it whether she wanted to or not.

"Or have you forgotten because it's been so long?"

Mr. Lobos turned from the door and walked away. Ebba lifted her head and smiled triumphantly at Mrs. Lobos in spite of everything that had gone on.

"How dare you," Mrs. Lobos boiled in a low ugly voice.

"How dare you, old woman," the doctor fired back. "And don't come to me again with your outrageous requests."

"You didn't have to do it," Mercedes said from the doorway, snapping her gum.

Doctor Vidal bent down, grabbed the metal tray and hurled it through the air. Luckily Mercedes turned just in time to take the impact on her backside. But she shrieked, which incited the parrot outside and created a high-pitched duet.

"It's payback, you foul slut, and if I have to, I'll do it again as I've done before, but I don't want to. It's a humiliation for everybody involved." Then he turned and looked Mrs. Lobos hard in the eye. "Go outside, Mrs. Lobos, and wait for the virgin to dress." Mrs. Lobos opened her mouth to speak but the doctor interrupted.

"No threats, Mrs. Lobos, or I'll tell your secrets and let them flap like flags in the wind." Mrs. Lobos was gone before he finished the sentence. Whimpering, Mercedes followed, but the doctor shouted.

"Get back here and help the girl!" Mercedes did as she was told under the watchful eye of the doctor who held up the stained glove for Ebba to see.

"This is blood and it's yours, understand?" Ebba nodded even though she didn't know what he was talking about. Doctor Vidal pulled off the glove and Mercedes undid the strap holding Ebba down on the table.

"Ask Hortence Grace to explain the business of monthly visits." Ebba looked at him blankly. She'd never heard of such a thing, but she nodded again as the doctor threw the gloves in the trash and told Mercedes to come to him at once which she did and Dr. Vidal gave her face a ringing slap. Then before she could respond he grabbed her big breasts and squeezed them hard and over and over until she moaned and then he pulled her face close to his and kissed her full on the mouth. After that he wheeled himself to the door, but turned back.

"I'm sorry if I hurt you," he said to Ebba. Then he wheeled himself out of the room followed by Mercedes who shut the door quietly leaving Ebba sitting on the table tangled in the sheet.

PINK ROSES

After Mercedes drove Dr. Vidal away in the doctor's old truck, Mr. Lobos sat on his narrow bed staring at the pink roses he'd brought for Ebba scattered all over the floor. He was numb to everything except the memory of Ebba crying out. After a while the wind began blowing through the open window, softly at first, then harder and harder until it was coming in gusts, lifting the curtains like untethered sails on a rudderless boat.

Finally Mr. Lobos got up to fasten the banging shutter, crushing the pink buds under the soles of his shiny black shoes, smashing the green stems and leaves and making stains all over the tile floor. He stood in the open window with the swirling curtains and looked at the churning circles of dust whirling around the courtyard. He watched one of the maids struggle to bolt the outside door, but he didn't move. He couldn't. He was frozen in the scream of Ebba that kept ringing in his ears.

In a desperate gesture to make it go away, he reached out, grabbed the banging shutter, pulled it closed, bolted it shut, locked it tight, locked himself inside his room with the narrow bed. It was like closing the lid of a coffin.

Then he lay down on the floor, on top of the roses he'd smashed with his shiny black shoes and wept for Ebba.

Joan Tewkesbury

Ebba sat in the sheets and stared at the door. She hadn't moved since the doctor left. She felt like a piece of green fruit that had been torn open too soon. Her white angel costume soiled with K-Y jelly was still hiked up around her waist. Outside the open window the sky was turning dark and the smell of rain was in the air. Ebba shuddered. She glanced at her forlorn white cotton underpants, a sad little mound of softness meant to cover and protect, left on the chair where Mercedes had dropped them. Ebba looked away.

The rain was starting to fall. It blew in the window so she reached down, took hold of the bunched up sheet and wiped the gooey jelly from between her legs. She rubbed and wiped until she was raw. Then still holding her dress up around her waist, she jumped off the table and hurried to the slice of mirror on the back of the door to see if she was all there. It was too dark to look for particulars, but as far as she could tell nothing had been taken or was gone. She twisted around to check her backside. It seemed fine and without a mark, unlike the time her mother hit her with her father's shoe.

Relieved, Ebba let the skirt fall and cover her, then hurried to the open window, thrust herself out into the falling rain, turned her face up to the sky and opened her mouth. She waited until a few large drops speared her tongue then turned around. Her abandoned underpants, directly in front of the open window, were getting wet, absorbing the water and turning into a limp, soaking wad. Ebba picked them up by the elastic, held them between her thumb and forefinger the way you'd hold a dead rat by its tail and left the room, went in the opposite direction of the sound of a vacuum cleaner, left a trail of drips on the red tile floor as she hurried down the long hall to a door at the end that was slightly ajar. The rain underscored the sound of someone snoring. Curious, Ebba carefully opened the door and looked inside. Mrs. Lobos lay like a lump in the four-poster bed, her body rising and falling with each harsh wheeze.

Ebba stepped into the room and tiptoed to a huge, hand-carved chest. She dropped the sopping wet underwear on the Persian rug and ever so gently opened one of the drawers. It was full of blankets and assorted candy bars from the United States. Ebba reached in and took a Milky Way and two Almond Joys then shut the drawer just as Mrs. Lobos stirred in her sleep. Ebba ducked down below the foot of the high bed.

After several squeaks from the springs under the mattress, Mrs. Lobos resumed snoring so Ebba eased back up, opened another drawer and spread out before her in neat rows like a garden, was an orderly array of Mrs. Lobos' underwear. Stacks of white step-ins, long black cotton stockings, black slips to cover her bony frame, undershirts for the cold and way in the back, tucked under all the rest was something edged in lace. Ebba managed to grab a corner and pulled out a pair of ivory silk step-ins trimmed conservatively in handmade lace from Belgium, a long-ago gift from Mrs. Lobos' husband Mr. Lobos. They had been purchased by him in Spain but never worn.

Outside, the rain was subsiding, but inside the snoring had taken on a new intensity so Ebba slipped into the lace-trimmed drawers and attached them at the waist with the tiny mother-of-pearl button. As far as she was concerned this was perfection and divine retribution rolled into one. Besides, she'd never felt anything so soft next to her skin except for the pale yellow silk shawl.

After she adjusted her dress she picked up the soaking wet underpants, folded them twice and shoved them into one of the neat rows in the back. Then she took a carefully folded black slip and placed it on top of the wet bundle, tucked it in around the edges, pushed the whole business even further to the rear and even more quietly than before, closed the drawer. Given the climate, humidity would take care of the rest. In no time at all everything would be rank with mildew and stink.

Ebba managed a tiny smile then picked up the candy bars and turned to leave but stopped when she saw the yellow silk shawl draped over a chair by the door. Quietly and without giving it a second thought, Ebba slid the slippery silk off its resting place, gathered it into a ball and hurried out of the room amidst the resounding snarls of Mrs. Lobos' snooze.

WAITING TO LEAVE

The rain had started again so Ebba sat by the window in the gardener's shed stroking the fringe on Mrs. Lobos' pale yellow silk shawl while she waited for a lull. She was trying to remember which dirt road led to the giant head of the General sitting in the patchy grass. She'd made up her mind it was time to go and was convinced that if she found the hill with the head she could get back home.

She bit into one of the apples she'd stolen from the kitchen and thought about the look on Mr. Lobos' face when he'd stood in the doorway and she was on the table. She had expected him to put a stop to what was going on. She had expected him to push aside the doctor's chair. She had expected him to shout at his mother, to tell her this was all wrong and to get out of his sight, but he hadn't. He'd just held on to a bouquet of pink rosebuds for dear life and looked at the floor. Ebba wondered what was wrong with a full-grown man who couldn't even shout at his mother.

Ebba lifted the brown bitter seeds out of their little membrane cases with the tip of her tongue. She chewed each one and spit the husks on the floor. How could an old man put his hand inside of her like that? And who'd given him permission? She certainly hadn't. She wasn't a chicken waiting to be gutted and stuffed. Ebba bit down hard on what was left of the core, shredded the stem into strings with her teeth and spit those out too and wondered why anyone would search inside there for something they were trying to find.

Ebba got up. Rain or no rain it was time to go. She poked around the shed, found an old cloth bag hanging on a hook and decided it was just right to hold her apples and candy. Then she folded the pale yellow shawl into a neat square, tucked in the fringe and stuffed it down the front of her dress. The gardener's old hat hung on the back of a rickety chair so she took that too, plopped it on her head and looped the bag over her shoulder. After a moment or two, she took a deep breath and opened the door. The rain was warm and soft and wasn't falling hard. So before she let herself think about the lovely white room that looked out at the blue-green ocean or the two tiny quail that had been cooked in sugar and oranges and served on a delicate china plate or the tinkling crystals on the enormous chandelier that hung over the baby grand piano in the sitting room that she never got to touch, Ebba forced herself to remember Mr. Lobos frozen at the door. Made herself remember the doctor's probing and the sound

of her very own scream and finally, after she'd remembered all that, Ebba reached up, adjusted the gardener's old hat and ran outside into the rain. She ran to the gate, ran out of the yard to the banyan tree on the other side of the wall and took off down the road.

All the while, unbeknownst to Ebba as she was running through the rain, Mrs. Lobos stood in her bedroom window watching her through a pair of high-powered binoculars, mumbling, "hideous, wretched pest," under her breath until Ebba was out of sight. When she was absolutely sure that Ebba wasn't going to turn around and come back, Mrs. Lobos put down the glasses and smiled. Then she picked up the phone she kept hidden in the drawer of her bedside table and dialed the General's private number. It rang six times before someone picked it up.

"What?" a man with a sharp nasty voice shouted at the other end of the line.

"To talk to my brother," Mrs. Lobos replied equally sharp, equally loud and more impatient.

"He's playing tennis," the man said.

"Is this Aldo?" Mrs. Lobos snapped.

"Why do you care?" he barked back.

"There is something I need you to do, a problem I need you to get rid of," she said matter of factly and went on to describe Ebba in detail down to the white dress with angel wings, the gardener's hat and the direction where she seemed to be headed.

After a bit more discussion regarding how soon and how much, Mrs. Lobos hung up the phone and put it back in the drawer. Then she got down on her knees by the side of her bed, crossed herself several times and thanked every saint she'd ever heard of. The horrid brat was gone and soon it would be forever.

Bad Timing

Juanita Chavez stood at Rosa Guillermo's gate with her mother who came once a week to do Rosa Guillermo's ironing and had insisted that Juanita come too. After all, widow or not, if Juanita was going to live at home she had to make some sort of contribution. One more mouth to feed was one more mouth too much as far as Juanita's mother was concerned.

Needless to say it was a great surprise for both women when Rosa Guillermo came to the gate and saw who was there. Moments went by like lifetimes as Rosa Guillermo and Juanita Chavez looked at one another through the spaces in the iron gate but didn't say a word. Finally, Juanita's mother who was impatient to get inside and get on with her work announced, "My daughter, Juanita Chavez," and gestured as if Juanita was something for sale. "Her husband went up in smoke." Both women, well aware of the facts, didn't move a muscle.

"So now she lives with me," Juanita's mother finished in a tone that let everyone know this was a terrible burden. There was another long silence.

Finally, "Oh..." was all Rosa Guillermo could manage. Juanita didn't bother with any kind of answer as something had caught her eye. Across the small court yard a young military couple was standing in Rosa Guillermo's doorway with a thin little boy, a thin little boy who looked terribly familiar. Juanita shaded her eyes to get a better look and discovered he was none other than her temporary son, Pablito. Juanita turned to Rosa Guillermo to speak her surprise, but Rosa Guillermo managed to interrupt with a "Don't you dare say a word" look while she crooned... "Perhaps you could come back in a half an hour?"

Since Juanita's mother hadn't noticed either her daughter's surprise or Rosa Guillermo's gloomy glance, she pushed her way through the iron gate and shook her head.

"No can do," she said firmly. "Two other houses full of shirts waiting for me and her." Then she grabbed Juanita by the arm and pulled her inside as Juanita twisted around to get a better look.

Flustered and worried, Rosa Guillermo rushed ahead stammering excuses to the young couple as she urged them into the tiny living room and hoped that Pablito wouldn't get a glimpse of his first "substitute mother."

Lucky for Rosa Guillermo, Juanita in her attempt to see better, stubbed her toe and had to recover while her mother chastised her loudly for being so clumsy. Pretending to be in great pain, Juanita sat down on the garden bench and looked at the couple through the dining room window as they tried to engage her Pablito in conversation but had no success. They'd been told the boy was shy, but the young military man was extremely determined and seemed to think he could solve the problem by talking louder.

"How are you today?" he kept shouting over and over. But Bernardo's Ariel and Juanita's Pablito just looked at the floor and didn't reply.

Trapped in bad timing with no predictable end in sight, Rosa Guillermo ran back and forth between the potential parents and Juanita Chavez like someone caught between a fire and a flood. Eventually, she began to feel rather faint, but Juanita, smoldering silently, sat still as a sphinx and let her mother paint her injured toe with tincture of iodine before she pulled Juanita to her feet.

"Time's a wasting," her mother said. "Let's go."

After Juanita's mother marched them inside, Rosa Guillermo herded them into the kitchen then deliberately planted herself between Juanita and the living room situation making it impossible for Juanita to see.

"Iced tea?" she offered in her most condescending tone. "It's so hot, a cool drink would be nice while you work."

Juanita burned Rosa Guillermo with a look, but her mother, always eager to get something more because she thought she deserved it, picked up two glasses and told Juanita to fill them to the top from the pitcher on the sink. Juanita added heaping teaspoons of sugar and sprigs of fresh mint for good measure while her mother set up the ironing board and told Juanita to grab the box of starch in the cupboard.

From this position Juanita turned and watched Rosa Guillermo usher the young military couple, with her Pablito, across the small courtyard to the iron gate where Rosa Guillermo shook their hands and waved goodbye to the poorly matched threesome. Finally, as Juanita handed her mother the starch, she realized that the baby picture contest had nothing to do with labels on baby food jars.

Rosa Guillermo, after she stopped waving and closed the iron grillwork gate, walked back inside wondering how she was going to convince Juanita Chavez that everything that had ever happened to Juanita Chavez was entirely Juanita's own fault.

Mrs. Marquez stood on her kitchen table wearing red high heels and turning an inch at a time so Hortence Grace could pin the hem of the brand new green satin dress embossed with red cabbage roses. It had more shimmer, more shine and more eye-catching quality than any of Olivia's old yard sale gowns had ever thought of having.

Finally, when Hortence Grace was finished, she stepped back to give her handiwork a critical look and realized that Mrs. Marquez, dressed in this dress, looked exactly like the large ceramic urn with hand painted flowers in the lobby of the Hotel Las Flores where she and Bernardo had spent their wedding night.

"Maybe you could put a rose on each sleeve," Mrs. Marquez offered. She was truly a victim of her own bad taste.

"The dress is already covered with roses," Hortence Grace said firmly. She stuck out her hand to help Mrs. Marquez, teetering dangerously in her high heels, down off the table.

"But those roses are flat," Mrs. Marquez replied. She skipped Hortence Grace's hand and leaned heavily on her shoulder.

"With roses on the sleeves my shoulders wouldn't seem so narrow."

By the time she made it to the floor she was out of breath, so Hortence Grace studied Mrs. Marquez' barrel shape and shook her head.

"I recommend you leave the dress alone or Raymond Valdez won't be able to find you in all the roses and shine."

Mrs. Marquez gave Hortence Grace an imperious look. She hated to admit it, but she knew that Hortence Grace was right. "I'll just have to wear them in my hair," she sighed.

Hortence Grace nodded her approval, then undid the opening for the zipper and removed the pins.

"So, it'll be finished right away?" Mrs. Marquez pressed.

"As we discussed..."

"Discussed? What did we discuss?" Mrs. Marquez interrupted.

"The dress is yours after we speak to Olivia."

"Olivia Gomez?"

"Surely you didn't forget?" Hortence Grace smiled and pushed pins into the tomato shaped pincushion poised on her wrist.

Mrs. Marquez moved closer to the sliver of mirror on the wall and twirled. Raymond Valdez would not be able to resist her. She looked like a movie star in this dress. Perhaps she would finally get to wear the diamond ring he'd kept from his long ago engagement to a girl who'd turned him down for a mortician. Hortence Grace snapped her fingers and broke the spell. "Mrs. Marquez?"

"What?" Mrs. Marquez yelped.

"You do remember our arrangement?"

Mrs. Marquez sighed. This wasn't going to be easy. She didn't care for situations where she didn't have the upper hand, let alone being called on to keep up her end of a bargain she'd never intended to keep in the first place. Besides, Olivia was too unpredictable, too lost in the landscape of her own body for Mrs. Marquez' taste. Servicing oneself for pleasure was a sin according to the church and the laws of nature.

"Mrs. Marquez?" Hortence Grace said, clapping her hands to get her attention.

"I heard you the first time," Mrs. Marquez snapped. "I'll see what I can do...."

"And I will too," Hortence Grace said.

Then she stepped behind Mrs. Marquez, pulled out the two remaining pins in the shoulders and watched both sides, front and back, fall to the floor.

Surprised, Mrs. Marquez let out a little whoop. She felt very bare in her two-sizes-too-small, black slip but she turned to Hortence Grace with a brand new really good idea.

"Maybe in the meantime, you could leave me the dress and I could show it to Raymond."

Mrs. Marquez was so transparent Hortence Grace started to laugh and scooped the two pieces up off the floor.

"And get someone else to sew up the sides, put in the zipper and stitch up the hem," Hortence Grace said.

Caught, Mrs. Marquez tried to cover her scheme with a hollow laugh.

"You're not going back on your promise?" Hortence Grace asked, feigning shock.

Mrs. Marquez tried feigning shock right back and shook her head no.

"Besides, why spoil the impact?" Hortence Grace smiled. Then stepping closer to Mrs. Marquez, she used her most intimate woman-to-woman tone. "This dress needs to be a surprise to insure the desired effect."

Mrs. Marquez looked at Hortence Grace darkly before she pulled a handkerchief out of her cleavage and blew her nose. Once again she knew Hortence Grace was right.

Mrs. Marquez kept her eyes on the shimmery dress as Hortence Grace folded it over her arm and opened the door to let the sun work its magic on the shiny fabric. She didn't feel a tinge of remorse for what she'd done even if Hortence Grace did look just like her son.

Mrs. Marquez grabbed her old dress and slipped it over her head. No getting around it, Hortence Grace was not going to be put off.

"Well then, wait." Mrs. Marquez grumbled as she opened a kitchen drawer and removed the blue pillow covering a telephone buried in a deep wooden bowl. "I'll call her now," she said and started to dial.

Hortence Grace managed to hide her surprise. As far as she knew there were no phones at the top of the mountain except for the mayor and maybe the priest. Mrs. Marquez looked at Hortence Grace and patted the receiver as she listened to the rings ring. Once, twice, three times... "A gift from Raymond," she muttered then counted out loud. "Four, five, six. No one's there," she said, but just as she started to hang up...

"Who is it?" blared out of the earpiece.

Hortence Grace smiled triumphantly, but Mrs. Marquez looked as if she'd been bitten by a snake.

"Olivia?" she asked in a tremulous tone.

"What do you want?" came the reply.

Mrs. Marquez turned her back on Hortence Grace but snuck little looks at the shiny dress as she mumbled into the mouthpiece.

"Hortence Grace wants to have a meeting."

"Speak up if you want me to hear what you're saying."

"Hortence Grace wants to see you," Mrs. Marquez almost shouted.

"What?!" Olivia sounded perturbed.

Then in urgent hushed tones, Mrs. Marquez blatantly lied. "She admires your strength. How you've survived since the killing of the mayor, and the loss..."

"Hortence Grace, my cousin-in-law?!" Olivia interrupted loudly.

"Frankly, I think she's looking for tips," Mrs. Marquez whispered.

"Tips?!" Olivia's voice pierced out of the earpiece.

"Tips?!" Hortence Grace repeated from the doorway just as loudly. Mrs. Marquez turned and gave her a dirty look as Olivia shouted.

"What the hell are you talking about?"

Mrs. Marquez turned back and started to croon spontaneous lies to the kitchen chair. Lie number one, Hortence Grace said a relative of the mistress was going to move Olivia out of the mistress' house. Lie number two, it was a woman. Lie number three, Hortence Grace said Johnny

Orteez would rig the election... on and on... Mrs. Marquez told Olivia at least fifteen things that weren't true but finally Olivia's curiosity was piqued enough for her to shout. "Enough! Come Tuesday at three."

So before Olivia could change her mind, Mrs. Marquez hung up fast and turned to Hortence Grace still stroking the dress.

"Done!" she announced. Hortence Grace nodded but Mrs. Marquez went on.

"So... you'll come here with the dress..."

"After you go with me," Hortence Grace interrupted.

Mrs. Marquez shook her head emphatically no.

"That wasn't part of the deal."

"Oh yes it was," Hortence Grace responded firmly.

"But I'd just be a nuisance," Mrs. Marquez tried to demur.

"Oh, no, no, no. I look forward to your help."

"Help? What help... how?"

"I don't know how to get there."

Mrs. Marquez was losing her patience. "She's Bernardo's cousin, for God's sake."

"But Li Choo was not."

"Well, I don't know either," Mrs. Marquez lied again.

Hortence Grace shrugged and started to walk away. "Fine. I'll just throw this thing in the trash."

Panicked, Mrs. Marquez yelled, "Stop!"

Hortence Grace turned back, watched Mrs. Marquez put the phone in the bowl under the pillow and shut the kitchen drawer.

"Be here Tuesday at two."

Hortence Grace nodded then hurried down the path. For the first time in ages, she felt a little shimmery, like the dress.

THE FUNERAL PARTY

It was dark and still raining. Ebba was soaking wet and beginning to lose confidence in her escape. The dry, dusty landscape had transformed itself into rivulets of mud that slurped between her toes. When she stopped to get her bearings an orange neon sign gleamed CANTINA in the window of a sinking shack and since it was the only thing around with a roof Ebba decided to go inside and get out of the rain. She wove her way through the potholes filled with water and a few parked cars and when she reached the portal, three wet dogs huddled by the door barely looked up as she hurried inside.

The small candlelit room was swollen with too many people. A funeral procession had come to a halt during the downpour and they, like Ebba, had had to seek shelter. A man perched on a stool under a tin can light was wrapped around his guitar and singing. His eyes were closed as he let note after note slip between his fingers and lips so his heart could pour out of his mouth.

"I send you prayers on the threads of my song.
May angels lift your spirits above the dark reason of this day..."

Ebba watched him open his eyes and look at the young husband and wife rocking a tiny white coffin cradled between them in time to the music. Inside, under a blanket of orange blossoms and roses, laid their dead baby girl.

"May angels caress you and rejoin your torn hearts with love."

The music was so reassuring Ebba let it lull her into momentary calm and when it ended the last few notes seemed to hang in air. After a moment or two the audience came out of their trance and began to clap and shout for more. What they wanted even more than the music was the spell that the singer had cast. Unfortunately the young father and mother were too numb to notice. After the singer bowed and acknowledged the applause he went to the couple, spoke to them softly and wiped the young mother's tears away with his thumb. Then he and the young father put the lid back on the coffin and sealed it tight.

"The songs will keep her safe," the singer said as the young couple took hold of his hands and murmured their thanks.

"Better to sing to the sweet soul of your baby than to anyone else," he smiled. Ebba, standing nearby, was wringing water out of her wings when the singer turned in her direction.

"Nothing worse for an angel than a rainy day."

Ebba looked at him levelly. "It's just a costume," she said in her best, leave-me-alone tone. But the singer ignored it.

"Do you need help?" he asked, extending his hand. Ebba took note of his calloused fingers and his kind gray eyes but shook her head no.

"What's your name?" he asked.

Ebba looked at the floor.

"Phillipa Marie, but you can call me Ebba."

"Ebba was the name of my cousin," he said.

Ebba was surprised. She'd never heard of anyone else named Ebba. She looked him up and down and decided he was safe. "Who are you?" she asked.

"Jesus Fidel, and are you hungry?" he answered. Ebba shrugged, she was too shy to say yes.

"Well I am," he said jumping over her shyness. "Besides it never hurts to eat when it's offered."

He walked her to the dimly lit bar and onto a stool before he asked Marie Monterey, the stern-faced woman behind the counter, what there was to eat.

"Some eggs, some cheese or peanut butter and tortillas."

"One of each," the singer ordered, "and a glass of milk."

Marie Monterey looked at Ebba and shook her head. "Milk is for the kids."

"This is not an old lady," Jesus said.

Marie Monterey sighed. The whole rain business and funeral people was putting a strain on her kitchen.

"No offense little girl, but we got some babies in the crowd."

Ebba nodded. "I could have a Coke," she said.

"And I'll have a plate of tomatoes with salt and flan and a beer."

Marie Monterey made a face at the unlikely combination, but Jesus just laughed. Then he patted Ebba on the back and went back to his stool under the tiny tin can light. He picked up his guitar, ruffled his fingers over the strings and as Ebba took the first bite of her tortilla sandwich, Jesus began to sing soothingly, using his voice to calm the room full of people.

Ebba watched him as she took more bites and tried to swallow the lump in her throat that had nothing to do with eating peanut butter. The music had taken her by surprise and she was fighting hard to hold back a flood of longing that had nothing to do with weather.

A Visit to Bernardo in the Rain

Bernardo woke with a start. Rain was pounding on the roof but the headlights of a car were sweeping across the bedroom wall as it circled the courtyard. Hortence Grace stirred in her sleep, but Bernardo patted her gently, waiting until she rolled over on her side before he eased out of bed and pulled on his trousers. He hurried into the kitchen, took his shotgun down from its rack then slipped outside, slid into the shadows as the driver of the black sedan stepped into the rain, snapped a large black umbrella firmly into place to shield himself against the downpour and hurried across the courtyard trying to avoid the deeper puddles but when he reached the portal he stopped. Mr. Lobos was looking down the double barrel of Bernardo's shotgun.

Startled, he took a few steps back and landed in a lake-sized hole filled with water, but he didn't say a word. Neither did Bernardo. He just stood in the dark and looked at Mr. Lobos' frightened face as he waited for him to say who he was. After a very long pause Mr. Lobos finally spoke.

"I've come about the girl," he said as water seeped into his shoes and soaked his white socks. "She ran away." Bernardo lowered the gun just a little. "I thought she might have come here."

Bernardo still didn't speak, so Mr. Lobos shifted his soggy feet and continued. "She was at my mother's."

Bernardo narrowed his eyes. "What girl?" Bernardo said softly. He wanted Mr. Lobos to say a name.

"Ebba," Mr. Lobos said just as softly.

"Who are you?"

"Mr. Lobos," Mr. Lobos said. He'd forgotten to say his name.

"My mother is the sister of the General and we live in Josefina."

Mr. Lobos extended his hand, but Bernardo just continued to look at Mr. Lobos over the barrel of his gun. After a moment or two, Mr. Lobos withdrew his hand and the two men just stood without talking.

"Why was she at your mother's?" Bernardo finally asked. Mr. Lobos sighed and looked at his feet.

"I had spoken to the priest."

Bernardo cocked his gun, which caught Mr. Lobos completely off guard.

"Why?"

Mr. Lobos hesitated, trying to make his answer sound better than it was.

"About custodial permission." The rain was coming down harder so it was very loud. Bernardo leaned forward thinking he hadn't heard.

"Custodial what?" Bernardo asked.

"Permission to keep her," Mr. Lobos said, clearing his throat. Incredulous, Bernardo took a step back. Tired of the interrogation, Mr. Lobos looked at Bernardo and bluntly stated his case.

"I asked for permission to take her." Bernardo lowered the gun. This was beyond his comprehension.

"Ebba is just a girl."

Mr. Lobos looked at Bernardo and nodded. He didn't know what else to say, besides he was sick of standing in the water so, gun or no gun, Mr. Lobos stepped out of the rain and ducked under the portal.

"Someone in the military found her the night of the movie. He was going to take her. I heard her screaming."

Bernardo shook his head. None of this was a great surprise. "I told her she couldn't go."

"Well, she was there and I took her home."

"Who gave you permission?"

"Permission? There was no time for permission. She was about to be snatched. You of all people should know..."

Mr. Lobos didn't finish the sentence. Bernardo looked at him as if to speak but just nodded instead.

"Is she here?" Mr. Lobos asked.

"No," Bernardo whispered as he shook his head.

Uncertain about what to do next, the men continued to stand without speaking until the wind changed direction and drenched them both. Finally, Bernardo put down his gun, walked to the kitchen door and motioned for Mr. Lobos to leave his umbrella by the bench and come inside.

Mr. Lobos sat across from Bernardo in a red kitchen chair hand-painted with purple morning glories. Bernardo sat on the bench he'd put together out of leftover wood from Elena Cordova's bedroom suite. The gun was back in its rack and a bottle of mescal sat between them on a table covered with yellow oilcloth. After the third glass of the wormy drink, Mr. Lobos gave a brief account of Ebba's activities at his mother's house including the new pink dress and lunch with Olivia. He did not mention anything about his mother's slap, the visit from Doctor Vidal to validate her virginity or the feelings Ebba aroused in him, but he did tell Bernardo how much

Ebba and his mother had hated each other at first sight, which Bernardo said, smiling for the first time, didn't surprise him at all.

After that there was nothing more to mention so the two of them sat in silence, each lost in his own thoughts enhanced by the potent drink and the sound of falling rain. Finally, Mr. Lobos put down his glass and looked around the room.

"Do you have a picture of your son? Ebba told me he was taken."

Bernardo poured himself another drink and drank it down.

"They came and ripped him out of our arms." He said it so fiercely it sounded like a sob so Mr. Lobos waited a moment before he continued.

"Maybe if I had a picture..."

Before Mr. Lobos could finish his thought Bernardo grabbed the basket from the shelf behind him and rummaged through the pictures. When he found the one of Ariel he placed it face up on the table, and as Mr. Lobos lifted it to the light, Bernardo handed him the picture of Ebba, too. At first glance, Mr. Lobos didn't pay much attention, but when he looked again he swallowed his breath and started to choke. It was the same picture Ebba had found when it flew in the back seat.

Bernardo got up and pounded him on the back, told him to lift his arms over his head and poured him some water, but even after Mr. Lobos caught his breath he could barely speak.

"Where did these come from?" he whispered.

"A helicopter on the night of St. Augustine. They fell out and spread all over the sky. These landed in the garden."

Mr. Lobos looked at the pictures one more time.

"Would you mind if I take them?"

Bernardo shook his head no, so Mr. Lobos stood up and jammed them in his pocket.

"I have to go," he said and started to cough.

Bernardo handed him another glass of water, which Mr. Lobos finished in great big gulps as he let his mind sort through the catalog of names and connections locked in his head. He drained his glass of mescal and put it down on the table.

"I'll let you know what happens," he said and bolted out the door. Then he ran across the courtyard to his car and drove away before Bernardo could tell him that he'd forgotten his umbrella.

Overnight in the Cantina

The rain continued to pour, so the funeral party was spending the night inside the small cantina whether they wanted to or not. Some slept, some talked in their sleep, others played cards or gossiped in whispers, but all of them took turns watching over the dead baby so the young couple could get some rest. At one point an old man woke from a fitful dream and pointed at Ebba who was holding the tiny casket in the corner.

"Transplants and research," he cautioned in a raspy whisper. Ebba had no idea what he was talking about.

"Cut out your parts. Liver, heart, eyes, kidneys. Anything you got that works they give to somebody else. You're not much except for your parts."

Ebba remembered the story Bernardo told about the artist's eyes and froze. Jesus Fidel reached out and gave the old man's arm a swat.

"Stop the talk, old man," the singer hissed. "You don't know."

"Yes I do," the old man sniped back. "I see what they leave in the ditch..."

"Enough," the singer said sharply.

"I'll say what I want," the old man grumbled then got up and moved away. Terrified, Ebba watched him go.

"Don't listen to that," the singer was trying to be reassuring. "You don't have to worry," he said, knowing full well that she did. Ebba knew it too, but just kept rocking the little coffin in time to the falling rain.

"How about some sleep?" Jesus suggested.

Ebba shook her head no.

"I like holding the little girl," she said.

Jesus looked at her and smiled.

"You're not so old. Certainly not a baby, but you're still a girl."

Ebba looked at Jesus and changed the subject. "Maybe you could sing about the angel again."

Jesus nodded and reached for his guitar. He had sense enough to know that she'd run out of responses. He touched the strings softly and sang.

"I send you prayers on the threads of my song and devotion to soothe your pain.
May angels lift you from the dark reason of this day..."

Ebba leaned back against the plaster wall, closed her eyes and went to sleep holding the baby in the coffin close to her heart.

Rosa Guillermo woke with a start. Someone was banging on the door. For a moment she lay in the dark and listened to the rain pounding on the roof and decided that that was the sound she'd heard, but just as she rolled over to go back to sleep she heard a man shout, "Open up!" in a loud, booming voice. Rosa Guillermo was alone in her brother's house, alone in her narrow bed. It had been a while since she'd shared a bed with her one-and-only lover, the lover her brother had paid twelve thousand pesos to and sent away because he didn't like him taking up so much of his sister's time.

"Open the door right now!" the man shouted again.

Silently she slipped out of the sheets, found her brother's bathrobe at the bottom of the bed and pulled it on as she hurried to the window, but all she could see was a curtain of rain. "Now!" the man demanded more loudly than before.

Uncertain of what might happen next she ran to the door and flicked on the light, opened the peephole and peered outside. She couldn't see a thing.

"Let me in," the man insisted, pounding the door with his fists.

"What do you want?" Rosa Guillermo asked, stalling for time.

She was taking the gun out of the box on the shelf above the door that her brother kept for just such occasions.

"Not you!" came the reply.

Rosa Guillermo made sure the chain was secure before she unlocked the locks and lifted the gun, placed her finger on the trigger before she opened the door a crack, but Mr. Lobos was quick. He pushed his finger into the narrow space and lifted the chain. Then he swatted the gun out of Rosa Guillermo's hand and as it fell to the floor he pushed the door open all the way and stepped inside.

"Where is she?" Mr. Lobos asked in a low controlled tone that barely capped his anger. Rosa Guillermo clutched her brother's robe around her body as if it would protect her.

"Who?" she replied.

"The girl," Mr. Lobos said. Then he reached down and picked up the gun, removed the bullets, put them in his pocket and deliberately waited until Rosa Guillermo returned the gun to the box on the shelf above the door. He didn't like Rosa Guillermo or her brother, Ricardo. He was suspicious of bureaucrats; they always got in the way. As far as he was concerned, their investment in fear, rigidity and rules was just like religion when sameness and order becomes a crutch. The Guillermos took righteous delight in the literal interpretation of every nuance of every idea or utterance no matter the subject or subtlety. In the grand scheme of things, pigs are more wily than sheep and as far as Mr. Lobos was concerned, the Guillermos were sheep.

"What girl?" Rosa Guillermo asked impatiently.

Mr. Lobos didn't bother to answer. Uninvited, he started to walk down the hall of the modest government house.

"You'll wake my brother," Rosa Guillermo whispered sternly.

Mr. Lobos gave her a blistering look. "No one is here but yourself or he would have answered the door."

Rosa Guillermo lifted her head defiantly, but decided not to say anything more. She didn't like Mr. Lobos any more than he liked her. Relatives of politicians in power were demanding and unpredictable.

Mr. Lobos continued to roam. He poked his head in every closet and cupboard with Rosa Guillermo close behind tying and retying her brother's robe more tightly. When he turned into the kitchen, Mr. Lobos stopped. A pile of government papers was sitting on the table.

"Those don't concern you," Rosa Guillermo said.

She tried to push past him, but Mr. Lobos stuck out his arm to stop her and walked to the stack. *Adoption Application,* each one said. He turned and looked at Rosa Guillermo huddled in the doorway and smiled. He turned each one over and read the facts of each couple aloud, each applicant more forlorn than the last.

"You're not supposed to do that," Rosa Guillermo said firmly.

Mr. Lobos didn't even look up. He searched through the entire stack before he demanded, "Where did you take her?"

Finally, Rosa Guillermo, who really didn't like men, starting with her brother, lost her temper.

"You expect me to read your mind? I don't know what you're talking about! You men are all alike. You expect me to make things right when they're wrong. Meanwhile you let us down with your overrated self-importance." All of her pent up frustrations came out in a rush; she couldn't stop them and she finished with a flourish. "The whole world will never recuperate from the diminished capacity of men."

Mr. Lobos dismissed her outrage with a wave of his hand and pulled Ebba's picture out of his pocket, held it up so she would have to give it her full attention. Rosa Guillermo sighed. She always, always gave in to the person wearing pants. It was a trait she learned from her mother. She moved to the table and reached for her glasses, put them on and gave the picture a hard look. After a moment or two she put the glasses back on the table, turned her back and shrugged. But before she could walk away, Mr. Lobos grabbed her by the shoulder and pushed her up against the wall where he held the picture in front of her face as he reviewed the details.

"The daughter of Carlotta Pavon. She lived with Bernardo DeVille and his wife after you kidnapped their son..."

Rosa Guillermo tried not to panic. "I don't know what you're talking about."

Mr. Lobos put his fingers around her throat and moved in close. He practically left his words on her lips as he whispered, "Yes, you do."

Without any warning, Rosa Guillermo's eyes rolled back in her head and she passed out cold from fear and anticipation, crumbled to the floor like a sack of potatoes. Mr. Lobos sighed in disgust. He looked down at her limp body and touched her arm with the toe of his shoe but she just remained in a state of unconscious panic. Certain he didn't want to be there when she woke up, Mr. Lobos took the bullets out of his pocket and put them back in the box with the gun, then walked outside into the pouring rain.

When Rosa Guillermo finally came to, the front door was standing wide open and rain was blowing into the hall. It took a while, but after she got her bearings and figured out where she was and why, she managed to get up, slam the door shut and lock it before she made her way back to her narrow bed and crawled inside, folded herself into the sheets like a letter stuffed into an envelope that was too small and tried to put the encounter with Mr. Lobos out of her mind.

A KNOCK AT THE DOOR OF MRS. MARQUEZ

Mrs. Marquez was wide awake wondering where Raymond was. She'd fallen asleep on the couch at ten, then awakened at two in a smear of lipstick and mascara. Angry, she'd called Raymond's house, but there wasn't an answer. Hoping he might still turn up, she'd removed her corset, redone her makeup and put on the sheer, blue baby doll nightgown with the marabou trim. She'd been saving it for the honeymoon she was sure she was going to have with Raymond after he saw her in the new shiny green dress, but figured, what the hell, tonight was just as good a night as any.

She had just stretched out on the sturdy double bed when she heard the knock and her heart skipped a beat as she got up and hurried to greet him, late or not, with open arms. She flung open the door spewing sweet nothings in a soft scolding tone.

"You know I don't like it when you don't come when you say you will, but never mind, all is forgiven..." She stood backlit in the threshold and let the wind blow rain against the sheer nightgown that clung to her naked body like molting skin.

"It's not who you think," Mr. Lobos announced firmly at exactly the same time Mrs. Marquez realized it for herself.

She ducked behind the door quickly and closed it until there was just a crack to look out and see Mr. Lobos' face.

"Why the hell are you here?" she snapped in an entirely different tone.

"Where's the girl?" Mr. Lobos jumped right in.

"What girl?" Mrs. Marquez lobbed right back. "I don't know what you're talking about."

She started to shut the door, but Mr. Lobos stopped it with his hand ending her hopes for a grand slam fueled by the momentum of her rage and disappointment. Finally, Mrs. Marquez gave up on shutting the door and looked up at him innocently.

"Who?"

Mr. Lobos wanted to wring her neck. "Ebba," he growled.

"Last I heard, she was with you," Mrs. Marquez muttered.

Mr. Lobos pushed on the door and opened it wider.

"Rosa Guillermo said you made a deal..." he lied.

"A deal? I don't know what you're talking about," she lied right back.

"Don't be coy, Mrs. Marquez. Everyone knows about your unofficial position."

"What's that supposed to mean?" She was trying hard to ignore what Mr. Lobos was saying.

"That you're capable of anything."

Mrs. Marquez peered out into the rain and her preoccupation with Raymond overcame her.

"I bet the truck broke down," she said.

"What?" Mr. Lobos had no idea what she was talking about.

"Maybe he's flooded in a ditch or drowned," she panicked. Mr. Lobos took a step toward Mrs. Marquez, which pushed aside her concerns about Raymond Valdez and made her wonder if Mr. Lobos really knew about her collusion with her cousin and Rosa Guillermo.

"I don't have no unofficial position. So go away."

Instead, Mr. Lobos pushed on the door she was using as a barricade, caught her off guard and found himself standing right next to Mrs. Marquez in revealing damp blue. Now afraid, she shrieked as she picked up an old sweater hanging on a hook by the door and held it up in front of her like a curtain.

"I don't know nothing," she whimpered. Mr. Lobos looked at her and let her squirm in the long silence, let the time hang, let it get longer and longer. Finally, before she could stop her desperation, she blurted out, "Have you seen Raymond Valdez?"

Mr. Lobos looked at her and laughed.

"You're pathetic, Mrs. Marquez." That was worse than a slap in the face.

Humiliated, she shouted, "Get out!"

But he was already on his way and as soon as he cleared the threshold, Mrs. Marquez got to slam the door with her long awaited frustrated slam and as she slid the deadbolt into place her misplaced rage fueled a plan to get rid of Ebba.

She ran to the telephone buried in the bowl to call her cousin Johnny but because she was feeling more anxious and abandoned than ever, she dialed Raymond's number instead. It rang ten times against the sound of the pouring rain, each ring making her more anxious than the last, more vulnerable and needy, more frightened, more angry. She finally erupted with a huge sob just as Raymond picked up the phone on the eleventh ring and answered with a sleepy, "Hello?"

"Where the hell are you?!" she blasted into the receiver before she could stop herself.

"What?" Raymond whispered.

"Oh God," Mrs. Marquez sobbed. "I didn't mean... I mean... I've been so worried. You were supposed..."

Without further hesitation, Raymond jumped in with an excuse. "The truck broke down... I just got home..."

"Oh no," she panicked, but was relieved. "Are you all right?"

"Well..."

"I mean, what happened?"

"Well, I..."

On a roll, she couldn't stop herself. "You have to come right now," she interrupted. "Mr. Lobos barged in and threatened me." She hiccupped a sob.

"The truck is stuck," he interjected.

"Well fix it!" she shouted.

"In the rain? It's after three..."

Mrs. Marquez was inconsolable. "But what about me? I was all ready..."

On the other end of the phone Raymond Valdez sighed and looked into Juanita Chavez' dreamy brown eyes, her naked upturned breasts... ripe... abundant...

"Ripe," fell out of Raymond's mouth before he knew what happened.

"What?" Mrs. Marquez sobbed into the phone.

"Pipe," he recovered. "I was laying pipe when the rain got so heavy and I got trapped in the ditch... and the water..."

Raymond was running out of details when Juanita moved closer, smiled before she leaned down and clamped her lips around Raymond's cock, took his free hand and placed it on her left breast which was slightly larger than the right, and encouraged him to fondle her with vigor as she progressed up and down on his rise, not missing a stroke.

"Oh... the flooding," Raymond exclaimed just as he was about to burst.

"Oh my God," Mrs. Marquez replied.

"Oh my God," Raymond shouted whether he wanted to or not.

"Yes, yes. Thanks be to God, you're safe," she cried out.

"Tomorrow, I'll talk to you tomorrow," Raymond said and hung up the phone in a fumble.

In her kitchen, Mrs. Marquez had wanted to linger in the details and his voice. She'd wanted to repent for her rant, but Raymond had hung up the phone leaving her feeling unfinished and alone. Shivering, she pulled off the wet, clinging garment and got into bed to try to let the rain pound out her doubts.

Joan Tewkesbury

Raymond, on the other hand, at the height of his anticipation, rerouted Juanita and entered her for the seventh time that night. Then he laid back to watch her abundant breasts dance in the air with a life of their own as she rode him in time to the rain and looked into his dreamy eyes with her dreamy eyes, shouting "Yes!" at the top of her lungs as he exploded like a melon splitting in the sun, spilling its seeds.

Daybreak

Morning sun peeked through the cantina windows dribbling pale light on everyone asleep on the floor, so it came as a sudden and great shock when the front door was flung open with a bang and two men in dark suits stood on the threshold shouting and waving guns.

"Everybody up!" they yelled. "And hurry!"

Uncertain of where they were, people woke with a start, but Jesus got up with the grace of a cat, slipped into his jacket as he stepped over the waking bodies and stepped right up to the men in suits.

"Can I help you?" he offered.

"If we need help, we'll say so," they said, looking around. "We're looking for a kid."

After Ebba had fallen asleep, Marie Monterey lifted the coffin out of Ebba's arms and the old man with the raspy voice had covered her with his coat so Ebba was out of sight. But she was awake, her heart pounding and her body rigid with fear.

"Sirs. This family is in mourning," Jesus said, pointing to the young couple sitting on the ground. "Yesterday the funeral of their first-born was interrupted due to the pouring rain and their only child... their little angel... is dead in that coffin."

He pointed to the tiny white casket, but the men ignored him and scanned the lumpy shapes on the floor. Jesus smiled, towering over them with his handsome height.

"I would suggest that you apologize to the bereaved for waking them so rudely after a sleepless night and be on your way."

One of the men looked at the singer menacingly and pointed his gun.

"Who are you with your big speech and your etiquette instructions?"

"Jesus Fidel," the singer said calmly.

"The one on TV from Spain and Brazil?" the other man turned and asked in disbelief. Jesus smiled feigning graciousness.

"I am here to sing for the General on his birthday," he said. Suddenly the room became very quiet.

"So I am asking you to leave and give these poor people some peace. Otherwise I will contact my cousin to discuss your unfortunate mistake."

"Who gives a shit about a call to your cousin," the first man said as he raised his gun and started to move into the room.

"The General," Jesus smiled. "He is the General's nephew."

The men looked at each other and after a moment they turned and started to the door, but then the one who had recognized him stopped, stuck his gun down the front of his pants and came back.

"Could you make an autograph for my sister?"

Without giving it a second thought, Jesus reached out and grabbed a pen off the counter.

"Her name is Carolina and..." The man started to say something else, but Jesus took hold of his shoulders, unbuttoned the jacket of his suit and before the man could stop him, he wrote:

"To Carolina from Jesus Francisco Fidel," across the front of the man's bright white shirt. The man was so shocked he couldn't speak. Jesus just smiled and put the pen back on the counter.

"Now," Jesus said, "you can do something for me." Still speechless, the man kept looking from Jesus to his shirt.

"We're in a hurry!" the other man yelled and walked back to see what was going on.

"To make up for the rude intrusion," Jesus said, "I'd consider accepting a contribution on behalf of the dead baby's parents and I think it should be substantial. Otherwise..." He let his voice trail off but shrugged a "you never know what could happen" shrug.

The men turned to each other in disbelief, but the one with the autographed shirt started pulling on his mustache aware that everyone in the room was watching, even Ebba who was buried under the old man's coat.

"Wait just a minute," the first man said. "You're the one who ruined his shirt."

Jesus started to laugh. He laughed so hard that he couldn't stop laughing and pretty soon the whole room was laughing too, so the men, having no other choice, dug into their pockets and slapped cash down on Marie Monterey's counter. After that, they walked out the door. Jesus followed, thanking them profusely and watching them slop through the muddy parking lot, then climb into the Johnny-mobile with Johnny at the wheel, and drive away with the loudspeakers blaring... "You Ain't Nothin' But a Hound Dog."

CAUGHT

The same morning sun streamed through Mrs. Marquez' window as she hauled her aching, sleepless body out of bed and decided to go see if her beloved Raymond had survived the rain. Besides, she had a low-down feeling in her belly that something wasn't right.

She managed to hitch a ride with Mr. Bravo who was on his way down the mountain to take portraits of military men and their families for a monthly magazine. Eager to be on time, he was more than miffed to find Mrs. Marquez sitting uninvited in his truck, begging to be dropped off at the house of Raymond Valdez because of some story about trouble Raymond had had with his truck. Only because it was on the way did Mr. Bravo consider it, and when mud threatened to sink them twice on the rain-rutted road he regretted it even though he managed to spin free each time they sank.

Unfortunately, dropping off Mrs. Marquez in front of Raymond's house did not go as smoothly. Just as Mr. Bravo pulled up next to the reputed stuck truck, which looked clean as a whistle, the ancient wood gate to Raymond's hacienda opened wide and out stepped Juanita Chavez beaming with afterglow. Raymond didn't look so bad himself until he lifted his head and saw Mrs. Marquez marching toward the guilty pair with her arms outstretched and her red fingernails stabbing the air like daggers.

"What's this? What's this?!" she kept shouting over and over.

Wisely, Juanita Chavez took a step back, put the door between herself and the unfolding events so she could watch. Raymond lifted his arms in a gesture of innocent explanation.

"Juanita Chavez was caught in the downpour," he said. "Stranded by the side of the road where my truck slipped into the mud. I had no choice but to save her from a watery destiny," he finished with a flourish.

"Liar!" Mrs. Marquez screamed even before he was finished.

Then she backed up and flew at him, ready to tear out his eyes, rip open his skin and bite him repeatedly. She knew in her bones that the whole mud, ditch-slipping, Juanita stranded on the side of the road story was completely made up. Raymond's arms took the brunt of the battle. He even managed to stand after she jumped on his back and hung around his neck like a snake, wrapping her short chubby legs around his waist while she kicked his kidneys with her high heels.

"Liar, liar, liar, liar!!" she screamed in his ear.

Mr. Bravo had just decided to drive away quick so he wouldn't be late, but when Raymond fell down under the weight of Mrs. Marquez he turned off the ignition and rushed to try to pry her off before she killed him. It wasn't easy. She was determined and focused and full of rage.

"No one else," she kept shouting. "No one else will have you... Not ever... no one else... ever, ever, ever!!!" Then she turned and started to attack Mr. Bravo too.

Suddenly, there was a loud clang and Mrs. Marquez went limp. Fortunately, Juanita Chavez had come to the rescue with an iron skillet and hit Mrs. Marquez over the head knocking her out cold. Silence echoed around the tiny courtyard until Mr. Bravo looked at his watch.

"I have to go," he said.

"But what about her?" Raymond panicked. Mr. Bravo shrugged. "Maybe you should have thought it through."

Juanita leaned down to check Mrs. Marquez' breathing. "She's fine, the old bat," Juanita said without an ounce of pity.

Raymond got to his feet and looked at Mr. Bravo in complete desperation.

"Please, can you take her..."

Mr. Bravo didn't let Raymond finish his sentence. "No. Absolutely not. I'm late and now it's up to you. I tried to save your life already. That's enough goodwill for one day," he said, turning to go.

"Wait!" Raymond shouted.

"What?" Mr. Bravo shouted back.

"Just help me put her in the back of my truck."

"Why?!" Juanita yelled. She didn't like where this was headed. But Raymond had a plan. He turned to Juanita and took her by the hand.

"I'll take her back and you go with him."

"What?" Mr. Bravo choked.

"Drop Juanita at her mother's. It's on the way." Mr. Bravo rolled his eyes. He hated complication and other people's messes.

"Drop me at my mother's?!" Juanita didn't like this plan at all. Raymond looked at the ground and sighed.

"It's the safest thing I can think of," he replied. "Now please just help me lift her into the truck."

So, after a moment, when Juanita thought it over and realized that Raymond was right, all of them lifted and strained and finally managed to hoist Mrs. Marquez into the flatbed of Raymond's truck. Then there was a brief tearful goodbye before Juanita climbed in beside Mr. Bravo and hugged the door as they headed to her mother's.

Raymond Valdez, on the other hand, drove straight to the manger in back of the church where he and Mrs. Marquez had had their last encounter in the hay and managed, just barely, to lift her up and slide her into the straw. Shortly after he drove away, Mrs. Marquez started to come to. There was ringing in her ears and spots before her eyes but her biggest confusion, besides the lump on her head, was about where she was and why she was in the hay-filled manger.

M arie Monterey pulled Ebba into the kitchen and cut the still soggy wings off Ebba's costume with her poultry shears. Then she tied a white tablecloth around Ebba's shoulders like a shawl and sent her off with the funeral procession.

Still wearing the gardener's damp hat, Ebba beat the cymbal as she walked behind the two drummers imitating their slow pace. Behind her, a quartet of boys carried the tiny coffin followed by the young father and mother, Jesus Fidel and a very young priest. All the rest of the mourners brought up the rear, parading down the muddy road that was beginning to dry in the bright sun. Out of respect, cars and trucks and horse-driven wagons slowed down and pulled to the side of the road and Ebba was careful to notice the General's monumental head decorated with empty bullet casings as the procession turned into the special cemetery for babies and children.

The service was short and led by the nervous young priest. He'd never conducted a newborn's burial before and was so despondent he could hardly contain his emotions. He kept wondering out loud why God would use creation's time for something so short-lived. At the end of the prayer, Jesus sang another song to soothe the souls of all those present. Then after a final amen everyone gathered around the young couple to comfort and console them; but the singer took Ebba aside, pulled the money the men had slammed down on the counter out of his pocket and counted it into her hand.

"There is enough for the bus and a little bit extra."

"But what about them?" Ebba said, looking at the young mother and father.

Jesus pulled another bundle of bills out of his other pocket and smiled. "This is for them."

Ebba looked up at him and nodded, whispered her thanks and took off the gardener's hat, put the money inside and plopped it back on her head as Jesus continued giving her instructions.

"I want you to go to the market and buy bunches of white paper flowers before you get on the bus."

"Why?" Ebba asked adjusting the pale silk shawl still stuffed down the front of her dress.

"To say your mother just died and you're going to the funeral."

"But she's dead already."

"Then it won't be a lie and people will know you're expected." Suddenly Ebba thought about the old man with the raspy voice.

"What if they want my liver or my eyes or my heart?

"Who?" Jesus asked.

"The men who came to the cantina."

"Did you see them?" Ebba nodded yes.

"Then you make sure you don't see them again."

"But what if they find me first?"

Jesus thought carefully before he answered. "In my opinion..."

Ebba nodded.

"You're much too smart and too much trouble, but after you get the flowers, wait for the bus at the stop under the banyan tree and don't talk to anyone unless you have to."

"What if I get the wrong one?" Ebba was starting to panic.

"There is only one bus and it only goes up to Elena."

Ebba sighed. All she'd cared about before was running away. Now that she'd had a taste of protection she wanted more. Jesus sensed her wanting with compassion, but he had to go. He bent down to reassure her.

"You were brave enough to escape wherever you were so I know you'll be fine."

"I'll miss the music," she whispered.

"Then sing the song. Sing it to yourself to keep you safe."

After that, Jesus stood up, patted her head and turned her in the direction where she needed to go. Ebba, with just one glance back and a short wave, started off on the paved road to town but he waited until she was out of sight before he hurried away.

Bernardo and Dr. Vidal go for a Ride

Bernardo stood by himself in the empty waiting room at the clinic looking at the photograph his father had taken of Dr. Vidal now hanging on the waiting room wall.

"I'm glad you could come on such short notice." Dr. Vidal said from behind the velvet curtain.

"It was my day to come to town," Bernardo replied.

"Where we are going happens twice a week," the doctor continued, "but I thought we should go today."

Bernardo muttered "all right" as he stepped closer to the picture to get a better look.

"What happened to your horse?" he asked.

"They shot him out from under me," the doctor said and pushed the curtain aside so he could roll into the room.

"It was unnecessary and cruel and when he didn't die your father used his gun to put him out of his misery."

Bernardo nodded. "He hated to see anything suffer."

"He was very precise," the doctor said as he started to search through the mess on Mercedes' desk. "Were you close?" he asked.

Bernardo smiled and shook his head. "I believe the camera was first, then my mother, my sister, then me."

"Obviously you didn't warm to it," the doctor said matter of factly.

"I didn't have the patience to wait to stop time."

"Too bad we can't make others like what we like the same way we like it."

Finally he found what he was looking for in a plastic bag and placed it on his lap as he started rolling to the front door.

"Come along," he motioned. "Let's hurry before that miserable woman returns."

Outside, Bernardo lifted the old doctor smelling of women's cologne into Gloria's front seat, secured his wheelchair in the back and off they went bumping down the road.

"Your father, is he still alive?" the doctor asked, shouting to be heard.

Bernardo shook his head and shouted back. "Dead. He died at the border. A bomb went off as the shutter dropped and he was blown to bits. His last image was a flash, a likely likeness of his passion and spirit."

The doctor gave Bernardo a jaundiced look.

"Don't be so romantic. He was a voyeur and a thief, grabbing what he could get. He liked the chase. He was a collector of moments, a truly selfish pursuit."

Bernardo smiled. "I thought you said you liked him."

"I did. He was a mercenary, like me."

Bernardo swerved sharply to avoid a huge pothole in the road while he defended his father.

"He photographed you at the peak of your cause."

The old doctor clutched the dashboard and re-adjusted his false teeth.

"Sorry to dampen your theory," he laughed. "I was in uniform but I didn't have a cause, just a disguise to cover the mischief of the church."

Not wanting to hear any details regarding the doctor's previous business, Bernardo kept his eyes straight ahead but the doctor rattled on.

"However I'm glad your father didn't live to endure the fate of your sister."

Bernardo glanced at Dr. Vidal darkly.

"What do you know about the fate of my sister?"

The doctor turned to him and shrugged. "That the General is very proud of your table and chairs."

Bernardo looked back at the road and the whirling dust as Dr. Vidal rearranged his limp legs and looked out the window. His standing days, his "Glory Days," hadn't drifted to the surface of his memory in quite some time. He yawned and then turned back to Bernardo as they bounced along.

"And you? What about your passion, Bernardo?"

Bernardo looked at him and shook his head, "I'm a simple man, doctor."

"Your wife, your children..."

"Are quite enough," Bernardo interjected. "At the moment I'm living in a cave of loss so they are about all I can keep track of."

The doctor sighed. "A wife and children... I can honestly say I've not been so abundantly blessed."

Bernardo's jaw clenched involuntarily but he kept silent and after that nothing was said until the doctor took out his perfumed handkerchief to blow his nose, looked out of Gloria's dusty windshield and saw the approaching fork in the road.

"What you are about to see won't be pleasant," he said and pointed to the left.

"That way, Bernardo. That is where we have to go."

Hortence Grace retraced her steps, marched through the house looking everywhere for the piece of antique lace she used to cover her head when she went to church to pray for Ariel. She opened drawers, looked in closets, opened all the cupboards. Finally she opened Rebecca's door and there it was hanging as a backdrop at an altar Rebecca had made out of the wooden box Tobias had given to Ariel to use for his toys.

Filled with remorse, Hortence Grace leaned against the door. After Ariel disappeared, Rebecca and Tobias had slipped quietly into the background of her day-to-day thoughts, and after Ebba disappeared their only function was to stay out of sight so they wouldn't be taken too. They had ceased to be children and had become objects, liabilities locked away in their rooms, only brought out if there was enough protection.

Hortence Grace walked to the altar and looked at the things Rebecca had gathered. A photograph of Ariel and one of Tobias, one of Ariel's trucks, four St. Jude prayer cards, a bowl of rose petals in water and a tiny piece of cloth that she'd cut from a seam in Ebba's blue cotton dress. Hortence Grace got down on her knees in front of the tiny shrine and asked God to forgive her. She said ten Hail Marys in a row, and when she finished she saw Rebecca standing beside her. Rebecca, the good girl, the girl who did exactly as she was told. Rebecca the child who never caused anyone to worry. Rebecca the pure soul, the rare result of a union of love.

"I took your lace," she said softly.

Hortence Grace got up and embraced her daughter as Rebecca whispered from the circle of her mother's arms.

"To pray for Tobias."

"Tobias..." Hortence Grace didn't understand.

"The mothers and fathers hate him."

"What mothers and fathers?"

"The ones whose children are gone."

"But what right do they have to hate Tobias?"

"He's here. They see him every day."

"Oh my God," Hortence Grace shook her head.

She realized that she and Bernardo had been so preoccupied that their sadness had turned into a blanket that covered them up and they had fallen asleep. Rebecca gazed at the shrine from the safety of her mother's roomy body as Hortence Grace took a deep breath.

"It's time to wake up," she said out loud and kissed Rebecca. "I'll wear the doily your grandmother crocheted on the living room chair. Handwork soothed her so it will soothe me. Besides, I don't think God cares what I wear on my head."

Then she started out the door, a new burst of fury in her step and a new notion in her head.

"No more grieving," she said. "I'm sick of tears."

bba had been waiting for the bus for over an hour. Seeking shelter against the scorching sun, she stood entwined like a snake in the large bouquet of white paper flowers Jesus had told her to buy while everyone else huddled in clumps around the sprawling roots of the banyan tree. She tried to occupy her thoughts with the list of things Jesus had told her to do but she was distracted.

Floating through the air from somewhere was the sound of whistling. It wasn't a song, just the same few notes over and over like a benediction in church. But it wasn't that either. This whistling had more spunk, like a march, and those same over and over notes grabbed your attention and invaded your thoughts. At first it had been distant but now it was closer and louder and pretty soon all traffic was forced to stop for the throng of whistling people shuffling their way into the street, trailing a lumpy cascade of used shoes hanging from ropes tied around their waists.

"Shoes of the dead passing by!" someone shouted.

Everyone waiting under the tree got up and scurried across the parched pavement like a battalion of roaches clacking to the curb to get a better look. Some people even began to whistle those same few notes over and over, but mostly they were quiet and took off their hats out of respect.

With so many people walking in the street, traffic was bunched up behind them but finally as the last whistling stragglers passed, dragging shoes of every description, the rickety bus could be seen laboring along, looping around donkey carts and cars and trucks older by decades than Ebba's dead mother.

"Bus is coming," shouted the same man that had shouted before.

Suddenly everyone curbside mobilized, forgot the whistling people trailing shoes and clustered into a bunch ready to board the approaching bus. Ebba began to panic. What if she couldn't get on? What if there wasn't room? What if she had to wait several days for the next bus to come? Realizing there was no alternative, she pushed her panic aside, stood up straight and studied her options. Sit outside on the roof in the fresh air with baskets of produce, suitcases, a few boys and old men or be jammed inside where it was stuffy and hot with the women, crying babies, chickens and pigs.

By the time the bus lurched to a stop the sound of whistling had drifted away and Ebba pushed to the front and up the rusty metal stairs.

"Girls and women sit inside," an old woman yelled. "You've got no business riding on the roof."

But Ebba ignored her, clung to her white paper flowers and buried herself in a stack of retread tires as the unshaven conductor puffed past.

"Fares," he shouted in a loud voice. Ebba thrust out her arm like a sword, the money clenched in her fist.

"How far?" the conductor yelled over the noise of the bus's clanking engine and honking horns in the street below.

Ebba burst into tears, just as she'd been coached.

"To the grave of my dead mother," she sniffed.

The conductor hated crying of any kind so he took her money without any questions but looked down at her heaving shoulders.

"See you get off where you need to because I don't know where she's buried." Then he walked to the stairs, weary to death of his routine. What the hell did he care about some kid's dead mother? As a parting gesture he kicked a basket of ripe tomatoes off the roof splattering red pulp and seeds all over the street.

On the Ride to the Soccer Stadium

Bernardo and the doctor rattled along the ragged road to the abandoned soccer stadium. Teams had stopped coming to play because the General refused to give up the sterling silver Winner's Cup. In the past, ever since 1928, it had traveled from winner's town to winner's town. Ten years ago Josefina's team had been the winner, and for several years after that, but when they finally lost, the trophy was never surrendered because the General pretended he couldn't find it. In truth, he wouldn't let it out of his sight.

Finally, the Soccer Association decided it was easier to wait for the General to die rather than die trying to remove it from his house. Retaliation to those who didn't go along with the General's slightest whim was swift and brutal. The last man who had tried to reason with the General regarding the huge cup was found dead in a ditch holding his tongue in his hands because it had been cut out of his mouth.

It was rumored the General used the trophy as a catch-all for loose change which he donated once a year to the parish priests so they could buy Spanish brandy and Cuban cigars. Payback for the exoneration of the General's sins and to spread the word that the General was a generous man.

Dr. Vidal was unraveling the history of his tyrannical assistant over the noise of the truck. "I had just lost my wife when this woman came on a tourist ship from Panama City. She'd run out of money so the captain called me. She had a little problem, he said, so as a favor to him I made an appointment to see her. But as soon as he was sure that she had reached my office, he left the dock and sailed away, leaving her stranded. She was exotic and loud. I thought she was very festive... at first." The doctor waved his perfumed handkerchief in the air in a festive manner.

"She had a terrible burn. It seems that she'd fallen asleep in the sun and her big bare breasts, which she had unveiled on several occasions for the captain, were bright red." The doctor stopped to blow his nose before he went on.

"I had to ice them to ease the swelling and I tried to be gentle as I rolled her generous assets in the clattering cubes but she seemed to enjoy the pain." The doctor sighed and closed his eyes, replaying the sequence in his memory. Then he smiled. "She had a mouth like a pump. Anyway, I hate

Ebba and the Green Dresses of Olivia Gomez in a Time of Conflict and War   195

her and she hates me, but I keep her. She likes the money I stick on her rump after she's greased herself up. She likes to take off her clothes and slide around on a rubber sheet."

They'd reached another fork in the road so Bernardo used this opportunity to change the subject.

"Which way do we go?"

The doctor cleared his throat and looked around, sat up higher in the seat and pointed. "To the left and pull right up to the gate. They know me," he smiled.

Hortence Grace rounded the corner on her way to church and saw the bullet-shaped sedan that had taken Ebba away from the cemetery. She stopped, pretended to adjust the doily bobby-pinned to her hair and peered in the tinted windows but all she saw was a man asleep in the driver's seat. His head was thrown back and his mouth wide open because he was snoring. Hortence Grace decided that the owner must be inside so she hurried up the steps and into the cool dark vestibule.

The place seemed to be empty so she walked to the very first pew, genuflected, got down on her knees and prepared to pray.

"I can't stand much more of this!" she heard a woman shout. It was coming from the confessional cubicle that she herself intended to enter.

"You have to talk to my son. My brother won't help. He doesn't have time for his sister."

Then Hortence Grace heard the priest.

"Mrs. Lobos, please... lower your voice in the house of God. He doesn't listen if you shout."

"And you don't listen unless I do!"

"That's not true, Mrs. Lobos. Now, a few Hail Marys should set everything straight."

"Hailing the Virgin Mother has nothing whatsoever to do with my son."

"Mrs. Lobos, where is your faith?"

"Faith?" Mrs. Lobos choked out a laugh and then got serious.

"Speak to him Father, or I'll have you removed." Then she yanked back the black velvet curtain on the confession cubicle, walked into the sacristy where Hortence Grace appeared to be deep in prayer and stormed out of the church.

Hortence Grace, who'd heard every word, counted to ten, crossed herself quickly and rushed outside just missing Father Lyle who emerged from his side of the confessional worried that someone might have overheard the outburst. Seeing that no one was there, he breathed a sigh of relief and to settle his churning stomach, pulled a flask of Calvados from his robe pocket and took several sips before going back to wait for the next sinner.

Outside, Hortence Grace lingered at the top of the stairs to watch Mrs. Lobos get into the car that the driver then struggled to turn around in the narrow street. Finally, after several forwards and backs and scraping the car's bumper against the church wall he drove out of town as Hortence Grace took off her shoes and ran all the way home.

Bernardo's face was streaked with sweat as he struggled to carry the doctor up the steep stadium steps. Dr. Vidal had held up the plastic bag he'd found on Mercedes' desk and told the guard at the gate that he was the doctor of the Chief Inspector and delivering a package that required giving it to the Chief Inspector in person. Without asking any more questions the guard had pushed the lever that opened the metal fence and told Bernardo to park his truck by the stairs because the elevator wasn't working.

They were midway to the top when the doctor told Bernardo to stop. "The press box is right over here," the doctor pointed to a door a few steps from where they were standing. "After you put me down and catch your breath, leave the package on the shelf on the door. I bring the Chief Inspector Ritz crackers," the old man smiled. "They're his favorite and I know where to get them." Bernardo nodded, pulled a clean white handkerchief out of his pocket and wiped his face. The doctor shook his head.

"Only men with wives or overly attentive mothers have the luxury of a handkerchief that's been ironed."

Bernardo didn't answer. He just put the handkerchief back in his pocket, placed the package on the shelf and leaned down to scoop the old man up in his arms, but the doctor shook his head.

"Actually you can leave me here," he whispered. "I've seen what you're about to see." Bernardo looked at him suspiciously but the doctor just laughed.

"Don't worry Bernardo. You're with me." After taking a moment to think it over, Bernardo climbed the rest of the steps and stepped under the rickety roof that provided the uppermost seats a few splinters of shade. Even so, the sun beat down on Bernardo's back as he looked around the stadium and realized it was shabby and falling apart. The glory days of championship soccer were definitely over. The seats were broken and sagging, the shattered scoreboard was missing its letters and numbers... everything was in a state of decay except the stadium floor, which was covered with sawdust and neat as a pin. Uncertain of what he was supposed to see, Bernardo looked down at Dr. Vidal and shrugged, but the doctor just motioned to take another look. This time as Bernardo turned back there was a slight breeze and he noticed an indistinguishable stench. He leaned over the safety railing and noticed a fringe of dark dirt bordering the newly dug trench rimming the stadium floor. An air-horn honked a short nasty blast into the quiet.

Bernardo almost jumped out of his skin but watched as a battered dump truck with a canvas cover drove though one of the tunnels into the stadium and puffed its way around the periphery.

Four men suddenly appeared with shovels to guide the truck as it backed up to the open trench, ground the gears and the fully loaded truck started to tilt with a resounding screech to its full 90 degrees so its clandestine cargo could slide into the ground. Then the four men with shovels pulled their white sanitation masks over their faces and went to work.

That's when Bernardo thought he saw a body. It was just a glimpse, but it certainly seemed like that was what it was. He rubbed his eyes. Perhaps it was just the heat or his imagination, but the sliding cargo kept filling the ditch and he saw another shape just like the first, then two more. The last were fully exposed...men with their hands tied behind their backs. Now Bernardo understood the faint stench and that the men wearing masks were layering the carpet of decaying bodies on the stadium floor with sawdust and lye.

Bernardo eased back to the stairs and hung onto the railing so he wouldn't collapse. The doctor called out in a cheery whisper.

"Time to go. Time to come back to me now," he said just as Bernardo's knees buckled.

"Easy, Bernardo. Maybe you should sit down on the step."

Bernardo's breath caught in his throat and he started to retch. His insides rolled over, spewed out of him in a hot stream and cascaded down the stairs in tear-shaped trails.

"What the hell is going on?!"

A man was shouting from inside the press box, now used as the command center for whatever was going on down below. He opened the door with the plastic bag on the shelf full of crackers.

It was Sergeant Ruiz, the black-haired officer that had stood in the door of Rosa Guillermo's living room with his wife. Sergeant Ruiz, the most recent recipient of Bernardo's son Ariel, whom he and his wife had named Thomas after Sergeant Ruiz' father's father. The doctor reached out and grabbed the Sergeant's sleeve as he stepped outside.

"Bad pork and the elevator is broken. Too many stairs. My assistant's not used to the stairs."

"Then why the hell is he up there," the Sergeant snapped.

"He didn't want to put me and now you in the middle of his mess," the doctor said innocently. "Give us a moment," he continued, "then have someone come with a hose."

As Bernardo continued to retch, the doctor waved at Sergeant Ruiz as if to say this lowly function was far too mundane for a man of the Sergeant's stature to stand and watch. Then he told the Sergeant the purpose of the visit.

"What you see on the shelf is for the Chief Inspector. I am his doctor and we are very old friends."

Sergeant Ruiz picked up the plastic bag and averted his eyes. The sight of someone puking always made him gag.

"Well, tell your assistant to hurry up," the Sergeant said. Then he darted back inside his air-conditioned box and slammed the door on all of the discoveries he might have made.

Bernardo took out his handkerchief and wiped his mouth. He looked at the doctor and started to speak but the doctor held up his hand and put his finger to his lips.

"Later for talk, right now is for breathing." Bernardo nodded and gulped in air. Finally he got to his feet and maneuvered around the putrid path to the doctor where he managed to gather him up and start back down the stairs.

"I've seen the girl," the doctor whispered hoarsely, "the one you brought with her mother, she's alive. I've seen her myself."

Bernardo reeled back from shock upon shock and the smell of the doctor's cologne. He tripped and stumbled, but caught himself just in time.

"We should sit down," the doctor ordered. Bernardo managed to find a scrap of shade for the doctor who handed him a flask and motioned to Bernardo to have a drink. After a moment Bernardo handed it back and whispered.

"What about my son?"

The doctor fanned himself with his perfumed hankie. "That is another matter. He's alive but I have no idea where." A sob escaped before Bernardo could stop it. Panicked, the doctor reached across and covered Bernardo's mouth with his hand and spoke in a low voice.

"Patience, Bernardo. At least you know he's alive." Anguished, Bernardo looked at the doctor then out into the arena.

"And my sister..."

Dr. Vidal didn't say a word, just sat still as a stone and shook his head while Bernardo choked back another sob.

"What is this?" He muttered faintly.

"Hell," the doctor rasped and took a drink from the flask before he put it back in his pocket. Neither of them moved until the stadium truck blasted a nasty, sharp honk.

"Time to go," the doctor announced. Bernardo nodded, took a last look around before he stood and picked up the doctor, cradled him against his chest like an old baby and hurried down the stairs as the doctor whispered in his ear. "I'm sorry Bernardo, but I thought you should know."

M r. Bravo stood in the General's garden under a large green umbrella photographing family after family standing next to a life-size replica of the General made out of cardboard and wood. A hand-painted dove with glass eyes was attached to the General's cardboard shoulder rounding out the tableau. Fathers in uniforms displaying their medals and young mothers in matronly dresses with matching shoes, purses and hats held small babies or expressionless children who bore no resemblance to the parents whatsoever. Everyone seemed so anxious and fearful that Mr. Bravo went out of his way to straighten an officer's tie or adjust the angle of a wife's chin, a baby's blanket, a little girl's bow, or entice a young boy to take his hands out of his pockets. He tried all sorts of things to invite a smile or make them laugh, but all of his finger-snapping and crossed-eyed trickery didn't inspire a single change on their blank faces.

"Something's not right," he thought to himself as he looked through the lens of his box camera.

Nobody made any noise; the children didn't play, there wasn't any laughter or music and no one disobeyed. There weren't even any birds in this garden, or bees. Occasionally a fly would buzz around someone's head, but nothing as majestic as a butterfly or a moth or a ladybug flew over the wall. Not even a spider or a trail of ants.

"Odd," Mr. Bravo muttered to himself as he ducked down and threw the black cloth over his head to photograph the third to last family in line. Just to be safe he always snapped another frame before Rosa Guillermo could step in to shoo the family away and shout "Next!" at the top of her lungs. Then with the help of a young soldier wearing a gun, the next family waiting in line was ushered into the tableaux.

"Over here and hurry," Rosa Guillermo motioned, fluttering her hands.

Another young solider sat at a large metal table writing down names and addresses.

"Fer-nan-dez," Rosa Guillermo enunciated tightly as she whisked the now photographed family to the refreshment table where plates of cookies and pitchers of red punch in paper cups sat on top of a festive paper tablecloth.

"Refreshments," she offered as she checked her watch and said to no one in particular, "Has anyone seen Sergeant Ruiz and his wife?" But no one answered and the Ruiz family was certainly nowhere in sight.

Rosa Guillermo hurried back to Mr. Bravo focusing the camera. She looked at the new family in front of the lens and pretended they were lovely.

"Lovely," she said out loud and nodded to Mr. Bravo, "I'll be right back," as she rushed away to find out if anyone had called the stadium where Sergeant Ruiz was stationed to see when he was coming.

Mr. Bravo shook his head. Lovely was the wrong word to describe dull eyes and numb expressions. He began to wonder if someone was spiking the punch, but he took the picture and the extra frame and that of the next family and the one after that before Rosa Guillermo came back in a fit of frustration.

"They've been held up," she said as if it were a personal affront. "Now there won't be a picture and we need every family to be photographed."

Mr. Bravo shrugged. "I could go to their house," he suggested.

Rosa Guillermo looked at him as if he'd saved her from eternal damnation. "You would?"

"If it's not too far."

"It's on the base."

"Shouldn't be a problem," Mr. Bravo said, packing up his camera. Rosa Guillermo went on and on extolling his kindness with effusive phrases as she wrote down Sergeant Ruiz' address and told the young soldiers to help Mr. Bravo load his equipment into his truck. Then just before Mr. Bravo turned the key in the ignition, Rosa Guillermo had an inspired idea.

"Excuse me, Mr. Bravo. But tomorrow night, would you be free?" Mr. Bravo looked puzzled.

"It's the General's birthday and photographs might be a nice touch."

"You mean, photograph the General?"

The General hadn't been photographed in years.

"No, Mr. Bravo, the guests. We'll give you a corner and set it up." Not particularly thrilling, he thought, and was getting ready to say no.

"And of course we'll pay..."

So without a moment's hesitation, Mr. Bravo settled on a price and took off in the direction of the base but just as he disappeared around the corner, Sergeant Ruiz drove right up to the garden with his wife and new son Thomas which threw Rosa Guillermo's rigid plan right out the window. She tried her best to cover her dissatisfaction as he told her about having to clean up after some guy who'd puked all over the stairs. She kept nodding understandingly until she saw the boy run to the statue of the General and reach up to touch the glass eye of the dove.

"Don't!" flew right out of her tight mouth. Everyone froze as she tried to recover.

"If it fell, I wouldn't want you to get hurt," she gushed.

The Sergeant's new son, Thomas, stared at her unflinchingly and pulled away when she hurried over and tried to take his hand. Rosa Guillermo sighed and shook her head.

"The photographer just left," she said. "He's on his way to your house…"

"They'll never let him in the gate," Sergeant Ruiz replied. "Ever since Chavez misplaced those kids nobody gets inside without papers."

"Oh," Rosa Guillermo visibly sagged then suddenly remembered what she had in her purse.

"Wait," she trilled. "I brought a camera, just in case."

So after a lot of fretful focusing and repositioning the family to catch the remaining light, Rosa Guillermo snapped a shot. In fact she took four just to be safe, but in every single one the sun hitting the glass eye of the dove bounced a reflection into the lens of her camera and blotted out the face of Sergeant Ruiz' new son with a big white dot.

The Pink Blanket

Hortence Grace was cooking a chicken she'd killed for supper, basting it with sugar and salt and fresh lime and chili and butter, a pinch of pepper, a square of bitter chocolate and other secret spices. She was creating a memorable meal to celebrate her newfound fury. For the first time in weeks she felt alive, like waking from a dark troubled sleep. When she heard Gloria rumble into the courtyard, she ran from the stove, ran out the door, ran into the courtyard where Bernardo saw her running with her arms outstretched, so he turned off the ignition and ran to meet her too and they embraced in the fading sun as if they had just met and fallen in love.

Revelations of the day spilled out of their mouths like a fountain of butterflies, everything except Bernardo's trip with the doctor. That, he decided to keep to himself, decided not to burden Hortence Grace with what he'd seen and only tell her what the doctor had told him... Ariel was still alive.

Together they visited Rebecca and her altar. Together they talked to Tobias, but only about the health of Pasqual, his favorite dog. Hortence Grace decided, just like Bernardo, not to burden her husband with the secret of Tobias and why he had to hide. Together they fed the chickens and pigs and then together all of them sat down at the table outside and ate Hortence Grace's memorable meal with a little red wine and music from Ebba's Victrola.

Finally, when they were sure Rebecca and Tobias had fallen asleep, Hortence Grace and Bernardo pulled out the pink blanket, the one that Ariel had been conceived on, and unfurled it in the garden. Then they took off all their clothes and made love under the stars and the moon, accidentally rolling off the blanket onto the ground as they pounded into each other's flesh over and over and fell asleep in a bed of wild sweet peas. Just before dawn they woke up covered in mud and started to laugh. Then they turned on the hose and washed each other off, let the water flood them as they slammed into each other one last time before running into the house to make coffee which they took outside and drank as the sun crept up over the morning glory covered wall.

Joan Tewkesbury

BAD SMELL AND AN UNRULY PARROT

An occasional sour stink had begun to make its presence known in the bedroom of Mrs. Lobos. The penetrating effects of Ebba's wet underwear tucked in the unused drawer were quietly worming their way into the maroon velvet drapes, the dark-blue Persian rug, the heirloom bedspread from Spain, the ivory linen sheets from Italy, and the ivory silk lampshades not to mention all of the clothes in all of the drawers. Since the weather had been cool, the magnitude of the rancid smell hadn't really had the opportunity to explode into its full pungent potential. Besides, Mrs. Lobos assumed that the scent had come with the rain so she lit perfumed candles and waited for the sun to come out and dry away the mysterious offending odor.

The first time Mrs. Lobos really noticed a full foul whiff, she was waking from her afternoon siesta and it gave her a fright. What if it was coming from herself? What if the great matriarch Lobos was starting to decay? She'd rushed out of bed and into the bathroom where she stripped off all of her clothes and as best she could, checked out every hair, nail, crevice and fold of her well-cared-for old body. She sniffed, searched, studied and spared no crease until she realized that she might be bent but every limb was lean and taut and the gamey odor was not coming from her. The relief she felt was palpable but she still took a precautionary soak in a tub of perfume and poured Chanel Number Five into a small porcelain bowl the consistency of an eggshell, which she left on the marble sink to work some magic.

After that she went on another systematic search for her pale yellow silk shawl. When it first disappeared she'd rummaged through the big chest of drawers, but missed Ebba's damp cotton underwear because the deposit was just a few hours old and tucked in the back. Though she never hung her shawl, she hunted for it in the closet and looked in her mother's chest at the foot of the bed and on the hat rack in the hall. She even checked Mr. Lobos' closet and the chest at the foot of his bed that had belonged to his father. Mrs. Lobos ransacked every room in the house and after turning everything upside down, she called all of the help into the kitchen and accused them of stealing her favorite garment.

"It's the only hint of color, the only ray of sun permitted to a widow who must always wear black," she whined. "So who took it and how could you be so cruel?"

Then she sobbed a dry sob, a sort of goose-like honk, as she remembered the silver-haired banker, a friend of her dead husband's, who had professed his love while probing her secret chamber on the couch in the living room after a dinner party given in his honor and after her husband had gone to bed, passed out really, from too much to drink.

The banker's fingers had found their way into an uncharted interior zone that Mrs. Lobos never knew existed. His fingers had unlocked the inside of her insides and given her the most joyous surprise of her adult life. However, he had disappeared after that dinner party night never to be heard from again except for the pale yellow silk shawl, which he had sent from Paris with a note thanking her and Mr. Lobos "for such a lovely time."

Mrs. Lobos had worn the shawl ever since. Day in and day out, it was a constant reminder of what her body was capable of. On one occasion she had even tried, discreetly of course, to place her husband's fingers at the departure point of the banker's exploration, hoping he would be curious and venture inside, but he'd been shocked and pulled away quick as if his hand had been seared on something extremely hot. After that he'd rolled over on his side to face the window. She had cried, softly of course, so he wouldn't know but in the morning he was gone, crept away in the night when he was sure she had fallen asleep, vowing never to return. After all, they had a son. He decided that she was just one step away from the deviant behavior of a particular kind of woman that the priests had warned him about when he was a boy.

With nothing further between them, Mrs. Lobos became hollow and holy, an acolyte of the church, a stickler for details and rules and literal righteous meaning in every nuance. She decided joy only brought pain. However, she wore the shawl like a coded message, a concealed hope for some kind word or some sign but it never came, so she wore it to remind herself that once there had been magic and she was determined not to forget.

"Who took it?" she demanded at the very minute the parrot started to scream, "Cuckoo, Cuckoo!"

"God," thought Mrs. Lobos, "I hate that bird." Her attention divided, she dismissed the help and hurried down the hall shaking her fist and yelling, "Shut up, shut up, shut up, you rotten fowl!"

The parrot had been a gift from her brother the General because the bird had been given to him and he hated it too. Some cruise ship captain had left it as a token of his appreciation. Truth be told, someone had given the parrot to the captain and he didn't want it either.

"Cuckoo, Cuckoo," it shrieked over and over and over.

Finally Mrs. Lobos looked up and screamed, "I will kill you! I will skin you and boil you in oil so you'll shut up and there will be a great festival because everyone hates you!"

The bird started to laugh, then screamed... "Hates you, hates you, hates you." Then he ruffled his feathers, extended his wings and boldly shat on the red tile floor. "All gone, all gone," he screamed.

Mrs. Lobos picked up the broom and started to swat the perch. Her intent was to topple and kill, but the parrot outwitted her by flying out the open door into the courtyard which he circled twice before landing in the tamarisk tree blooming lacy pink flowers and screamed, "Dance with me, honey," three times in a row.

"You son-of-a-bitch," Mrs. Lobos snarled.

She looked around to see if anyone had heard her but there was nothing but emptiness everywhere. She threw down the broom with so much force it chipped a tile and she made her way to the shed to find the gardener so he could get out the hose. She'd heard someone say if a parrot's feathers got wet they couldn't fly, so she devised a plan. She and the gardener would trap the beastly bird and drown the pest.

BLACKMAIL

Hortence Grace was standing inside of Olivia's closet, actually Li Choo's closet with all of the kimonos and underwear and diaphanous doodads. Mrs. Marquez' finished dress was folded neatly over her arm and she was holding a Zippo lighter in her hand. As she surveyed her surroundings she was calm and still, unlike Olivia who was standing in the center of the room spilling flesh and shouting one thing right after the other at the top of her lungs.

"What on earth are you doing? What is going on? How dare you threaten me like this!" And... "Get out of my closet!!!"

Mrs. Marquez stood frozen in the doorway, shocked and stunned and angry. Never mind Hortence Grace standing in Olivia's closet. How dare Hortence Grace hold Mrs. Marquez' new dress hostage after all the trouble Mrs. Marquez had gone to arrange this arranged meeting?

"And you," Olivia turned to Mrs. Marquez and pointed. "You put her up to this!"

"Me?!" Mrs. Marquez shouted. "I did not!"

Olivia clomped along the tile floor overflowing Li Choo's marabou-covered "Come Fuck Me" flip-flop high heels and tried to slap Mrs. Marquez, but only struck air because Mrs. Marquez saw her coming and ducked.

"How dare you!" Olivia shrieked.

"How dare yourself!" Mrs. Marquez shrieked back.

Hortence Grace cleared her throat and spoke in a loud, clear voice. "Ladies!"

Both women turned.

"You're missing the point."

Olivia blinked but Mrs. Marquez fumed. "I don't know what this is about, but how dare you include my dress in your own private revolution."

Hortence Grace looked at her and shook her head. "It's not your dress yet, Mrs. Marquez. Only when I hand this dress to you and say to you 'here is your dress,' will it be yours. So... once again, Olivia. Where is my son and your cousin, by the way?"

"Distant cousin, not by much," Olivia defended.

"And what has happened to Ebba?" Hortence Grace continued.

"That brat," muttered Mrs. Marquez, feigning innocence.

"I told you. I don't know!" Olivia shouted.

Joan Tewkesbury

Hoping to deflect her lie, Olivia stared right into the eyes of Hortence Grace with false self-righteous fury and tried to put the lunch at Mrs. Lobos' house out of her mind, as if it had never happened. Hortence Grace wasn't buying the loud indignant voice or the infuriated look. She studied Olivia calmly and flipped open the Zippo.

"If you want to keep all of these spider webbed, 'what-cha-ma-call-its' from going up in smoke, you'll mention the name of someone for me to talk to." Mrs. Marquez opened her eyes wide and blinked several times, trying to maintain the look of an innocent bystander as she bent down and picked up a bobby pin that had fallen on the floor.

"I don't know what you're talking about," Olivia lied again, making herself sound more offended than before.

Hortence Grace pulled a delicate salmon-colored brassiere and matching G-string that looked like a slingshot off a hook, flicked the lighter, lit the lace and tossed the whole burning business into the middle of the tile floor.

"Oh God, no! My favorite ones!" Olivia cried out in shock. She rushed as best she could in the too-small flip-flopping shoes, to the little pile of flames and tried to stamp them out. When that didn't work, she tried to pick up the undies with her pudgy little fingers, but they were so hot she dropped them on the tile floor, fell to her knees and watched them turn to ash. Olivia looked up at Hortence Grace with tear-filled eyes.

"How could you?"

Amazed at Olivia's heartfelt reaction over a pile of threads, Hortence Grace remained unmoved and reached into the closet again where she found something filmy in purple and moved it toward the flame.

"No!" Olivia wailed in desperation.

"Oh, for heaven's sake," Mrs. Marquez exclaimed, commenting on everything at once.

That's when Hortence Grace moved the flame from under the underwear to the hem of Mrs. Marquez' new dress.

"Stop!" Mrs. Marquez screamed in horror. Then she rushed to Olivia, pulled her to her feet and hissed.

"Get up, for God's sake and say something, or I will."

"Me? What am I supposed to tell her?" Olivia sobbed pitifully.

"Tell her about the lunch."

Olivia stopped crying at once, narrowed her eyes and looked at Mrs. Marquez coldly.

"What lunch?"

"The lunch!" Mrs. Marquez snapped, watching the flame begin to scorch the dress.

"Who said anything about lunch?" Olivia flared.

"Who doesn't matter," Mrs. Marquez said, realizing she'd already let the cat out of the bag.

"How do you know about lunch?" Olivia was working herself into a frenzy.

Hortence Grace looked at the women with the detachment of a prison guard and continued to brush the hem of Mrs. Marquez' new dress as she walked toward the closet. She was sick and tired of this ridiculous wrangling.

"Stop!" Olivia screamed at the top of her lungs. Hortence Grace turned around and there was a very long moment where no one moved or said a word. Finally, Olivia leaned over and whispered in Mrs. Marquez' ear so Mrs. Marquez nodded and made her way to Olivia's overflowing desk. Hortence Grace blew out the flame and closed the lid, waited for Mrs. Marquez to find a pen and a piece of paper which she brought to Olivia who grabbed them out of her hand. Then Olivia wrote something down, folded the paper into a tight square which she handed to Mrs. Marquez who walked back to Hortence Grace while Olivia seethed soberly.

"I never told you this name, understand... just because Bernardo is a relative in the distance..."

"Actually your third cousin," Mrs. Marquez offered.

"Just you shut up!" Olivia exploded and got very red in the face.

Hortence Grace didn't say a word, just flipped the Zippo back open, placed it under the clothes then nodded to Mrs. Marquez.

"Open it up so I can see, but don't you dare look."

Mrs. Marquez did as she was told. She tried to act nonchalant but her hands were shaking so badly she dropped the paper.

"How can you be so clumsy?!" Olivia shouted, still red in the face.

"Use both hands," Hortence Grace coached.

Finally Mrs. Marquez bent down and, using both hands, picked up the paper and turned her head. Hortence Grace read the name Rosa Guillermo, once, twice, three times, until it was engraved in her memory. Then she lit the Zippo, moved it to the paper and watched it go up in flames. Mrs. Marquez yelped and let it drop to the floor where it burned itself out. After that, Hortence Grace backed away from the closet and the two speechless women then went to the door and looked at them darkly.

"We'll never speak of this," she said and started to go.

"Wait a minute," Mrs. Marquez yelled. "What about my dress?"
Hortence Grace turned around.

"In due time, Mrs. Marquez. I'll need to repair the hem…"

She held up the dress so the women could see the burnt edge.

"Unless you want to wear it like this…"

Mrs. Marquez opened her mouth to speak, but decided not to, so Hortence Grace folded the dress back over her arm and walked right out of the house.

The Birthday Party

On special occasions the enormous iron gate in the shape of the General's mouth, and the only entrance from the street to the General's estate, was left open as if it was giving a speech. To the General's way of thinking it was the perfect way to enter a party. Once inside, guests were greeted by armed guards bordering the gaslit path, Mariachi musicians playing loud music, tables sinking under the weight of too much food and ice sculpture replicas of the General's head replaced frequently so they wouldn't melt. Waiters carrying trays of vintage champagne moved among the guests and the wandering peacocks who occasionally called out because it was mating season.

Since the General continued to be covered with a blanket of blame regarding the Kind Predecessor's death, he brought a chorus of singers to perform operatic selections at intervals even though the General couldn't stand that kind of music. It was his tip-of-the-hat tribute to try to whitewash the disastrous event. "Who knew Jorge Maximo couldn't drive a tractor?" the General would innocently intone to any one who would listen so he could relinquish all responsibility for the fatal stunt.

A silk-draped gazebo with sheer curtains stood in the center of the ballroom floor so the General could sit inside; see everything going on in every direction and occasionally wave to the crowd while remaining mysterious. In truth it was the General's beacon of protection against germs. Of late, according to the General's manservant Raoul, the General was more terrified of microbes than an assassin's bullet. In fact, again according to Raoul, the General was so afraid to breathe everyday air he now wore a mask and only inhaled pure oxygen from the compact green tanks that accompanied him everywhere.

In another corner, Mr. Bravo, standing on a box, was taking portraits of the overdressed guests in front of a garden tableau even though it took every ounce of self-restraint not to turn his camera around and photograph everything he'd been told not to, including Mrs. Lobos sitting on a tiny gold leaf chair by the gazebo steps sipping Scotch. She was waiting for a lull in the parade of sycophant well-wishers standing in line to wave at her brother through the curtains and wish him a long life.

Mrs. Lobos hated her brother for various reasons, but most of all because she was a woman and he was a man. After her husband died and because she was a woman, therefore a second class citizen according to the authorities, and because her brother was the General and a man, he was entitled by law to take charge of her husband's estate which included the money, the house, her son, his education and anything she wanted to buy including the clothes on her back. Every aspect of her life he governed except for the parrot and it was understood that if Mrs. Lobos wanted to continue living life in the manner to which she had become accustomed, she was obliged to keep her opinions to herself but right now she was brimming with suspicion.

Why was her brother hiding behind those ridiculous curtains? Allowing himself to be isolated like a pupa in a cocoon was odd. And why was he waving like that? Not seeing him up close and personal gave her the creeps. He loved being in public and puffing out his chest to support the mountain of medals he'd purchased from a mail order catalogue. Fully convinced that something secret was going on, Mrs. Lobos downed the rest of her Scotch in one big swallow, stood up and pushed her way to the head of the line.

Beyond the crowd, Mr. Lobos stood at a mirrored table eyeing a towering cake. Then using his thumb as a spoon, he scooped chocolate frosting from the bottom layer and watched the General's Commander, accompanied by the not so attractive winner of the Central Committee Beauty Pageant, stop to talk to Father Lyle and Johnny Orteez who stood next to Rosa Guillermo sipping punch. He allowed himself another thumbful of frosting as Mercedes, sparkling in sequins and leopard skin mules, pushed Doctor Vidal onto the dance floor and when they reached a tall woman spray-painted silver she made sure the doctor was face to face with the woman's lively silver crotch undulating in time to the music.

"Cousin Lobos?"

Mr. Lobos turned around. Jesus Fidel was approaching, smiling a great warm smile. Mr. Lobos smiled back, something he did so rarely that it hurt his cheeks. The two men laughed and embraced. It had been a long time.

"How are you?" Jesus asked.

"A bit older," Mr. Lobos smiled. Jesus took a step back and looked him over.

"Still in the business of your mother?"

Mr. Lobos smiled then laughed a short stabbing laugh that plunged into the air like a dagger. "Unfortunately yes," he replied and Jesus nodded.

"I have my own hardship there. A mother without a husband is like a boat without a rudder."

At that very moment Olivia, swathed in a kimono of purple silk made especially to accommodate the increasing enormity of her sprawl, pushed in front of Jesus to look at the cake and almost knocked him over. She'd stopped all pretense of dressing as a widow. In fact she'd stuffed all those clothes in the incinerator of her old house and burned them up. Unfortunately for Mr. Lobos she caught his eye as he turned to avoid her.

"Where's the kid?" Olivia blurted out. She couldn't resist but neither could Jesus.

"Is that you, Olivia Gomez?" he asked. Olivia turned and gave him an imperious look until she remembered who he was. Then she stuck her finger in his chest menacingly.

"Your family is responsible for the death of my husband."

Jesus laughed and dismissed the attack. "And you're looking expansive and very well-dressed."

"How I dress is none of your business," she said, ignoring his tone.

"And the death of your husband isn't mine. We don't go in for afternoon murder."

Olivia had had a few margaritas so she pointed her purse at Mr. Lobos and giggled. "But you have other perversions."

"It seems like you have a few of your own," Jesus countered and Mr. Lobos, having heard enough, turned to Olivia and spoke in a low, threatening tone.

"Walk away, Mrs. Gomez, or I'll have you removed."

But Olivia laughed and gave as good as she got. "You have no power here," she taunted. "Your mother might, but not you." Then she turned and announced to anyone who cared to listen. "He's fixated on a kid."

Mr. Lobos nodded to one of the guards.

"Some brat from Elena because no woman wants a man who can't stand up to his mother..."

"Can you stand up to his mother, Mrs. Gomez?" Jesus smiled.

But before Olivia could respond, Sergeant Ruiz arrived with his partner and Mr. Lobos turned to him and spoke very politely.

"Would you please take the mayor's widow to the front of the line? She would like to give birthday greetings to my uncle before she leaves."

Olivia turned and spoke to Mr. Lobos from the back of her heart. "The only thing I want to give the General is a way out of his misguided existence." Then she hurried away before the guards could grab her but they followed closely, not letting her out of their sight.

"What kid?" Jesus was curious about what Olivia had set in motion.

The band was playing something sentimental so Mr. Lobos sighed and looked at his hands. He cleared his throat and considered telling a lie. "It's complicated," was all that he could manage but when he looked back up at Jesus, the truth jumped out of his mouth with unadorned honesty. "A girl named Ebba."

Jesus swallowed his surprise but didn't want to jump to conclusions. After a moment he asked, "Perhaps she gives you a little bit of joy?"

Caught off guard, Mr. Lobos blinked. He'd never thought about joy. Joy wasn't something he'd ever considered. He shrugged, but there was a hint of possibility in his gesture.

"Potential... Promise... A new beginning?" Jesus continued.

Mr. Lobos looked at his cousin with a sense of wonder, a feeling he'd only felt once or twice and only fleetingly when he was a boy.

"I don't know," he replied, a slight tingle of "perhaps" in his voice, a tone he wasn't familiar with.

"So where is she, this... joy?" Jesus persisted instead of revealing any details or facts. Mr. Lobos looked worried.

"I don't know... she ran away in a white dress."

"A white dress..."

Mr. Lobos interrupted full of anticipation. "With wings. Have you seen her?"

The band continued to play as Jesus looked at Mr. Lobos but decided against telling the whole story so he shrugged. "Perhaps..." he ventured. "Perhaps it was she, waiting for a bus. I seem to recall a white dress... but it could have been someone else, a bride maybe, with a veil not wings. You're sure about the wings?"

Mr. Lobos nodded then slumped in his suit, drifted from hope into gloom and resignation.

"Lobos," Jesus said sharply. "Quit building dungeons in the sky." Mr. Lobos looked at Jesus who leaned closer but kept all of his information to himself.

"No need to rush into the dark while there's still light."

Mr. Lobos shook his head and spoke the truth. "No reason not to."

Jesus looked at his cousin in dismay. "Change the climate, Lobos. Bad weather doesn't have to be a constant condition. Think about others. Think about mothers and fathers living with inconsolable grief while you search for your little piece of joy. Meanwhile it's time to sing 'Happy Birthday' to our unworthy uncle." Then Jesus turned and walked away with his secret leaving Mr. Lobos trying to swim to the surface of his confusion.

THE BIRTHDAY SURPRISE

Mrs. Lobos had been waiting for twenty minutes and was losing patience fast, especially when Olivia Gomez marched up the gazebo steps with military escorts and flounced to the head of the line. But, much to Mrs. Lobos' delight, the gazebo guards rushed up and stopped her, denied her permission to get near the sheer curtain let alone go inside. For whatever reason, they said Olivia's birthday visit was a possible plot, a threat against the state and the General himself. After all, she was the widow of the dead mayor and might be carrying a bomb in all that purple silk. Besides, wearing bathrobes, getting rid of her children... who could be certain of what Olivia was up to?

Olivia shouted and stamped her foot, which shook the curtained gazebo with collapsible force, but more guards arrived and Sergeant Ruiz threatened to put her in prison. In retaliation, Olivia shouted, "Just you try," and hit the youngest and skinniest soldier with her purse so Sergeant Ruiz grabbed her arm and ushered her out of the building.

Though delighted with Olivia's inglorious dismissal, Mrs. Lobos' suspicious nature now went into high alert. Something about that gauzy chamber was wrong; she could feel it in her bones.

"I send you congratulations on the threads of my song...

A song to adorn this moment's celebration and the bright reason of this day."

The reconstituted song of Jesus Fidel drifted across the ballroom. Everyone seemed transported by his voice but he sang with his eyes closed so he didn't have to see who he was singing to or come to terms with or try to understand the cruel man who was also his uncle. His uncle who had stolen another man's last heartbeats and stuffed the overworked muscle into a jar. A tangible reminder that it was possible to seize power by way of fear.

Mrs. Lobos sighed. The song bored her. Jesus' voice was nice but it had always been nice. When he was a child, her sister had sent him to Spain and Vienna to sing for God. Mrs. Lobos had prayed hard not to be petty and that her son would develop a talent too, but Jesus had been born with his. Even she couldn't dispute that kind of gift.

Mrs. Lobos looked around. Everyone, including the guards, was completely transfixed by Jesus' soothing tones. So gathering her gumption she decided now was the time to find out what was going on behind the gauzy curtain.

"All good wishes to you and may laughter and happiness fill your heart with joy."

The last note of the song lingered, suspended itself in the air as Mrs. Lobos slipped inside the sheer cocoon.

Applause broke the silence, thunderous applause and shouts of, "Bravo, Bravo! Sing more! Bravo!" which completely camouflaged Mrs. Lobos' shout of shock. Her piercing "Oh my God!" went completely unnoticed in the grand scheme of birthday party entertainment. There in front of her was her brother laid out like a corpse. He appeared to be breathing but comatose. His head was raised and he was propped up on an electric lounge chair in a position posturing life. A plastic tube ran from the compact green tank into his nose, whispering oxygen through his nostrils and pushing vapors toward his lungs. Beside the tank, a mechanical attachment was rigged to the General's arm on a timer, lifting it up on alternate cycles. Three minutes, then every seven, sending his fingers fluttering through the air in a random gesture that resembled a wave. Mrs. Lobos covered her mouth so no other sound could escape. She couldn't believe what she was seeing so she stepped a little closer and discovered that the General was a dummy.

When the whole ballroom swelled with "Happy Birthday to you," she noticed a trap door by the electric lounge chair. After a bit of a struggle, she managed to pull it open and creep down the interior unguarded steps to the ballroom floor where, because of her diminutive size, she slipped unnoticed through the gazebo bunting and into the crowd, but luck was not on her side.

In an unfortunate coincidence, all of the toilets at the party had backed up at once and Raymond Valdez was summoned to come right away to unclog the pipes. So because it was a party, he brought the new love of his life, Juanita Chavez and his assistant Salvador Ernesto to help with the big flush. Salvador brought the object of his grand passion, Lilly Narada dressed in something skintight and yellow that clung to her bell pepper body.

In fact, if Lilly's white fox chubby hadn't slipped off her shoulder and onto the floor she would have missed seeing Mrs. Lobos slither away from the gazebo. And, noticing the look on Mrs. Lobos' face, Lilly picked up her fur and rushed right over to tell Mrs. Lobos that just that morning she had seen it in the cards. Mrs. Lobos was going to experience a terrible shock.

BLOWOUT

There was a sharp, nasty explosion of rubber and metal and Ebba woke with a start. After a terrible thud and bumping with furious flapping, violent slapping, dragging and sparking against dirt and rocks, a lashing lurch caused a jolting stop and a drop to one side. As a result, an enormous sack of jalapeno peppers split open and engulfed Ebba in a mountain of waxy green.

"A fucking flat," someone shouted.

Confused, Ebba looked up at the star-filled sky. After a moment she remembered she was on the roof of the bus going to Elena. The driver, now attempting to limp up the mountain on three wheels and a rim, finally lost control and the bus plunged into a ditch, pitching Ebba into a metal luggage rack where she gashed her arm and it started to bleed.

For a few moments it was still as a tomb. The driver had been knocked unconscious and people were trapped inside, but little by little men started to shout, pigs began to squeal, women screamed, children cried and the chaotic noise burst into the quiet like a bunch of rockets.

Except for Ebba, the passengers on the roof hurried to the ground shouting impotent instructions in the dark.

"Push the handle, push down on the handle! It opens the door!"

Then the men started yelling at the women inside to move across the aisle, to the side nearest the road so their accumulated weight wouldn't cause the bus to roll over.

Ebba watched blood from the gash drip onto her dress so she tore a strip off the hem using her teeth and wound it tight around her arm the way she'd watched Hortence Grace wrap Bernardo's arm after an accident with his saw.

On the ground below, the door finally banged open, but the bus made another shift so there was a lot more screaming as everyone inside hurried onto the road. Finally after they dragged the unconscious driver out of his seat, the bus groaned, slid down deeper and wedged itself firmly in the ditch. A few men dropped into the trench in order to jostle the bus into a more upright position. Back and forth, back and forth, they pushed and pushed and on the roof Ebba was tossed from one side to the other, her white funeral flowers spilling all over the place as she struggled to keep from falling off.

Down below, the women's excited voices, shrill and piercing with after-the-fact terror, filled the deserted road as they reviewed the entire experience in contradicting detail.

"The last curve, the first puncture, the explosive blast, the twisting, the bus out of control, the tossing inside. The slide. The drop."

Finally, with the help of a few robust younger girls, whose combined weight was more than all of the men, they managed to attach chains and ropes and slowly, bit by bit, pull and push the old bus back onto the road.

After the initial cheer that comes with such an accomplishment, obscenities unraveled like firecrackers on a string and blame ignited in a blaze.

"The driver was a dunce, the driver was a son of a bitch, the driver was drunk, the driver was deranged, he was getting a divorce, he was suicidal..." Finally the driver came to, but someone punched him in the jaw so he passed out all over again just as the younger men rushed up to the roof to the heap of retread tires mixed with Ebba's flowers.

"Looks like Hermillio's front yard," one of them said. Then all of them started to laugh. They had survived. They were alive and all that was left to do was change the tire. After they finally found one with a little bit of tread they went to work. They could hardly wait to get to the next cantina so they could tell everybody about the colossal crash.

"The massive accident, the near death experience, the uncertainty, the danger, the peril, the heroism of the bus driver..."

Someone had revived him with a little tequila and now he was turning the facts into a mythic tale of gigantic proportions.

"The pitch dark night... Everyone sound asleep... Suddenly, bandits with guns, the cause of the first swerve and only his supreme skill kept them from sliding off the mountain, the explosion, the saving of terrified women and children from the enormous depth of the ditch..." choruses and choruses of story. Soon someone with a guitar was setting it to song.

Ebba yawned and decided that now was as good a time as any to relieve herself in the bushes. She adjusted her hat and jumped to the ground as one of the women started to sing so no one noticed Ebba as she ran up the side of the mountain and disappeared.

ATTEMPTED ROBBERY

Mrs. Marquez thought she was about to die or pass out. The road up to Hortence Grace and Bernardo's house was steep and the chain on her pink bicycle kept slipping. Besides it was dark as pitch, but she didn't dare turn on the wobbly light even though she'd fallen over once already and didn't want to do it again. Finally, when she could see the shape of the house, she got off the bike and walked it to the gate, leaned it against a post and hurried across the courtyard trying not to crunch the gravel.

The closer she got the faster her heart beat and the more leaden her legs. When she reached the portal, one of Bernardo's peacocks screamed and scared her to death, caused her to step backwards and twist her ankle.

"Shit!" she hissed. In pain, she limped to the long bench against the wall and knocked over a bucket of bulbs waiting to be planted in the garden. Luckily the peacocks screamed again and covered the noise, but Tobias was a very light sleeper so he woke with a start, hurried to his window and watched the lumpy shape of Mrs. Marquez move to the back door. Without waiting another moment, Tobias picked up his flashlight and darted into the hall, but he didn't turn it on. Unlike Mrs. Marquez, he moved like a cat and knew his way in the dark.

Once inside, Mrs. Marquez looked around. She had no idea where Hortence Grace kept her sewing. She'd only been to the house one time and since she had no sense of direction, she couldn't remember a thing about which room was where. Confident she would figure it out, she opened a door and found herself in Bernardo's workshop filled with wood and large machinery. Then as she turned to go, she ran right into the blunt metal end of a lathe and took the impact in her belly.

"Whuff!" she bellowed. This time no peacock screamed to cover the noise so she stood screwed to the spot and tried to catch her breath.

"Son-of-a-bitch," she muttered.

Tobias moved swiftly from the other end of the house, slid in and out of the doorways until he found a corner where he could wait for the lumpy shape to come out of his father's workshop and make itself known.

Mrs. Marquez, doubled over and limping, struggled into the dark hall where she decided that moving straight ahead would be her best bet. Still hidden, Tobias determined that the lumpy shape was a woman even before he smelled her "Jungle Gardenia" perfume and decided to wait to see what she was up to. In her twisted logic she had decided to steal the unfinished dress from Hortence Grace. She would get someone else to fix the hem, put it on, go to Raymond's house, dazzle him with its shine, win him back and live happily ever after.

Mrs. Marquez glanced in Tobias' room, but it was too dark to see his empty unmade bed. She looked in Rebecca's room too and the kitchen, the living room. Not a trace of what she was after. Finally she turned and saw the open door at the end of the hall and caught a glimpse of her new dress, draped over a chair.

Overcoming her various aches and pains, she rushed forward as quickly as she could and entered the bedroom of Bernardo and Hortence Grace. She was so intent on what she was about to do that she didn't even look to see where she was and just as she reached out to claim the dress, Tobias turned on his flashlight and caught her red-handed.

"Oh my God," Mrs. Marquez cried out and dropped the dress on the floor. She tried to dodge the beam of light but came face to face with the double barrel of Bernardo's gun. He'd been waiting since the first tiny crunch of gravel. Behind him, Hortence Grace stood, shielding her eyes from the light.

"Mrs. Marquez?" she asked in disbelief.

"What!" Mrs. Marquez snapped. The jig was up.

"What on earth are you doing?" Hortence Grace asked as she lifted the dress off the floor.

Mrs. Marquez watched Hortence Grace fold the garment over her arm and broke down in utter despair.

"You have no idea." She began to cry. Hortence Grace cleared space in the chair and helped Mrs. Marquez sit down so she could rock her broken heart.

"He's... he's... been sidetracked," she sobbed. Hortence Grace immediately understood. She motioned to Bernardo to put down the gun and told Tobias to turn out the light, help Mrs. Marquez to the kitchen and put on the kettle for a cup of chamomile tea. Finally, when Mrs. Marquez was out of sight, Hortence Grace dropped the dress into her cedar chest and locked the lock with a special key.

In the kitchen, Mrs. Marquez drank the tea and displayed her desperation in a variety of ways. Hortence Grace kept nodding with considerable compassion given the circumstances, while Tobias loaded the pink bicycle into Gloria's flatbed and Bernardo started the engine so they could take her home.

In no hurry to go, Mrs. Marquez limped very slowly out to the truck. She had really enjoyed the conversation and care. Without Raymond there really wasn't anything to do. Not that they had ever done much but a little of not-a-lot was better than nothing at all.

Dark was turning to dawn. The bus was finally back on the road inching its way up the steepest part of the mountain when a grey sedan breezed past on the narrow incline, cut them off and forced the bus to stop so quickly it tossed most of the sleeping passengers onto the floor. The brakes were so worn they started to slip and the hand brake wasn't holding so the bus began to roll back down the hill and everyone started screaming.

One of the men dressed in a shiny suit got out of the car and shot a hole in the front tire which brought the bus to an immediate halt. Given what they'd all gone through with the flat, the driver was so enraged he shouted his complaints to the man when he boarded the bus. However, he shut right up when he saw the drawn gun. A second man, also dressed in a suit but shorter, climbed in right behind the first and turned on a high-powered light which he shined in everyone's faces. Row by row, seat by seat, he checked the floor, disturbed grandmothers, children, chickens and a couple of pigs but what he was looking for didn't seem to be there. That's when the first man shouted.

"Look on the roof!" and continued to point his gun at the crowd.

Everyone was quiet, listening as the short man climbed up the stairs and overturned anything still standing. Baskets of produce, fruit, then the luggage, the tires... anything that he could kick, spill or throw. He was looking for Ebba, but all he found were a few white paper flowers, which he added to the mess below.

Then because he hadn't found her, he pulled two men trying to sleep to their feet and forced them down the steep steps at gunpoint. Once on the ground he pushed them into the back seat of the grey sedan and shot holes in the rest of the bus tires. After that he and his partner drove away with the two men, leaving everyone on the bus silent and stranded in the middle of the road.

Back at the ditch, where the women had sung songs in the road while the men fixed the flat, Ebba, despite all of the noise and commotion, had crept under a pinion tree and fallen asleep. Now the sun was rising and after waking up to the sound of the birds, she looked around and realized that the bus was gone. She was completely alone except for a row of ants. She exhaled a shaky little sigh and blinked. She took off her hat and found a few coins, but who knew when there would be another bus or if it would stop. Frightened or not, Ebba decided now was not the time to wait around or take chances on the road. She clamped on the hat, crawled out from under the tree and started to climb up the steep mountain wishing that she had a drink of water.

Joan Tewkesbury

A Very Bad Stink

It was hot. The air was heavy and humid and still without a whisper of wind. An intense, rancid smell, so foul it took your breath away, filled the bedroom of Mrs. Lobos and made her gag as she rolled over in bed. Her eyes darted over the pillows and sheets half expecting to see something dead. After a moment, she got up and ran to the window, threw open the wooden shutters, but there was nothing out there but flat morning light and hazy gray sky. It was already hot at seven.

"Graciella!" She yelled, pulling her robe off the chair and slipping her arms through the sleeves as she rushed into the hall. "Lobos!" she shouted, stopping to bang on his door. Then with no thought or consideration, she threw it open, but her son wasn't there and the bed was neatly made.

"Lobos?" she shrieked her surprise. "Dammit... where are you?"

She started back down the hall, running into Graciella and all of the household staff, including the gardener, coming as fast as they could.

"Where's my son?" Mrs. Lobos demanded.

Everyone looked blank and shrugged except for Graciella who blurted. "Gone."

"Gone? Gone... where?"

Now Graciella shrugged, but suddenly she was distracted.

"Boy. Something sure stink bad."

Mrs. Lobos didn't know where to put her rage first.

"That's why I called!" Now all of them covered their noses with aprons or sleeves or anything else that was handy, and confirmed.

"Pew... smell very bad stink."

"Then find it and get rid of it!" Mrs. Lobos shrieked.

The gardener deciding to go first, took a deep breath, tied his handkerchief over his nose, hoping to dull the smell of whatever it was, and trudged across the threshold into Mrs. Lobos' room with the others close behind. Once inside, the pregnant cook had to turn back for fear of being sick, but the rest of them determined that the odious odor was coming from the chifforobe. So, gagging and coughing, they began to investigate drawer by drawer.

Nothing in the world offended Mrs. Lobos more than others rummaging so probingly through her personal belongings. Folding and putting away was one thing, but this was extreme invasion and she had no choice. She certainly didn't want to be the one to discover the source of the god-awful smell. Drawer by drawer, article by article, Graciella made piles on the floor of stuff to throw away or wash while Mrs. Lobos stood in the doorway covering her nose and mouth with a tiny towel to make sure nothing was taken.

Finally, when Graciella opened Mrs. Lobos' not-for-everyday-use underwear drawer, the smell was so rancid they had to rush into the hall for a gulp of not-quite-so-smelly air before going back to find the sour source. Step-in by step-in, some of them already tinged with mold, Graciella delicately removed all of the underpants row by row.

Fed up with how much time it was taking, Mrs. Lobos rushed in and pushed Graciella out of the way. She thrust her hand all the way to the back and felt something warm and soft and moist. She shuddered, but gathered her courage, grabbed the glob and pulled it from its hiding place. Ebba's once white cotton underpants, still a little damp and reeking with putrid stench, had turned a bilious shade of mildew green. Mrs. Lobos' horrified scream rocked the room as she dropped the garment in the middle of the floor, rushed to the bathroom and slammed the door just as her stomach rolled over and turned inside out. She barely made it to the bowl. Inside the bedroom Graciella picked up Ebba's revenge with the rest of the things to be burned and assigned the burden of removing the chifforobe to the gardener and one of his helpers so it could be destroyed.

Inside the bathroom, rolled up in a rug, Mrs. Lobos tossed herself from side to side, bellowing blasphemies so loud that it caught the attention of the parrot that had never been recaptured and was living wild in a nearby tree. Cocking his head, he caught the riff of her rage and began to bellow back an exact replication only a few decibels louder and brighter.

Frightened by the sound, Mrs. Lobos stopped her cavalcade of fury but when she determined that the echo was the parrot and determined the parrot's exact location, she picked up the crystal soap dish that weighed several pounds and ran out of the bathroom, ran out of her room, ran down the hall to the front door and out into the courtyard.

As luck would have it, the parrot was so absorbed in his own baleful bellow he never saw it coming. By the sheer will and focus of her intensity, Mrs. Lobos pitched the heavy soap dish into the tree just as the bird shifted his position and made direct contact with the oncoming hunk of Baccarat which knocked him out cold.

After a shocked squawk and a shattering explosion of broken glass on the flagstone below, there was a silent fall and a terrible thud. The parrot hit the ground, broke his neck and died. Needless to say, Mrs. Lobos responded with stunned disbelief, which threw her into such disarray she sat down and wept because she'd murdered the bird.

QUEASY

Walking up the road to Rosa Guillermo's house, Juanita began to feel queasy. She and her mother were on their way to clean house and iron shirts, but all of a sudden the smell of Juanita's own Coty cologne was making her sick or maybe it was the pork tamale her mother kept nibbling like a candy bar, but whatever it was, she had to duck into the scrub.

"What the hell is going on now?" her mother sniped. Juanita was too sick to answer so her mother sat down by the side of the road and finished her tamale.

"Come on quick, we gotta go," she shouted into the bushes. A moment later Juanita emerged, pale and shaky.

"I can't," she said as her knees buckled and she fell to the ground scaring her mother to death.

"You hot? You got the grippe?" she asked. Juanita's mother started fanning her daughter with her purse. Juanita shook her head and shrugged so her mother eased her into a little piece of shade under a bush.

"You eat something funny?" Juanita rolled her eyes. Worried, Juanita's mother looked at her watch.

"Well, I gotta go or we don't get paid."

Juanita just nodded. "I'll stay," she whispered.

Her mother shook her head. "What if somebody comes?"

Juanita waved her off. At that moment her only desire was to die, but to make her mother feel better she tucked her legs up under the bush. It wasn't perfect but it would have to do.

"No rides from strangers," her mother warned.

Juanita nodded. She was very sleepy.

"I'll tell Rosa Guillermo, maybe she could come in her car..."

Juanita shrugged. She really didn't care as long as she could lie down right now and sleep. Her mother tried to cover her worry with cheer.

"Okay... goodbye... too-da-loo." Juanita waved weakly. Her mother waved back then darted onto the road and ran the rest of the way to work.

Juanita, on the other hand, went straight into dreamless sleep and didn't move for an hour and fifteen minutes, so when she woke up she felt as if she'd never been sick. Easing out from under the bush she stretched and after brushing herself off, started up the road.

She hadn't gone very far when she heard a horn honk. Having been carefully coached by her late husband, she moved way to the side, put the scraggly bushes between herself and the car driving by, but there was another honk and someone called her name. A quick look sideways revealed Mr. Bravo in his truck.

"Want a ride?" he called out cheerfully. "You shouldn't be walking alone..."

Before Mr. Bravo could finish his sentence, Juanita was climbing into the truck and telling him how grateful she was for the lift.

THE NOTE

Mrs. Marquez stood pounding her fists on Raymond's front gate but no one answered. His truck wasn't there either. She walked around to the back of his house and thought about scaling the wall but the neighbors' mangy dog appeared baring its teeth, so she hurried back to the front and stood wondering what to do. Finally, after checking her watch a couple of times, Mrs. Marquez opened her purse and took out some paper, searched for a pen and hoped for inspiration. She would write a note; but what to say? After thinking and thinking she finally wrote...

DEAREST RAYMOND, IF I HAVE DONE
ANYTHING TO OFFEND YOU... I AM
SORRY...

She stopped and looked at what she had written. Maybe Raymond had found out she'd stolen Bernardo's kid's picture. For a split second she panicked. She wadded up her first attempt, tossed it into her purse and searched for another piece of paper. All she could find was a recipe for coconut cake, but it was blank on the back so she started over.

DEAREST RAYMOND, WHERE HAVE
YOU BEEN? I AM FOREVER YOUR
MARIA... A THOUSAND
REVOLUTIONS AROUND YOUR
PECKER...
I AM GIVING YOU ME WITH LOVE...

Then she applied more red lipstick and kissed the words with her gooey lips. After that she folded the note and pushed it into a crack in the gate. She kissed the gate too and let out a little sob before she turned and hurried away.

Joan Tewkesbury

Juanita's mother was ironing in Rosa Guillermo's kitchen while Mr. Lobos stood in the living room yelling...

"What do you mean, you don't know? Of course you know. You plan every contest, every abduction, every barren couple's match-made baby..." He took a deep breath and yelled even louder.

"Where is she?!"

"I must advise you to lower your voice," Rosa Guillermo shouted back.

Mr. Lobos laughed a dry laugh.

"Do you think that you're a secret? You think no one knows what you do? What you traffic?"

Juanita's mother adjusted the angle of the ironing board so that she could get a better look. She'd never been aware of the "government goings-on" of her boss. Rosa Guillermo feigned innocence and smiled.

"Mr. Lobos, why are you so upset? Maybe you'd like a nice cup of tea..."

Mr. Lobos turned around, picked up a paper-thin teacup and saucer on a nearby table and dropped them on the tile floor. Shattered Limoges went everywhere. Rosa Guillermo tried not to flinch. It was the last in a set belonging to her great-grandmother.

"I'm not interested in tea," Mr. Lobos said darkly. He began to prowl around the room, stopped at the bookshelves, opened every book, searched the pages.

"Just what are you looking for?" she asked in a high-pitched whine just as he found it. "There it is... There... that's it!" He laughed, beside himself with discovery. Suddenly she realized what he was after and shouted in a completely different tone. "Don't! Don't you dare touch that!"

She tried to put herself between Mr. Lobos and the thick book stored inside the glass front cabinet requiring a key. Too late. Mr. Lobos had already used his elbow to break the pane.

"Stop...!" Rosa Guillermo yelled. She started to hit him with a needlepoint pillow she'd given to her brother for his birthday, but Mr. Lobos grabbed it and threw it on the floor with the broken Limoges. He held her off with one hand while delicately withdrawing the volume he was after with the other.

"You have no right to destroy my house!" She started to go for her brother's gun, but Mr. Lobos took hold of her arm and whirled her around until they were face to face.

"Why don't we look at this together," he smiled. Then he glimpsed at Juanita's mother peeking around the kitchen corner. "Maybe she would like to see it too."

Rosa Guillermo looked up and caught Juanita's mother snooping. "Just you keep ironing," she shouted. "This doesn't concern you!"

Juanita's mother did as she was told. She even turned her back, but that was so she could watch Mr. Lobos in the kitchen mirror as he sat down and squeezed right up next to Rosa Guillermo on the faded blue couch.

"Would you like to open the book or should I?" he asked. Rosa Guillermo looked at him with enough hate to cause an explosion. He just laughed and lifted the cover.

"NEWBORNS AND BABIES," it said. After that, pages of pictures of babies that all seemed to look the same so he moved to the next category.

"CHILDREN THREE TO SIX." Mr. Lobos looked at these more closely... Boys, girls, some fat, mostly thin, but all with haunted eyes. A few with black "post-it" dots, stuck to their faces.

"I assume these have been taken," Mr. Lobos said, already guessing the answer.

"It means that they are dead," Rosa Guillermo stated the facts. Mr. Lobos gave her a long look and shook his head.

"This wasn't my idea," she said in her defense. "He's your uncle."

"That may be true, but I don't do his bidding," Mr. Lobos replied and turned the page. "SIX AND OLDER," it announced.

Mr. Lobos looked and looked, but found nothing of interest there either. Next he poured over the "NEW FAMILY" pictures taken by Mr. Bravo including the snapshot of Sergeant Ruiz, his wife and new child, taken by Rosa Guillermo. The face of the Ariel was so obliterated by a spear of light he couldn't make out any features. Mr. Lobos closed the book. He pulled the paper pictures out of his pocket, placed them on the table then grabbed Rosa Guillermo by the bun on the back of her head, twisted her around and forced her to focus.

"What about these?" he pointed. "What about her?"

Rosa Guillermo looked at Ebba's face. It seemed familiar, but she couldn't remember why or where she'd seen it.

"Where'd you get this?" she asked and tried to break free. Mr. Lobos tightened his grip.

"And him?" Mr. Lobos was pointing to Ariel. She let out a gasp before she could stop herself.

"What? What do you know with your college education?"

"Nothing," she said, trying to cover her tracks and imagining he would believe her. "You're hurting me," she wailed.

Mr. Lobos drove his knuckle into the soft spot at the base of her skull.

"Do you know this boy?" Rosa Guillermo let out a loud cry. The pain threw her off guard and in her struggle to keep all of her information locked up tight behind her lips, one name escaped whether she wanted it to or not. "Mrs. Marquez... she knew the boy."

Then she pulled free, pointed to the door and shouted with flourish. "Get out of my house!" But Mr. Lobos was already going to the door with the book tucked under his arm and the paper pictures back in his pocket.

"You can't take that book!" she screamed. Mr. Lobos ignored her. He stuck his head in the kitchen and told Juanita's mother to have a nice afternoon then walked outside, moved across the courtyard whistling tunelessly. Juanita's mother smiled, opened a fresh stick of gum and continued to iron the pillowcases and sheets while Rosa Guillermo wept on the tile floor with the broken china and tried to load her brother's gun.

THE PROGNOSIS

Hortence Grace sat on Dr. Vidal's examination table looking into Bernardo's eyes. The doctor was roaming around her fully clothed body with a stethoscope; last stop at the region near her belly to listen to the percussive symphony inside.

After a moment or two he handed the instrument to Bernardo and showed him exactly where to place it to hear the sound best. Bernardo did exactly as he was told... waited... listened... Finally he looked at Hortence Grace and smiled as Dr. Vidal announced, "Twins."

Exhausted, hot, barely able to lift one foot in front of the other, Ebba moved sluggishly through the scrubby trees. So far she'd been safe in the clumpy camouflage, but up ahead a two-tone brown van sat partially hidden in a bunch of ragged piñon trees rocking back and forth in time to the loud music underscoring the moaning and groaning inside. Ebba stopped right where she was and didn't move a muscle. It was hard to determine what form of human torture was going on in the two-tone container. Edging closer to the blackout windows trimmed in chrome she began to hear a woman's voice.

"Yes, yes, yes," the woman yipped, then..."God, oh God, oh God, don't you dare stop!"

Ebba wondered if it was some sort of religious celebration like the Penitentes with whips but whoever it was seemed too distracted to harm her, so she moved closer to see if she could see inside the long window in back. At first it was only shapes moving in a blur of shifting and turning, but then everything paused on the intense deep note of a female moan.

Ebba mashed her nose right up against the tinted glass and recognized Mercedes, naked and sweating, sitting astride a shortish man shaped like a barrel also naked and sweating. He was covered in body hair like fur, from his neck to his ankles. The pause didn't last very long. In fact it only seemed to provoke an even greater series of athletic maneuvers as Mercedes called out.

"Oh Commander... Command me, Commander..."

First up, then down, then up and down and up and down in double time, then triple. The whole van began to squeak and tremble and shake, squeak and tremble and shake and Mercedes' famous flapping breasts took on a life of their own threatening to smack whatever got in the way, but then the Commander took charge. In one heroic shift, he lifted himself and Mercedes off the bed and spun her around until she, now on all fours, was facing Ebba still watching in the tinted window. Behind Mercedes, the Commander was up on his knees moving with the speed of a pneumatic drill, slapping her big bouncing butt and shouting... "Uh, uh, uh..." All this in time to the music's beat. Then bending over Mercedes' back he grabbed her giant breasts, which for some reason, caused her to arch back and shout... "Uh, uh, uh..." in another key. Faster and faster, racing on and on, their duet louder and louder, so caught up in the ride of a lifetime that they never saw what they were facing in the tinted window.

Ebba was glued to the spot. Torn between boredom and suspense, she couldn't believe her eyes. Their voices got louder and louder with every undulating thrust until there seemed to be a final monstrous whoop crescendo of everything all at once and the rocking van shuddered to a stop followed by a giant crash because the bed lost its mooring and fell to the floor just as the music ended.

For some reason that Ebba didn't understand, the couple inside started to shriek with laughter. They laughed so hard they were having a hard time catching their breath. Fearing the worst, Ebba darted away from the window hoping that whatever it was she'd just witnessed would get Mercedes in a whole lot of trouble.

As Ebba started up the steep hill behind the van she heard the music start again so she started to run and when she got up to the top she tripped and fell into a company of crows that went clacking into the sky, disgruntled over the disruption of their dinner. Looking up from the ground, Ebba came face to face with their feast. Face to face with one of the men riding with her on the roof of the bus, only someone had scooped out his eyes and he was missing his ears along with his hands that had been cut off and stuffed in his mouth where his tongue used to be.

Ebba's scream ripped into the dirty, dry silence as she got up and ran away.

MRS. LOBOS GOES TO VISIT HER BROTHER

Olivia looked at Mrs. Lobos in the rearview mirror of the Packard. She was pale and tucked up in the corner of the back seat like a mummy.

"Watch it!" Mrs. Lobos shouted sternly. Olivia barely missed running over the armed guard at the General's gate. She was getting better but still hadn't quite mastered the finer points of driving, yet she did manage to stop just in time and roll down the window.

"We're here to see the General," Olivia said imperiously.

The disgruntled guard looked in the back seat.

"Who's that?" the guard demanded, recoiling from Olivia's "Joy" perfume.

"The General's sister and me... Olivia Gomez."

Mrs. Lobos rolled down her window and shouted at the guard.

"Hermina Lobos. I'm the one he's going to see. This woman is just the driver."

Olivia rolled her eyes, but the guard had already checked his clipboard so without further discussion he pressed a button and opened the electronic gate. Olivia stalled the engine, started it again and ground the gears, but lurched inside just before the gate clanged shut. She drove up the long driveway bordered by lush green lawns and manicured by gardeners spread all over the grass like ornamental birds. She parked in the assigned space without incident where two guards met and escorted them up the stairs to the huge house.

One of the maids let them inside and ushered them into the main meeting hall designed for discussions between heads of state or people from other countries, which were few and far between since the soccer "Winner's Cup" fiasco. Now it seemed the only use of the room was for workmen involved in estate upkeep and repair. Today it was Raymond trying to fix the drain in the powder room.

Twenty minutes passed before an earnest young soldier entered with a tray of coffee and cakes.

"Where is he?" Mrs. Lobos demanded. The young man ignored her question, clicked his heels and walked out of the room. Olivia attacked the dainty little cakes with gusto.

"Is that all you ever think about?" Mrs. Lobos demanded. Olivia ignored the remark and poured herself a cup of coffee.

"You're big as a barn," Mrs. Lobos continued.

"Coffee with cream and sugar?" Olivia asked Mrs. Lobos politely.

"Black. I take my coffee black," Mrs. Lobos snapped. She grabbed the coffee Olivia had just poured for herself right out of her hand, sipped a sip and made a face.

"A dog wouldn't drink this swill."

Olivia didn't care. She poured another cup, which she drank down demurely, her little finger crooked. It was filling a void.

After more long waiting, the door opened at the other end of the room and Father Lyle stepped inside smiling a worried smile.

"Good morning ladies. Sorry to keep you waiting, but I hope you enjoyed the cakes," he said, directing his remarks to Olivia. Mrs. Lobos was already on her feet.

"I came to see my brother, not you."

"Well..." the priest started to say.

"Where the hell is he?"

"Mrs. Lobos, please. There is no need for that kind of language..."

"Then cut the baloney," Olivia said with a mouthful of cake.

"That'll be enough out of you!" Mrs. Lobos threatened. She was not about to be upstaged by Olivia Gomez. But Olivia didn't care. She just shrugged and kept on chewing while Father Lyle started over.

"Mrs. Lobos..."

"I want to know what's going on," she interrupted.

"Well... quite a lot..." was all he managed to get out before a terrible crash cut him off and everyone jumped. Raymond had dropped his wrench.

"Sorry," Raymond called out from the powder room floor.

"And shut the door!" Mrs. Lobos shouted. Which Raymond did as Mrs. Lobos stood up and started to pace.

"I want to know about my brother's health," she barked.

"Well, Mrs. Lobos..."

"I want to know what's with the oxygen and the dummy with the electric hand. I want to know if my brother is real or stuffed. I want answers and I want them now."

Then she coughed, leaned on the arm of the chair, started breathing heavily and her eyes seemed to bulge. Father Lyle, thinking she might faint, got up quickly to help but to his relief she was already settling into the seat. He handed her a glass of water and sat down too.

"As you know," he said softly, "there have been numerous threats on your brother's life."

"It's not a wonder," Olivia interjected. Both Mrs. Lobos and the priest ignored her remark. He continued and nodded in Olivia's direction.

"In the past little while, ever since the death of your husband, Mr. Gomez... the threats have gotten worse... so..."

"So? So what?" Mrs. Lobos interrupted.

"So, I've been told to tell you that every precaution has been put in place to protect the General's immune system."

"What does stabbed or shot have to do with his immune system?"

"That's just the point..." the priest tried to explain.

"What's the point? The tank turns into a bulletproof vest? The electric arm turns into a gun?"

"Mrs. Lobos! Let me finish!" Father Lyle said firmly. He was fed up. Mrs. Lobos gave him a withering look but leaned back and gave him her full attention.

"Every effort is being made to keep your brother alive. Possibly these methods don't suit you and you will never understand... but... he is being looked after by the best in the 'looking after' business. Should there be any change, you'll be the first to know."

Mrs. Lobos didn't respond. She pulled out her handkerchief, faintly scented with mildew, and dabbed her eyes.

"He and my son are all I have left." The priest nodded and assumed an attitude of patient compassion as Olivia continued to work on the cake. Feeling more in charge, Father Lyle talked more about the General's condition, explained that right now, at this very moment, the General was in the hands of specialists so there was nothing to fear.

Indeed it was true. Right then, at that very moment, a team of specialists was testing a better, less mechanical wave for the mechanical arm of the life-sized mechanical General mannequin. And hidden from view in one of the gardens below, the General, fit as a fiddle, was at work with another specialist, Pancho, a direct descendant of Pancho Gonzales, on the General's tennis serve.

It was the General's most sincere wish that when things calmed down and weren't so uncertain, he would enter the "National Tennis Tournament" and win another silver cup to stand alongside the one for soccer. In the meantime he hoped to win some money from his opponent, the Commander, who emerged from the locker room, flushed and late and a little bit tired, but ready to play.

Drink Coca-Cola

Mr. Bravo helped Juanita into Dr. Vidal's office. He was going to leave her in the waiting room but there was so much shouting behind the green velvet curtain he felt compelled to stay.

"You're not the boss of me," Mercedes was yelling.

"When I say nine, I mean nine," the doctor yelled right back. There was a loud smack and Mercedes burst out of the drawn curtain holding her cheek.

"You shop worn sow!" Dr. Vidal shouted.

"And you can't get it up!" She screamed right back, not noticing anyone or anything except her broken fingernail.

"Then get out," Dr. Vidal growled. He rolled into the room like he'd been shot from a cannon, pulled off his belt and lashed out at her backside with a snap.

"Dog in heat!" He yelled and made a direct hit. "Did you ride him like a bucking bronco?" He shouted over her yelp.

Mr. Bravo cleared his throat as doctor and nurse stopped to catch their breath and realized they weren't alone. A big silence captured the room until finally Mr. Bravo pointed at Juanita. "She's not well."

"I fainted," Juanita nodded hesitantly.

This gave Dr. Vidal, who was having difficulty restoring his dignity, something to focus on. He cleared his throat. "Anything else?" he asked.

"I got sick, it's the third morning in a row..."

At that very moment Mercedes opened a bottle of fixative to repair her broken nail, which overwhelmed the room with its sharp chemical smell. Juanita blanched and Dr. Vidal handed her the wastebasket just as she started to retch. After that, he wrestled the fixative out of Mercedes' hand and tossed it out the door into the street.

"Nooo!" Mercedes cried mournfully as if he'd thrown her child in front of a moving car. Mercedes started to run to retrieve it but the doctor caught her by her arm and smiled coldly. "Prepare the patient Mercedes, and bring her a cola." Then he gave Juanita a reassuring pat.

"Best thing for morning sickness is Coca-Cola."

"Morning sickness?" Juanita whispered. Dr. Vidal nodded with authority then handed the fouled wastebasket to Mercedes. After that he pulled the curtain aside and motioned to wide-eyed Juanita. "Won't you come in," he smiled.

Joan Tewkesbury

L illy turned over the last three cards in the spread and placed them in a formation that seemed revelatory. As far as she was concerned it put everything into perspective.

"That's it!" she shouted.

"What? What's it?" Mrs. Marquez wanted to know as she hunched closer to Lilly.

"There's a kid."

"A kid?"

"He's waiting in the wings."

"Whose wings?"

Lilly gave Mrs. Marquez a jaundiced look. "His mother's. She's pregnant."

"I am not," Mrs. Marquez defended.

"Nobody said you were."

"Then how can he be waiting if I'm not pregnant?"

"Are you nuts?" Lilly tossed out, full of impatience.

"Then who...?" Suddenly, Mrs. Marquez drew back in her chair and looked at Lilly in disbelief.

"No!"

"Yes," Lilly confirmed.

"How the hell can you know something like that?!" Mrs. Marquez was becoming hysterical. This was nothing Lilly hadn't experienced before. People hated to hear the truth. Lilly pointed her red fingernail at three configurations of cards in the spread.

"There, there and there," she said. "Fertile, fertile, and baby." Then she pointed to three other places.

"Soul mate, soul mate, fertile."

That was it. Mrs. Marquez stood up and yelled right in Lilly's face.

"She is not! I'm the one. I'm the soul mate! He belongs to my soul and I'm his mate. All that stuff you say you see is lies!"

Mrs. Marquez reached across and swept all the cards off the table with the back of her hand, which Lilly grabbed and squeezed as hard as she could. Then she stood pulling Mrs. Marquez to her feet until they were nose to nose and Lilly said in a threatening tone...

"Don't touch the tarot."

"You're hurting my hand," Mrs. Marquez whined.

"Good," Lilly said in a low rumble.

"And I'll touch what I want," Mrs. Marquez sniffed.

"No. No you won't." Lilly was emphatic. "You got bad karma. You got bad plans AND bad karma, so I want you to go home."

Mrs. Marquez jerked her hand out of Lilly's grip.

"And I want my money back."

"Not a chance."

Mrs. Marquez was not about to give up.

"You told me lies because you're jealous."

Lilly erupted with a huge laugh. "You got a mind going round like a hamster wheel. Now get out," Lilly said firmly.

Realizing she didn't have a leg to stand on, Mrs. Marquez picked up her purse, marched out the door and up the stairs.

"I hope somebody poisons you and your miserable dogs," she yelled as she opened the door. Lilly just laughed, turned the ghetto blaster to her favorite station, cranked up the volume and picked her cards up off the floor.

Outside, Mrs. Marquez drew her pistol out of her purse and shot the snarling dogs with soapy water as she hurried to get on her bike parked just outside the gate.

Before Raymond could bring the truck to a full stop at his gate, Juanita rushed to open his door.

"You have such good news!" she exclaimed. Raymond was grinning with gladness to see her and started to laugh. It couldn't be helped. Her joy was so contagious he slid off the seat, put his arms around her and she danced him around the truck while she told him that she, Juanita Chavez and he, Raymond Valdez, were going to have a baby.

"A what?!" Raymond stopped dancing.

Never in his whole life had Raymond ever thought about leaving anything of himself or his relatives behind. Before he met Juanita he'd felt like an old man with no future at forty-six and now... now Juanita was saying something about a baby.

"A baby," she repeated. She was staring up at him like a child, but she spoke like a woman.

"Mine?" he whispered. "My baby?" He didn't dare say it out loud for fear he was dreaming, but calmly and quietly she nodded yes.

"Mine," he said again out loud, but softly.

Turning this reality over and over, Raymond shook his head while Juanita watched him absorb the news, waited anxiously with quiet anticipation for the outcome of his response.

"My baby?!!" He shouted. "Your baby and mine!" Juanita just looked at him and nodded, so he picked her up and spun her around. "Your baby and mine!" He said over and over. Then he started to dance to the music of his shouting and danced Juanita around the truck. In his whole life he had never expected such a miracle. And Juanita, who had always wanted to believe in miracles but had never had the opportunity, felt like one had finally arrived. For the first time in her life she felt rich. So rich, in fact, she expected yellow canaries to come flying out of her mouth bursting with song.

Rescued

Ebba was borderline delirious by the time she reached the top of the mountain. So delirious she thought she saw the entrance to the cemetery but decided it was an illusion. Weak and afraid of who might find her and take her away, she decided to run to the gate to see if it was real. She made herself reach down to touch the red geraniums growing where Louisa Ortega had died. They were fragrant and soft and not an illusion. She was so relieved tears started rolling down her cheeks. Then she ran to the cemetery spigot, turned on the water and drank until she thought she might burst.

Ebba took off the gardener's hat and washed her face, hands and feet, let the water run through her hair but the tears wouldn't stop so she lay down on a nearby bench and hiccupped soft sobs in time to the music of Mr. Escalante's guitar. She closed her eyes but the image of what was left of the face of the man in the dirt wouldn't go away and when a truck stopped at the cemetery gate she panicked and slipped off the bench, hurried to her mother's grave, laid down and curled up in a ball.

Mr. Bravo got out of his truck and slammed the door. He was exhausted. The business between women and men was overwhelming. The expectations, the disappointments, everybody getting mad... the yelling and crying. Of course he was the first to admit that in these matters he had no experience, but everything he'd seen between Raymond and Mrs. Marquez and Juanita and Dr. Vidal and the nurse made him grateful that he was content to live alone with no children. Besides, why risk having kids if someone was just going to steal them?

So much ado about creating some little replica of yourself that usually caused trouble. Why all the excitement? After all, it wasn't like Juanita had just been welcomed into the gates of heaven by God. Mr. Bravo shook his head. He needed to go see his mother. He took a deep breath and carefully stepped around the headstones so as not to disturb the dead and hurried to her grave.

This was the place where he came when he needed a rest from life. Besides, he'd found a wreath of fuchsia plastic flowers at the market in Josefina with "Beloved" scrawled in day-glow letters at the top and was eager to place it close to his mother's heart. When he passed Mr. Escalante he tipped his hat and whispered his thanks for serenading the souls. Mr. Escalante just smiled and kept on playing.

When Mr. Bravo arrived at his mother's marker he placed the wreath on the ground, got down on his knees and prayed for protection. He was beginning to feel it might be necessary. He also asked Jesus to thank God for his recent employment even if it was for the government. After he crossed himself he stood up and noticed Ebba curled up in a ball next to the geraniums Hortence Grace had planted on her mother's grave.

He remembered something about her being gone and everyone's concern so he started toward her but worried Ebba might become apprehensive he stopped and called out.

"Excuse me, but are you all right?"

Ebba just nodded. She was too afraid and exhausted to form words. She hunched under the gardener's old hat and tucked tighter into her dirty dress. Mr. Bravo moved a little closer.

"It's all right," he said softly, the way you'd talk to a frightened dog.

"I'm not going to hurt you," he continued, "but maybe I could help." Ebba wasn't exactly certain what to say but he was short so she figured she could always run away if she had to.

"Have we met before?" he asked. "I'm Mr. Bravo."

Ebba nodded and remembered that he was running the movie projector at the festival of St. Augustine, but they had never been formally introduced.

"I'm Ebba," she whispered. Mr. Bravo extended his hand. After a moment Ebba reluctantly extended hers.

"Perhaps I could drive you home. I did know your mother. I never took her photograph or yours, but I've passed your house many times..."

Ebba's tears came on so fast they rendered her more speechless than before, so Mr. Bravo helped her to her feet. He put his arm around her so she could sob on his shoulder and they walked to the truck, gently encouraged by the music from Mr. Escalante's guitar.

M rs. Marquez parked the pink bicycle by her back door and walked inside.

"It's about time," Mrs. Lobos shouted, scaring Mrs. Marquez to death. She was sitting in a chair at Mrs. Marquez' kitchen table.

"Oh my God," Mrs. Marquez clutched her heart and gasped. One surprise after another was beginning to take its toll.

"Why are you here?" Mrs. Marquez said trying to catch her breath.

"I want you to arrange an accident."

Mrs. Marquez poured herself a glass of water from the jug and drank it down in a single gulp.

"I'd certainly like a glass of water too," Mrs. Lobos whined, "but that jug's too heavy for my delicate wrist." Mrs. Marquez picked up the jug and a glass and poured begrudgingly, splashing water on Mrs. Lobos' purse.

"Watch what you're doing," Mrs. Lobos bristled.

Mrs. Marquez was too hot to care. She took off her shoes and plugged in the electric fan. She had been looking forward to a nap.

"How'd you get here?" she yawned.

"Olivia. She's dropping that worthless priest at church."

Because Mrs. Marquez was not inclined to share, Mrs. Lobos moved her chair closer to the fan so she could benefit from the breeze.

"What kind of accident?"

"A tragic accident," Mrs. Lobos was emphatic.

"Who?" Mrs. Marquez poured herself another glass of water.

"She's right next door." Mrs. Lobos pointed with her thumb.

Mrs. Marquez rolled her eyes. "That again? She's not even here."

"She is responsible for the death of my parrot." Mrs. Lobos looked at Mrs. Marquez and smirked.

"And now she's loose and running around," Mrs. Lobos said defensively.

Mrs. Marquez shook her head. "Look, I got a lot of bad rigamarole on my plate, a lot of problems of my own."

"So this will be one less thing," Mrs. Lobos reasoned.

"She's not on my plate; she's on yours."

"Well, what about her mother? What about that?" Mrs. Lobos reminded.

There was a very long pause. Mrs. Marquez leaned further back in her chair to get the full benefit of the fan while she thought it over. Finally, after a few more gulps of water, she leaned forward and spoke very softly.

"Just what kind of tragic accident do you have in mind?"

SERENDIPITY

Olivia sat outside the Church of Martyrs. She'd dropped Father Lyle off hours ago, but she was still waiting for the guy from the gas station to come and change the Packard's flat tire. She'd phoned Mrs. Marquez from the rectory to say she'd be late and Mrs. Lobos had thrown a fit so Olivia just hung up. She was sick and tired of being at Mrs. Lobos' beck and call and listening to all those hush-hush, delicate conversations like they'd had with the priest. Who cared how long the General might last? In fact, maybe he should die so everyone could start from scratch.

Finally, as the sun blasted its last almost ready to set hot glare, some kid who could barely see over the steering wheel of his truck arrived to take off the tire. He whistled long and low out of respect and admiration for the Packard, but Olivia was in no mood for pleasantries or to hear the history of the world's best built car so she just pointed to the trunk and told him to hurry up.

As the kid went to work, Olivia moved to the last tiny triangle of shade on the church steps. She took one of Li Choo's fans out of her purse and waved it vigorously, hoping for a hint of circulation just as Raymond drove up in his truck with Juanita sitting right beside him. Both of them were grinning from ear to ear as he hurried to open Juanita's door and help her, ever so gently, up the stairs to the church. Before Olivia could grab hold of her fleeting speculation, she saw Father Lyle appear on the landing with Bernardo and Hortence Grace.

"Father Lyle!" Raymond called out excitedly.

"Raymond Valdez," the priest replied as Juanita and Raymond hurried to greet him.

"We want to get married right away." The priest tried to suppress some gas as he cleared his throat. He was still having trouble with his bowels.

"Well, that's very nice, but Juanita has only just become a widow. We believe grief should last for at least a year." He looked Juanita up and down.

"By the way, Juanita. I see you are not wearing black."

From her seat on the stairs, Olivia rolled her eyes and crossed her legs, which caught the attention of Hortence Grace who chose to wait before she said hello. In the meantime Juanita interjected proudly.

"We're going to have a baby," she said.

"A baby?" Father Lyle gulped, caught completely off guard.

"In December," she grinned.

"Just like Jesus," Raymond remarked and really meant it.

Father Lyle shook his head and smiled a tight little smile. "Well... this does put things in a different category."

Simultaneously, Olivia and Hortence Grace looked at each other, pictured Mrs. Marquez hearing the news and shook their heads. Bernardo, on the other hand, was grinning at Juanita and shaking Raymond's hand.

"It might be helpful for you to talk to my wife," Bernardo said. Hortence Grace turned back and looked into the young woman's eyes. Then she smiled and patted her own stomach.

"Twins. Our fourth and fifth so I'm happy to offer any advice." Juanita's eyes filled with tears.

"My mother isn't going to believe it has finally happened."

Father Lyle fluffed his robe to avoid all of this female chatter. He fiddled with his rosary and adjusted his privates. Being surrounded by so much fecundity made him nervous.

"Hey, Mrs.!" The kid at the car was holding up the flat tire. Everyone on the landing turned and watched Olivia waddle down the stairs. She had hoped to avoid being seen but she was way too large for that. Besides, Bernardo couldn't resist announcing...

"Olivia... New cousins!"

"Distant cousins!" she shouted back.

Then after trying to avoid seeing Raymond and realizing it just wasn't possible, she shouted to him too.

"My lips are sealed!" rang out across the steps as she pressed her fingers to her lips and threw away an imaginary key. Once she got to the kid at the car she gave him some money, promised to pick up the damaged tire another day and waved to everyone on the steps. It was a deliberate attempt to seem friendly before she got in the car and drove away.

After that, Father Lyle invited Bernardo and Hortence Grace and Juanita and Raymond Valdez into the tiny chapel inside the church so they could pray for healthy babies with big baptisms and big donations. Secretly, all of this news made him very excited. There hadn't been a christening in the village for a very long time.

Homecoming

I t was dark by the time Mr. Bravo pulled up in front of Ebba's house. She'd fallen asleep so he was careful to touch her gently so she wouldn't be afraid.

"You're home," he said in a quiet voice. It took a moment for her to wake up from dreaming that she was swimming in the ocean, but finally she lifted her head and looked around.

"Would you like me to take you inside?" Mr. Bravo asked.

Ebba nodded. She had no idea what to expect.

Mr. Bravo picked up a brown paper bag as he got out of the truck.

"Leftover lunch," he said. "Not much, but I imagine you'll be hungry." Ebba nodded again and followed Mr. Bravo numbly as he opened her front door and stepped inside. After he lit a candle he walked her through every single room. Fortunately, nothing had changed while she was gone except for a layer of dusty pink dirt that the wind had blown in through one of the open windows.

Mr. Bravo righted a wooden chair that had fallen over so Ebba could sit down and went outside to the well where he filled a pitcher with water and brought it inside.

"Now?" he asked, "Will you be all right?"

Ebba nodded. She was too tired to speak.

"Then I'll go on so you can get some rest." Again she nodded, but before he got very far, Ebba slid off the chair, reached around his back and hugged him as hard as she could. Caught off guard, he turned and looked into her drawn grateful face.

"Thank you," she managed to whisper.

He patted her awkwardly and smiled.

"Now you'll be safe." Ebba nodded and tried not to cry as Mr. Bravo told her she would feel better in the morning and after cautioning her to lock the door behind him, he said good night and walked outside.

Before he got into his truck he looked up at the moon and smiled. Two rescues, a domestic squabble, the announcement of a new life and the gratitude of a young girl. He was exhausted, but for the first time in his life he felt tall.

Inside the house, Ebba bolted the door and took a few sips of water. She hurried to her tiny room, pulled the yellow silk shawl out of the front of her dress and draped it over the wooden chair. Then she lay down on her bed and was fast asleep before Mr. Bravo started his truck and drove away.

REDISTRIBUTION

B right and early, Juanita's mother was at Rosa Guillermo's house trying to finish the mountain of laundry left over from the day before because her daughter had never shown up. She hadn't come home last night either, so Juanita's mother was glad to have a quiet place to worry, but the bell on Rosa Guillermo's front gate began to ring vigorously and shattered the solitude.

"Get the gate," Rosa Guillermo shouted from her office.

Juanita's mother sighed, but she put up the iron and walked to the gate, unlatched the latch and opened it a crack.

"We're here to see Rosa Guillermo," Bernardo said politely. Figuring it was official, Juanita's mother nodded and brought Bernardo and Hortence Grace through the courtyard and into the living room.

"Yes," Rosa Guillermo said rounding the corner, looking puzzled. "Who are you and what do you want?"

She had no idea who these people were and wished she had some sort of security rigged to stop strangers from ringing the bell and coming inside. Hortence Grace took a step forward, refusing to be put off by Rosa Guillermo's chilly tone.

"We were told that you might be able to help us locate our son."

"What?" Rosa Guillermo sounded appropriately shocked. "You must have the wrong house," she said, smiling condescendingly, and made a move toward the door.

"Rosa Guillermo?" Bernardo asked, picking a letter off the table and holding it up so she could see. "Rosa Guillermo is the name of the person that we were told we would find at this address." Rosa Guillermo walked to Bernardo and grabbed the letter out of his hand.

"Who gave you that information?"

"It's of no importance," Hortence Grace said.

Then she smiled condescendingly. Two could play at this game. "Begging your pardon, but I don't know you from any other peasant I might pass on the street." Bernardo laughed. Then he looked at her darkly.

"But now we know you and what you do for a living."

Rosa Guillermo raised an eyebrow and decided to be curt.

"Then be quick. What is it you want?"

"Our son," Bernardo replied.

"Your son?" Rosa Guillermo laughed. "Why would I know anything about your son?"

"Because you are the broker in charge of redistribution."

"I beg your pardon," Rosa Guillermo blanched.

"Assistant to the General in his Program of Redistribution."

The way Bernardo said it made her sound very official. It also made her very uneasy. She started to fuss with the buttons on the front of her dress.

"I have no idea what you're talking about," she said.

"Perhaps this will help," Hortence Grace said as she lifted an envelope out of her purse, pulled out the picture of Ariel and placed it on the table, but before Rosa Guillermo could take a very good look they heard Juanita's mother shout.

"Where on earth have you been?!"

Everyone turned. Juanita was trying to sneak in the front door without being seen and hurry into the kitchen. Hortence Grace smiled and so did Bernardo.

"Señora Chavez?"

"Señora?" Juanita answered with sweet surprise. Her tone pulled the rug right out from under her mother's wrath.

"How are you today?" Hortence Grace asked.

"Much better with the cola I drank first thing this morning."

Rosa Guillermo was stunned. This wasn't right. Since when was Sergeant Chavez' widow, her cleaning lady's daughter, a friend of this woman with the picture and this man with a braid? Rosa Guillermo jumped right in to attack with self-righteous bravado. Instead, what she was thinking flew out of her mouth.

"Excuse me, but why is the woman in the kitchen your mother?"

Juanita looked at Rosa Guillermo as if she was crazy.

"She was very worried," Rosa Guillermo said, trying to put the words back in her mouth and cover her tracks.

Juanita ignored Rosa Guillermo and turned to Hortence Grace.

"What brings you here?"

"That is none of your business!" Rosa Guillermo interrupted. A wet dishtowel unfurled with a resounding snap. Juanita's mother had stepped into the living room using her kitchen weapon to slap her daughter with well-placed blows, snap after snap.

"Oweee!" Juanita howled.

"Go right now and hurry," her mother barked and gave Juanita a shove. Not approving of this sort of treatment, Hortence Grace interrupted the fracas and answered Juanita's question.

"We came to see about our son," she announced. Suddenly the room was quiet as a church.

"He was kidnapped," Bernardo boomed.

"Stolen?" Juanita asked, suddenly very curious.

"I think it's time for you to leave," Rosa Guillermo said.

Sensing impending disaster, she tried to round up Bernardo and Hortence Grace as if they were cattle.

"But you haven't even looked at his picture." Hortence Grace walked back to the table and picked up the paper, waved it in front of Rosa Guillermo's face making her very uncomfortable and angry.

"Why should I look at a picture?" She tried to pretend that she hadn't seen it before and reached out to grab it. Instead, it fluttered to the floor right in front of Juanita who stooped to pick it up.

"Don't you dare!" Rosa Guillermo shouted. The noise was so loud, two candlesticks quaked. Surprised by the intensity of the command, Juanita's mother decided to move closer to see what her daughter had found.

"Give that here!" Rosa Guillermo bellowed and lunged for the paper, but it was too late. Both mother and daughter looked up from the picture with reverence and said, "Pablito..."

Bernardo and Hortence Grace had no idea what was going on, but Rosa Guillermo panicked. This living room coincidence was the worst possible coincidence of any coincidence that could ever have happened.

"That is my Pablito," Juanita said. She advanced on Rosa Guillermo like an inferno. "My Pablito that you gave to me was their son?"

Juanita made a grab for Rosa Guillermo's throat, but Bernardo pulled her aside when Rosa Guillermo started to hyperventilate. Hortence Grace turned to Juanita's mother and asked her to please go get a paper bag, then turned back to Juanita.

"Pablito? Your Pablito?"

By the time the bag arrived for the stricken Rose Guillermo to blow into, Juanita had blurted out the entire tale from its start in the General's garden to its finish when Rosa Guillermo had taken the boy away from the front porch of her burned-up husband's house. Overwhelmed and covered in a clammy sweat, Rosa Guillermo kept blowing in the bag to avoid speaking. But Juanita wasn't finished.

"... And she knows where he is now because I was standing in the kitchen..." Rosa Guillermo stopped blowing, "... and watched her give him to someone else."

Rosa Guillermo collapsed. Juanita's mother panicked, turned on her daughter and lashed out.

"Now we're both gonna die!" she screamed. "You and your big mouth." Before she could wind up and strike Juanita again Bernardo grabbed the wet towel Juanita's mother used for snapping and put it on Rosa Guillermo's head.

Heartsick and full of remorse, Juanita turned to Hortence Grace, got down on her knees and took hold of her hands.

"I am so sorry," she said. "We didn't know." Hortence Grace shook her head and helped Juanita stand back up.

"Don't be silly, there was nothing for you to know and this is a blessing because he's alive."

"No wonder he never spoke," Juanita whispered.

"Never?" Bernardo asked. Juanita shook her head.

"He was just too sad. Poor little Pablito."

"Ariel," Hortence Grace corrected.

Juanita's mother's eyes filled with tears. "And me. I was getting ready to be so proud to have a grandson so beautiful..."

Hortence Grace looked at Juanita as if to say, now would be a good time to tell her, as she poured a glass of water for Rosa Guillermo who was starting to come to. Juanita nodded and took a deep breath, put her arm around her mother and whispered.

"You can get ready again."

"What's that supposed to mean?" her mother muttered tearfully.

"Because in nine months you'll have one of your own."

It took a few minutes, but by the time Juanita's mother finally understood what Juanita was saying, she hugged her daughter all the way back to the kitchen.

Rosa Guillermo kept sliding in and out of the endless stars and echoes circling around in her head until Bernardo, caught between joy and despair, leaned down and in his best, kindest voice whispered, "You'll take us to him as soon as you feel able."

That is when Rosa Guillermo looked into his face, closed her eyes and fainted all over again.

THE STOLEN HEART

M r. Lobos sat across from Dr. Vidal who was listening to the sounds of the General's heart as the General, reclining on a leather lounge while recovering from plastic surgery to lift his droopy eyelids and pin back his ears, smoked a cigar. They were in the General's sitting room where photographs of the General filled every inch of every wall even though some had been taken before he'd had implants added to his thinning black hair. In each he was pictured next to an unholy parade of minor dignitaries and "tenth-tier" Pan National politicians from all over the place. The presence of women in the photographs was scarce but all of them were blonde.

The photograph in the most prominent position, the one you couldn't miss even if you wanted to, was of the General with his idol General Noriega holding a live lobster waving its claws. It was signed, "To my forever compadre. From the man you look up to." Clearly it had been taken before Noriega had been sent off to prison in the United States. But the General's two most important possessions, the ones that he never let out of his sight, were in glass jars sitting right beside him on a low table handcrafted by Bernardo DeVille. The smaller one contained the Kind Predecessor's heart. The other was full of human ears.

"So... Lobos. Are you happy?" the General asked as he puffed on his cigar and blew smoke in the doctor's face. Mr. Lobos ignored the question.

"My mother's convinced you're already dead."

The General smiled. "Good. I never liked my sister."

The doctor released the blood pressure pump on the General's arm then unwrapped the cuff and shook his head. "Her conviction may come true."

The General peeked at the doctor from his reconstructed eyes and whispered coyly. "More fellatio... is that what you recommend?" The doctor pretended to be busy writing things down but the General started to laugh which triggered a fit of serious coughing.

"You might want to give up the Cubans," the doctor cautioned.

"The Cubans... that's very funny," the General wheezed between bouts of breathlessness. Then he picked up a heavy medical book sitting next to him on the lounge and slammed it down on the doctor's withered thigh.

There was a tense moment of silence and then Dr. Vidal laughed. Not at all the response the General was seeking.

"What's so damned funny?" the General gasped.

"I'm paralyzed, General, I don't feel a thing."

"Pity," the General pouted darkly and put the book on the table with the jars. The doctor waited until the General relit his cigar then grabbed the General's arm and gave it a thorough perusal.

"What now?" the General demanded sternly but the doctor didn't answer.

"I consider this as an invasion!" The General's voice went up an octave.

"It's time to test your blood," Dr. Vidal reminded matter of factly. The General inhaled sharply and panicked.

"Blood? You never mentioned anything about blood!"

"Don't be such a baby. We do this every month." Dr. Vidal had already bound the General's arm with rubber tubing and the needle was poised to insert a shunt.

"Wait!" the General cried out, surprised by the doctor's strength and speed but Dr. Vidal just grinned.

"Why prolong the anticipation?" Then he jammed the needle into the General's arm, deliberately missing the vein.

"Oh my God!" the General cried out from his stiff, new, plastic surgery face.

"I am so sorry," the doctor seemed sincerely contrite as he withdrew the needle then plunged the shunt into a vital vein.

"Stop! Please," the General whimpered and started to tremble then sank low on the lounge.

Mr. Lobos looked out into the garden from the open window and wondered if Ebba was all right.

"I can't stand it," the General whined but Dr. Vidal didn't say a word, just kept filling one tube after another with the General's blood, tube after tube, seven altogether.

"Considering your condition be grateful you have it to give," the doctor commented dryly.

"What condition?" the General cowered, feigned innocence, pretended not to know what the doctor was talking about.

"The one you've got," Dr. Vidal answered curtly.

Mr. Lobos smiled at the General knowingly, which made the General mad but there wasn't much he could do about it.

"Someday I'll kill you," the General said hoarsely to Dr. Vidal.

"No you won't," the doctor replied as he pulled the needle out of the General's arm and waved it in his face.

"No one but me knows how to keep you alive."

This was a fact. The General was suffering from the advanced stages of something severe he'd picked up from some woman or other in the days when he was Minister of Public Relations and traveled from one country to another. Worse than the unfortunate recurring symptoms, Dr. Vidal had made the General tell him, in graphic detail, what vile things he'd done to contract the disease.

"Until I find someone to replace you," the General snarled.

"Then hurry," Dr. Vidal said and opened a tiny vial of something powdery and white, poured it into a glass of orange juice and stirred it with his thumb.

Mr. Lobos sneezed three times in a row not bothering to cover his face. The General ducked, covered his head with his arm and shouted, "You worthless son-of-my-sister! You know how susceptible I am." While in this position and before the General could stop him, Mr. Lobos picked the small jar containing the Kind Predecessor's heart off the table and held it up to the light.

"Put that down!" the General bellowed. He stood up to grab the jar out of his nephew's hand but his knees buckled so he sat back down whether he wanted to or not. Dr. Vidal handed the General the glass of orange juice.

"You forgot this," he said. Trembling and fearful, the General gulped it down as Mr. Lobos walked to the window tossing the jar from one hand to the other with a rhythmic snap, snap, snap.

"Stop that!" the General roared and stuck out his hand. "I want you to give me back my heart!" But Mr. Lobos just continued the rhythmic snap, snap, snap.

"It's not your heart," Mr. Lobos said. "You took it, remember? You took your Predecessor's heart. Then you tried to take his wife, but she shot herself instead."

"She did not," the General shouted.

Mr. Lobos wasn't listening. "Then to get even, you took the body parts of her children, and then other people's children..."

"You should talk about taking children!" the General interrupted.

Mr. Lobos looked at the General darkly and tossed the jar up in the air, caught it with one hand. The General gasped. Mr. Lobos smiled and tossed the jar a little higher.

"Stop!" The General shouted. Mr. Lobos caught it and tossed the jar higher. "Lobos!" the General shouted again.

Mr. Lobos looked at his uncle and threw the jar even higher, let it fall free through the air.

"No! Oh, my God... Don't!" he pleaded.

"That's what people cry as their children are ripped out of their arms and taken away..."

"I'm not the one that does that!" the General lied again.

The jar was falling fast, fast, fast to the floor.

"What about all those ears in the jar? Who do they belong to?"

"Stop!" The General's ragged scream pierced the air.

At the very last minute, just as the jar was about to hit the floor Mr. Lobos reached out and caught it, held it in front of his uncle's distorted new face.

"Uncle General, you've manufactured a mess." Hoping to get his heart back the General nodded foolishly. He looked so pathetic Mr. Lobos could hardly stand the sight of him, but fixed him with a lethal stare. Then he held up the jar and shook it.

"Maybe I should feed it to the dogs."

That did it. Nephew or not, Mr. Lobos had stepped over the line. The General was so enraged he opened the drawer in the low table and pulled out his gun, pointed it at Mr. Lobos but was having terrible trouble holding it steady.

"You shit son of my sister! I'll kill you!" he yelled. Mr. Lobos smiled and started tossing the jar back and forth all over again... snap, snap, snap...

"Same thing you did to my father?"

Back and forth...Snap, snap, snap...

"The whole story, everything included on the ten o'clock news right before Daniella Perez's telanovela." Mr. Lobos continued, tossing the jar. Snap, snap, snap.

"Dog food or the ten o'clock night news? Dog food or the news..."

"Enough!" the General interrupted. His fury was so intense that his grip gave way and he dropped the gun. Then his whole body collapsed into an unconscious heap. Dr. Vidal looked at Mr. Lobos and smiled thinly.

"I always give him something to relax."

"Thoughtful," Mr. Lobos nodded.

Then he slipped the jar with the heart into his pocket, helped Dr. Vidal pack up his case and collect all seven vials of the General's blood. As he wheeled the doctor out of the room, he was whistling, "I'll Build A Stairway to Paradise," slightly off key.

Joan Tewkesbury

$\mathcal{E}$bba woke up early in the morning and looked around. It took a moment before she remembered that she was home in her own bed and because it was so quiet she shouted, "Hello?" just to hear a voice and convince herself that her mother wasn't going to answer.

She crawled out of bed, found the sack with Mr. Bravo's leftover lunch and ate everything including the crumbs. It had been a long time since she'd had anything to eat. After that she ran outside to fill the washtub by the well. The sun was just coming up when she stepped into the cold water and scrubbed every inch of her shivering self with soap and a brush. She stuck her head under the spigot to wash her hair and then scrubbed herself all over again.

When she finished, she wrapped up in a towel and dumped the water around the big tree, watched it soak into the ground and tried to force every recent memory to go with it. After that she picked up the battered angel dress along with the gardener's old hat and tossed them into the incinerator. She lit a match, set them on fire and waited until everything went up in smoke before going inside to look for her favorite blue dress.

She found it on her mother's bed where Hortence Grace had left it. She shook it out and slipped it over her head but it wouldn't go over her shoulders. When she finally managed to pull it off she put it on the floor and stepped into it, eased it over her hips, jammed her arms in the sleeves, but even after all that it still didn't fit.

Ebba walked to the sliver of mirror attached on the door of her mother's closet. Before the blue dress had covered her knees and was loose around the waist. Now it was creeping up toward her thighs and way too tight across her chest. She couldn't figure out what was going on. The dress hadn't been washed while she was gone so it hadn't shrunk. Ebba stepped closer to the mirror and saw something new. "What in the world is that?" she asked the image. Where it used to be flat as a board, two small mounds were making an appearance on her chest. Ebba stepped a step closer and said out loud, "This is a mistake."

She turned upside down, struggled out of the dress then stood up and studied herself in detail. Things were changing everywhere. Not only was she taller with the beginnings of bulges, there was the start of a waist and when she lifted her arm and looked really close, she discovered a thin patch of dark hair. "Oh no..." Ebba whispered as she picked up the blue dress and clutched it to her chest, sat down on her mother's bed and ceased all further exploration. Her eyes filled with tears but after a moment she thought about her options. Finally, she got up and walked to her mother's closet. Three dresses were hanging on the rod, each one a different size to accommodate her mother's ongoing struggle from thin to fat to thin again. One by one, Ebba took them off the hangers and tried them on. Finally she decided on the oldest one. It was faded, but at least it was blue.

Ebba brushed her hair, wove it into the usual fat braid and looked down at her feet. She had no shoes so she went back to the closet and found a pair of her father's huaraches, the only thing he'd left behind, and put them on. Then she put her old, blue dress on a hanger and hung it over the only existing picture of her mother and father. It was her way of saying goodbye to what had barely been there in the first place.

When she was finished, Ebba found Mrs. Lobos' pale yellow silk shawl and wrapped it around her new body, did a couple of twirls, then decided to save it for a special occasion. Besides, losing the safety of her old blue dress and entering the realm of her mother's closet was enough for one day.

REUNION

On the way to where they were going, Rosa Guillermo asked Bernardo and Hortence Grace to stop at Mr. Bravo's house. She had a roll of film from the General's birthday party that needed immediate attention. Bernardo kept Gloria's engine running while Rosa Guillermo hurried to find Mr. Bravo but he wasn't there, so she pushed the plain brown envelope through a crack in his door and got back into the truck.

After Rosa Guillermo showed her pass to the guards at the gate, they finally arrived at the home of Sergeant Ruiz, but no one was there either, so the three of them sat crammed in Gloria's front seat without speaking. There was nothing to say. The women fanned themselves with their purses hoping to stir the hot air and break the terrible tension, but it didn't do any good, so they just waited as the sun got lower and lower in the sky.

Bernardo, seemingly calm, stared straight ahead willing Sergeant Ruiz to hurry up and come home. Finally, at the end of the winding street, they all watched a government green car move closer and closer until it pulled into Sergeant Ruiz' driveway at exactly six o'clock. But before it could come to a stop, the back door flew open and Ariel ran across the small manicured lawn with his arms outstretched, shouting "Poppa... Poppa!" at the top of his lungs.

Bernardo was already outside running to retrieve his son and hold him next to his heart.

"Poppa... Poppa!" Ariel sobbed.

When they reached one another, Bernardo got down on his knees and Ariel jumped into his father's arms, held on for dear life, wouldn't let go, Bernardo's endearing whispers straining against the sobbing of his son.

"It's all right. It's all right. I have you now." Over and over, Bernardo rocking and rocking, whispering to Ariel who couldn't stop gulping the words, "Poppa... Poppa!" again and again.

"Thomas!" Sergeant Ruiz stamped his foot. Not certain of what was going on, he and his wife stood rigidly by the car.

"Come here at once," he yelled in a tone better suited for giving orders to soldiers. Bernardo got up off his knees and stood in the center of the manicured grass holding Ariel wrapped tightly around Bernardo's neck, clinging to him, not letting go, whispering, "Poppa" over and over in Bernardo's ear.

"What the hell is going on?!" Sergeant Ruiz stepped forward and shouted. That's when Ariel saw Hortence Grace running to join them.

"Momma!" Ariel cried and started to sob.

Calmly, Hortence Grace stepped right in and gathered her son into her roomy body, let him reclaim the rightful place he'd been ripped from.

"I said, what the hell is going on?" Sergeant Ruiz shouted again.

"This boy is our son," Bernardo interrupted firmly. "I am his father." Sergeant Ruiz was incredulous and his wife started to weep.

"Stop that!" He turned to her and yelled. And she did. She choked on her fear and shock and shut right up.

Though shaky, Rosa Guillermo had gotten out of the truck too and now she was standing somewhere between Bernardo and Hortence Grace with their reunited son and Sergeant Ruiz yelling at his wife.

"I'm so sorry," Rosa Guillermo said. "There's been a mistake." Then she smiled tightly and tried to sound cheerful.

"A mistake?" Sergeant Ruiz was incensed.

"His cousin," she pointed to Bernardo. "His cousin, Olivia Gomez married to the Mayor... Octavio Gomez..."

"The mayor?" Sergeant Ruiz interrupted. "What the hell does the mayor have to do with anything? He's dead."

Rosa Guillermo continued with Bernardo's pedigree as if nothing was the matter.

" ...a direct descendant of the General himself," even though the last part was a lie.

"You mean they took the wrong kid," Sergeant Ruiz jumped ahead.

"It was a mistake," she confirmed, nodding her head. She was trying her best not to feel faint.

"A mistake!" Sergeant Ruiz' words came out like an explosion.

"And we're just supposed to take your word that this is true?"

"My word," Bernardo interjected.

Sergeant Ruiz was overwhelmed with menace.

"Your word, her word, what difference does it make?" Then he sighed and looked down at the ground and took a step back.

"You have no idea what we've been through," he said, becoming very self-righteous.

Incredulous, Bernardo gripped the Sergeant with his gaze and spoke in a low soft voice. "And the boy? What about the boy and what he's been through?"

Sergeant Ruiz broke into Bernardo's recrimination with a small corner of his memory. "Have I seen you before?"

Joan Tewkesbury

Bernardo had already remembered Sergeant Ruiz at the stadium, but he refused to be pulled off course.

"Perhaps you've seen me with my son."

"Your son... he's my son and he belongs to me."

Sergeant Ruiz was on the verge of losing control. Bernardo turned to Hortence Grace and put his arm around her.

"It's time to go," he said. The Sergeant took a step forward trying to maintain control. "Go? Who said anything about going?"

"I did," Bernardo's answer was emphatic.

"Do you know who I am?" The Sergeant shouted. This was not a salvageable situation.

"Unfortunately, I do." Bernardo said and motioned to Hortence Grace to take Ariel and get into the truck then he turned to Rosa Guillermo. "Come along. We'll drop you at home." From where she was standing back by the car, Sergeant Ruiz' wife let out a little cry.

"We're not done here," Sergeant Ruiz snapped. Then he turned to his frightened wife and shouted. "Get the hell in the house!" Which she did except for stopping at the front door to wave a little wave.

"Goodbye, Thomas," she cried and burst into tears.

"Go!" Sergeant Ruiz raged and started after her, but she managed to slip inside and slam the door before he could reach her, so the Sergeant turned back and grabbed Rosa Guillermo by the arm, pulled her close to his face.

"You stupid cunt. I don't care who he belongs to. He's mine."

Rosa Guillermo started to shake. "I'm sorry," was the most she could manage.

"So am I." The Sergeant's nasty tone slashed through her like a knife, but he turned to Bernardo and smiled.

"It was you and the doctor, wasn't it? You were the one puking on the steps..." Bernardo didn't respond so Sergeant Ruiz just laughed. It was vile.

"You better get your family and go. Miss Guillermo and I will need to work out the details." Rosa Guillermo went pale with panic and looked from one man to the other.

"We can wait," Bernardo offered.

"Don't," Sergeant Ruiz' answer was final. He pulled out his gun.

Bernardo looked at Rosa Guillermo who was trembling like a leaf. Then he looked at the gun Sergeant Ruiz was pointing at his head.

"I'll take her back when we're done," the Sergeant smiled. Bernardo turned to Rosa Guillermo and tried to look calm, but the Sergeant had cocked his gun and began to count.

"One... two... three..." Rosa Guillermo just looked over his head. She had no choice in this outcome.

"Four... five..."

"We'll see you at home," Bernardo said, fearing the worst. Rosa Guillermo didn't answer.

"Six... seven... eight..."

Bernardo walked to his truck, got inside, turned the key in Gloria's ignition and drove away before the Sergeant could change his mind. Now that he had his son, he would never give him back.

After Bernardo's truck disappeared, Sergeant Ruiz wrapped Rosa Guillermo's arm tight behind her back and drove his gun into her soft middle. When her eyes started to roll back in her head he refused to let her faint, refused to let her go unconscious as he dragged her across the small manicured lawn to the car and whispered in her ear.

"How about we go for a little ride."

PICTURES

M r. Bravo stood on his bench in the dark room, riveted by the images floating to the surface of the developing solution and onto his paper. They were grisly and loathsome and incomprehensible.

Pictures of children's fear, frozen faces, but no image showing the reason. Pictures of children watching things children should never see. Things they were too young to understand. Laughing with shock as soldiers mounted anguished women. Uniformed men pushing cattle prods into the private soft skin of grown men, sodomy and things too dimly lit to comprehend that required electricity and wires. Faces wrenched in agony and terror. Military men standing in a row. Snappy military jackets, snappy salutes, snappy smiles, twinkling eyes, no trousers, just dangling dicks, except for one man holding his part like a gun, his foot on the bare backside of a woman and laughing like he'd downed big game on safari. Tractors crossing the stadium floor, scooping up something hard to make out. Was it human remains? These were the images on the roll of film that Rosa Guillermo had shoved in the crack of Mr. Bravo's kitchen door.

Mr. Bravo felt ill. He pulled the pictures out of the bath and hung the last print on the rack to dry. Then he turned out the light and locked the door behind him. He was so stunned by what he'd seen he forgot to fix his supper. Instead, he took the stack of photographs from the General's birthday party, laid them out on his kitchen table and studied every face with a magnifying glass. He went back and forth from person to person, couple to couple, women in long dresses, men in tuxedos and cummerbunds. No trace of military here. But Mr. Bravo was an expert in human faces so after a while he made a few discoveries.

Seven of the men standing next to their well-dressed wives were the smiling soldiers without pants. Three more, including those seven, were involved in the rapes. Nine more, pictured sweetly with their fiancées, were nine of the eleven wielding the cattle prods. Mr. Bravo shuddered. He got up to get a drink of water and as he looked out of the window, he remembered something else. He hurried back to his desk and brought out all the portraits of fathers and mothers and their newly adopted children. Once again he studied the faces with the magnifying glass and this discovery didn't take very long. Mr. Bravo picked everything up and hurried back into the darkroom.

What was apparent in the family portraits was positive proof that the terrified children pictured in Rosa Guillermo's roll of film were now the adopted sons and daughters of the men pictured in all of the party poses. The snapshots of the torment and torture that had taken the lives of their real parents so their children could be given to military men and their wives who couldn't conceive on their own. As an extra bonus for the government, these same children became children in training for the General's Children's Army.

Mr. Bravo put down the magnifying glass and stared into space, then walked out of the darkroom, leaving everything inside. This time he double-locked the door.

Outside, he sat down on the running board of his truck and gazed up at the stars. All these years he had used his camera like a suit of armor to keep the world away. Used it so he wouldn't have to participate in other people's complications. Now all of his protection had betrayed him. His camera wasn't a shield. It was a window.

A few days later Mrs. Marquez was back at Raymond's house banging on the courtyard door, but he wasn't home. She discovered the note she had written, wadded up and dropped in the dirt. After considering several possibilities she decided to pick it up and reread what she had written. It made her cry, but when she was finished she put it in her patent leather purse and closed the metal clasp with a click. Something about that click filled her with irrational fury. All of a sudden she wasn't just mad, she was furious.

Mrs. Marquez looked around the courtyard for something to get her hands on, a weapon, something to throw but nothing she saw could do much damage until she tripped over a hoe on the ground where Raymond usually parked his truck. She kicked it out of the way at first but then she gave it a second look and picked it up. With a spectacular rush of excitement Mrs. Marquez swung the hoe through the air. This object of wood and metal was much more than just a tool for digging in the dirt. This was a weapon. Mrs. Marquez lifted the hoe higher, took aim and swinging it as hard as she could hacked out a hunk of Raymond's courtyard door.

"Son of a bitch!" She yelled as if she'd just hacked a hunk out of Raymond.

"You shit!" she hollered, swinging the hoe again and again.

Mrs. Marquez swung and chipped and hacked. New energy started coursing through her veins. Never before had assault brought such satisfaction and pleasing results. Suddenly she stopped and took a look at the damage, took a look at what she was holding. There was a very long pause and then Mrs. Marquez, her eyes blazing with an even better idea, started to laugh. She hoisted the hoe over her shoulder, adjusted her purse and took off down the road.

STRIKING A BARGAIN

Raymond Valdez was so nervous he could hardly be heard as he asked Juanita's mother for permission to marry her daughter.

Juanita's mother had prepared herself to say no. As far as she was concerned Juanita had too many high falutin ideas and needed to be knocked down a peg or two. After all, she'd already lived in a house with running water, indoor plumbing and a husband who, in a fair world, should have married her, not Juanita. Lord knows she'd done her best to seduce him but he wasn't interested in anything but her daughter's tits. It was disgusting. In a plot to win him over, Juanita's mother had, on more than one occasion, offered him a glimpse of her own ample assets but he never even looked. Now Juanita was knocked up by this plumber when she'd hardly had time to be the widow of the first guy, Sergeant Chavez.

"I love your daughter very much," Raymond said. His voice was cracking like a teenage boy. "I want very much to protect her from the storms of life."

"Yeah? What about the kid?" Juanita's mother blurted. Raymond looked up at her through his thick dark lashes.

"If you please, I was just getting to that part." Surprised, Juanita's mother was momentarily pulled off her path of resentment.

"For a long time I have hoped for a blessed baby. To have a wife and a baby all at once is a miracle, don't you agree?" Juanita's mother shrugged, not sure how to respond. In her usual way of evaluation she figured that what he was saying was bullshit.

"Happens every day," she blurted again. But when she saw the look on his face she tried to stuff what she'd said back in her mouth. It was apparent that Raymond Valdez really meant what he was saying.

"Not to me," he said in a low, sincere voice.

Raymond Valdez looked around the room crowded with stuff and, being a businessman, decided to take another tack.

"And for you," he said pausing dramatically, "indoor plumbing and a beautiful blue commode."

"Commode? What the hell's a commode?"

"A toilet," Raymond translated. Juanita's mother's mouth flew open. "A blue toilet?"

Raymond nodded.

"I have it in my truck..."

Before he could finish his sentence, Juanita's mother was out the door to take a look at the bright blue porcelain prize riding majestically in the flatbed of Raymond's 1948 Ford.

"Jesus, Mary and Joseph," Juanita's mother exclaimed.

She crossed herself twice just as Juanita emerged from the communal outhouse looking pale from the morning ritual of tossing her cookies. Raymond rushed to her side and helped her to a bench under a tree.

"Where'd you get it?" Juanita's mother demanded.

Juanita's mother wanted details, but she started circling the truck, rhapsodizing about what she would tell the neighbors to make them jealous.

"Especially ordered..." Raymond replied.

"How did you know blue is my favorite color?" she trilled. Now Juanita's mother was climbing up on the running board to get a better look. As far as she was concerned, this was trading up for her daughter.

Raymond shrugged as he offered Juanita a sip of cola and decided to remain vague about the details of the toilet. He figured she wouldn't like it as much if she knew it had been for Li Choo, paid for and then rejected because it was the wrong shade of blue. Then, because she'd been killed before Raymond had a chance to send it back, he'd decided to save it for a rainy day.

"Can you install it?" Juanita's mother asked. Raymond looked at his watch then back to the Juanita's mother, oozing grandiose greed.

"I suppose now is as good a time as any," he said, getting up.

He was eager to close the deal before she changed her mind, so he pulled a paper and pen out of his pocket and motioned to Juanita's mother to meet him at the hood of the truck.

"I'll need you to sign right here," he pointed.

"Sign what?" Juanita's mother asked, her back stiffening up like a board.

"The receipt for the toilet, so it's in your name," he lied.

He held out the pen and Juanita's mother signed with a great big X, letting Raymond know that she couldn't read or she would have noticed the entire sentence.

"I HEREBY ACCEPT THIS BLUE COMMODE
IN EXCHANGE FOR JUANITA'S HAND IN
MARRIAGE TO RAYMOND VALDEZ.
EFFECTIVE IMMEDIATELY."

After signing, she handed back the pen and he shook her hand before he folded the paper and put it in his pocket.

"So I will speak to Father Lyle about a date."

"What date? A date for what?" Juanita's mother seemed to be having a memory lapse.

"For the marriage of your daughter to me," Raymond reminded.

"Who said anything about that?"

Juanita's mother, hoping for more stuff, tried to seem like she didn't understand.

"You took the toilet," Raymond prompted.

"You think I would trade my daughter for that?" Raymond didn't say a word. He'd been wondering the same thing. She pointed indignantly to the beautiful blue object gleaming in the sun. "You think you can buy my daughter?"

Raymond pulled out the paper and tore it in half, dropped it on the ground, blew a kiss to Juanita, started to get in his truck.

"Wait!" Juanita's mother panicked, unveiling her fake forgetting.

"Don't do that!" she cried. She rushed over and bent down, picked up the pieces of paper, put them in Raymond's hand and spoke in a whisper.

"She's all yours. I just wanted her to think I put up a fight."

Raymond looked at her. He couldn't believe her insatiable coveting was that blatant but he pretended to be part of her conspiracy. Now he turned to Juanita so her mother couldn't see his exuberant smile and blew two gigantic kisses before he reached for his tools and followed her mother inside.

Mrs. Marquez swung the hoe over her head and let it crash into the dirt, hacking the heads off the geraniums growing on Ebba's mother's grave. This time she was determined to get to those dresses if it was the last thing she did. Nothing had been the same since they went underground. At least when the dresses were in Ebba's mother's closet Raymond had remained a possibility. They could change hands, live in someone else's closet if given the opportunity but as long as they were buried under all that dirt they weren't going anywhere and she would never be able to get Raymond back.

Obviously he was living under some sort of spell concocted by that Juanita woman, certainly a witch, to get even with Mrs. Marquez because Bernardo's kid didn't like her and wouldn't talk. Not that she, Maria Marquez, had had anything to do with any of that, of course, but one thing was for certain: if she, Maria Marquez, was important enough to have that pain-in-the-ass kid of Bernardo's stolen, Juanita had better watch her step.

In fact, the more Mrs. Marquez thought about it, the more she decided the whole thing was Ebba's fault. All of it would have been avoidable if Ebba had just given her one of those green satin dresses after her mother died. Actually, everything that had happened was Carlotta Pavon's fault. She wouldn't share those dresses so she was the one to blame. Therefore, it was only right and fair and with a clear conscience that she dig up the Olivia Gomez' dresses and wear them in order to break the spell the witch Juanita had cast.

Swing after swing, hack after hack, sweating and grunting, Mrs. Marquez threw herself into the activity of grave destruction.

"You pig's mother," she shouted. "You shriveled lizard's heart," she cried out between swings. "It's your fault he's with someone else, your fault, you selfish pig's mother!"

"What do you have against the pig?"

Mr. Escalante managed to interject his question between hoe strokes of grave bashing when he walked up behind her and scared her to death.

"What?!" Mrs. Marquez shouted. She was so surprised she lost her flow, lost her grip, lost her hoe.

"It's a sin to desecrate the resting place of eternal sleep," Mr. Escalante said with a worried look. He stepped around the mess and brushed off the dirt that had landed on his suit.

"The souls don't like it," he said.

"Souls don't give a shit," Mrs. Marquez snapped. "They're dead."

"Excuse me," Mr. Escalante said, "but they care very much."

Mrs. Marquez wasn't fazed. She reached down to grab the hoe, but Mr. Escalante beat her to it. He picked it up and threw it across the graves like a javelin.

"You smelly old coot!" Mrs. Marquez yelled and marched off to retrieve it. Mr. Escalante sighed and looked down at the dirt and geranium bits at his feet. The soil was hard and full of rocks so Mrs. Marquez' efforts had scarcely made a dent. A little replanting and it would be good as new, but just as Mrs. Marquez strode back with the hoe to start all over again Mr. Escalante gasped.

"Oh now what?" Mrs. Marquez said, extremely annoyed.

Mr. Escalante couldn't speak so he pointed. Coming up from the various divots and dents, the same thing that happened when Hortence Grace had asked Ebba's mother for a sign, water tinged with silver and pink was bubbling up around Ebba's mother's grave and oozing up through the cracks.

"Oh my God!" Mrs. Marquez cried and dropped the hoe. Terrified, she turned and started to run. She ran across all of the graves and then she ran down the path, ran right out of the cemetery gates shouting, "Oh my God!" over and over.

She thought she might be having a heart attack, but she kept running. "Oh my God!" echoing after her like a song as she disappeared around the bend.

Meanwhile the water bubbling up around Ebba's mother's grave subsided and stopped. In fact, all of a sudden the ground was dry, not even damp. All that remained of the watery episode were little rings of silver shimmer around all of the hoe holes. Mr. Escalante, convinced he'd witnessed a miracle, replaced all the dirt and geranium and used the hoe to smooth out ruffles in the soil. When he finished he was sure that he heard a lovely long sigh of appreciation so he picked up his guitar and started to sing...

In My Adobe Hacienda..." He did this to reassure and calm the spirit below as well as his own, up above.

When Mr. Bravo arrived in Bernardo's courtyard and got out of his truck he had to stop and rub his eyes. Clearly he hadn't been paying attention when he drove through the gate. Clearly this was a mirage. There was music and dancing and everyone was laughing. Tobias was playing his tin whistle for Hortence Grace and Rebecca who were twirling round and round with Ebba, a little bit shy in a new pale-blue dress and all of them were trying to entertain Ariel, the most unexpected sight of all. He was taller than before but he was in Bernardo's arms, clinging with his head tucked down in his father's neck while everyone was doing their best to make him smile or laugh or just make a sound. Any kind of sound would do.

Mr. Bravo shook his head. All of this good news didn't coincide with the envelope full of photographs he was holding in his hand. Hortence Grace caught sight of him and rushed right over, her arms outstretched and full of excitement even though Mr. Bravo thought he must be dreaming.

"Oh, Mr. Bravo, I know. It looks too good to be true." Then she embraced him with a hug and smiled reassuringly.

"You're just in time for refreshments." She put her hand on his shoulder and led him to the kitchen full of everyone's loud talk and laughter. Everyone except Ariel, who couldn't speak, couldn't let go of the knot he'd become hanging around Bernardo's neck. Yes, he was back but trapped between the world of right now and whatever had gone on where he had been taken.

There was lemonade and cookies for the children. The grown-ups drank a congratulatory mescal to thank Mr. Bravo for bringing Ebba home safely and Hortence Grace played with Ariel's hair while she told Mr. Bravo the story of how they finally found him as if it were a fairy tale. Only when she got to the part about holding him in her arms after such a long time, did Ariel release his grip around Bernardo's neck and crawl into his mother's lap where she gathered him up and rocked him like a baby and he touched her cheeks that were wet with tears. All of them took turns trying to coax him to come back to rejoin his life as it was before but nothing they did worked. Finally Mr. Bravo had to turn away and wipe his eyes on his sleeve.

Bernardo asked Ebba about her adventure so she told them about Jesus singing in the cantina to the little girl in the coffin and the bus falling in the ditch and the great big women helping to push it out and how she fell asleep in the bushes. But she didn't tell them about Mr. Lobos or his mother or Dr. Vidal or Mercedes and the Commander in the back of the van or the dead man with no ears or eyes with his hands stuffed in his mouth. Instead she told them about Mr. Bravo at the cemetery and taking her home and eating his leftover lunch.

When she finished and everybody laughed with relief, Rebecca put her arm around Ebba's shoulders and told her how glad she was Ebba was with them again and Ebba, to her own surprise, turned to Rebecca and hugged her tight. She'd never felt so much like she was part of anything like a family before.

After Mr. Bravo finished his drink and ate a cookie, he said that he didn't mean to be rude but he needed to speak with Bernardo alone. What he had to say was serious and not appropriate for the children so Hortence Grace and Tobias got everyone together and started out the door until Ariel realized Bernardo wasn't coming, and went white as a sheet trembling with terror.

"No Poppa, no!!!"

His scared-to-death scream pierced through the hubbub and dispelled any notion that Ariel would be back to normal in no time at all. Bernardo got up and put his arm around Ariel and Hortence Grace and bunched all the others into a tight circle to corral them out the door as he tried to reassure Ariel that this circle was his cocoon, his shield, his protection. With them he would always be safe. Finally because Ariel couldn't be calmed Bernardo steered everyone to the shed where they put Ariel in his old red wagon so they could wheel him back and forth in front of the window where Bernardo would be sitting.

Once Bernardo came back in the kitchen, Mr. Bravo laid all the pictures out on the table and in silence they looked at them one by one. Then Mr. Bravo showed Bernardo how they fit together. Family portraits, soldiers, uniformed and in cummerbunds, their wives in long dresses. Children's haunted faces, torture, rape, the General's birthday party. Mr. Bravo stared out the window at Ariel in the wagon and a sob from his heart slipped out of his mouth.

"I don't know what to do."

Bernardo turned the pictures face down on the table, poured each of them another glass of mescal and told Mr. Bravo the real story of Ariel's return. About Rosa Guillermo at her house. About making her go with them to take back their son.

"She had one request, to drop off the film. We had to go to your house so she could drop off a roll of film. 'Pictures of the General's party,' she said."

Carefully, Bernardo started to pile the condemning pictures in a stack. "May I keep these?" he asked. Mr. Bravo nodded and helped put them back in the envelope. Bernardo retrieved an old tin box hidden in a hole behind the photograph of his father.

"This way you'll know where they are," he said. Mr. Bravo nodded again as they placed the envelope inside the box. When he was finished, Bernardo thanked Mr. Bravo and thanked him for his help, assuring him that he wouldn't tell a soul until the time was right.

THE DELIVERY OF THE DRESS

I t was late afternoon and Mrs. Marquez stood squinting at herself in the
narrow mirror while Hortence Grace made final adjustments on the
new dress. Mrs. Marquez hadn't quite recovered from the events at Ebba's
mother's grave but to have this dress in her Raymond Valdez arsenal would
soothe the situation. At first she was mad because Hortence Grace had
promised she would never tell a living soul about the telephone, but after
Bernardo assured her that this was a one-time-only emergency and it would
never happen again, Mrs. Marquez, against her better judgment and
because she wanted the dress, had dug into the bowl and pulled out the
phone.

"Turn please," Hortence Grace said, checking the hem with the sounds
of Ariel's terrified screams still ringing in her ears. She was beginning to
understand that his fear was now a permanent guest in their house and it
filled her with dread. Down on the floor, snipping a few hanging threads,
Hortence Grace had no idea that Mrs. Marquez had put the whole Ariel
tragedy in motion. Neither did Bernardo hunched over the phone, or Mr.
Bravo who they had left at home trying his best to reassure Ariel, promising
to stay until Hortence Grace and Bernardo came back, even though it had
little or no impact on Ariel's alarming fear.

Finally it was Tobias who made up a game that convinced his brother
they would keep him safe while Hortence Grace and Bernardo were gone.
Rebecca, Tobias, Ebba and Ariel would hide in the boy's bedroom closet
with a flashlight and a book. Mr. Bravo, sitting on the other side of the
door with a string of firecrackers and a machete, was the guard and if
anything threatened or was dangerous, he would knock five times, light
the firecrackers, stand on the bed with the weapon to whack whoever got
close and Tobias would hide Ariel in the laundry basket and cover him up.
After a full demonstration, complete with reading and knocking, lighting
firecrackers, jumping up on the bed and covering Ariel in the basket, Ariel,
though still hiccuping sobs, had kissed Hortence Grace and Bernardo
goodbye and let them leave.

"Turn please," Hortence Grace said again.

She glanced at Bernardo nodding into the receiver then motioning,
letting her know that he had reached Mr. Lobos and was speaking directly
to him. Mrs. Marquez had no idea who he was talking to. She was only
concerned with herself and the dress. Hortence Grace adjusted the sleeves

making sure they were even, then looked at Mrs. Marquez in the mirror and said with calm authority, "It's done."

Mrs. Marquez turned on the light and stepped closer to the mirror, gave herself a hard appraising look and twisted around to see the back. Suddenly she wasn't so sure. "Do you think it's too much?"

"Too much what?"

"Too much dress," Mrs. Marquez said. She was stirring the air with her hands. Hortence Grace shrugged.

"It's exactly what you said you wanted."

Suddenly Mrs. Marquez was filled with self-doubt. She couldn't decide. "The green's okay?"

"It's the same green you tried to dig up."

Mrs. Marquez gave Hortence Grace a hard look, hoping the news of her latest graveyard episode hadn't traveled.

"What a wonderful dress," Bernardo smiled. He was turning around and hanging up the receiver, putting the phone back in the bowl in the drawer. Mrs. Marquez smiled. At last, validation from a man, the only thing that counted. The only way you knew if something was really right or wrong was to hear it from a man.

Out of nowhere, there was a knock at the door. Bernardo looked at Hortence Grace and hoped it wasn't Mr. Bravo with all of the children. Mrs. Marquez just looked annoyed.

"Now who is that?" she said to Bernardo.

He took a deep breath, walked to the door and opened it. Raymond Valdez was standing outside in the fading light. He looked at Bernardo and nodded shyly.

"May I come in?" Relieved, Bernardo grinned and stepped aside so Raymond could enter.

"It's Raymond Valdez," he announced. Mrs. Marquez gasped with surprise and tried to pull herself together, tried to get her stomach out of her throat as Hortence Grace looked at Raymond and smiled her most welcoming smile.

"How nice to see you," she said. Then Hortence Grace stepped aside so Raymond could get the full effect of Mrs. Marquez in the brand new green dress with red cabbage roses, but she could tell by the look on his face something else was on his mind.

"What a wonderful dress," he said, full of relief. At least he had something nice to say right off the bat.

"Thank you," Mrs. Marquez mumbled. She was trying to work up a little bit of bravado to cover the uncertainty of being caught without a plan.

"Is it new?" Raymond asked. He was trying to fill the air with the sound of something besides his anxiety.

"Yes," Mrs. Marquez said. "It was made especially for me."

Gradually, Mrs. Marquez' imperious façade was catching up, trying to build enough momentum to take on its usual tone.

"How nice," was all Raymond could manage. He was starting to worry about what he knew was to come.

"Well, thank you so much for the favor," Bernardo said. Eager to leave, he deliberately didn't mention the phone.

"Just don't make it a habit," she sniped. Then she looked at Hortence Grace with a, "this-dress-better-work," look as Hortence Grace walked to Bernardo.

"It's time for us to go," she smiled.

After a round of goodbyes they slipped out the door without a single thank you from Mrs. Marquez who, when the door finally closed, ran to Raymond and threw her arms around his neck.

"Oh, my darling, oh my own. Oh, Raymond, my Raymond... I love you. You are the treasure of my life," she bellowed. Raymond stood still as a post and tried to get a word in edgewise.

"Maria... Maria... a..." but it was impossible.

Mrs. Marquez was so caught up in her own scenario she was missing all of the signals. In her mind, God was on her side. First the delivery of the dress, then the delivery of Raymond just like clockwork... one, two, three. And boy, she thought, had she ever been right about the color green as she grabbed Raymond's hands and tried to engage him in some sort of twirling dance to show off how beautifully she and the dress moved together. Just like she and Raymond would move together now that he was here and would certainly want to stay always and forever after seeing the intoxicating image of her in this gown. Maybe Hortence Grace had been right...

"Maria!" Raymond finally had to shout to get her attention.

Then he pulled his hands out of hers. He didn't like this approach, but she'd left him no choice. Affected by his harsh tone, Mrs. Marquez stopped spinning and smiling. In fact, she almost stopped breathing. She'd never heard so much volume come out of Raymond before.

"I think we should sit down." He said this as calmly as he could for a man not used to this sort of thing.

"Would you like something to drink?" Mrs. Marquez asked. She sensed something was coming and was trying to throw him off track.

"No... No, thank you," he declined firmly.

"A snack?" This was going to be even harder than he had anticipated.

"Maria... I have something to say."

Finally Mrs. Marquez sat down and fluffed out her dress but Raymond didn't notice. He sat down in the chair right across from her, took a deep breath and plunged right in.

"I wanted you to be the first to know..."

"Know what?" she interrupted.

"Please... Please don't interrupt," he implored. "This is very difficult." A moment went by. Then Mrs. Marquez sat forward in her chair so she could inhale his every breath and watch his every move.

"I wanted you to be the first to know that Juanita Chavez is going to have a baby."

"So?" Mrs. Marquez shrugged.

"My baby..." Raymond said softly. Mrs. Marquez looked at Raymond like she'd been shot.

"Your baby..." she whispered.

"So she and I are going to be married..."

"What?!" blared out of her mouth in a blast. "You're going to be what?!"

"Married," he said with a little more volume. Mrs. Marquez exploded out of her chair.

"No, you're not!" she yelled.

Raymond used this as a cue to stand up and wish that the floor would just open up and swallow him.

"Yes, Maria. We are," he contradicted softly. Mrs. Marquez started to shake with rage and look for something to throw.

"She's a slut!" Mrs. Marquez shouted as she found the tea pot and flung it in Raymond's direction. Luckily he ducked so the pot missed him and crashed against the door, spraying tea all over the walls and dribbling down on the floor.

"I'll kill you," she raged. She was already on her way to the drawer in the kitchen where she kept the gun.

Raymond sensing it was now or never, rushed to the door and ran outside to his truck. He jumped inside just as Mrs. Marquez found the gun buried under all of her kitchen utensils. Hearing the truck's engine turn over was the final blow. She ran outside as he was backing away, lifted the gun, took careful aim and fired but nothing happened, just a click. Much to her dismay she'd forgotten there were no bullets in the chamber. Mrs.

Marquez let out such a loud howl, shock waves rippled out to the setting sun. After that she started to sob.

In an absolutely tormented state she ran back inside the house churning with fury. Uncertain of what to do or where to begin, she started in the kitchen, dumped every drawer, every container and every shelf out onto the floor. Then she tore apart every closet, chest and cabinet and finally, after she had turned the rest of the house upside down and thrown every single thing including the bed into the center of the room, Mrs. Marquez collapsed on top of the heap and sobbed inconsolable sobs all over her brand new dress.

The Drop

A small dirty car driving in the dark without lights skidded around the corner onto Rosa Guillermo's narrow street and almost hit a tree. Whoever was at the wheel stepped on the gas and in the middle of the block, without slowing down or the slightest hesitation, a car door flew open and Rosa Guillermo was tossed out of the back seat. She landed on the walkway in front of her courtyard gate like a sack of shit.

After the initial thud the only sound was the car's squealing tires as it turned the corner. Then it was still except for the brand new baby that started to cry in the house next door. It was 3 a.m., time for the baby's middle of the night feeding.

On the ground, Rosa Guillermo lay in the moonlight, her face tilted up toward the stars. Her mouth was wide open, stuck in a soundless scream without her tongue. Her eyes were gone, gouged out. So was her heart and she was naked. Her body twitched, but she was dead. Her battered arm was just settling after the fall. All the other damage couldn't be fully assessed until it got light.

Just then, Johnny Orteez pulled up in the Johnny-mobile. He was drunk. He'd just been to a cousin's wedding and was hoping Rosa Guillermo would let him sleep on her couch. He was too tired to drive and he didn't want to sleep in the van. It wasn't good for his image. He switched off the engine and stepped into the street, unzipped his pants and took a piss. He began to hum, "Love Me Tender," under his breath as he finished his business and hurried to the gate, but stopped when he saw the lump on the ground. It took a moment before he concluded that whatever-it-was wasn't a bag of trash. He looked around to see if he was being seen, but he wasn't. Everything was perfectly quiet. Even the baby next door had stopped crying and fallen asleep. Johnny Orteez took a deep breath and approached whatever-it-was cautiously, only going close enough to the lump to see that it was a body.

He shook his head. The impact of what he was seeing was having a hard time penetrating his stupor. He decided that it was just a dog someone had run over and thrown to the side of the road. Still very drunk he yawned and hiccupped all at once and started to walk around the whatever-it-was, and go inside but about halfway, the body twitched and shifted in its uncertain position. Johnny Orteez stopped in his tracks. Suddenly he was sober. Now that he was close he could see Rosa Guillermo's open mouth and eyeless face and whatever else that had happened to her mangled body. He was so afraid he let out a little cry and choked on his own saliva.

Johnny Orteez turned and ran to the Johnny-mobile, jumped inside, slammed the door, turned the key in the ignition and drove away fast, leaving Rosa Guillermo alone in the moonlight.

"Damn it!" Olivia yelled.

Someone was urgently ringing the bell by the gate and banging on the door, which irritated Olivia to no end. She was right in the middle of the last episode of her favorite telenovela starring Daniella Perez, the most popular actress in nighttime soaps. She had finally worked out the right readjustment of the rabbit ear antenna with aluminum foil and a rubber band to get rid of the snow on Li Choo's thirteen-inch television set, so she didn't want to be bothered.

"Go away!" she shouted. But the banging and bell ringing continued so she yelled to the hired help... "Get the door!" She was determined to ignore everything but the television stars professing their undying love. In fact she was so engrossed she missed the argument between the housekeeper and whoever had barged inside until he was standing right there. Johnny Orteez, looking pale, was too horror-stricken to speak.

"What the hell?" Olivia said.

She pulled the black silk robe around her hammy backside and sat straight up in bed, searching under the satin cased pillows for her switchblade as he stepped closer.

"Don't come any further," Olivia commanded. So he stopped, but he was breathless with fear.

"What? What the hell is it?" Olivia didn't like what she was looking at. "Can't you see I'm busy?"

Johnny Orteez was having trouble forming words.

"Come on... speak up. Why are you here at this hour?"

"Something bad," he finally managed to mumble.

"What? And for God's sake talk louder." Olivia had fumbled around and finally found her knife.

"She's dead."

"She? She who?"

"Rosa Guillermo."

"Rosa Guillermo?" Olivia was puzzled.

"Rosa Guillermo is dead."

"Dead?" Olivia strained forward to make sure she was hearing him right. Johnny Orteez just nodded, he was in such a state of shock. So was Olivia, but she wanted the dirt. Facts didn't interest her, but she was blatantly curious for all of the descriptive details, most especially ones that she could embellish.

"Why?" She was hoping to get the ball rolling, but he could only shrug because he was shaking.

"Where?"

"Dumped in front of her house."

"Dumped?"

Johnny Orteez nodded and then he whispered, "Like a sack of garbage."

Olivia got up off the bed. She slipped the knife into her robe pocket as dramatic music swelled out of the television set.

"They cut out her heart," he continued. Olivia's mouth fell open and she sat back down on the bed. This was something altogether different.

"And her eyes. Other things too... I couldn't see what else, it was dark..." His voice trailed off. All of a sudden Olivia felt shaky.

"My God," she whispered.

Daniella Perez's voice blared, "How could you do this to me?" from the television set. For the first time, Olivia was scared.

"I didn't know who to tell," Johnny interjected.

Olivia blinked. "Why would someone cut out her heart?"

Johnny Orteez could only shrug, but then he wondered... "Should I call her brother, or the Commander, or..." His voice just stopped. He and Olivia looked at each other while someone on television selling toothpaste talked about gleaming white teeth.

Finally Olivia got up and spoke very low. "Go home," she said. "Go home and don't tell anyone anything about nothing and don't call anybody and if somebody asks, you don't know what you never saw and if anyone says they saw you seeing it, call them a liar and get away fast."

Johnny Orteez snapped to. Something in the tone of Olivia's voice gave him courage and direction, a path to follow.

"And don't tell nobody you came here. But if anybody asks, you were bringing me a book. Tell them 'Gone with the Wind.' But you and me, we never talked about this... Understand?" Riveted to her every word, Johnny Orteez nodded.

"Now go." Olivia pointed to the door.

He was gone so fast it seemed like he'd never been there. After a few moments Olivia got back into bed. The beginning of the end of the telenovela dilemma was just starting so Olivia hadn't missed much, but she just stared at the screen. The thought of Rosa Guillermo dumped like garbage in front of her gate refused to leave her mind.

Joan Tewkesbury

Mr. Lobos entered the Church of Martyrs and looked around, tried to adjust to the dark, but the sound of someone weeping inconsolably inside the confessional stopped him cold. A sharp whistle pierced through the sorrow. Mr. Lobos turned and saw Bernardo sitting in a pew in the back so he slid in beside him before he noticed Mr. Bravo kneeling on the prayer rail. Spread out in front of him where you fold your hands to pray were all of the Rosa Guillermo pictures Mr. Bravo had exposed.

The weeping from the confessional got louder as Bernardo handed Mr. Lobos a flashlight so he could get a better look and Mr. Bravo pointed out who went with what. Mr. Lobos, who usually wasn't affected by much, was having a hard time. On one hand he couldn't believe what he was seeing, on the other hand, he could.

The metal curtain rings of the confession cubicle slid across the metal rod and all of them jumped. Mr. Bravo gathered up the pictures and dropped them in his pocket. Bernardo managed to extinguish the light just as Father Lyle stepped out of the booth followed by Johnny Orteez drenched with sweat. Father Lyle didn't see the three men sitting in the back and he was still trying to be helpful, wracking his brain for something to diminish this poor man's panic. Something this dramatic could loosen the tongue and have dangerous ramifications. As a priest he'd seen so much that he was numb to other people's shock at the defiling of the human body and it ceased to stir him.

Finally he put his hand on Johnny Orteez' shoulder and looked in his eyes. "Go with God, young man," was the extent of his message.

That's when Mr. Lobos stood up and, without genuflecting, walked right down the center aisle of the sacristy to Father Lyle and Johnny Orteez hovering near the altar as Mr. Bravo and Bernardo eased into the shadows to watch.

"Good morning, Father Lyle," Mr. Lobos said in a loud voice.

"Mr. Lobos?" Father Lyle was very surprised. Mr. Lobos nodded to Johnny Orteez who stood still as stone like he was glued to the spot. Mr. Lobos pulled a jar out of his pocket, held it up to the light so Father Lyle could get a good look at what was inside.

"I was hoping, Father Lyle, that you could keep this heart." Johnny Orteez looked up, blanched and started to shout.

"Oh my God, it's hers. I knew it. It's Rosa Guiller...!!!" Father Lyle covered Johnny's mouth with his hand to shush him.

"Mr. Orteez, no shouting in the house of the Lord."

Mr. Lobos looked at the two of them curiously.

"He's suffered a terrible shock." Father Lyle was trying to pretend they hadn't heard any part of Rosa Guillermo's name.

From the shadows in the back, Bernardo and Mr. Bravo watched the priest ease Johnny Orteez into the nearest pew as Mr. Lobos continued to hold out the jar so both of them could see.

"This heart is the heart of our Kind Predecessor, not the heart of anyone else. It is the heart The General removed while it was still beating. Until now, it has never left his side." Johnny Orteez started to shake, but Mr. Lobos continued.

"But now it's time to keep it on the altar of this church."

Father Lyle looked horrified. "Why on earth would I do that?"

The priest had no desire to be on the receiving end of the General's revenge or wrath but Mr. Lobos spoke in his most humble, sincere tone.

"Who better to protect a kindly heart than a man of God in the house of God for the good of all of God's people?" Mr. Lobos walked up to the holy table. He placed the heart next to the box of bones of a lesser-known saint and made sure the jar would always be in plain sight under the single shaft of artificial light. Then he turned to Father Lyle.

"Tell everyone the General has given this gift for the good of the people in the parish."

Father Lyle was suspicious, but he tried to sound calm. "What if the General changes his mind and wants the heart back?"

Mr. Lobos shrugged. "I've told him if he does, I'll feed it to his dogs."

That's when Johnny Orteez got up and ran out of the church.

The Discovery

Rosa Guillermo was still on the ground where she'd been tossed. Everything was exactly the same as the night before except for the flies and an old blue baby blanket someone had thrown over her bloody privates.

Bernardo covered his nose and mouth with his handkerchief and rolled her over. She'd been gutted like a chicken, cut from her neck to her pubic bone. Anything usable was gone. Eyes, heart, liver, kidneys and lungs... even her ears and breasts. Drawn on her flank with a felt tip marker, a picture of a dog mounting a woman carefully detailed to look like Rosa Guillermo and "You're No Virgin Mother" scrawled across what was left of her chest.

Mr. Bravo had to walk away, but Mr. Lobos took a clinical approach and after examining the grisly mess asked Mr. Bravo to come back with his camera. Like it or not, he had to take pictures otherwise they'd have no proof and no one would believe them. After they helped Mr. Bravo set up the camera and he snapped the first photograph, Mr. Lobos went to see if one of the neighbors had a phone. In a matter of minutes Juanita and her mother rounded the corner on their way to Rosa Guillermo's house to go to work.

Seeing them out of the corner of his eye, Bernardo ran to intercept so they wouldn't have to confront the situation. Unfortunately they'd caught a glimpse and the smell of something dead and their impulse was to see more than a woman's blood-smeared foot sticking out from under a blue baby blanket. Bernardo managed to get in the way, told them to go and not come back and not to tell anyone they had even come here on this day or yesterday or any other day this week or that they knew anything about anything at all. They could be blamed, held accountable, or responsible, and taken away.

Juanita's mother got it immediately, understood just from the tone of Bernardo's voice and seeing the little guy taking pictures and recognizing Mr. Lobos crossing the street. It certainly was time to go, but Juanita, who never believed anything any more unless she saw it with her own eyes, wanted confirmation, some kind of proof. After all, it was just Bernardo's word about what they had glimpsed on the ground. Maybe it was something that she wanted to know about. She had been a Sergeant's wife. Bernardo was a very nice man, but she was smart enough to figure out that whatever it was, wasn't right.

"I want to see what's going on!" she shouted.

That's when her mother smashed her hand across her daughter's mouth. "Enough!" Her mother's voice was low and serious and just right. She grabbed her daughter by the arm and steered her back to the corner.

Juanita let out a wail so her mother smacked her and told her to shut up. After that she grabbed Juanita by the hair so she couldn't turn around and look. Bernardo didn't move until they were out of sight.

When Mr. Bravo said he was finished, Bernardo helped Mr. Lobos help Mr. Bravo load everything back in his truck.

"Be quick," Mr. Lobos said. Then all of them climbed inside and Mr. Bravo gave Bernardo the keys and as they drove away they passed the ancient ambulance coming in the other direction, its raspy siren blaring and missing every other note.

The General sat in Lilly's underground living room while the General's Commander stood right next to him and held the General's jar of ears. Lilly looked at the General's tarot spread and whistled low down and slow.

"You better lean back and relax. You got a big mess here."

The General wasn't used to taking orders, but he was desperate or he wouldn't have come in the first place. He motioned to the Commander who handed him the jar, which he put in his lap and cradled like a baby.

"What the hell is that?" Lilly wanted to know.

The General shrugged. "Ears. I'm lost without my heart," he whined.

"You can say that again." Lilly looked at him sternly. "You got strange ideas about what to hang on to." The General loosened his grip on the jar a little as Lilly shook her head. "Uh, uh, uh..."

"What?!" The General was edgy, to say the least.

"Trouble, trouble, trouble," Lilly said. "Your big wave is about to crash and you could drown." The General started to sweat.

"If you could just tell me about my heart."

"Why?" Lilly asked.

"Because it keeps me safe."

"It's not even yours." Lilly started to laugh. Then she stopped. "Are you nuts?"

The Commander reached out to give Lilly a smack, but Lilly saw it coming and threw her ice tea in his face.

"Don't mess around," Lilly advised. "You just never know what will happen." The General motioned to the Commander, dripping with tea, to back off. Lilly leaned down to get closer to the General's paranoia.

"He's no help, you know. No help whatsoever."

The General shrugged.

"And whose idea was that dummy you got rigged up?" This took the General completely by surprise.

"Well..." the General waffled.

"Mine," the Commander jumped right in.

"You're a fool," Lilly said and reshuffled the cards.

"Now wait just a minute," the General said. He didn't take kindly to the truth.

"Why? You came here to ask questions. You think I'm gonna lie?"

The General pulled out his gun and put it on the table, but Lilly just yawned. "Fine. Shoot me. Then you'll really be in a dinky canoe way out in the ocean with no paddle." Torn between superstition and practicality, the General took a moment to think. He chose superstition and holstered his gun, but Lilly was adamant.

"Put that thing on the table. I want it right out here in the open."

The Commander shook his head. He was still wiping off tea with a towel, but the General sighed and did what Lilly said. The Commander sighed too and looked out the window at the row of mangy dogs sitting in the dirt.

"You got big ideas, but no plans and that other guy's heart you carry around in a jar... it don't do squat."

"Yes it does!" the General cried out, sounding desperate. Lilly looked into his panicked eyes then shook her head.

"You got a big ambition with the wrong map and being a pig-headed tyrant don't win you no prizes."

The General had had enough humiliation. He lost his composure and pounded his fist on the table.

"Where is my heart?!"

Every dog sitting outside got up, bared its teeth as they came right up to the window and growled.

"HIS heart," Lilly corrected.

"MY heart," he snarled. So did the dogs outside, which made the Commander very nervous.

"HIS heart is someplace safe and in plain sight," Lilly said.

"What kind of stupid riddle is that?" he yelled getting red in the face.

"Just what I said," Lilly smiled, turned over another couple of cards and laughed.

"What's so goddamn funny?"

"Somebody took it to church."

"You son-of-a-bitch, that is a lie." He reached for the gun but Lilly beat him to it and put it in her lap. Then she continued with a menacing tone.

"What you got is a long, awful life ahead unless maybe somebody does you a favor and pulls the plug. I suggest you got a lot to make up for, so you better get started."

"You bitch!" the General shouted. Then he picked up his jar of ears and stood. He'd had enough of her abuse.

"That'll be four hundred fifty," Lilly said.

"Well, I'm not gonna pay," the General announced.

Lilly smiled. "Yes, you will. It's bad luck not to pay the visionary."

Joan Tewkesbury

"You're a witch, not a visionary."

Now Lilly stood up and leaned in close. They were exactly the same height. "General, get ready to do some heavy lifting. Bad luck is about to take a long ride on your back."

At this point the Commander, who was more superstitious than smart, dug into his pockets because the General never carried cash, and produced a couple of bills which he tossed on the table. Lilly just laughed.

"You gotta be kidding." She motioned for more so the Commander was forced to dig deeper and give her all the cash that he had. After she thanked him she walked to the door and held up the gun.

"You got one of these, Commander?"

The Commander nodded.

"Shoot my dogs on the way out and I'll shoot you."

The Commander got the picture so he nodded again. He couldn't wait to leave. This whole tarot card business gave him the creeps. Lilly turned to the General and gave him some food for thought.

"As to the heart, I don't lie General. I see things you can't even imagine. I even know your father killed your mother so he could fuck her sister..."

The General blanched, but she continued.

"The cards told me that. They told me a lot of other stuff too, so if I'm kind enough to tell you where that stupid heart is staying, you better believe me it's true." Now Lilly opened the door. She waited for the Commander and the General to climb the stairs before she said the last thing that she had to say.

"I'll have the gun delivered."

At this point the General didn't care. He just wanted to get the hell away. He stormed through the pack of mangy dogs and after Lilly counted to twenty she fired the gun in the air which scattered the dogs and scared the shit out of the General and his Commander as they got into their armored car and drove away.

Go Boil Water

Mrs. Marquez was in a stupor. Still dressed in her shiny new dress, she hadn't moved off the heap of stuff she'd thrown on the floor during last night's fury. Even when the phone rang at noon from the depths of its bowl she hadn't bothered to answer. There wasn't anybody she cared to talk to. Not even Raymond Valdez if he came crawling back on his hands and knees. Mrs. Marquez didn't move even a little when Olivia and Mrs. Lobos arrived in Olivia's Packard for a prearranged meeting and, finding Mrs. Marquez' front door standing wide open, just walked right in.

"My God, what a dump," Olivia said as she looked around. Emptied out drawers, overturned table, flipped over chairs, knives and forks side by side with the dirty clothes, shoes, dishes and bowls, an assortment of Hamburger Helper, corn meal and the mattress with its pillows and sheets tossed on top of the pile.

"Mrs. Marquez?" Olivia called out.

Mrs. Lobos stepped over several broken plates and some pots and pans. "What a sty," she announced.

Mrs. Marquez heard every word, but she didn't answer. She was too lost in her loss.

"What do you think happened?" Olivia wondered.

"Well, she's got nothing worth stealing," Mrs. Lobos said, picking up the odd item or two then tossing it back on the mountain of mess.

Expecting the worst ever since the late night visit from Johnny Orteez, Olivia moved further into the house and caught a glimpse of the shiny-green, cabbage rose, puffed sleeve sticking out from under an old fur coat.

"Oh for heaven's sake," she frowned as she lifted it up, unaware that Mrs. Marquez was buried beneath it. "This is my mink!"

Mrs. Lobos shook her head. "Yard sale memorabilia?"

"I can remember," Olivia said, searching through the pockets and seeing a little more of the dress.

"Good Lord. That's just awful."

"What?" Mrs. Lobos said.

"That," Olivia pointed boldly then bent over and lifted the skirt to feel the shiny fabric. Mrs. Marquez decided she'd heard enough and pulled the dress right out of Olivia's hand.

"Oh my God!" Olivia shrieked.

"What?" Mrs. Lobos said, and rushed over just in time to see Mrs. Marquez' leg move across her assortment of possessions. "Oh my God!" she cried out.

Mrs. Marquez didn't say a word, didn't whisper, didn't even blink.

"She's a ghost!" Mrs. Lobos yelled even louder. Olivia hurried to Mrs. Marquez and felt for a pulse, tried to see into her vacant eyes.

"Maria, what happened?"

Slowly, Mrs. Marquez raised herself up on one elbow and tried to get her bearings, but Mrs. Lobos, impatient to get down to business jumped right in.

"We're here to discuss the details of the 'tragic accident.'"

"Stop it," Olivia snapped. "Can't you see something's wrong?"

Mrs. Lobos looked around at the chaotic jumble and took an imperious tone. "Her business, not ours," she said.

Olivia had had enough. She pointed at her and ordered, "Mrs. Lobos, put on the kettle and boil some water. This woman needs a strong cup of coffee."

"Me?" Mrs. Lobos couldn't believe what she was hearing.

"Unless you'd prefer to tend to Mrs. Marquez?"

No sooner had the words come out of Olivia's mouth, than Mrs. Lobos began to look for a pot to fill with water. Olivia, uncertain of what could have caused this rampage and hoping in her heart it had nothing to do with the business of Rosa Guillermo or some other plot, helped Mrs. Marquez get to her feet and eased her into the only upright chair, where she sat staring into space and not speaking and remaining in some sort of trance.

PICTURES AT AN EXHIBITION

In the late afternoon, when everything in front of Rosa Guillermo's courtyard gate, including Rosa Guillermo, had been cleaned up so it looked like nothing on earth had ever happened, Bernardo and Mr. Bravo appeared like two city workers preparing her wall for a fresh coat of paint. They caulked the cracks, primed the plaster from bottom to top just like an artist would prepare a surface to paint an important mural. They blocked off the sidewalk with signs that read... CAUTION WET PAINT... so no one could get close enough to see what they were up to and when the sun finally sank, the two of them, careful as curators, hung their exhibit of facts on the wall.

A special selection of photographs: men, women and children, terrified faces, torture, rape, tractors and limbs, men in tuxedos and women in long dresses singing "Happy Birthday" at the General's birthday party, soldiers without pants, new families in the General's garden and featured prominently in the middle row, right at adult eye level so you couldn't miss it, photographs of Rosa Guillermo filleted and gutted and without most of her body parts. All that remained of the thirty-year-old woman was a bloody, hacked-up mess.

After they finished, they painted over the pictures with something like a transparent suit of armor so sturdy it repelled paint from a brush or a spray can and wouldn't wash off. Something Mr. Lobos had stolen from the maintenance station, a product developed by leading chemists to protect the General's propaganda posters from graffiti or other forms of destruction.

It was dark when they took away the ladders and signs and stuffed their overalls in Mr. Bravo's truck, so they went to the local cantina for something to eat and a couple of beers. By the time they walked back toward Rosa Guillermo's gate, what they saw surprised them.

A steady stream of people, silent and holding candles, was waiting in a line that extended around the block to look at the pictures on the wall. And as they recognized a face or a relative's child in someone else's arms there was disbelief and then gasping and moaning and horrified confirmation. What they suspected was true. Witnessing Rosa Guillermo's fate some of them whispered, "She got what she deserved," but after the woman next door placed a bouquet of flowers by the gate, others left prayer cards and then more and more flowers until another neighbor, worried about all the strangers in the street, called the authorities.

Finally, when the police arrived, in no rush because they were finishing their dinner and the circumstances didn't seem very important, they were driven back by a group of grandmothers who pelted them with garbage and rocks and anything else they could get their hands on. Grossly outnumbered, the police decided to leave. Let the General's army take care of the situation. Seeing this as a kind of victory, the people on the block and around the corner split into shifts to guard and protect the exhibition of facts.

Bernardo and Mr. Bravo got into Mr. Bravo's truck and drove away without saying a word.

GARDENIAS FROM THE GARDEN

Mr. Lobos stood in Ebba's open doorway looking at Ebba, dressed in her mother's pale blue dress and his mother's yellow silk shawl. His arms were full of gardenias he'd picked in his mother's garden. Ebba seemed fine but different, yet he wasn't sure why. Something was new and whatever it was was confusing yet familiar, but it made him shy, and she was shy too, so neither of them spoke until finally he remembered to hand her the flowers. Delighted, she buried herself in the bouquet and the fragrance thrilled her so much she almost forgot to ask him to come inside.

"Won't you come in?" she said so softly she could barely be heard. Mr. Lobos nodded, stepped into the narrow hall and watched her fill bowl after bowl with the flowers, placing them in every room so their perfume could spread all over the house.

"I'm sorry," Mr. Lobos said.

Those were the very first words out of his mouth after Ebba poured him a glass of lemonade flavored with rose petals she'd brought from Hortence Grace and Bernardo's garden. Her braid fell across her chest like a beauty queen banner and she looked at him through her lashes over the rim of her glass.

"I didn't know what my mother had in mind," he continued, shaking his head.

"Mothers have a life of their own," Ebba said with authority.

Mr. Lobos nodded and gazed at her in the glow of several jelly glass candles. "You have a new dress."

Ebba took a gardenia from one of the bowls and put it in her hair.

"Mine was too small," she replied, surprised that he had noticed.

"The color is nice," he said.

Ebba shrugged.

"So are the flowers," she said and took another sip of lemonade.

Then Mr. Lobos sipped his lemonade too, and both of them sat wrapped in the gardenia smell and the quiet. Finally Mr. Lobos put his glass down on the table and asked, "How is Ariel?"

Ebba shook her head. "Not the same," she said, realizing she wasn't either. All of a sudden the image of the dead man's face without his eyes and tongue, floated across her memory like a curtain.

"Ebba..." Mr. Lobos said. Ebba turned to him, but the image wouldn't go away.

Joan Tewkesbury

"Ebba?" Mr. Lobos asked.

This time she made no response whatsoever so Mr. Lobos got up and knelt down by her chair, took hold of her hands and after a moment or two Ebba started to sob and collapsed into the nape of his neck. Mr. Lobos took her in his arms, sat down on the floor, let her slide into his lap and then rocked her, tried to bring her back to before, even though he knew that would never be again. He was almost afraid to touch her but he held her anyway, let her sobs course through his body as if they belonged to him and tried to figure out when she had become part of his heart.

At that exact moment there was a bang at the door and then it slammed open, revealing his mother and Olivia Gomez. After the initial shock of what she was seeing, Mrs. Lobos shouted at the top of her lungs, "What are you doing?!"

Mr. Lobos didn't move, didn't answer and Ebba just stayed lodged in the nape of his neck. "I saw your car," Mrs. Lobos continued to shout.

Mr. Lobos turned to his mother and interrupted. "And why was that an invitation to enter someone's house without knocking?"

"Because..." she took a moment. "You are my son!"

Mr. Lobos shook his head. "Maybe when I lived in your womb, but certainly not now."

Then he got up and helped Ebba back into the chair, stood with his hand on Ebba's shoulder as he looked at Olivia.

"Obviously you showed her the way."

"Your mother didn't need a map." Olivia had had quite enough of all these people. First, Mrs. Marquez and now this ongoing family drama. She slipped out of her too tight shoes to let her feet have a rest as Mr. Lobos walked to his mother.

"It's time for you to go home and leave everyone alone," he said.

Ebba wiped her eyes and stood up. "Would you like a glass of lemonade?" she asked politely.

That's when Mrs. Lobos saw her pale yellow silk shawl draped around Ebba's body.

Mrs. Lobos inhaled a huge scoop of air in preparation to stretch full height and shriek her disapproval, but instead she froze. Instantly she was locked in the silent grip of a paralyzing stroke. The only sound she was able to utter came out as a croak and then she went stiff as a plank.

"Oh my God!" Olivia cried.

Mr. Lobos just shook his head. Somehow he'd always known it was just a matter of time. "It's a stroke," he said and looked at Olivia. "I'll need you to help me put her in your car..."

"My car?" Olivia sounded desperate. "She's your mother."

"Your car," Mr. Lobos said firmly.

Olivia struggled back into her shoes, furious to have to be the one to have to tend to this sort of emergency.

"Go straight to the hospital. I'll go get the doctor."

"What about the kid?" Olivia wanted to know. She was having difficulty helping lift Mrs. Lobos who, for someone so tiny, seemed heavy as lead. Mr. Lobos ignored her question.

"Just drive fast, Mrs. Gomez. I'll take care of the rest."

Once Mrs. Lobos was in the back seat of the Packard, Ebba unwound the silk shawl and placed it on top of its original owner hoping it might revive her, but it had no effect at all. As soon as Olivia's car was out of sight, Mr. Lobos took Ebba to Bernardo and Hortence Grace. No matter what happened to his mother, he wanted Ebba to be safe.

News of the photographs displayed on Rosa Guillermo's wall had traveled fast. In fact, the wall was becoming a kind of word-of-mouth shrine and people were traveling from all over everywhere to take a look.

Because the General determined it was too dangerous to go see the wall for himself, he commanded the Commander to tell Mr. Bravo to take pictures of the pictures but Mr. Bravo was never at home when they knocked. Actually he was. He just didn't answer. He was busy in the darkroom printing more of those pictures to put on flyers to give away.

Consequently the Commander, who never thought things through, commanded one of his uniformed aides to come with him to the site. The Commander would take pictures himself with his old Brownie camera. Unfortunately as soon as the Commander stepped out of his government green vehicle the neighbors pelted him with pig droppings and anything else that was handy. The only photograph the Commander managed to take was of the men with kerchief-covered faces overturning his truck and setting it on fire but it was out of focus.

THE FIRE

L ater in the day when Bernardo was driving Gloria home he began to smell smoke and as they rounded the curve near the top of the mountain he saw orange flames forking near the ridge. Thick gray smoke began to form a blanket making it impossible to see so he pulled Gloria onto the shoulder and got out of the truck. Then he covered his nose and mouth with his handkerchief and walked up the road.

At first he thought that it was Ebba's house going up in flames but as he got closer he realized it was the house of Mrs. Marquez. A bucket brigade was in progress but it wasn't enough to combat this sort of blaze. One of the men carrying water said Mrs. Marquez had been burning rubbish in the back yard: letters, clothes, pictures, a few pieces of furniture and other odds and ends when an unexpected burst of wind had fanned the flames which changed direction and moved quickly to the house.

One of the other men reported seeing Mrs. Marquez in a fancy green dress, waving a cape at the flames like a matador, but when the fire didn't respond to her veronicas she'd run back in the house and hadn't been seen since.

Bernardo rolled up his sleeves and relieved the man pumping water from the portable pump to fill the buckets but it was too late. By the time the wind stopped blowing and the fire died down the house had burned to the ground. All that remained were the cremated remains of Mrs. Marquez sitting upright in a metal chair that was molded to her body. She was charred beyond recognition except for one unexplainable detail. The brand new green dress was burnt to a crisp, but one red cabbage rose remained entirely intact, perfect in fact, and not even singed by the fire.

Joan Tewkesbury

THE HOSPITAL VISIT

By the time the General's limo pulled up to the front of the not-so-state-of-the-art hospital in Josefina, every car in his motorcade was covered with garbage and rotten eggs thrown by local residents lining the streets. And when the General got out of the car and stepped inside the bulletproof popemobile waiting to take him into the building, someone threw a dirty diaper that slapped against the window and smeared shit down the bulletproof glass where it clung and flapped like a banner letting everyone know that the General was arriving to see his sister in a perfumed cloud of baby poop.

Inside Mrs. Lobos' private room, her stiff-as-a-board body was laid out on a mechanical bed; medical apparatus clogged every inch of available space. Permanently paralyzed because of the massive stroke, she stared straight up at the ceiling. Her gaping mouth, a large dark hollow, didn't work and never would again. Tucked in a corner, amongst large funereal arrangements of flowers that the Commander kept readjusting, Mr. Lobos stood with Dr. Vidal and Olivia Gomez watching the Commander try to orchestrate some sort of photo opportunity with a local newspaper reporter out in the hall. "GENERAL VISITS SISTER WITH STROKE," the Commander dictated loudly as he stepped into Mrs. Lobos' room leaving the door wide open so the reporter could take a bedside photograph of the devoted brother and his sick sister. Mr. Lobos waited until the reporter announced, "Ready? One, two, three..." then kicked the door shut just as the camera clicked, wiping out the General's public relations photo op. The General, disguised in bright blue scrubs and looking desperate, had managed to sneak into his sister's room without being noticed. Juggling the jar of ears he carried around like a baby, he'd turned to Mr. Lobos and before asking about his sister's condition, pleaded with him to give back the heart, and promised he'd take care of anything Mr. Lobos wanted him to take care of, but Mr. Lobos had just smiled.

"My thanks, Uncle, but there's nothing left to do."

In an attempt to appear relieved like he knew exactly what Mr. Lobos was talking about, the General nodded. Then he turned and handed the jar of ears to the Commander as Olivia, hidden amongst the calla lilies and yellow hibiscus, piped up from the corner.

"So, General? Seen the pictures on Rosa Guillermo's wall?"

The General got busy trying to get out of the bright blue scrubs so he could ignore her as she smiled.

"And the ones of you waving in the tent?"

The General decided to turn a blind eye to the whole topic and grabbed the jar of ears back from the Commander as Dr. Vidal looked up from Mrs. Lobos' pulse and sighed.

"It was bound to happen," he said, without saying which thing he was referring to.

The General found his handkerchief and blew his nose. "Allergies," he said to the doctor before he finally asked, "How's my sister?"

"Trapped," the doctor said. "Her body won't do what she wants, but she understands everything that's going on." Dr. Vidal patted her arm as if it was a piece of wood and whispered, "Just like living in a coffin."

The General turned and looked at Mr. Lobos with a thin mean smile. "Must be a big relief. No more business of your mother. Finally, free." Then he paused for dramatic effect and added himself into the situation. "Actually now both of us are free of her clutches."

Mr. Lobos didn't answer; he just smiled that same thin mean smile right back. Not knowing what else to say the General cleared his throat. He didn't like all of this innuendo and beating around the bush so after a moment or two he picked up where he'd left off at the beginning.

"So about my heart..."

"I don't have it," Mr. Lobos interrupted, matter of factly. The General flinched.

"What do you mean, you don't have it?"

Mr. Lobos shook his head. "I don't."

The General was so alarmed he felt weak. He looked around, found the only chair in the room and sat down.

"I gave it to the church," Mr. Lobos said.

"The church?" The General was stunned. Everything Lilly had said she saw in the cards was flickering before his eyes in neon.

"On your behalf, of course." Mr. Lobos said. "With special visiting privileges any time you want."

"Visiting privileges?"

Mr. Lobos nodded.

"It's sitting on the altar at the Church of Martyrs under a beam of light."

"A beam of light?!" The General's fury was starting to mount.

Mr. Lobos continued sincerely, "Private sittings for you and the heart to be followed with public viewings so everyone can mend after this prolonged period of fear and sadness and grief."

The General stood up like a bear aroused during hibernation and knocked over the chair.

"You son of a bitch!" he yelled.

Mr. Lobos held up his hand. "General, please. Not in front of the ladies."

"Ladies?" the General snarled, pointing at the women in the room.

"This one is a vegetable and this one..." the General stepped closer to Olivia, "is nothing but a widow."

Unable to resist, Olivia grabbed hold of his finger and gave it a nasty little twist. "That's what you think," she smiled as the General jerked back from her grip.

"Don't touch me!" he shouted fiercely. Then he righted the chair and sat back down, shifted the jar of ears from his left arm to his right and yelled to no one in particular but the whole world in general, "You shit!"

Dr. Vidal used this opportunity to roll his chair intrusively between the General and the Commander and leaned in as close as he could to the Commander's ear.

"She's all yours," he whispered with a friendly smile.

The Commander panicked as he watched Olivia pull a fan out of her great big purse. "Her?" he croaked.

The doctor laughed a don't-be-ridiculous laugh. "Don't be a fool, Commander. I'm talking about Mercedes."

"Mercedes?" The Commander tried to indicate by his innocent tone that he didn't know anyone named Mercedes and had no idea who the doctor was talking about.

"Yes. Mercedes. Mercedes, my nurse, in your van." The doctor chuckled. "When you broke the bed?"

Horrified, the Commander clammed right up.

"Consider it a gift," the doctor smiled just as Mr. Lobos opened the great big box of candy the General had brought to give to his sister.

The doctor's announcement came as a shock to the Commander who wasn't ready for anything more permanent than a few athletic rounds with Mercedes' abundant body. He certainly wasn't looking to make a commitment, so to avoid saying anything that might change the his and her hit-and-run status, he reached out for the box of candy.

Unfortunately, he had to wait for the General who was rummaging through the entire selection. When he finally found two chocolate covered cherries he popped them into his mouth, but Olivia, who wasn't choosy, reached across the Commander, grabbed the box and a whole handful of sweets then offered it to Dr. Vidal who declined because he was busy doing something else. When it finally came to the Commander his choices were sticky and chewy so he stuffed all of them into his mouth to use as a deterrent to talking.

The General whose eyes were still a little tight from plastic surgery bent over to remove the bright blue surgical covers disguising his expensive Italian leather shoes. Dr. Vidal, who'd been waiting for just the right opportunity, turned around quick, took careful aim and jammed a hypodermic needle, filled-to-the brim with something unfortunate for your body, right through the General's trousers and into the General's bent over backside.

"What the hell?!" the General yelled and right then and there, from the depths of his dark heart, the General knew that whatever had just happened was something unusually bad and that life as it had been a moment before would never be the same again. Clutching the jar of ears to his heart, the General decided he better leave while he still thought he could so he stood up but suddenly his body started to jerk involuntarily and sent him crashing into all of his sister's medical equipment and gasping for air. Still a little bit conscious, he struggled to stand but this time he dropped the heavy glass jar, fell to the floor and found himself thrashing around in a puddle of ears and shattered glass.

"Paraquat!" Dr. Vidal announced triumphantly when he turned to the stunned Commander who couldn't say a word because his mouth was jammed full of half chewed candy.

"In a couple of days he'll be as stiff as his sister. Then his organs will shut down and that will be the end of that."

Mr. Lobos stepped over the General who couldn't stop convulsing and flailing and stood by his mother's bed. "There are some things you need to attend to," Mr. Lobos said looking at the Commander trying to swallow the chocolate mess in his mouth. "First you'll tell the journalist from the paper that the General is so overcome by his sister's condition he's decided to stay in the hospital to be by her side."

The General, still having spasms and thrashing around in ears and broken glass, was speechless as Mr. Lobos pointed to him on the floor.

"Next, you'll take over all government responsibilities but Olivia Gomez will function as your second in command." Hearing every word the General rolled his eyes frantically as Mr. Lobos continued to address the Commander, who was in shock.

"It won't exactly be business as usual, Commander, but Mercedes will be on your arm, by your side."

The Commander was starting to feel lightheaded and sick. None of this was good news. He tried to perk up and waved his hand to interrupt. "Ah... that part... about Mercedes... I'm not so sure about that."

Dr. Vidal smiled as he fussed with the hypodermic needle. "You'll get used to it, Commander. It doesn't take long."

Mr. Lobos reached out and placed his hand on the Commander's shoulder. "And everyone will learn to love you because you're going to right all wrongs with your generous heart."

Then Mr. Lobos started for the door but stopped. He looked down at the General surrounded by ears and broken glass and turned to the Commander.

"Maybe you should ask the nurse to come and bring a mop..."

ABDUCTION, FUNERAL, FUNERAL AND A WEDDING

Just before dawn on the morning of Rosa Guillermo's funeral, Sergeant Ruiz was dragged out of his house in his pajamas by a group of men, their faces covered in flour sack masks with holes cut around the eyes so they could see. The Sergeant's pathetic, terrified wife managed to escape out the back door with her husband's coat thrown over the nightgown she was wearing and her purse. She was never seen again and no one ever found out where she went.

At the funeral service, conducted by Father Lyle at the Church of Martyrs, people came from as far away as Mexico City, including a television anchor named Lupe Perez, a friend of Rosa Guillermo's brother who was too afraid to come himself. For whatever reason, there was a determined group of women from Josefina whom Rosa Guillermo had only met once, passing around a petition to turn Rosa Guillermo into some sort of saint. Another group from Elena argued that Rosa Guillermo of all people didn't deserve sainthood, that only Bernardo's sister Gloria, who had never been found or heard about since she went missing had those kind of qualifications.

Olivia came in the Packard with a wreath of orange plastic flowers but got there late. The Commander, filling in for the "grief-stricken General" arrived with Mercedes on his arm and pushing Dr. Vidal in his chair. Dr. Vidal was asked by Lupe Perez from the television news to give them a statement.

"God rest her soul," Dr. Vidal said without emotion. Then he sneezed and motioned for Mercedes and the Commander to roll him away.

No one, it seemed, wanted to dwell on Rosa Guillermo's long career in "Family Redistribution" and not one of the families she put together showed up to pay their respects. Neither did Bernardo and Hortence Grace and their children, or Ebba, or Mr. Bravo, or Mr. Lobos, or Raymond Valdez, Juanita Chavez, her mother or Johnny Orteez.

After the service the television anchor, Lupe Perez from Mexico City, was doing her best to dismiss the truth, wrap the whole thing up and tie it with a bow so everyone could put it behind them. She blabbed on and on to her one-man crew in front of the little church.

"No one wants to piece together the past," she smiled into the camera.

"What's done is finished," she said, "the facts are on the wall. Let the pictures tell the story. Heaven knows, in the uncertain times of conflict and war, it helps us to reach out and make a martyr."

Then she smiled an earnest, benevolent smile and tried to stop Father Lyle for a statement as he rushed out of church, but he waved her off saying he was just too busy for talk and when she looked around to find someone else, the place was empty. Everyone had moved on to the cemetery to listen to Mr. Escalante trying to soothe Rosa Guillermo's soul with his guitar. Reluctantly, Lupe Perez and her one-man crew shoved all their camera equipment into Lupe's tiny Toyota and headed back to Mexico City.

Next on Father Lyle's schedule, that same day in the afternoon, was the memorial service for Mrs. Marquez. Because there was really nothing left of her to bury, it was classified by default a cremation since the ashes had already been scattered by the wind at the scene of the fire. The service was small. Out of respect, Raymond Valdez took care of the costs but didn't attend. A few neighbors came, and Olivia out of sympathy and guilt, and Johnny Orteez who announced after the brief service that he was going to visit relatives in San Miguel.

Mr. Escalante reported that when he came back from the cemetery, late in the day after the Mrs. Marquez' send-off, Carlotta Pavon's grave site had been rimmed in a shimmering green halo that hovered over the dirt and stayed there until dark. No one bothered to believe him except for Hortence Grace, but she was too busy to go see for herself and Ebba was too afraid. She figured if that was what her mother wanted to do from under the ground, it was none of Ebba's business.

Finally and gratefully, on the Saturday following the two celebrations of death and rounding out the week for Father Lyle, was the wedding of Juanita Chavez to Raymond Valdez. This time everyone showed up, including Lilly and Salvador with three or four of her nasty-looking, better-behaved dogs. Olivia even wore a dress and Ebba and Rebecca and Tobias and Ariel, still clinging to his father's neck, wore new clothes made by Hortence Grace including new dresses for Juanita, Juanita's mother and one for herself because the twins in her belly were beginning to be very big. The doctor came with the Commander and Mercedes, and Mr. Lobos arrived with more gardenias from his mother's garden for the bride.

Thankfully, the General and Mrs. Lobos were still speechless and confined to their beds, in the not so state-of-the-art hospital. As predicted by Dr. Vidal, the General's body was shutting down bit by bit. Organ after organ was beginning to shrink, but slowly, so there was a lot of time for the General to reflect while experiencing these biological events and review his not so wonderful life. Mrs. Lobos was simply still as a stone and would remain that way for years to come unless someone had the courage to pull the plug.

Meanwhile, at church, shortly after the bridesmaids, Ebba and Rebecca, walked down the aisle, Bernardo gave Juanita away to Raymond Valdez and Father Lyle pronounced them man and wife and new baby.

THE WEDDING PICTURE

After Mr. Bravo took the bride and groom outside for their wedding portrait, three children from Rebecca's catechism class discovered the body of Sergeant Ruiz stuffed in the manger behind the church where Mrs. Marquez and Raymond Valdez had had their last intimate encounter. Every single one of his bones had been broken so he would fit in the baby Jesus crib. He looked just like a sardine stuffed in a can. Because there was so much blood, it was difficult to determine the rest of the damage, but it appeared to be extreme, and it was so hot the ants and flies were making inroads wherever they could.

Finally, two policemen arrived in a government green truck and wrapped yellow stay-away tape around the entire Christmas crèche. They were bossy and self-important and walked around waving their arms as they told people not to leave because they had important questions to ask and wanted answers. But instead of the crowd leaving they gathered around the uniformed men in a tight clump which made the uniformed men very nervous. Several times the policemen told the crowd to step back in a threatening tone, but no one moved or paid the slightest bit of attention.

Finally after Father Lyle let the tension build between the crowd and the police he stepped forward with the Commander, made the Commander stand right beside him, and told the police they were interrupting a wedding.

"No one is in the mood for questions," Father Lyle said.

"Not in the mood?" one policeman shouted while the other nervously picked his teeth.

That's when Mr. Lobos stepped to the front and in a low, calm voice told them to go away or they'd end up like the man in the manger. Needless to say, the uniformed men took great offense.

"Who gives you such a big, low voice, like you are someone important?" said the one not picking his teeth.

"I told him it was all right," the Commander smiled with a hint of uncertain menace. The policemen, realizing that it was the Commander and noticing Lilly's dogs, took a step back.

"Perhaps you'd like a glass of punch," Juanita's mother offered.

She couldn't resist a man in uniform. The officers glanced at the group then looked at one another and decided that if the Commander didn't care about the guy in the manger, why rush? They accepted the punch, drank it right down, wished the bride and groom a long and happy life and then, to save face and look official, they picked up the manger stuffed with Sergeant Ruiz, put it in the back of their truck and drove away.

Just as soon as they turned at the corner, Lilly made Salvador set fire to the rest of the holy family just in case the policemen came back to look for clues.

THE RECEPTION WITH MUSIC,
THE CHILDREN'S ARMY, AND SINGING

After the flames in the manger, great plumes of white smoke hovered over the church and the wedding party as they walked to the dance floor in the field of flowers. Everyone walked except Raymond, who drove Juanita in his truck decorated with pink whirligigs and red ribbon streamers.

Juanita's mother whined and squeezed out a few tears because she wanted to ride in the truck too, but Lilly took her aside and told her to stop being such a pain in the ass or she would make sure she would have continuous bad luck and never meet the man of her dreams. Juanita's mother wasn't really interested in a man of her dreams, so she continued to pout but wiped her eyes and pulled herself together.

By the time everyone arrived the sun was sinking behind the mountain and the canopy of Christmas lights crisscrossing the wooden floor were lit and twinkling. Bernardo's uncle and his band, including Mr. Escalante and Jesus Fidel, were seated on top of the bus and ready to get started. Mr. Lobos had called his cousin and asked, as a special favor, if he would come and sing not only for the bride and groom, but to celebrate the end of the General, even though the General wasn't quite dead, and on a personal note, to rejoice in the ongoing silence of his mother who was resting uncomfortably in the hospital next to her brother. It had taken some delicate maneuvering to rearrange his schedule, but by early afternoon Jesus Fidel drove up the mountain not only to sing but to see the frozen relatives for himself.

After the wedding toast with champagne stolen by Mr. Lobos from the General's treasured wine cellar, they cut the cake, blindfolded the bride and groom and spun them around until they were dizzy. Then someone handed each of them a broom but Juanita was the one who managed a direct hit and broke the wedding piñata, spilling candy and coins all over the floor. And finally, after all of that, the music got started.

"May angels lift your hearts to be joined by love," Jesus sang.

As the song drifted over the canopy of tiny lights and across the flowery field, everyone was so enchanted that they joined in and sang at the top of their lungs. When the song was over and after the applause, Jesus looked down from the top of the bus and was relieved to see Ebba smiling and clapping so he called out her name and waved. Ebba laughed and waved back. Then she introduced him to Hortence Grace and Rebecca and Tobias and Bernardo and Ariel who clung even more tightly to his father's neck. Jesus looked at Bernardo understanding everything there was to understand without anyone having to go through any sort of explanation.

"Maybe he would like to come up and help with the music?"

Bernardo looked at his son, then up at the singer.

"Maybe if the two of us came together," he smiled, so Tobias brought the ladder and Bernardo put Ariel on his back then climbed to the top of the bus.

They settled into a chair just as the musicians started to play the traditional wedding song but down below Juanita's mother was still pouting as she watched everyone watching Juanita and Raymond glide gracefully around the floor. Lilly, sensing it was time to nip Juanita's mother's jealousy in the bud, leaned over and whispered in Salvador's ear who looked at Lilly in horror and shook his head no, but Lilly insisted, so poor Salvador got up and asked Juanita's mother to dance.

As they moved onto the floor, so did everyone else including Mr. Lobos who took hold of Ebba and Rebecca's hands and turned them round and round as they circled the bride and groom. On top of the bus, Bernardo and Jesus Fidel helped Ariel shake the tambourine as he watched Hortence Grace try to avoid being stepped on by her partner Tobias who was just getting the hang of dancing.

When the song was finished Salvador eased Juanita's mother into a chair so he could rush right back to Lilly fast. Ebba walked to the back of the bus with Mr. Lobos for a glass of punch but as she reached out to pick up a glass, she saw the priest out of the corner of her eye and stopped dead in her tracks.

A little ways away from the festivities, Father Lyle, surrounded by a group of children from the Children's Army, some of them survivors of Sergeant Chavez' unfortunate roadside mistake, was being escorted away from the crowd toward a government green truck.

Mr. Lobos reached out for Ebba protectively, pulled her close to his side and kept his arm around her shoulder as they watched the uniformed children usher the priest away from the celebration whether he wanted to go or not. They were not using guns but making their point of moving him right along with firm politeness. Because of the music, no one had heard the vehicle approach, but now everything had stopped and everyone was watching.

"Best thing is keep the music playing," Lilly yelled up at the musicians and waved her arms like a conductor. "Besides, they're in for a big not-so-hot surprise."

That's when she put her fingers in her mouth and whistled a whistle so sharp it hurt your teeth, which alerted her dogs and set them off like a starter's gun at a race.

"Play and don't stop!" she shouted at the musicians.

So they did, and loud, played in time to the dogs running and snarling and biting and knocking kids down, snapping and barking and growling and scaring those miniature soldiers of the General's army out of their wits, ripping their uniforms, confusing their focus, making them run into the truck to keep from being caught in the jaws of Lilly's nasty looking, ferocious dogs who were jumping and hurling themselves against the doors and tires, until one of the Children's Army started the engine and took off leaving the priest, shaking and passing wind profusely, to deal with the dogs and the attack, all done in time to the music.

Lilly whistled that lethal whistle again and everything stopped, the dogs, the music and everyone's breathing. The only thing moving was the government green truck driving away at as many miles an hour as it could manage. In the silence all of the men and some of the musicians including Jesus Fidel started to run to Father Lyle who was still standing despite the whole ordeal, but his hair looked as if it had turned white.

"Getting even for the man in the manger," he whispered hoarsely to the men when they reached him.

Mr. Lobos pulled a flask out of his pocket and handed it to the priest. Then he and Raymond and all of the others led him back up the hill to the bus and a chair, where the dogs milled around him protectively. After the priest sat down and Hortence Grace brought him a glass of punch, the most beautiful grand sound of someone singing slipped into the confusion. It was such a wonderful voice that grandfathers and grandmothers hugged each other and tears rolled down their cheeks. Even the dogs seemed to smile as they clustered more closely around the priest's feet and began to howl their approval of Ebba's song.

"Magnificent!" someone yelled.

"The singing angel is filling the air," someone else said, and Bernardo's uncle was so excited he cried out, "It's Elena Cordova! Elena Cordova is here and she's singing!"

"But it's not!" Rebecca shouted, much to everyone's surprise. Then she turned and pointed to Ebba standing on one of the musician's chairs with her arms outstretched and music pouring out of her mouth and Ariel was so caught up in the sound that he let go of his grip on Bernardo's neck and smiled for the first time since he'd been home.

Dreaming Blue Silk

That night Ebba dreamed that she and Mr. Lobos were standing in the field of wildflowers by the dance floor and he gave her a present, handing her a thick square of something wrapped in red tissue paper with a red ribbon that he took out of his pocket.

"What's this?" she asked in the dream, and in the dream Mr. Lobos told her to open it and find out. Then he smiled and watched her undo the ribbon and pull apart the paper until she found a small square of very pale blue silk, which opened like a flower when she lifted it out of its red nest. Ebba was so surprised she gasped and a very pale blue silk shawl streaming silk fringe filled her lap and spilled down her legs in a cascade of softness so soft it thrilled her. And in the dream Mr. Lobos was so delighted he actually laughed and watched as she stood up, wrapped the new treasure around her naked new body and turned around and around thanking him in every direction until he caught her in all of that softness and wrapped himself around Ebba and the blue silk shawl, turning himself into her and her into him, into each other together with laughing and falling and rolling over and over in the field of flowers until the shawl slipped away, the way silk does, and then there she was with her naked new body under the stars with Mr. Lobos' soft voice whispering in her ear, "You're safe Ebba, you're safe here with me, Ebba..."

After that, in the dream Ebba looked up at the trees blooming feathery yellow flowers that pushed toward the dark blue sky like fireworks. Tucked amongst the blooms, a small spotted owl was perched on a branch looking down at Ebba, keeping watch, keeping track, looking back to see what was coming, ruffling its feathers in the soft breeze, soft like the silk and the soft sounds of Mr. Lobos as he explored her new body in the dream...

In the morning Ebba woke up in her own bed and the first thing she saw in her tiny room was a pale blue silk shawl streaming pale silk fringe across the back of a chair and spilling onto the floor, cascading in every direction and shimmering highlights from the rays of sun pouring through Ebba's bedroom window as the scent of night blooming flowers seemed determined not to drift away.

A little friendly advice:

Don't clip the wings of your chickens
they have as much right to fly as anyone
certain housewives
indulge in this diabolic practice
it is better to lose a chicken
than commit the unpardonable sin
of believing ourselves capable
of improving on the plan of the Creator:
if He in his infinite wisdom
provided them with wings
he must have had a powerfully good reason
even if it seems ridiculous to us.

Nicanor Parra

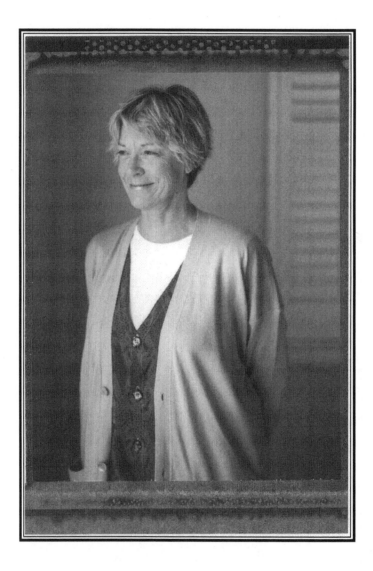

Joan Tewkesbury

ABOUT THE AUTHOR

Writer/Director Joan Tewkesbury began her career at age ten as a dancer in The Unfinished Dance. A few years later she appeared as an ostrich, an Indian and Mary Martin's flying understudy in Jerome Robbins' *Peter Pan*. She attended University of Southern California, became a choreographer, a theatre director, a script supervisor for Robert Altman's "McCabe and Mrs. Miller," then a writer of feature films, "Thieves Like Us" and "Nashville" and the director of "Old Boyfriends" which was presented at Director's Fortnight at the Cannes Film Festival.

She has also written and directed numerous projects for cable and network television: "The Tenth Month," "Acorn People," "Cold Sassy Tree," "Sudie and Simpson," "Wild Texas Wind," the HBO series "The Stranger," "On Promised Land," and "Elysian Fields," and was a consulting producer for the CBS series, "The Guardian."

For the theatre she wrote and directed "Dance Card" for the Oregon Ballet theatre, wrote and directed "Jammed," presented at the Edinburgh Festival, and wrote and directed "Retrospective" at the Manhattan Theatre Source.

Ten years ago she developed a class, "Designed Obstacles, Spontaneous Response" which she has taught at Art Center, American Film Institute, Bard College, Chapel Hill, UCLA, NALIP and various filmmaker labs and immersions throughout the United States, Israel and Europe.

She participates as a creative advisor for the Sundance Native Lab, the Sundance Institute and is teaching her class for the Writers of Milagro at Los Luceros in Alcalde, New Mexico.

Her work has been honored by the Writers Guild, Humanitas, Golden Globes, the British Academy Awards, Cable Ace, an Academy Awards Best Picture nomination for "Nashville" and the Los Angeles Critics award for best original screenplay.

She has two grown children, Robin and Peter Maguire, six grandchildren and lives in Northern New Mexico.

Ebba and the Green Dresses of Olivia Gomez in a Time of Conflict and War is her first novel.